THE WYCHERLEYS

ANNALIESE AVERY

Praise for THE WYCHERLEYS:

'I'm obsessed with this captivating and fiercely romantic book. Annaliese Avery cleverly weaves a magical world of family curses, glittering ballgowns and characters you can't help but fall in love with. A beautiful story, beautifully written.'
– Kathryn Foxfield, author of *Good Girls Die First*

'Avery has created an inventive escapist fantasy where magical ability meets societal nobility, where forged alliances are life-changing, and for cursed outcast Aurelia Wycherley, potentially lifesaving. With a swoon-worthy Regency setting, feuding families and deadly curses, a wickedly fun opposite-sides-of-the-same-coin heroine and hero, treachery and backstabbing galore and more than a little romance, *The Wycherleys* will surely be the talk of the Season! Perfect for reading by candlelight in the back of a darkened ballroom while you wait for your mysterious paramour to find you and spirit you away!'
– Melinda Salisbury, author of *Her Dark Wings*

'From the first perfect line, *The Wycherleys* had me hooked. It's the perfect swoon-worthy fantasy-romance featuring everything I love: wonderfully drawn characters to fall and root for, an alternate history with ballgowns and broomsticks, curses, magic with a clever twist, and a world I'd love to visit.'
– Dominique Valente, author of the Starfell series

'A fun, tense, enemies-to-lovers romance with magic and plenty of secrets. Nothing is as it seems. It had me gripped from the first page.'
– Zeena Gosrani, author of *This Dark Heart*

'I am utterly captivated by this addictive and swoony fantasy romance! Aurelia is brave, bold and wears her curse proudly. Jules is Mr Darcy for a new generation. They set the standard for courtship. If you're not committing felonies together, is it love?'
– Rosie Talbot, author of *Sixteen Souls*

THE WYCHERLEYS

ANNALIESE AVERY

SIMON & SCHUSTER

London New York Amsterdam/Antwerp Sydney/Melbourne Toronto New Delhi

First published in Great Britain in 2025 by Simon & Schuster UK Ltd

1 3 5 7 9 10 8 6 4 2

Simon & Schuster UK Ltd
1st Floor, 222 Gray's Inn Road
London WC1X 8HB

www.simonandschuster.co.uk
www.simonandschuster.com.au
www.simonandschuster.co.in

Simon & Schuster Australia, Sydney
Simon & Schuster India, New Delhi

The authorised representative in the EEA is Simon & Schuster
Netherlands BV, Herculesplein 96, 3584 AA Utrecht, Netherlands.
info@simonandschuster.nl

A CIP catalogue record for this book
is available from the British Library.

PB ISBN 978-1-3985-3626-5
eBook ISBN 978-1-3985-3627-2
eAudio ISBN 978-1-3985-3628-9

Typeset in the UK by Sorrel Packham

Printed and bound in the UK
using 100% renewable electricity
at CPI Group (UK) Ltd

MIX
Paper | Supporting
responsible forestry
FSC® C013604
FSC
www.fsc.org

For Helen Boyle, agent extraordinaire
and the only person I'd want to tether my magic to.

THE WHEEL
OF THE YEAR

PROLOGUE

Tuesday the 13th July 1813

Great Aunt Antoinette was dead, but the curse she had carried was very much alive. Not that I knew this as I stood in the gardens of Hemlock Square awaiting the arrival of my magic. I had just turned seventeen, and the Thunder Moon was as full and blinding as my blissful ignorance.

I should have been terrified, but instead I was excited . . . and expectant. We Wycherleys are powerful witches with a line that stretches back to the First Age of Magic; I was sure that I would be all a Wycherley witch should be.

My magic rose in me, lifting me into the air. The power strummed through me and I felt more alive than ever; connected to the world and everything in it.

When the pain started, I thought it was part of the magic; even when I was screaming up to the stars. I did not know that Great Aunt Antoinette was no longer of this world. I did not know that the family curse that she had carried was free to seek out and curse another Wycherley. To curse me.

In the early days of the Third Age of Magic, over a century and a half ago, my ancestor Mathilde Wycherley was cursed by her magical tether, Heston Nightly. It was a powerful, hereditary curse which did not stop with Mathilde, but sought out other Wycherley women. One of us must always carry the curse . . . until our bloodline is no more.

My family watched on: my older brother, Vaughn, and our mother, Nell, her magical tether, Frances, standing close by her. They all saw it happen, saw the curse take hold. Soft, grey smoke-like tendrils appeared around me, growing thicker and darker in the light from the full moon. They reached for me as I soared higher into the air, as if my magic knew what was coming and was trying to fly me to safety. But the curse smothered me. I tried to scream, but no sound came out.

It was as if the tentacles of smoke had form and feeling. Small, sharp barbed hooks drove into my skin, clinging to me, consuming me, burrowing their way into me like worms.

Vaughn says that my hair turned white with shock all at once, but Mother says it was more gradual, as if the colour from the once chestnut strands was pushed out by the curse. I didn't notice it. But I did feel the intense pain in my eyes as they filled with the grey mist that was becoming part of me.

As my body descended, returning to the ground, I felt the

power of my magic vibrating through me. The joy of *having* magic filled every part of me as the pain disappeared in an instant. It was as if the world had just opened, expanded with the promise of endless possibilities. But one look at my family told me that something was wrong.

From that moment on I felt betrayed by my magic. So deep and powerful, and yet so cursed. I will not get to keep it for long; magic needs to be tethered, and no witch is going to want to join their magic to mine, to suffer the effects of my curse.

My magic will leave me in a few years, and all because of a witch named Nightly.

HER MAJESTY THE PRINCESS REGENT,
GEORGIANNA,
AND THE ROYAL MAGICAL COUNCIL
REQUEST THE PRESENCE OF

Ms Aurelia Wycherley

AT THE MABON PRESENTATION TO CELEBRATE
THE BEGINNING OF THE MAGICAL SEASON

ON THURSDAY THE 23RD SEPTEMBER 1813
AT CARLTON PALACE.

ARRIVALS FROM 5 P.M., CARRIAGES AT MIDNIGHT.

AS A FIRST SEASON DEBUTANTE OF MAGIC,
YOU ARE REQUIRED TO WEAR WHITE TO THE PRESENTATION.

FOR THE KINGDOM AND THE MAGIC.

MABON

The Most Magical Season –
A Debutantes' Guide

by Cathleen Kelly
and Kate Walker

Mabon signals the start of the Magical Season. Every witch remembers their debutante years fondly: the magic, the balls, the trials and, for a lucky few . . . the romance.

However, love is of secondary importance; we all know that where a magic match is concerned the heart need not be involved.

The primary goal of the Season is to find a witch whose magic and character are strong and compatible with yours, so that you may create a lifetime of magic together. As such it is important to seek out the right witch. Binding one's magic to another is not a task that should be undertaken lightly, as imperative as it may be.

Of course, almost every witch secures their match in time.

Since the necessary tradition of tethering was first introduced at the beginning of the Third Age of Magic, these authors can count on one hand each the number of witches who did not succeed in making a match.

But tarry not – three years you have to find your tether, and if you fail, you will lose your magic. So, dear Debutante of Magic, proceed with caution, but do indeed proceed, or you too will be a witch no more.

However, before there can be any magic making between a witch and their potential tether, first there is the presentation to the Crown. The pledging of one's magic between a witch and the kingdom, some may say that this is an even stronger bond than that of a witch and their tether.

One

Every witch worth their weight in salt knows that without a tether, they are not a witch at all.

Since the end of the Second Age of Magic and the Great Witch War when a devastating magical calamity occurred, the only way for a witch to keep the magic gifted to them on the full moon after their seventeenth birthday is to find another witch – a tether – to bind their magic to and share it with. I, Aurelia Wycherley, know that my magic was not gifted, far from it, just as I know that no witch will ever be able to match with me, even if they wanted to. Over the years, my ancestors had all tried and failed to break the hereditary curse that I am now the custodian of: a fate I had never thought would be mine. Great Aunt Antoinette was not so old that I had ever feared inheriting the curse from her, and besides, I have many cousins who could have been the unlucky ones. But, indeed, fate had me in mind.

The magic I carry is not only a curse to me, but to whoever I try to perform magic with too. It renders them sick and feeble . . . it is worse than worthless to other witches. However, I know in the marrow of my magic that I *am* worth more than my weight in salt, and more than the distrust and hostility that my fellow witches cast towards my curse.

I've dreamed of this moment since I was a little girl: of wearing a long white cape and travelling to Carlton Palace to be presented to the Crown, of taking my place in magical society, of finding my most perfect magical match. It was all but guaranteed for me; my family is one of the most powerful magical families in Briton, and, besides, I already had designs as to whom I would tether my magic to when it appeared. But as I sit in the carriage next to my older brother, Vaughn, I can't even muster a smile.

Vaughn shifts beside me and the two of us uphold the silence we've surrounded ourselves with since we left our home in Hemlock Square. I've got used to the silences. They'd started long before the spark of sadness that had landed on me this summer, the spark that soon spread through me hotter and more determined than any witch-fire. The distance between myself and Vaughn began long before last Mabon, even when Vaughn was wearing white, when he was presented to the Princess Regent, when he entered into magical society and left me, his annoying little sister, behind.

Things between us changed when our father died, almost four years ago. In that moment the world shifted; it lost a little of its magic and I lost a tether of a different kind, an anchor that had always held me steady – held us all steady: me, Vaughn, Mother, even Frances.

Today Vaughn wears the soft light grey of the second year, no longer a first year debutante dressed in white, nor donning the dark grey of the third year debutante with only a Season left to find a match for his magic. I know that a dark-grey cape will be the last that I'll ever wear. No one will want to form a tether with me. Even if they did, they are forbidden; the Royal Magical Council will not allow such a pollution of the kingdom's magic. Mother and Frances, despite being members of the council themselves, only just persuaded the other members and the Princess Regent to allow me to take my place as a debutante for the next three years. No other cursed member of my family was afforded such liberties, and if my mother was not who she is, then I doubt I would have either.

Vaughn glances over at me as we turn the corner, following the procession of carriages containing other witches, all making their way to Carlton Palace. He goes to say something then stops himself, that awkwardness lodged between us.

Today was supposed to be an exciting day of beginnings, but for me it only signals the beginning of my loss. Without a tether to anchor to, I'll have three years of good strong magic – four or five of any magic at all if I am lucky – before it is gone entirely.

As the carriage rolls on towards the debutante ball, I look

out of the window at the gathering dusk. My reflection shines against the darkness outside, my white hair pinned up around my face, the warm tones of my skin looking darker now against my hair and the unnatural smoke-grey of my eyes.

I look past my reflection to that of Vaughn's, his hair the chestnut brown mine once was, his eyes a darker shade of brown than mine had been.

Outside, the streets of London look a little quiet too. The non-magical folk of the ton know that the Season of the Witch starts this night, and most of them will keep away. Despite the Oath of Obedience – the pledge all witches make to the Crown, and the service every witch gives to protect the kingdom – we are still not a welcome sight, unless it is on the battlefields or high seas.

I hear the shouts first, the almost chant-like cries that, for a moment, make me think of a coven ceremony. The carriage slowly draws to a halt.

I push my face against the glass as Vaughn opens the door.

'Stay here,' he instructs as he jumps into the street.

No chance. I follow him, the soles of my soft shoes striking the ground, and I feel every indentation of cobbled stone as I pick my way up the line of carriages beside Vaughn.

'Fine, but stay close to me, and stay behind.' He moves in front, defending me with his body; his wandlet, a moment ago curled around his wrist, has responded to his call, snaking its way into his hand. I roll my eyes at him. I may not have my wandlet yet, and only have a handful of spells about me, but

I am a Wycherley and we are not the type to sit in carriages even when others do.

The chanting becomes louder as we walk, the sound coming from up ahead, just past the curve in the road.

As we make haste, I see the carriage that is holding everyone up, turned on its side. On top of the carriage stands a man holding a torch, trying to set it on fire. Around him is a group of people, all shouting and brandishing torches.

'Is someone in there?' I ask, nodding towards the overturned carriage as Vaughn stops next to a small knot of witches. They are all in grey – light and dark – and they see Vaughn before looking behind him to me. I should be used to the way they recoil, move away and whisper, like my curse is contagious. I look defiantly at them till they each turn away from me.

I realize that I am the only witch in white. I wish I had a wandlet, and something other than my cursed magic.

Vaughn's best friends, Martyn Galesburg and Layla Mistry, move towards him and the three of them engage in hushed conversation. Martyn gives me a sad smile, which is almost as bad as the stares and glances. There are other witches that I know by sight, but all of them are looking forward now, facing the group of protesters who have poured a line of salt on the floor between themselves and us, thinking that it will protect them. The truth is that salt only works as protection *for* witches, not protection *from* witches; to non-magical folk it's just seasoning.

'They must be members of the New Dawn,' I say to Vaughn as he re-joins me, assuring me that the carriage is empty. One of the protestors is waving a orange flag; on it is a black circle with a dot in the middle. I find it mildly amusing that these people who despise everything magical have chosen the magical and astronomical symbol for the sun to hide behind.

'Why can't they just leave us witches alone. And on a Sabbat as well.' Vaughn shakes his head in disgust.

The assembled witches don't move, standing firm and listening to the members of the New Dawn chanting for us all to burn. Wands glow with magic but the witches don't cast any spells, not till one of the protestors throws something.

Movement catches my eye and a tall witch with hair all the red-kissed browns of an autumn leaf lifts his arm and sways smoothly, almost lazily back on his right foot, sweeping a large circle with his left hand and raising a witch-wind that hits the small projectile and sends it back the way it came. It crosses the salt line and I watch as he joins hands with the witch next to him and together they cast a spell, their magic causing the object to explode, before some kind of liquid rains down on the protestor who threw it. They start to scream, as if their skin is burning. I have heard about the advancements in non-magical alchemy and how destructive it can be. I feel my temper rising as I realize that whatever was inside the bottle was destined for us witches.

The protestors retreat further behind the salt line, cursing us and screaming loudly. I shake my head at their words. I know curses, and what they are throwing our way is nothing but hate and small-minded fear.

The other witches have all shifted, taking up new stances, and I see Vaughn and Martyn have shed their gloves and linked hands. Through touch they will be able to perform the more complex secondary magic, stronger than a debutante witch can do alone, and something that, once tethered, a witch can perform all of the time without the need for physical contact.

The witches raise a wall of protective witch-wind following the example of the tall auburn-haired witch. He sizes up the line of witches before him, scanning each one as he walks between them and the protestors; like a military witch general of the Coven of Accord, till he reaches me. His eyes linger, but not in the fearful way of most. He looks at me as if I am something novel, amusing maybe, and the little jolt that runs through my body lets me know how much I have missed being looked upon with *anything* but fear or sadness.

Then the witch is moving towards me, his dark blue, unflinching eyes locked on to mine. He stops when he gets to Vaughn. 'Wycherley, what did you bring her with you for?'

My brother has never been quick to anger, but his eyes flash. 'Not that it is any of your concern, but she followed me,' Vaughn says.

'And you thought it wise to let her?'

'I didn't know the extent of the danger.' Vaughn narrows his eyes.

'Well, you do now. You should return to your carriage. She might follow you back like a little white sheep.'

'I'm not going anywhere. I may not have a wandlet, but I have my magic,' I tell him straight, feeling confident of my skills following the few lessons I have had at the Magical Arcade. The witch clenches his teeth in agitation. I doubt he is used to being told no, and I can tell that he's just about to say something unpleasant to me when another projectile flies towards us, bigger this time.

Vaughn and Martyn perform the same magic that the autumn-haired witch did, mirroring each other as they do, keeping their hands locked together and their wands moving in unison. I flinch as the huge object stops in mid-air. The tall auburn-haired witch links hands with the witch beside him and they perform the spell too, pushing the larger projectile back together with their secondary magic, aiding Vaughn and Martyn.

But then another missile appears.

Triggered by the magic around me, I feel my own stir, as if answering some call. Without a wandlet I have little control over its focus. I feel myself starting to rise up from the ground, just as I did on the full moon, my magic taking over.

I stop when a strong hand grasps my ankle and pulls me down to the ground with a jolt. The autumn-haired witch has me by the shoulders and pushes me roughly towards a nearby carriage.

Pulling open the door, he bundles me in. I round on him as he uses his magic to seal the door shut.

'How dare you manhandle me in such a manner. Let me out immediately,' I shout, feeling my anger rise and my indignation prick.

'Nightly?' one of the witches calls to him as he stalks away, turning his head once back to the carriage, flashing me an icy stare.

Nightly? I shoot my hands out against the window of the carriage, my magic splintering the glass into small pieces, but it holds in place and I wonder what type of spell he used to seal me in.

I push my face against the broken glass and watch as Vaughn and the others dodge out of the way of the projectiles, sending as many back as they can. The horses are bucking, the carriage rocking.

I see one of the witches point up and I follow their gaze. The black-clad witches of the Coven of Justice are a formidable sight. I watch as they swoop down on their broomsticks, then use their tethered magic to create walls of protection where the salt line is.

Ropes of light snake through the air, seeking out the protestors, binding them as the witches use knot magic to stop them from fleeing or doing any more harm. The Coven of Justice are so graceful, moving and bending their bodies

19

as they call upon their magic, drawing it through and out of them and into the world in a controlled and forceful manner.

My eyes wide, a smile on my lips, I can't help but think, *that will be me one day.* Then a twist of pain rises in me as I check myself. *That will never be me.*

I begin banging on the door the moment the witches of the Coven of Justice have rounded up the protestors. Vaughn and Martyn both place a hand on the carriage and unseal the door, the glass shattering out of the window frame as soon as the spell is broken.

I tumble from the carriage, and my stormy eyes seek out Nightly.

'Aurelia, don't! He's not worth it. No Nightly is!' Vaughn makes to grab me, but I know how to avoid him when I need to.

'Excuse me, *sir*. What in the name of all that is magical were you thinking?' I gesture towards the carriage as Nightly turns to look at me. His expression is lazy as he sweeps his hair to one side; it is too long and in need of a good cut.

I look up. Even though I am not particularly short, Nightly is a head taller than me and I instantly don't like that I have to look up at him. He lowers his head a little and whispers to me in a way that makes my blood boil.

'I was thinking of good magic and how you are untrained, how you lack a wandlet, how your magic is yet to be tamed. I was thinking that if you rose high into the sky then you would have been a clear target for those protestors in your white dress, with your white hair. I was thinking that you were foolish to have followed your brother and that he was foolish to have let you. That you placed him, yourself and the rest of us in more danger than we were already in. So, Wycherley, I removed you to a place where your presence would do no harm.'

He stands back up straight and looks down at me. I feel small and angry, because, annoyingly, he is right.

I am saved from making a reply by Vaughn, who is at my side and pulling me away. 'Now, Nightly, there's no need for that. It's not her fault that—'

'No, it's yours.' Nightly rounds on Vaughn and I feel my haunches rise; the magic in me stirs to defend my brother. 'She could have been hurt. Sisters are to be looked after and cherished; once lost she would be gone forever.'

Nightly doesn't wait for a reply but walks away, leaving me seething because, in a way, he is right again.

Two

The sun has almost set when we eventually pull up to the steps of Carlton Palace. Butterflies dance around in my stomach. I'm sure that if my circumstances had been different they would have filled my entire being, swooping in my chest, making me lose my breath with the excitement of being presented and the prospect of finding my tether. Instead, I step from the carriage with a defiant determination.

Cursed though it might be, my magic is mine. If tethering to another witch is not an option, then I will find another way to keep hold of it . . . I have to.

Things were not always this way for us witches. Magic was once free and stable, and often wild; in the First and Second Ages of Magic, no one had to tether. A witch would receive their magic on the full moon after their seventeenth birthday and, from that moment on, it would grow with them: a constant companion till their death. All of that changed in the Great Witch War. But there has to be a way for me to keep my magic, just as those early witches did.

The steps up to the palace are festooned with all the fruits and flowers of the harvest – the smell of sweet, ripe barley and corn mixed with that of the late-summer roses. I feel a lightness return to me as Vaughn offers me the crook of his arm. I take it as a carriage rolls into place behind us and Constance Prior exits alone; she is the only member of her family who is out as a debutante. The last of her older sisters, Faith, made a match last Season.

'Aurelia, what happened back there?' she calls out, her brown eyes large. I reach out my free hand to my best friend and she grasps it, lowering from the carriage.

'Protestors. The New Dawn,' Vaughn answers, as he holds out his other arm to her. Constance lets go of my hand and takes Vaughn's arm, we both flank him as we walk towards the steps of the palace. 'They've gone now,' Vaughn continues. 'We kept them at bay until the Coven of Justice arrived.'

I look past Vaughn to Constance who is looking impressed with my brother for helping to hold off the attack. She is wearing the most beautiful white gown. Where mine is plain, hers is made of a delicately patterned silk. The jewel tones of her deep brown skin shine out against it and her dark hair is pinned with small sprigs of white gypsophila. Her cape is of the same patterned silk with a soft fur trim and diamonds sparkle around her neck.

'You look beautiful,' I tell her, and notice that Vaughn obviously thinks so too as he's looking at Constance as if he's never seen her before – as if she isn't the same witch that pushed him in to the Thames two summers ago, or that used to chase him with frogs, playing as children in the gardens of Hemlock Square.

Constance blushes – at my words or Vaughn's gaze I can't quite decide – but I know how she feels about the dress she is wearing. As the seventh and youngest of the Prior-Okore sisters, everything that Constance owns has belonged to someone else before, indeed this dress has belonged to all of her sisters: Amity, Verity, Felicity, Honour, Joy and Faith. Each of them has worn it for their presentation, a Prior family tradition, but I'm sure that Constance has worn it the best of all of them.

'Come on, witches, this is your time to shine.' Vaughn smiles, but there's a sad tinge in his eyes.

Despite all the feelings running through me, I know that this moment will never come again so I take the time to savour it. At the top of the stairs the massive double doors are thrown open and we walk into a grand hallway decorated in all the colours and accoutrements of the season. As the setting sun pushes through the open doorway and its surrounding windows, it bathes the hall in a soft warmth that reaches up the double-curving staircase illuminating the curving railings of the stairs adorned with late summer wild flowers and sheafs of ripe golden corn. Cauldrons full of floral displays and seasonal fruits and seed litter the hall; glowing candles floating all around. I soak it all into me.

The stairs to the left are lined with grey-clad witches making a patchwork of light and dark greys, while every step to the right is occupied by a witch wearing white.

'I'll meet you after you've been presented.' Vaughn gives my arm a little squeeze and, bowing a quick farewell to Constance, lets me go. I'm not sure I'm ready, and I stand for a moment watching him ascend the stairs on the left. I feel a small prickle of tears in the corner of my eyes as I realize that soon Vaughn will find a match, that he will create a tether and he and his witch will live a life of magic together, a life that I will never get to experience. I already feel so left behind; despite all of my intentions to find a way to keep my magic, the greater possibility that it will never happen harpoons my heart.

Vaughn turns his head and looks at me quizzically, motioning towards the other staircase where Constance is already halfway up. I give him a small smile, pull up my armour of determination and instantly feel more assured as I turn away . . . and manage to walk straight into Nightly. I apologize before I realize that it's him.

'I see you've arrived safely,' he says, glaring at Vaughn, who hesitates on the staircase, obviously contemplating if he should turn back and rescue me from Nightly.

'Now he's worried about you.' Nightly shakes his head, his autumn-coloured hair stirring like fallen leaves in a breeze.

'Mr Nightly, is there something that I can help you with?' The edge in my voice ready to cut, I shift my hands to my hips.

I can't tell if Nightly is amused, impressed or unfazed. 'I assure you, Ms Wycherley, there is nothing that you can help me with.' He moves off in the same direction as Vaughn, up the left-hand staircase with the other grey witches. I watch him go, my eyes burning into the back of him. He pulls the hood of his dark-grey cape up as he takes the steps two at a time, moving ahead of the witches in front of him.

As I take the right-hand staircase, copying his motion and pulling up the hood of my cloak, like all the other witches around me, I keep my eyes trained on him as I ascend. If I knew a hex to make him trip I would use it, a charm to bind his legs I would perform it, a spell to make his nose bleed I would cast it. When he reaches the top, he hesitates for a second, as if he can feel my ill will towards him. I think he might turn back, but then he is gone.

I would like to think that, like all good witches, I am learning to keep hold of my emotions – govern them and bring them under my power – but the truth is that there is something about Jules Nightly that really makes me wish I had a wandlet. We only met a few hours ago, although of course I knew *of* him. You didn't need to be a Wycherley to know who the Nightlys were.

'Are you all right, Aurelia?' Constance asks as she takes my arm and leads me into the large reception room at the top of the staircase, full of other first year debutantes. 'I don't mind telling you that I'm feeling nervous about being presented, but I'm only telling *you*. As far as anyone else knows, especially my sisters, I am fearless and completely in my comfort zone,' she adds with a smile.

Constance is walking quickly now, pulling me along towards a table where two purple-clad witches sit. Purple is for scholars – the Coven of Knowing – and these witches will record the name of every witch who is presented and swears their Oath of Obedience. I wonder how many of us there are this year; every year there are fewer witches in the world. Since the end of the First Age of Magic there has been a steady decline in witches and magic; before he died my father had been trying to figure out why that was, part of what he called 'the great problem'.

'Names,' one of the witches says without looking up at us.

'Constance Prior.'

'Aurelia Wycherley.'

Now both of the witches look up from their list and stare at me. I'm used to people taking note when they hear my last name – with a family as well-known as mine and a mother on the Royal Magical Council, it's unavoidable – but I might not ever get used to the way they look at me now.

The witch closer to me regains her composure first. She is older than my mother and the look on her portly face is one of pity, another thing I am yet to get used to. 'You will be called in alphabetical order. You might have a bit of a wait,

Ms Prior, Ms Wycherley more so.'

Constance and I head towards the side of the room, witches scatter out of the way of us. I hold my head up. I don't intend to let them see how much it hurts. And it really does hurt, especially when I see Sebastian Crenshaw and he looks away sharply, suddenly very interested in the cuff of his jacket.

'I swear, Aurelia, as soon as I learn the really strong hexes, I am going to visit Sebastian Crenshaw and hex him so badly he won't know what to do with himself.'

'It's fine,' I tell Constance, although it is most definitely not fine. The pain in my chest and the clenching of my stomach tell me so.

The three of us used to be close, and recently Sebastian and I had become more than friends. Where Constance has her sisters and I have Vaughn, Sebastian has us. *Had* us. I thought the three of us were unbreakable. We all live in Hemlock Square and when we were little, we would play pretend magic. The three of us were always part of the black-clad Coven of Justice, and in our games we had refused to tether unless it was a binding of three – which of course was not possible – but we were young, and it felt as if magic had no limits then. As we grew, we would talk about the magic we would receive and how we would be debutantes together.

I can't remember exactly when my feelings towards Sebastian changed – sometime shortly after my father had died. Sebastian had been there for me, consoling me when my family were locked in their own grief. Constance was away with her family, visiting her father's relatives for the summer. I had felt so alone, save for Sebastian. After that, our friendship shifted, becoming something that makes my heart flutter to remember.

Constance, the eldest of us three, had come into her magic first, on the Frost Moon. I remember pushing my face against the window and watching as her family gathered out on the green in the middle of Hemlock Square. All of them huddled together in the cold, celebrating loudly as her magic manifested. Sebastian's magic had arrived the month after, under the light of the Worm Moon, just his parents looking on. Once the two of them had their magic, they would visit the Arcade together, leaving me behind as they went to practise their primary magic. I had been so eager to join them.

I know that Constance and Sebastian were watching me on that Thunder Moon over two months ago, that they saw the curse take me.

Constance was already there when I hit the ground. Her eyes wide and worried, she held my hand as Mother tended to me. I saw Sebastian too, watching from the window. We haven't spoken since. I've tried, but his avoidance has been as tight as a cork in a bottle of eye of newt. So now I've given up trying. It hurts too much. It was supposed to be the three of us debuting together and the two of us tethering, but now that will never happen, and one of us – me – will be left behind forever.

I'm roused from my memories by a flutter of activity as one of the witches who was collecting names opens a large set of double doors. I instantly move forward, taking Constance with me; I look through the open doors and over a small balcony, down a long twisting staircase to a grand hall that, at the far end, holds a raised platform with a throne upon it. Sitting on the throne is the Princess Regent. She is a beautiful young woman, her gown embroidered in the colours of the season and her hair piled fashionably around the golden crown that sits on her head. I can't hold back the stirring of excitement in me that is at odds with the look on the princess's face, bored and disinterested.

Constance gives my arm a squeeze and I smile at her. The buzzing voices of the witches around us have faded into a whisper.

The purple-clad witch of the Coven of Knowing takes his list and walks out on to the balcony overlooking the hall.

'Ms Gretchen Archer,' he calls, his voice clear and high. I watch as Gretchen, a tall witch with fair cascading hair, takes a tentative step forward. With her jaw clenched – from resolve or to stop herself from being sick I'm not quite sure – she steps forward boldly.

A few long minutes later, the next witch is called, then the next, then the next.

Constance and I stand together. I avoid looking in Sebastian's direction and he in ours. When his name is called, I feel my chest clench. I know he's nervous; I can see by the way his shoulders pull together, his strides long as he pulls down the front of his delicately embroidered white waistcoat then sweeps his cloak back, adjusting the hood. When he gets to the top of the stairs, he pauses and begins to turn, and for a moment I think he's going to look at me and all will be as it should be between us. But then he's gone.

Constance lets out a long breath, shaking her head and staring at the space where Sebastian was. I know that she is about to launch into another verbal attack on him so I try to stop her in her tracks.

'What about her?' I say in a low voice, inclining my head to a witch sitting close to us.

'What about her?' Constance says.

'I've seen her at the Arcade, the instructors are always praising her footwork, I think her name is Hetty or Betty. She might be a good match,' I say.

'Hetty Wymondham, and no she wouldn't,' Constance says. 'Well, not for me anyway.' Constance's cheeks get a little darker.

I lean in close and whisper. 'Have the two of you tried to perform magic together?' I ask.

Constance shakes her head. 'No, nothing like that, it's just that Felicity made an unsuccessful offer to Hetty's brother, and she told me that if I was to accept any Wymondham, she would hex me out of the family.'

Constance pulls a face. Of all six of Constance's sisters, Felicity is the one that I have the utmost faith in being able to perform a fifth-degree hex.

There are fewer and fewer witches in the room, and soon enough Constance is called. She gives a little squeal and I hug her, whispering in her ear before she goes. 'You are going to find the most magical match.' I mean every word of it and will help her to find them if I can; she has always been there for me, cursed magic and all, and I'll always be there for her.

I hover near the doorway to watch, but the witches in purple shoo me away. I hear a little collective gasp from the crowd below and I know that they are all seeing what I see in Constance every day: she is beautiful inside and out and today she is shining brightly.

Before I know it, I'm the last in the room since no Yagis, Yateses or Yaxleys are being presented this year. And even though I've been waiting for almost two hours, it's still too soon when the witch calls my name.

I take a deep breath and steady myself. It feels as if there are a hundred steep steps down to the hall, although in reality there are far fewer. The room is silent, unnaturally so, and I can feel every eye on me as I take each step slowly. I seek out Vaughn in the crowd, he is nodding encouragingly. I give him a small smile, which quickly fades as I sweep my eyes around the hall. Most of the looks are a mixture of pity and fear, and some are downright hostile. I sweep my stormy eyes over the crowd and catch on the haughty face of Demelza Nightly, I can see where Jules gets his cheekbones from. If it weren't for her ancestor, I would not be cursed, and yet she is the one looking at me as if I have personally wronged her. I lift my chin a little higher before I look away from her.

The perimeter of the hall is filled with witches wearing all the colours of magic. Each of the six covens has their own colour: black for Justice, green for Nurturing, purple for Knowing, blue for Mysteries, red for Accord and yellow for Curiosity.

To one side stand the light and dark grey second and third year debutantes, with the newly received white-clad witches standing in front of them. I see Sebastian. He holds my gaze for the first time since I received my magic. It's me that looks away first, my stomach twisting, my heart hopeful. I remember that look, and I miss it. I hadn't realized quite how much till that moment.

I reach the bottom of the stairs and make my way towards the raised platform. Princess Georgianna is standing in front of her throne, behind her in an arc are twelve seats, ten of which are filled by a member of the Royal Magical Council, all dressed in the colours of the covens they represent. To her left stands my mother, Nell, and to her right Mother's tether, Frances, both dressed in the black of the Coven of Justice.

I keep my eyes on Mother now. Just as a distance formed between me and Vaughn when our father died, so one grew around our mother like a ring of salt. In the almost four years since his passing she has thrown herself into her work, and although she is still present, still part of our lives, it often feels like she isn't truly with us, as though part of her died with Father. My mother smiles at me with that hint of sadness in her gaze. Usually it makes me feel small, like I should shrink away and not let anyone see me, but everyone *can* see, everyone *is* looking at only me, so this time I stand tall and defiant. I stand as me, not the me that they see, but the one I know I am, the way I want to be seen.

It makes me feel powerful but, deeper than that, it makes me feel sure and happy, two things I haven't felt since I received my cursed magic. I steal a glance at my mother and smile as I see a look of pride where before was sadness.

Next to her, the Princess Regent recoils a little as I advance towards her, but I don't stop being me. I glance at Constance out of the corner of my eye and see her beaming at me. Directly behind my best friend I see Jules Nightly, fixing me with that inquisitive look of his, as if he is examining every inch of me for weakness. I give him the same look that I gave his mother, and he gives a small smile that I'm sure is meant to disarm me – I don't allow it to.

As I stop in front of the princess and her council, I make a low curtsy, then I pull back the hood of my cloak, freeing my white hair to cascade from my shoulders and down my back. The lowering of a witch's hood symbolizes their loyalty to the Crown.

The princess lifts a sword, Excalibur, from a simply carved chest; the blade is thin, shaped more like a needle than a weapon, the hilt is ornate and set with a large clear diamond. The princess points the blade at me, and I take a step closer to it so that it is in line with my heart.

'Do you, Ms Aurelia Hathor Wycherley, swear on your blood never to use the magic that courses through you to bring harm to the Crown and its people?'

'I swear it,' I say. Then I reach out a finger and press it against the sharp point of the blade. It pricks my finger, thick red blood coating the tip of the metal for a moment, and then I watch it move along a thin narrow groove in the blade, as if it is being pulled towards the hilt. For a moment the blood glistens, and then it is gone, absorbed. That's when I notice the diamond on the hilt has become a ruby, filled with my blood, the red swirling deep within it before it clears once more.

The princess passes the sword to my mother, who places it ceremoniously back in the wooden chest. When she turns towards me she gives me a small nod and a smile. Frances, who is on the other side of the princess, passes her a wooden wand with a crystal tip.

'Kneel, Ms Wycherley,' the Princess Regent commands, and for a moment I hesitate. Mother has always said that I do not do well with authority, and this command makes me feel like rebelling. But I do kneel before the princess, keeping my eyes levelled on her. Now I'm up close I realize that she isn't much older than Vaughn, but there is something about her manner – bored and superior – that makes me believe the rumours I have heard that, like her mother, she cares not for witches.

The Princess Regent holds out the wand to me and,

with the same finger that the sword pricked, I touch the tip of the crystal. Once again, my blood slides inside, creating a shimmering swirling strand that shines with all the colours of the rainbow, then turns dark as it twists with the potential of my magic – the swirling grey of my curse.

The princess looks a little taken aback and glances over to my mother who looks momentarily worried, before her face clears. 'It is a side effect of a family curse, nothing that can harm the Crown,' she whispers to the Princess Regent, who looks distastefully at the wand, then at me, and I wonder if what Mother has just said is true or something that she is guessing at.

I hold my hand open, and the princess looks grateful to release the wand, placing it in my open palm. Closing my fingers tight around it, I feel the wood becoming hot as it shifts and twists under my grip. It melds with my touch and begins to lengthen and stretch as it snakes its way out of my hand and around my wrist, where it will stay as a kind of twisted bracelet until I have need of it and the wandlet will respond. Carvings glow in the wood – colourful decorations and runes – and its crystal tip glows.

Excitement and comfort flow over me as I realize that the wandlet will always be there, ready for my call at a moment's notice, helping me to focus and command my magic in a way that, so far, has alluded me. It will even remain after my magic has gone; it will be inert, nothing more than jewellery, but it will still be there.

The Princess Regent gives me a small nod, my cue to stand up and follow the awaiting steward who leads me to where the other debutantes are standing.

Constance makes a little room and I stand beside her, the witches around her all moving away from me as if I have my own circle of protection and they cannot pass the ring of salt. Usually I would shrink at this, but I am done hiding and I am done feeling ashamed. This is the witch I am, whether or not I, or anyone else, like it.

The Princess Regent steps off the dais and walks to the centre of the hall. Just as every eye was on me, they are now firmly on her.

'Witches of the realm, we meet this Mabon night to greet not only the balance of the year, but the new witches of our world. From this day on, the days will shorten quickly, the nights will lengthen, the light will dim, and the darkness deepen. And that darkness is never far from our thoughts. It has been over one hundred and fifty years since the dawn of this Third Age of Magic, since the perpetrators of malevolent magic rose up against these blessed isles and plunged our people into depths of a magical war never seen before, and I hope never to be seen again.

'During that time my great-great-grandfather, called out from his palace to the witches of the lands and asked them to unite with him on the battlefield. Many of you here today carry the names and magic of those who stood against the darkness of malevolent magic, but many were lost in the war,

37

witch and non-magical alike. We are indebted to them all for the balance that they gave to the world.

'Today we measure this balance once more, as Mabon gives us equal amounts of light and darkness so we are reminded that we must all work together to ensure stability.

'On this day we give thanks to you, debutantes of magic, and your coven witch kin, for you bring the balance. With your light, with your magic. Since those warring days, the covens of this land have kept malevolence in check and one day it will fall to all of you to take your place among your fellow witches and continue to keep it at bay.

'When you do that, you will not be alone. From the moment of your tethering till the breaking of your string, you will share your magic with one other. Today marks the start of the search for your match. I wish you all the greatest of tetherings, for the kingdom and the magic.'

'For the kingdom and the magic,' call out the crowd.

Three

The princess makes her way back to her throne and is immediately surrounded by the Royal Magical Council as the hall descends into light chatter. Constance turns to me with a little squeal.

'Aurelia, you were magnificent. I have never seen anyone look so powerful. Cursed or not, I will be very surprised if there aren't one or two witches that are now thinking about trying their magic with yours.'

I seek out Sebastian and he looks away. I remember the look on his face when I was being presented and I desperately want him to look at me like that again.

Vaughn is already surrounded by a small knot of eager witches, no doubt filling up his dance card for the night.

'Do you still want to dance the first with me?' I ask Constance as I see a witch in light grey looking intently at her.

'Of course I do!' Constance rounds on me, her brow

furrowing. 'And, Aurelia Wycherley, if you think that I am dancing with you out of pity then you are wrong. I'm dancing with you because we have entered this debutante year together and there is no one else I would rather have my first dance with.'

The witch in light grey has struck up enough courage to approach. He ignores me at first, and Constance, although kind, is firm in pulling me into the conversation. I have to give him points for persisting and asking Connie for the second dance. But she leans in closer to him and I hear her say, 'I am sorry, but I could never dance with a witch who does not accept the company that I keep and, as your manner has been so cold towards my friend, I too must be cold with you.' I catch her wandlet glow and his lips turn blue as he begins to shiver then hug his arms around himself before walking off, stomping his feet I suspect as much to get them warm as to show his anger at being refused.

'You probably didn't need to hex him,' I say as the musicians take their places.

'Oh, I think I did.' Constance picks up my hand and leads me to the dance floor. 'Besides, it was barely a hex.'

We smile at each other as the music starts, and it is as if we are children again, playing at being witches, pretending to be at a ball, except now we are here and so is our magic. As I follow Constance's lead I swallow down that lump in my throat that keeps telling me that I will never be a proper witch, despite what I am determined to do. If this indeed is all I will have, three debutante years, then I am going to make the most of them.

Constance laughs as I spin her around, and we twirl and glide with the steps of the dance, the movements so close to those of magic that I feel my wandlet tingle on my wrist, and the same deep and certain sense of power that I get from performing magic fills every facet of my body.

When the second dance begins, we go again, and I'm sure that Constance would have made me dance a third if Vaughn hadn't come to intervene.

'It's kind of you to dance with me,' I tell him. Constance is now dancing with a witch in dark grey, she is smiling tentatively up at him as they hold each other awkwardly.

'I'm not dancing with you out of kindness, Aurelia. I'm doing it because you are my sister and, as someone recently told me, sisters are to be looked after.' I follow his line of sight straight to Jules Nightly who is standing near the back of the room, glaring at a witch in white who is talking to him animatedly, hopefully.

'You do look out for me,' I tell Vaughn, 'as I do you.'

'Before I got my magic, we were closer. In the last few years I've been off doing things that I thought were more important than spending time with my little sister, but after . . .' He raises a hand towards me and I know that he is gesturing towards my curse. 'Well, I was wrong and I'm sorry.' I look up at him a little shocked.

'It's fine, Vaughn. I understand. You had other things on

your mind. Magic and matching. Little sisters can be a bind when it comes to both of those things.' I smile at him.

'That is true,' he offers with a wink. 'But who knows what might happen this Season. We may only have this one Season together if I tether so I will be your guide through the more fun aspects of being a magical debutante. Things like visiting the Season Gardens – we shall go together on every opening day.' He looks at me expectantly and I can tell that he is pleased with himself.

'Umm, I don't know,' I tease. His face falls as he spins me around the hall. 'Will you promise to buy me sweet and sickly food and take me to see all the best features of the gardens?'

'The very best, and the sickliest, I promise.' His smile is back.

'Very well then, a family outing.' And I suddenly find myself looking forward to it in a way that I didn't when it was going to be just me and Constance.

After the dance, I insist that I need to sit the next one out. I don't want Constance and Vaughn to feel as if they need to play chaperone all night and I already know that no other witch is going to offer their hand to me.

As I sit, I watch them both dancing with their partners. Constance has loosened up now, she's laughing with a fellow witch in white, and leaning close to her as she whispers in her ear. I look for Vaughn again but instead I find Sebastian. He's dancing with a witch in light grey, and he turns him smoothly. I fight down the warm flush that is running through me. I'd thought that it would be us. That I would dance with

42

Sebastian at this ball and every ball to come. I only ever thought that it would be him and that our magic would be all the stronger because of the way I felt about him, because I had loved him. And, despite myself, I know I still do.

I feel my wandlet glow and vibrate. As the emotions in me shift, my magic stirs from longing to something else. *Warning.* Suddenly a boom rings out around the hall and for a moment I think my cursed magic has acted out as the glass in the windows blows inwards. My wandlet snakes into my hand, my fingers curling around it in its wand form, and instead of turning my back on the falling shards and hunkering low, like many around me, I give an instinctive flick of my wrist and sweep out my wand hand then lift it high. The edges of the small umbrella-like magical dome that I've created send the shards of multi-coloured glass that land on it sliding to the ground, the dome protecting me and those in the circle around me. I'm not the only one who has performed such a spell, around the hall there are glowing wand tips as the smell of magic fizzes in the air.

Screams and yells come thick and fast as smoke drifts from the back of the hall where the princess retired to and where my mother and the Royal Magical Council now are. Behind me there's a door that leads out into the gardens at the back of Carlton Palace, but instead I move further into the hall. Not only is Mother at the back, among the smoke and the chaos, but somewhere between me and her are Vaughn and Constance.

I pull my magic back into me and stumble forward, my wand glowing, ready. I call out, 'Vaughn! Constance!' My voice is lost in the maelstrom of terror as another blow rings out. Non-magical alchemy or malevolent magical attack, I'm not sure, but I think of the New Dawn's earlier protest.

It feels as if the building is being shaken by giants. I don't react as quickly with my magic when the next explosion rings out. I hit the floor; my knees and hands land hard on the glass splinters from the windows. I hear a mighty crash close by and curl myself inwards. One of the chandeliers has fallen from the ceiling and I curse as I get to my feet, running my hands down my white dress, covering it in lines of red blood as I try to dislodge the small pieces of glass that have pushed into my flesh.

'Vaughn! Constance!'

'Aurelia!'

I recognize the voice at once. 'Sebastian!' I call and push my way through the now hysterical debutante witches who are fleeing. Most have their wands in their hands as they stagger to freedom, some supporting other witches.

Sebastian is pinned under the fallen chandelier; I crouch beside him and assess the damage. The smoke is getting thicker now and I haven't yet learnt the moves of the spellcast to conjure a witch-wind. I hope another witch has the forethought to quell it before it engulfs us.

Blood is covering Sebastian's white stockings. As I reach out a hand to reassure him, he flinches from me, and I snatch

44

my hand back as quickly as I would from a fire.

'If I lift the chandelier, will you be able to pull yourself free?' I ask.

'I . . . I think so,' Sebastian says.

I stand up straight and take a step back, planting one foot in front of the other, just as the instructors at the Arcade have taught. With my wand in my hand, I lift my arms out in front of me. Then I pull my wand hand back from my outstretched empty hand, which feels as if it has a great weight in it. I lift that weight higher as I make a circular motion with my left arm. My movements are big and clunky but I know that over time, with practice and skill, they will become smoother. I feel my magic concentrating on the chandelier as it lifts, and my body feels the strain of it through my magic.

'Move, Sebastian,' I urge. But he isn't moving fast enough, and I can feel my magic slipping.

I see a dark-grey flash beside me and Jules Nightly swoops in and loops his hands under Sebastian's arms, dragging him free just in time, before I drop the chandelier with another crash.

Jules Nightly sits behind Sebastian, arms still hooked under him. 'Are you all right?' he asks, and when I look across, I realize that he is speaking to me, not to Sebastian. He's looking right into my stormy eyes, unflinching.

I don't get a chance to answer as Sebastian cranes his head to look up at Nightly. 'I . . . I don't think I can walk,' he says, as he looks numbly back down at his legs.

I stand up and move to help him but he flinches away, and that hurts more than all of the tiny shards of glass that are pressed into my palms and knees.

Nightly stands in one swift motion, pulling Sebastian with him, then he unceremoniously lifts him over his shoulder before turning to me.

'Follow me, Wycherley, keep your wand high,' he instructs. Reluctantly, I do as he says – the smoke is thicker now, covering the whole of the hall, obscuring the exit.

Nightly pauses. 'Do you know how to make a witch-wind?' he asks with a cough.

'No,' I say, eyes stinging.

'Place one foot out in front of the other and drive your hands down, and then up and out. Think about drawing energy up and through you and then away, make the energy light, think of the breeze you want to create caressing your face, tousling your hair.'

I do exactly as he says except it's *his* long hair I imagine being batted by the wind, streaming across his face and irritating him. The thought of it makes me smile as I raise a brisk witch-wind and manage to create a smokeless path a few steps ahead of him for us to follow.

'Good, keep it blowing,' Nightly shouts back, and I almost want to stop just to spite him. I can see Sebastian hoisted over his shoulder, his torso drooping down Nightly's back. He lifts his head to look at me. I ignore him and keep the witch-wind going, pushing Nightly's hair forward as well as the smoke, extending the path a little further out too. Sebastian drops his head but I keep my magic going.

I see a shape in the smoke and out stumbles Vaughn, his cloak over his mouth, Constance holding his hand as he guides her along. 'Aurelia, are you all right?' His eyes dart from me to Nightly, then Sebastian, before back to me again.

'Yes, are the both of you?' I ask, a little tight-lipped because I'm using all the concentration that I have to keep the witch-wind going.

Constance realizes and reaches for her wandlet. It snakes into her hand, the tip shining brightly, as she uses the same motions that I am making with my wand hand. Vaughn does the same.

I'm not sure that either of them think through what they are doing – that they are performing magic while holding hands. As they form a connection and send their magic out it is amplified, almost clearing the smoke from us to the exit. I have a strange feeling that I'm intruding as the two of them look at each other slowly, deeply, before dropping each other's hands as they remember themselves.

'That's some strong magic the two of you have together,' Nightly says with an approving nod as he walks on between Constance and Vaughn, making them move apart. Sebastian is squirming trying to see what happened.

I follow along behind Nightly, giving both Vaughn and Constance a curious look as I pass. But neither of them look at me; they have both become very interested in everything around them that is not each other.

As I follow Nightly out of the hall and on to the lawn at the back of the palace, he makes for a pair of witches clad in light green – apprentice healers from the Coven of Nurturing. They move forward, helping him lower Sebastian, who looks as if he's fainted, down to the ground. I go to crouch beside him, but then I hesitate. I'm not sure he would want to have me near him.

'She's hurt too,' Nightly says, nodding in my direction.

'I'm fine,' I say, but as I look down at my hands they are still bleeding, my wandlet is as covered in my blood as my dress is, and there are two large red stains where my knees are.

'Oh, my goodness, Aurelia!' Vaughn says, taking in all of the blood staining my white dress.

'It's fine honestly, I fell and . . . it's just glass.' I hold out my hands to show the small shards of glass stuck in them.

One of the pair of light-green clad witches moves over to me, he places both of his hands around my wrists, my palms facing upwards. He begins to say a spell just under his breath and I can feel the magic as it rushes into my hands and pulls out the pieces of glass. I notice his wandlet glowing on his wrist, as my skin heals over and the bleeding stops.

'I'm sorry, Ms,' he says and motions to the hem of my dress. My cheeks flush as I realize what he is asking and tentatively begin to pull my skirt up over my calves and knees. Vaughn turns around instantly to protect my modesty. I notice that

Nightly is not so quick, his eyes tracing my exposed flesh. I fix him with a defiant stare, catching him as he turns away, having enough sense to look a little sheepish.

The healer then gets me to sit as he places his hands above my knees and once again pulls the glass from me.

'Thank you,' I say and he smiles, pulling my dress firmly back down for me.

'Not at all.' It's only then that I realize that he didn't flinch once from me, at my cursed appearance.

I'm sitting next to Sebastian on the ground as he comes round, and, as he opens his eyes, he immediately scoots back from me.

'Hold still, you've broken your leg; I'm trying to fix it,' the other light-green witch tells Sebastian, who stops his squirming and starts staring intently at his leg.

Constance reaches out a hand to me and lifts me from the ground.

'Sebastian Crenshaw, you are a pathetic small-minded coxcomb,' she tells him.

The healers snigger and I'm sure Constance would have said more if Emery and Jackson hadn't just arrived in their sweeping black cloaks of Justice. Hobbs Emery and Nita Jackson are part of Mother and Frances' close coven. If the two of them are about then it's usually because there is trouble afoot.

'Nell and Frances have bid us bring you to them. You too, Ms Prior,' Jackson says. Her hair is raven black, long and straight, her skin the colour of warm chestnuts, whereas Emery's hair is all golden mid-length curls and their skin is a rosy pale pink. They make a stunning pair, both young witches, only a few years out of coven college. I get the impression that Mother is training them to take over from her and Frances one day.

As we walk off with them, I hold Constance's arm. Vaughn shoots a look behind him at Sebastian and says to me, 'Coxcomb indeed.'

I look back at Sebastian; I can't help myself and I feel like a fool for doing so. But it's Nightly's gaze that I find as he watches after us, that sheepish look replaced with his usual superior glare, probably wishing another curse upon me.

Four

The events of the day rush through my mind as I lie in bed: the protestors, being presented to the princess, feeling powerful, dancing with Constance and then the attack. Sebastian getting hurt, Nightly swooping in again and plucking him to safety. I turn over and hit the pillow with my fist, then push my face into it. Mabon and the presentation ball was supposed to be a positive experience, a celebration of all of the debutantes, of our introduction to magical society.

I shift my head and look at my wandlet and the runes carved on it. A few of them, I know: Berkana and Mannaz, growth and self-awareness. I could probably do with a bit of both. I twist the wandlet and frown at the symbol for the sun, the same symbol used by the New Dawn. A thrill of excitement runs through me as I conjure a witch-flame in the palm of my hand. Like my magic, it too is unique. My witch-flame burns black, glowing with a strange light that seems to shine from pulling in rather than radiating out. I let it run over my hand to the tip of my finger and light the candle next to my bed before extinguishing the flame in my palm. I find the eerie light comforting as it illuminates the bookcase, and I quickly find a small volume bound in midnight-blue cloth. The silver embossed lettering reads 'Gwynn, Pinder and Slight's Assemblage of Astronomical Attribution'.

On the first page of the book I find an index full of symbols and their corresponding pages. I quickly find 'The Sun'. What follows is a detailed explanation of the astronomical object, followed by its magical meaning and correspondence:

'When a witch encounters this sign as a symbol, the meaning is clear – just as the sun shines forth its light, so you shine forth yours. Your life and vitality are part of what makes you shine. Do not darken your light. But do not use your brightness to outshine all before you. Seek to become the highest vibration of magic that you can be; the purest of light – that which shines true but does not burn.'

I give a little 'huh' and close the book with more force than I mean to. The shadows of the curse that run through my magic feel as though they obscure all the light that I once had. My wandlet speaks of growth and self-awareness and light, but every day feels like a struggle not to fall into despair, not to be trapped and lost in the dark. Maybe I do need that sun more than I realize.

I gaze at the last symbol on my wandlet: a beautiful curling rune that I've never seen before. As I twist my wrist it flickers with a magical black flame, the same colour as my own witch-flame. I flick back to the index, and, when I can't find it there, I reach for another book, then another. I have a small pile of discarded books next to me when the need for sleep outstrips my curiosity and I crawl into bed, telling myself that I'll check the library for the rune tomorrow.

When I wake, I can feel that the protective wards around our house have been reinforced. After the attack at the palace, I am sure that every magical household did the same last night.

Mother and Frances are at the breakfast table when I enter. They are poring over some papers which Frances scoops into a pile as I approach, making room for me. Mother is on her feet, hugging me close and kissing the top of my head. She pulls away and holds me at arm's length. 'I am so sorry that your presentation was ruined.'

I kiss her on the cheek and say, 'At least we are all safe.' I walk around the table, hugging Frances and kissing her on the cheek too before taking my seat.

Mother is still scrutinizing me as I drink my tea, looking me over for any visible signs of injury from the day before. When Emery and Jackson took Vaughn and me to her and Frances, Mother had been frantic at the sight of the blood on my dress. Frances had to reassure her that everything was well in a voice that she often used to calm me when I was little. I feel that my mother carries around a lot of guilt about how little time she gets to spend with me and Vaughn – her job is demanding and there is always something pressing that she needs to deal with, but we both know how deeply she cares for us. Nell Wycherley might be a Coven Head, she may sit on the Royal Magical Council, but Vaughn and I both know that she is our mother first and will always be there for us.

I put down my teacup and look down at the pile of papers in the middle of the table. The *Daily Cauldron* is on top, the headline reads, 'ONE WITCH DEAD AS NEW DAWN ATTACKS ON MABON'.

I snap up the newspaper. 'Someone died?'

I scan the article as Frances says, 'Yes, but not at the palace.'

The body of Abel Jones, tether of Gilma Sinclair, was found late last night. Although the death of a lone witch may strike fear nowadays, in this case, Abel Jones' death does not appear to be linked to the serial murders of high-profile witches over the past three years. His death is not thought to be attributed to the murderer, currently being referred to as the Magimancer, by other, non-magical newspapers, but rather to the New Dawn. Although, this reporter must note that there are similarities between this and the deaths of the alleged victims of the Magimancer. See page nine for more details.

I turn through the pages. Mother and Frances will both be even more preoccupied this Season as they continue to try and find this Magimancer, I realize. I stop turning on page four where I see the drawing of a familiar scene: at the centre is a witch with long white hair, looking wild as she rises into the air. Around her are menacing protesters and flaming carriages, and there's a second witch holding on to her ankle, pulling her down.

The storms in my eyes churn because I know that the depiction is supposed to be me and Nightly.

In their attempt to disrupt the evening's proceedings, the New Dawn's protest held up many debutantes. However, the young witches of the ton took to their wands and held back the rebels. Mr Jules Nightly, son of Demelza Nightly, chief investigator of the Coven of Mysteries, and Oliver Hallow, an esteemed major general in the Coven of Accord, is reported to have led the charge, and Mr Nightly was even seen escorting Ms Aurelia Wycherley to safety! Readers will not need to be reminded about the ancient rivalry between these two powerful families, nor that the unfortunate Ms Wycherley, daughter of Nell Wycherley (Coven of Justice council member) and the late Ulric le Fay (lately of the Coven of Curiosity), inherited the family curse bestowed by Heston Nightly on Mathilde Wycherley and a select group of her descendants. Poor Ms

Wycherley's magic is thought to be tainted, and the fact that she needed to be rescued by the gallant Mr Nightly is evidence of this. We do indeed live in strange times, but this Nightly intervention might be the strangest act of all! I'm sure that if Nell Wycherley doesn't have anything to say about this interaction between Mr Nightly and Ms Wycherley, then Demelza Nightly most certainly will.

I fold the paper, feeling my cheeks flush as I seek out my mother's gaze to see if she does indeed have anything to say. She lifts one eyebrow, then says, 'There are more pressing matters than a silly news story about the Nightlys.'

She's right, of course, and my thoughts return to the dead witch. The mention of my father has also left a lump in my chest.

It's been almost four years since he died, since I found him lying on the floor at the bottom of the stairs to our family arcade, his life and his magic gone from him. An accident, a trip and fall, and he was gone. In that short time we have become a family of four – me, Vaughn, Mother and Frances – where we were once a family of six. Most witches tether for magic or status. My father tethered for both, my mother too, in a way. The illusive love match, when both heart and magic are in union, is hard to find. It is more common for witches to tether for magic and to marry for love.

Most magical families are blended, with witches and their tethers creating large extended families. Our family was a little different, but not uncommon: Mother loved Father *and* Frances, and the three of them loved me and Vaughn.

Father's tether, Jonathan Reid, was part of our family, but it was always different. He never lived with us; he had his own family, a wife, Christina Thorn, and a son, Kit Thorn, who is some years older than me and Vaughn. Jonathan had definitely only tethered for magic and the influence that my father's family had. The le Fays were more prominent in magical history than both the Nightlys and the Wycherleys, although not as well known in this Third Age of Magic.

Sometimes Father and Jonathan would endure long periods of absence from each other, usually after a fight about something or other. Their magic was strongest together but, as Mother often remarked, they were not always good for one another.

It has not escaped me that I lost them both when my father died. When a witch dies, the magic held between them and their tether dies too, so Father's death took Jonathan's magic away from him, and Jonathan, faced with the loss of his tether and his magic, withdrew from us completely, from his own family also, becoming estranged from all who cared for him and quitting England entirely to travel Europe.

Mother was a mess after Father passed; it had been Frances who held us all together. Frances, who is dispassionate and practical and even now is making her tea as if it were a potion, had scooped us all up, comforted and cared for us in her own way.

Not for the first time since I've received my curse, I think about seeking Jonathan out. After all, he lives without magic, he can tell me what it will be like if the worst happens, if I can't find a solution to my problem. However, none of us have any idea where he is.

I smooth over the folded newspaper, suddenly not wanting to read the details of the dead witch's murder. 'Was it the New Dawn who attacked the presentation last night?' I ask.

Mother and Frances glance at one another and I already know that they are not going to tell me all that they know. There are so many important things that they can't share, I understand that. I can't share everything that I'm holding on to with them either: they would think me foolish at the impossibility of my desire to find a way to keep my magic.

'The New Dawn are taking responsibility for the attack; they issued a statement to the non-magical press. As you can imagine, they have each taken that and run with it in whichever direction they feel fit.' Mother sips her tea noisily.

I don't need my mother to explain. There are more than a few papers that report the rumours, that the King's illness is actually due to him being magically muddled, that some malevolent leaning witch has cursed or hexed him, which of course is impossible. The oath all debutantes make would never allow anything like that; however, the queen and Princess Regent believe the rumours and from that stems their not-so secret dislike of witches. At the same time, they need us and our magic, as the recent war with France has shown.

'Destabilization: that's what the New Dawn were no doubt after,' Frances offers. 'Acting out against us. Trying to stop the ceremony, dismissing our traditions. Showing their displeasure that the Princess Regent was there, seeming to support us.

'Some fear they are trying to incite another witch war, turn the non-magical community against us, turn us witches against one another, against the Crown! The last time that happened, witches burned and malevolent magic rose, taking hold and changing magic forever.'

I give a little shudder as I think of the war that ushered in this Third Age of Magic in which we live, and the final battle that changed magic forever, creating the need to tether.

'I'm just glad that no one was seriously hurt last night. I think young Sebastian Crenshaw bore the greatest injury,' Mother says. Frances gives a little 'humph' into her teacup as Mother reaches out and pats my arm. 'I heard that you rescued him – you and that Nightly boy. The two of you saw a lot of each other last night,' she adds with a purse of her lips.

'You should have left him there,' Vaughn says from behind me. Mother rolls her eyes.

'Nightly or Crenshaw?' I say with a glare in my brother's direction.

'You could have left either of them and none of us would have said a word against it. But, surprisingly, I meant Crenshaw, not Nightly, although . . .' Vaughn continues as he kisses Mother, then Frances, on the cheek and sits down between them, opposite me.

'Well, I think it just shows us how full of heart our Aurelia is, to help Crenshaw after he—' Frances begins.

'After he was a massive maggot and treated her like—' Vaughn interrupts.

'Like I'm cursed! Which is to be expected because . . . well . . . I am,' I say loudly. Everyone goes a little too quiet.

'Damn Jules Nightly and his stupid ancestor,' Vaughn says in a low voice.

Five

The world feels as if it has been put on hold for the next few days. The Arcade, where I'm desperate to try out my magic now that I have access to a wandlet, is closed, as is the library that I have been so eager to explore. Everything feels off limits and Mother insists that Vaughn and I stay in. 'We must set an example. The heart of the Magical Court was attacked, and as Frances and I are members of the council, we can't ask debutantes to limit their activities if the two of you don't follow suit.'

But Vaughn and I not going out doesn't mean that I can't let anyone in, and so for the three days that we are under house arrest, Constance's frequent visits are kept secret. Never one to do as she is bid, she enters through the rear garden with a stealth that only a youngest child of a large family can achieve. The three of us practise our magic in our family arcade – a small, magically protected vaulted room in the basement of the house.

As well as the staircase entrance, our arcade has doors on three of the five sides: one that leads out to the herboritum and courtyard garden beyond, and one to the broom room. The third door, a door that, when I was little, had been as open and welcoming as the other thresholds, is now locked. It is the entrance to my father's spellorium and has been magically sealed shut since the day he died – no one can get in, and we've all tried. Mother even sought specialist advice through her connections on the council, but to no avail. Our best guess is that Father used a deeply powerful spell that was so in tune with his own magic that only he could open it. And as he and his magic are gone, so is the means by which to open the spellorium.

Sometimes the thought of the room beyond makes me feel uneasy, but mostly it makes me feel sad. Father would spend hours in his spellorium, researching and cataloguing, trying new spells and rediscovering lost ones from the First and Second Ages of Magic.

The spellorium always felt like a place where anything was possible. But now, there's no more Father, no more spells, no more discoveries.

On the fourth day after Mabon, Vaughn charges into my room before I'm even up and dressed.

'What a fine morning,' he declares as he throws open the curtains. I pull the covers up over my head to shut out the light as I sink down into the warmth of my bed.

'Aurelia Hathor Wycherley, the Autumn Gardens are finally opening today, and I have a promise to fulfil, so up you get,' he barks.

My heart lifts. Vaughn leaves the room, and I scamper out of bed and proceed to get dressed in record time. This is something I can finally get excited about. As I pull on a thick white dress and smooth down the fabric at the front, I realize September is fast turning into October and the crisp bluebird sky carries in it a nibble of cold that, in a couple of months' time, will be a bite. I pull my cloak tightly around me.

My gloved hand is linked around Vaughn's arm as we follow a long parade of witches heading towards the gardens. As we turn a corner, so does a carriage that I recognize immediately; the Prior family sigil is on the door and Constance is looking out with a pained expression as her mama sits next to her. Two of her sisters, Verity and Amity, sit opposite.

Like all of the other witches they are travelling towards the gardens, and I resolve to make sure that Vaughn and I find her and save her. I'm formulating a plan in my head when I notice someone up ahead looking back in hurried glances. Sebastian is with a group of witches I don't know but I've seen about the Arcade – his new friends.

Vaughn looks from me to where I am staring. 'You really should just let me hex him!'

I squeeze Vaughn's arm. 'You can be very sweet and brotherly when you want to be,' I say to him. 'Despite what Nightly says.'

This launches Vaughn into a tirade against not just Jules Nightly, but the whole Nightly family, mostly for the actions of their ancestor Heston.

'Even if the Nightlys are dealing with their own misfortune, it is nothing compared to the misfortunes they have placed upon us . . . upon you,' he finishes, glancing in my direction.

I pretend not to see the look he gives me, bitterness and sadness mixed in one. 'What misfortune is this?' I ask, trying to recall hearing anything scandalous about the Nightlys beyond the usual.

'The Season before my debutante year, at Ostara, Evelyn Nightly made her pledges to a witch; I do not know the particulars of the match, I was not myself with magic yet. I heard that they tied the first knot of tethering but, when Beltane came, he broke it, jilting her and finding another. Hardly anyone speaks of it now, no one wants to be reminded of the fate of an untethered witch.'

'That's terrible.'

'Evelyn was in her last Season. Apparently, her parents found her a willing match before Beltane ended, but she was heartbroken and refused.

'Demelza Nightly keeps her daughter away from magical society now and deals quickly with any gossipers. But Evelyn's magic is fading. I guess that's why some say that you should never form a magical match for love, only for the advancement of one's magic.'

'Gosh, poor Evelyn.' A million things run through my

head, but mostly I wonder how she could have thrown away her chance of keeping her magic, all because someone had thrown away their chance with her.

'Indeed, who would have thought a Nightly would stir up such sympathies. I guess love really does make people do the most foolish things,' Vaughn says. 'I hope I never tether for love.' I think that might be one of the saddest things that I've ever heard, despite the kernel of truth to it.

We continue walking in silence as I contemplate whether Vaughn is more likely to make a match for power or magic, if indeed love is off the table. The enchanted railings that mark the edge of the gardens run alongside us. I feel the magic streaming from them: a boundary holding in the magic of the gardens and keeping out all but witches. The black metal of the railings looks like twisting tree trunks with magically falling iron leaves that continue in a never-ending stream, twirling and crumpling as they make their way to the bottom only to start fluttering again from the top.

'That one's a gingko,' Vaughn points out. 'They have superb magical properties for healing and make quite a nice tea.'

He carries on pointing out leaves, telling me about them, and before I know it we're at the entrance to the gardens. I'm not surprised to see that it's flanked by two sets of witches from the Coven of Justice, and that dotted through the gardens are more black-cloaked witches. Since the attack, more of them are on the streets of the ton to guard us all, but that doesn't stop me from feeling a little wary as we pass into the gardens, their presence reminding me of what happened at the palace.

The trees are all on the turn, wearing crowns of copper, gold and bronze. The flowers are having their last burst of brilliance, filling the air with a musty sweetness; leaves crunch under my feet. There are small pavilions serving tea and cake, stalls of sweets, and walking vendors with treats to sell. Vaughn buys a bag of sweet peanut brittle and the two of us eat it as we pause by the amphitheatre and watch the players enact a scene from *The Tempest*.

'I haven't seen Constance yet,' Vaughn says as we walk towards a small knot of witches.

'No, but look, there's Martyn!' I wave and he smiles and waves back. Martyn is Vaughn's oldest friend. I often think of him as Vaughn's Constance. 'Come join us, Vaughn,' Martyn calls out. 'You too, Aurelia,' he adds, and I see a few of the witches he is with look a little horror-stricken as they turn away from me and Vaughn – but mostly from me.

'I can't, I'm on chaperone duties,' Vaughn replies with a cheerful wave to Martyn and a hard glare for the other witches.

I hold my head up and walk tall as we overtake where they are perched in an ornamental pagoda, looking out over the lake. If things had been different, these witches would have welcomed me into their circle with open arms, but all they give me are cold shoulders, harsh whispers, and looks that could wither. I set my stormy eyes on a future, one which I don't know how to make a reality . . . yet. One where I get to keep my magic and tell everyone who thinks little of me to go hex themselves.

I catch Vaughn looking back. 'You don't have to be stuck with me,' I whisper to him. 'I'm sure I'll find Constance soon – if you want to go with your friends, you can.'

'I'm not stuck with you, Aurelia. I wouldn't be spending time with you if I didn't want to.' I smile at him, happy to be close to him once again.

'So, besides Sebastian "soon to be hexed" Crenshaw, have any young witches taken your fancy?' Vaughn asks me and I look at him incredulously.

'Don't make fun of me, Vaughn, it's not fair.'

'I'm not,' he says, lifting his hands up in surrender.

'You know full well that even if the council allowed it, no one would ever tether with me. No one wants to be connected to cursed magic.'

'There has to be at least one witch in the world for you to tether with; if only the council hadn't forbidden it, I'm sure Constance would have . . .'

I stop walking and round on him. 'And you think I would let her? You were there, you saw what happened to her.' I shake a little as I remember Constance lying unconscious on the floor of my family arcade the day after I had received my magic, the day we had tried to perform secondary magic. She had been ill for almost a week.

Mother had to fight hard to let me be trained at the Arcade

67

at all, arguing that an untrained cursed witch was a bigger threat to magic-kind than a trained cursed witch. But when I had seen Constance lying there, I had to agree with the council, that maybe I should not be permitted to perform any magic.

No, I would never put someone that I love through the after-effects of my magic. And Vaughn puts too much importance on our family name and our mother's position if he thinks that the council would ever allow me to tether.

We both walk on in silence. I don't tell Vaughn that although I have no hope of tethering, I do have hope that I will find a way to keep my magic. He'd think me foolhardy for looking for an alternative to tethering, for searching for something that so many witches before me have failed to find, and I don't want him to dissuade me from what I am determined to do.

A slight wind picks up, rustling the trees. Leaves float from the branches down to the ground where they dance in eddies. And I feel hopeful with my wandlet on my wrist and my white debutante cloak around my shoulders. I squeeze Vaughn's arm.

'All will be well, you'll see. And there will be no need for us to be distant from one another as we have been. Let's not step away from each other, no matter what happens. Let's promise, magical matches or not, that we will always step up *for* each other,' I say, and he nods as he escorts me towards a small café with outdoor seating that looks over the lake and the small island in the centre of it. The island itself is off limits to all; it is the heart of the gardens and upon it is one of the last henges in England.

The sun is shining, and Vaughn moves towards an empty table. As we sit down, I can't help but notice that a few witches around us leave, their cake unfinished, their tea still warm. It's obvious that it is because of my presence.

I look around to find that Sebastian is sitting right behind us. Part of me is ridiculously grateful that he has not left, but another part wishes that he had. He looks fine after his ordeal at Mabon – a little pale maybe, but still handsome to me. His dark hair matches his eyes and I know that if he were to smile at me, the dimple in his left cheek would pull in.

A small pain in my chest rises as I think of it.

Vaughn said that there had to be at least one person in the world for me to tether with and I had always thought that would be Sebastian. A tiny part of me hopes maybe it still is. Maybe if we perform magic together, it will be compatible . . .

But judging by the way that he is sitting next to Emeline Hunt, her white gloved hand resting ever so delicately on his forearm, I don't think Sebastian has this same hope.

'Do you want to move?' Vaughn asks.

'No.' I'm resolute, even when I hear Sebastian talking to Emeline, speaking of the future, of Samhain and his hope that his magic finds her out. Our tea arrives and I hear him laughing at the things she says. I hear the scrape of a chair moving closer. I sip my tea and wish it was me he was moving towards.

Just when I think I can take no more, Martyn appears at our table and sits on the other side of Vaughn. Jolly Martyn fills the air and the space around him, and Vaughn's attention, with his smiles and his deep voice. I don't think I've ever seen him troubled a day in his life.

'Will you both excuse me for a moment?' I say and get up, looking for a rest room to compose myself.

I'm crying as I turn the corner of the café. I had thought that Sebastian loved me. I know I had loved him, that I still do, even though it hurts.

I rest my back against a tree and my sobs are soft and quiet as I slip down its trunk and look out across the lake. Sitting on the slightly damp ground, knowing that my white dress will be stained when I stand and not caring one bit, I allow myself to feel wretched.

I draw in a ragged breath as I hear a splash in the water in front of me.

Jules Nightly is wading through it, his back towards me, oblivious to my tears – thankfully. I don't need his scorn on top of my own pity.

He has his socks and shoes off, trousers pulled above his knees, and is ankle-deep in the lapping waters. His behaviour is odd, but the way that he moves through the water, like he is Poseidon himself and this is his realm, pulls my attention. He stops and hunches over, looking for something, his too-long hair flopping forward.

'Evelyn, I've found it!' Nightly calls, his voice full of

excitement. He turns his face with a smile that is a pure ray of joy. I feel like I'm intruding, like I'm seeing some unguarded part of Jules Nightly that he would not want me, or any Wycherley, to see.

Evelyn Nightly wades towards him. She is a tall young woman, her hair is also all the colours of autumn: copper, bronze and gold, with the same slight curl. She too has bare feet and her skirts are hitched up to show the curve of her calf.

I'm hidden from their eyeline by a collection of bushes, but I can see and hear them clearly.

'I told you to wait on the bank, I would have brought it to you,' Nightly says, an edge of exasperation in his voice.

'I know, but you're out here because of me. The least I can do is join you in the search,' Evelyn tells him, as he shoots a hand into the water and pulls out a fist full of green weeds.

'What do you think? Is this it?' I can hear the excitement in his voice.

Evelyn wades over and examines the plant. 'Yes, that's it.' She smiles at him but the edges of her mouth are tinged with sadness as she places a hand on her brother's. 'It'll be all right, you know; you really don't have to keep looking for the impossible. I . . . I need you to know that it's all right if I lose my magic, if you can't find a way for me to keep hold of it.'

Nightly looks up at her and, all of a sudden, he looks much younger than the dark-grey of his clothes – the dark-grey of a boy who is about to have his dreams shattered. Then, in a

71

blink, his hard exterior slips back into place.

'I will not fail. This is it, I'm sure of it.' The hope in his voice is infectious.

'You said that last time.' Evelyn's voice is gentle. I know by looking at her that she has moved past anger and arrived at the acceptance of her fading magic. In a way, I envy her that. I'm not sure I'll ever get there.

'I will not stop searching. I promise you, there *is* a way for witches to remain untethered and keep their powers, I know there is. I just need to find the right spell, or potion, or incantation. I'll storm the restricted section of the library if I have to. But who knows, maybe I have found the answer . . . with this.' He lifts the small, plain-looking green weed. 'We will save your magic, then Mother will have to change her tune.'

Evelyn lets out a mirthless laugh. 'I fear it will take more than a magical miracle for our mother to change her mind about anything!'

Jules crouches down and pulls another fistful of the weed from the lake, then places it in a jar that he fills with water.

'Even if you do find it, Jules, my magic is ebbing quickly. I don't know how much longer it will be with me.'

'Please don't give up on your magic, and don't give up on me,' her brother urges.

There is a long silence. I watch Nightly screw the lid on the jar tight and I know he is trying to contain his emotions.

'Are we done?' Evelyn says. 'I'd like to enjoy the gardens; I might not be able to get into the next one.'

'You will, and if I have anything to do with it, you'll be here with all your magic restored and for you to keep hold of forever.' The conviction in Nightly's voice strikes me. Evelyn Nightly is about to lose her magic and her brother is trying to find the key to keeping it, without tethering it. I feel my magic stirring. This is what I need. Whatever it is that Jules Nightly knows, I need to know it too.

Evelyn moves slowly towards the bank. Jules holds the jar up to the light and looks at it with a knowing smile, so different from his usual scowl.

But how am I ever going to get a Nightly to share the things that he knows with me: a Wycherley? Unless I can give him something he needs in return.

When I'm sure that the Nightlys have gone, I get up and walk back to the café, and I remember that Nightly said he would storm the restricted section of the library if he had to.

I smile broadly.

'What are you so happy about?' Vaughn asks as he and Martyn look up at me.

'Oh, nothing much,' I lie. Because I know exactly how to get Jules Nightly to give me what I need.

Six

It takes me a few days after seeing him at the gardens to track down Jules Nightly at the Royal Library of Magic.

I make my way across the sweeping piazza, the library doors magically parting as I approach them. I can smell the soft vanilla of old parchment and the spicy scent of magic as I stand in the foyer, breathing it all in.

The library sprawls over six floors; swirling staircases lead to long corridors that give way to endless rooms full of books and scrolls. I pull myself away from collections that I want to lose myself in, heading to where the witch at reception told me that I might find Nightly: fourth floor, ancient magical history.

The room is vast, double-heighted and stacked from floor to ceiling. There are shelves lining the spaces between the windows with books illuminated in a light that fluctuates as fluffy autumn clouds scuttle across the sky. In the darker corners of the room, the orbs of witch-fire float amid the gloom. Here are some of the oldest grimoires and spell scrolls in the building. I can feel how strong the magic inside them is; magic that has stayed the test of time.

Nightly is up a ladder with his back to me. His cravat is missing, shirt open at the neck and waistcoat buttoned tight. His muscular arms are bent and he's absorbed in a book as he balances with one leg higher than the other, pulling his grey trousers taut. My eyes read every line of him, and to my surprise, I feel more than my magic stirring.

A bell rings, signalling that the library will soon close, and I give a little start at the sound of it. He hears me but he doesn't turn his head from the pages. 'If you are looking for a match then you are sorely wasting your time. I am not interested in any notions of love or tethering, nor likely to be any time soon, so if that is your purpose then you should leave now and seek out my mother. She is taking full control of all things related to my tethering and ultimate happiness.' His tone reminds me of a guard dog, barking to frighten would-be intruders.

'I assure you, Mr Nightly, I am not interested in either of those things,' I declare.

He snaps the grimoire shut and rounds on me. He looks at me in that unshaking way of his, then he narrows his eyes. 'I don't believe you,' he replies, and I hear my voice in my head as I think, *He is right. I* am *interested in love and tethering – just not with him.*

'Ms Wycherley,' he says before placing his feet on the outside of the ladder rungs and sliding smoothly all the way down. 'Your brother really is a terrible chaperone.'

'Chaperones are not necessary in the library, just like in the Arcade or the spelloriums.'

'I know, but they should be. I've seen and heard things happen between the book stacks that would turn your hair white.' His eyes grow mischievous and my cheeks redden. 'If it wasn't already, of course,' he adds. 'If you are not here for matters of matching, then what are you here for?'

He is direct and I feel myself prickle at his manner. I let my shoulders sink and lift my chin as I tell myself that my need for Nightly's knowledge is greater than the hate the Wycherleys have towards his family.

I try to make my voice as direct as his, as disinterested and nonchalant. 'I just thought I'd check and see how your potion turned out,' I say, and he fixes me with a quizzical stare. I have him on the back foot and I like it.

'My potion?' He says the two words as if each one is new to him.

I nod and give him a knowing smile as he shakes his head and finds his composure again.

'I have no idea what . . .'

I take a step closer and show him a small dried-out piece of the lake weed that he and Evelyn had been collecting.

He glares at it, then at me, his eyes stormier than mine have ever been.

'I know what you are trying to do, Mr Nightly, and I want to help.'

For the second time I have Jules Nightly confused. I extend the weed to him and he takes it from my hand, his fingers grazing my palm.

'You, a Wycherley, want to help me?' He raises an eyebrow.

'Yes.' There is a pause and I can't tell if he is going to acquiesce or round on me.

'And what exactly is it that you think I need help with?'

I can hear the blood rushing through my head as I check that no one is near.

'You are seeking a way for your sister to keep her magic: a way that does not involve tethering and is more akin to the natural order of old magic, as things were in the First and Second Ages,' I say, then hold my breath because he is giving nothing away and I worry that I am wrong and Nightly will use this as a way to discredit my name.

Then he seems to soften. 'Yes, I am, and I can see why something like that would be attractive to you.' It feels like a slap and my wandlet is tingling in retaliation, snaking its way into the palm of my hand.

'I am not permitted to tether, but I don't see why I should let a curse dictate my future, my magic.'

'And to get what you want, you would seek out help from a Nightly?'

'I'm here, am I not?' The edge in my voice is noticeable.

'That you are.' There is another pause.

'Did it work? The potion?' The hope in my voice is high and desperate.

He shakes his head as he wraps his fingers around the dried plant and crumbles it in his palm.

'No. And I don't need any help.' He starts to turn his back on me, closing down the conversation.

'I beg to differ. Time is running out, Mr Nightly. Evelyn's magic is fading fast, is it not?'

'I don't need help, especially not from a Wycherley. My mother was livid when she found out that I had assisted you at Mabon, and I can imagine how she will react if she found out that you were here with me now,' he says again.

I give a long sigh of exasperation. 'Mr Nightly, we may share a common war, but we also share a common goal. If we pool our resources, we are more likely to succeed. I am not above using the most cunning persuasion that I can find to encourage you to work with me.'

'Cunning persuasion. Are you threatening me?'

'Yes, and bribing you too, if it will help.' He smiles for a second, an amused twist at the corner of his mouth. 'The threat comes in the form of my best friend, Constance Prior. She is connected to almost every witch in the ton, her social circle made large by her family's reputation and the excellent connections of her six older sisters. If I were to ask her to make it known that you, Mr Jules Nightly of Kestrel Lodge, were in the market for a match, you would not have a moment's peace between now and Ostara.

There would be no time to look for a cure at all!'

Nightly crosses his hands over his chest, his gaze practically shooting lightning bolts at me. 'That's not just cunning, that's downright nasty. And the bribery?'

I hold out an official letter, signed and sealed, from the Royal Magical Council, giving the two of us permission to access the restricted section of the library.

He reaches for it, and I move back. I can see how much this means to him, and I know what it might mean to his sister too.

'How did you get your mother to sign that?' he asks. 'I don't believe that Nell Wycherley would ever willingly sign her name to something that would be of advantage to a Nightly.'

'She didn't,' I reply. 'I forged her signature and her tether's too.' I can feel my cheeks flushing, I've never done such a thing before, but I've seen their signatures a thousand times and know them by heart. If Mother found out she would be furious, but this is important.

'Threats, bribery, forgery. You know, in light of this, I can see where we Nightlys get our hostility towards you Wycherleys!' His eyebrow rises again, and I want to hex him.

'Do we have a deal, Mr Nightly?'

Seven

T here are five arched entrances to the Grand
London Arcade spread about the ton, though I
have only ever used the one closest to Hemlock
Square, on Tonbridge Street. Beyond these entrances is the
Arcade: a secret space, somewhere else entirely.

The four other entrances are at Devonshire Court, Flint
Street, Randor Mews and Warwick Way. Mother once said
that if she ever told me the location of the secret interior of the
London Arcade that she would immediately combust. I don't
doubt that for a moment; some oaths have strong repercussions
when broken and a secret oath is one of the strongest.

The Tonbridge Street entrance is constructed of stone and
glass and magic. The glass shifts with patterns and colours
depending on many things: the time of day, the season,
the mood of the people within it, the experience of the city
around it.

Today the glass is full of birds, a mixed flock of small finches all darting around in ripples on the glass.

The five arches of the Arcade are never shut. Any tethered witch can access them at any time, but there are only certain times when a debutante is allowed in, one of which is to learn from one of the purple-clad witches from the Coven of Knowing. It's not usually this busy – not even during designated teaching times – but with this being the first class since our presentations, all of us white witches are eager to try our wandlets, and all the grey witches obviously want to assess us and see who might make a good tether.

Constance swears in a way that would have her mama reaching for her wandlet as she takes in the long line that we are at the back of.

'Can you see anyone that we know?' she asks, hopping about on tiptoes.

Being taller, I have a clear view. I see Vaughn as he slips through the arch, then my heart skips as I see Sebastian a little behind him, a different witch as his confidante today.

Seeing him makes me think of Jules Nightly and the way that he tried to dismiss me a few days before: *'If you are looking for a match then you are sorely wasting your time. I am not interested in any notions of love or tethering, nor likely to be any time soon.'*

Nightly hadn't reacted the way I thought he would to my threats, forgery and bribery. 'I'll consider your offer, Wycherley, and let you know by the end of the week,' he had said.

'I knew we should have got here earlier,' Constance is saying. 'We would have been at the head of the line by now if Mother hadn't wanted me to help her with brewing more cough medicine.'

'How is your father?' I ask.

'He's fine. Mother is just fussing. He says it's the British weather – damp and cold, that it lives in his bones and plagues him. He swears that cook's Waakye is all the remedy he needs, but never within my mother's hearing.' Constance lets out a frustrated sigh. 'As long as he is occupying my mother, that's fine by me. She's been trying to set me up with Sebastian again – can you believe it?'

I could.

'What did you tell her?'

'I told her that not for all the magic in the world would I tether with Sebastian "the worm" Crenshaw; that he is a pathetic little cretin with no backbone and even less magical aptitude.' She scowls.

'Not for all the magic in the world!' I say with a raised eyebrow and a teasing look at Constance.

'Never,' she says defiantly.

'All of it? Every last spark?' I tease some more.

'And what would I do with all that magic? I'd be miserable. Imagine if you were the only person in the whole world who could use magic. Everyone would come to you with their problems and expect you to fix them. You'd have no one to talk to about it because no one would understand, and to top

82

it all off you'd be tethered to a two-faced, friend-ditching, lily-livered coward!'

I can't help but smile at Constance's vehemence. I shake my head and follow her through the arch and into the Arcade. Inside is a huge domed area, a roof of carved rock soaring above it and a vast five-pointed star on the floor. Each point of the star is in line with the arched entrances. In between the tall arches that lead from the streets of London to the Arcade are smaller arches that lead off to practice spaces.

As the witches file in, they fill the enormous space. There are two witches standing in the centre of the pentacle on a raised platform – Linden Platz and Gerard Russo. Both are among the oldest and most well-respected witches in England, both of the Coven of Knowing, their robes such a deep purple, they almost look black.

Platz hits his staff on the floor of the Arcade, radiating out a small shock wave through all us debutantes, quieting us.

'Those of you in white, I extend formal greetings and welcome you into the world of witches and magic. Those of you returning, I am sorry to see you. The desired outcome of a debutante is to find a match, and all of you in grey have failed to achieve this.'

His words sound a little harsh, and I catch the eye of a girl in dark grey who is trying to make herself look small and less obvious.

'Unfortunately, you greys will not find any new instruction here. You have mastered your primary magic, there will be no more development for you until you form a tether and join a coven college. Of course, you will be expected to go over the basics once again, to refresh your skills, but they will not deepen until you take the next step with your magic.' He seeks each grey witch out in the crowd and holds their gaze for a beat while he speaks.

'As we move through the Season there will be opportunities for you to seek out possible matches. Once Samhain is over, you will be encouraged to form small bonds with other witches to test the viability of any connections you might feel are establishing.'

Russo steps forward to speak – his tone is lighter than Platz's, more nurturing and enthusiastic. 'However, we know that you are eager to perform secondary magic with another witch, and for you new debutantes, this is your first chance.'

There is murmuring around the room, maybe a few of the other witches in white like me are trying to hide that they have already tried secondary magic. I watch as Platz and Russo start to pair us. I look towards Sebastian and I'm surprised to see Constance standing near him. She was at my side a moment ago.

As the two purple-clad witches walk around the room pairing debutantes in close proximity to each other, I can't help but notice a gap forming as witches shift away from me.

Sebastian doesn't look happy about being paired with Constance, but Constance looks gleeful. I don't know what she's up to. I have seen her and Sebastian perform magic together in her family arcade . . . it had not been a success.

When Russo gets close, he pairs me with Mariah Kent. 'Sir, I can't perform magic with her, she's cursed.' Mariah fixes me with a terrified stare.

'Thank you for pointing this out to me, I would never have realized,' Russo says with a withering look that makes Mariah turn pink.

'I don't want to force anyone to perform magic with me, Mr Russo,' I intervene. 'I will observe, if that is all right with you?'

'It is not all right with me.' Russo looks from me to Mariah, who now looks like she might start crying.

'I won't do it. You can't make me,' she says.

Russo shakes his head. 'How very disappointing. Mr Liam Long, you will pair with Ms Wycherley.'

'No, I won't,' Liam says, crossing his arms.

I'd expected as much from my fellow witches, but it doesn't mean it hurts any less. Tears threaten to spill and a lump in my throat has me lifting my head high as I turn, set on leaving the Arcade before I actually start crying, when I walk straight into Jules Nightly.

I take a step back and look up at him.

'I will,' he says, 'I'll perform secondary magic with Ms Wycherley.' There is a sharp intake of breath from those around me, and I hear Mariah whisper, 'By the Magic, a Wycherley and a Nightly! That is never going to end well.'

I blink up at Jules Nightly and give him a hard stare, but I don't refuse. I want to perform secondary magic, and although I don't want to inflict suffering on anyone, he is a Nightly and is a willing participant . . . Or is he?

'Do you know what happens to those who perform magic with me?' I ask him straight.

He gives a small smile, then replies, 'I do.'

'Very well, I will let you both decide upon your wand hands.' Russo motions to me and Nightly before pairing Liam Long and Mariah Kent together and moving on.

'What are you doing?' I hiss at Nightly. I can feel my stormy eyes flashing, my magic rising.

'Moving my wandlet to my right hand. I can use either to perform magic, though I do favour my left, as do you.'

'That is not what I mean, and you know it, Nightly!' I bite out his last name in a way that Vaughn would be proud of.

'That's not a very nice way to say thank you,' he says, looking down at me, his infuriating hair flopping forward.

'Are you doing this out of pity . . . or revenge?'

'Definitely revenge. You are a Wycherley after all and you did try to bribe me with a forged library permission the other day.'

'Bribe you!' I say with a smile. 'Have you already forgotten about me threatening you too?'

'Oh no, I haven't forgotten those at all, in fact the threat of you has been on my mind a lot.' He moves to stand beside me, facing the centre of the pentacle and pulling off his gloves. I turn and do the same. 'You see, with or without Ms Prior's gossiping sisters, I have a gaggle of witches desperate to try their magic with me and I, as you know—'

'You are "not interested in any notions of love or tethering, nor likely to be any time soon",' I say in my best imitation of Nightly.

I don't look at him, but I can hear the smile in his voice as he says, 'Precisely.'

'So, you thought you'd terrorize me because I too am not interested.'

'Indeed. Amusingly, you are safe, neutral ground. I can perform magic with you, and they will keep their distance.' He extends his arm and I take in the empty space around us.

'Does this mean that you have accepted my—'

'Bribe? I'm still deciding, I told you I'd let you know by the end of the week; I am a witch of my word.'

Platz performs a small movement and large circles of salt appear around us all to keep our magic contained and us safe from the magic of others.

'We want you to perform a simple lower-level secondary magic spell. If nothing happens, don't worry,' Russo says. 'Only magic that is compatible will work. If your magic is mismatched, prepare yourselves for consequences – that is why we have the salt circles.'

I notice that all of the pairings have at least one witch in white.

'It is not about the spell itself really, it is the outcome of the spell that we will be observing,' Platz says. I've seen the beauty and harmony in a magical match, as well as the destruction and turmoil of mismatched magic. I think of

Constance and Vaughn and the way their magic worked in unison to clear the smoke during the attack. Luckily, my brother is on the other side of the Arcade, otherwise he would be protesting my pairing.

We are to perform a growth spell. Platz and Russo show us the movements: they join hands and then mirror each other as they take a small step to the side, then throw out their free arms before sweeping them to the front and raising them above them. Then they bring their arms back down to their sides with a flick of their wrists and pull their extended legs back. A small green shoot pushes up through the floor of the Arcade in front of me and Nightly; there is one inside every circle of salt, green and bright.

'Now it is your turn, perform the move as often as you need to, stop if it becomes . . . uncomfortable,' Russo instructs.

'We are expecting to see some growth. Anyone who can produce a bud will be assured that their magic is a fine match indeed,' Platz adds. 'If the seedling dies, then it's safe to say that your magic is incompatible.'

My hands are sweaty, my palms slick, fingers tingling as I look from the seedling to Nightly. He has his hand extended to me. 'If you please.'

I look at his hand. It feels like a betrayal to take it, as if I am crossing some line that no Wycherley has ever crossed before, but at the same time the pull of performing magic is strong.

'Very well.' I grasp his hand and instantly feel a tingle of magic move into me. I check to make sure that I can't see

Vaughn, worried about the lecture he and Mother will give me later.

Nightly lowers his voice to a whisper. 'Relax, breathe into the magic. With every in-breath imagine my energy, my magic, flowing into you; with every out-breath think of pushing your magic into me. In and out, in and out.'

We take a few deep breaths, and each time, I do as he instructs. I imagine myself filling with his magic. It is hot and bright, and as I breathe out, I imagine my magic flowing into him, dark, smoky and swirling. I feel his fingers tense around mine as I send my magic through them and into him, his breath catching a little as he breathes out.

We begin to perform the same movement that Platz and Russo demonstrated, flowing through the sequence twice before the shoot grows to a bush. Excitement swells in me, and in another movement, the bush is taller than Nightly, curving at the top to fit in the invisible bubble of protection that the salt ring provides. The magic feels delightful and a little intoxicating as it flows into every facet of me. I draw more of it to me, send more of my magic into Nightly. A fourth time and there are buds on the bush, a fifth and the buds bloom into beautiful deep red roses, filling the air with their heady scent. My whole being is full of magical potential – a strength and openness that I have never experienced before. The power of my and Nightly's secondary magic surprises me, its force a little overwhelming.

'Aurelia,' Nightly says, his voice strained, and I turn to look at him. His eyes are full of smoky tendrils and his skin looks a little ashen. I instantly let go of his hand and he falls to the ground, shaking, curling himself into a ball. I crouch beside him, his eyes still misty, his skin pale and a little shiny.

'I'm sorry. It will pass . . . eventually,' I tell him as I kneel beside him. 'The same thing happened with Constance, my magic leaving her incapacitated for . . . a while.'

After a few minutes his eyes brighten and clear, he sits up, shaking his head. 'Is . . . is this your cursed magic?' he asks.

I nod. 'When I performed magic with Constance, she was ill for a week.'

Platz has noticed. He clears our protective barrier and crouches next to Nightly, checking him over before looking at me from a distance, and I can see a look of questioning about him. Then he looks beyond me, assessing our rose bush.

The pairs whose magic is not compatible either stand in empty magical domes or, like Constance and Sebastian, are covered in dirt and bits of shrubbery from the explosive union of their mismatch. Those that found a match to their magic have grown their seedlings into small green plants, some have buds within their vivid green leaves and thorns, but none of the others have full blooms and ours is bigger than all of them put together.

'Impressive and surprising,' Platz says, admiring the roses.

Then we both watch as Nightly is sick on the floor. 'What a shame that the two of you are not compatible.'

Not that much of a shame, I think to myself. *He is, after all, a Nightly.*

Eight

watch Sebastian dancing with Liam Long at the first private event of the Season: the Prior-Okore ball. As is their custom when one of their daughters is in the Season, Constance's parents are throwing a lavish celebration. Their beautiful home is a riot of warmth and colour, and Merry Prior and Yemi Okore give me a warm welcome as I enter their house – Ms Prior pulls me into her embrace and I thank her and Mr Okore for inviting me. Constance's father smiles heartily at me and I am grateful that neither of them have ever treated me differently since my cursed magic descended on me.

Constance quickly pulls me to her side. 'My mother is practical and economical in all things except the Prior-Okore ball,' Constance says as she shows me around all of the many decorations that adorn the house and flavourful dishes that fill me up with their scent. I can't wait to sample them all.

The festivities are soon in full swing, the musicians play lively dances and there is a sweetness in the air that has nothing to do with the myriad flower arrangements throughout the house.

I am sure this is the only private ball that I will be invited to all Season, so I am determined to make the most of it. The ball is not only for debutantes; there are witches of all ages here and, as it is outside the confines of the Season's official engagements, we can wear whatever colour we want. Constance is in the middle of everything, dancing with everyone. She looks radiant in a beautiful jade green silk dress with bold silver detailing that makes her skin glow deep and rich. Matching drop silver earrings sway as she moves. If she doesn't find a match by Yule, there is something desperately wrong with the magical world.

She smiles as she dances with Emeline Hunt, who I like a little better now that Sebastian has moved on to other witches. I think he is determined to step out with everyone but me and Constance, whose mother has stopped pressing the issue after the rose explosion at the Arcade.

I am wearing a deep crimson dress that reminds me of the roses Nightly and I have conjured. I slightly regret my choice, and wish I knew how to perform a minor glamour so that I could change the colour. I stand out too much among the pale or bright colours everyone else is wearing.

Although, not *everyone*, I notice, as Jules Nightly enters the room wearing dark blue. Behind him, his parents walk arm in arm. Demelza Nightly looks as if she is inspecting every witch around her. Nightly's father looks as if he wants to apologize to every witch for it.

I can see that Jules and Evelyn are a mixture of both of their parents: Oliver Hallows' height and auburn hair, Demelza's bone structure and withering looks. Although right now, Jules just looks bored. His mother is introducing him to a small knot of witches, no doubt dealing with the important task of his future happiness. It's amusing to watch Nightly as his mother talks to the witches, scrutinizing them all, before setting her attention on one and trying to engage her son in conversation with them.

I'm smiling at his misfortune when he looks up and sees me, his eyes narrowing. He knows I'm making fun of him, and before I can look away he is making his apologies and striding towards me.

'Wycherley, care to dance?' He extends a hand and I look at it, then beyond him to the revolted look on his mother's face.

'Is she livid? Please tell me she is livid,' he whispers, conspiratorially.

'I think she is not so secretly hexing us both,' I say.

'Good, she's been on edge since we grew that rose bush. You know when Platz and Russo removed all the others, they couldn't get rid of ours? Every time someone goes near it they get spiked by flying thorns.'

'Really?' I look at him, disbelieving.

'Really. It seems cursed magic works in wonderful ways.' His hand is still extended, his mother still glaring at us.

'She's threatening to disown me for performing magic with a Wycherley.' I can believe that and wonder why he is testing her further. My own mother, although not as displeased as Demelza Nightly, has let me know that she was not happy with events. But I couldn't help feel that my mother was a little glad that I'd found anyone at all to perform magic with, that she'd thought I might pass the next three years only observing secondary magic. I'm sure she hopes this will encourage the boldness of others, after all, she does not want to encourage Jules Nightly.

'Saving you at Mabon was bad enough, but that rose bush has made my mother produce thorns I don't think even she knew she was capable of,' Nightly continues.

'I'm sorry, did you say that you saved me at Mabon? You must have me mixed up with Crenshaw because I'm pretty sure that you manhandled me and incarcerated me in a carriage.'

He gives a smile. 'If that is how you choose to recall it, I have no doubt that I had good reason for incarcerating you. After all, Wycherley, criminal behaviour is in your base nature.' He raises an eyebrow. 'Now, about that dance?'

'I don't know if I should,' I say, teasing. 'Apart from your mother's displeasure and the outrage that it would cause my own family, it doesn't feel dangerous enough for my felonious tendencies.'

'I assure you, my mother *is* danger, and I've heard enough

about Nell Wycherley to know that you would be in grave danger on two fronts.' He looks to his outstretched hand. 'Now, if you please. We can discuss our arrangement while we dance.'

'Arrangement?'

'The conditions of our . . . scheme.'

'Very well.'

We join the edge of the dance and follow the lead of the assembled pairs. The looks on some of their faces are even better than the one Demelza has on hers, and I am resolved not to look in my own mother's direction.

'Tomorrow,' Nightly says.

'Tomorrow?'

'Noon sharp, I will meet you at the Arcade.'

'I see,' I say. 'So you have decided to take me up on my offer of assistance.'

'I have decided to accept your bribe.'

I ignore that comment. 'And in exchange, for access to the restricted library and all the knowledge that it holds, you will share everything that you know with me?'

He spins away from me and we part for a few beats as we pass our neighbouring couple in the dance before we are united once more.

'I will, but I think that my contribution, my information, is vital to what will come next, and because of this I am going to need something else from you,' he says.

I raise an eyebrow as we move close then spin out, passing a second pair.

'And what extortion might you want to pull from my bribery?' I ask. He is in front of me once more, my hand in his, his other on my waist, mine holding my dress.

'You.'

'Me?' I put a foot wrong in the dance and almost step on his.

'Look at how incensed my mother is. You are a Wycherley, I am a Nightly, she sees it as a personal attack on our bloodlines that we are . . . courting.'

'But we are not.'

'She seems to think so.'

'Whatever gave her that idea?'

Nightly spins me in the dance then pulls me close and puts his lips to my ear and whispers, 'I did.'

'Why?'

'I just told you.' We push away from each other again, circling a pair of witches.

'No, you didn't, not really.' My voice is a high whisper at his audacity.

'Evelyn. I know you understand the particulars of her . . . magical future. When it all came about, my mother cast her out. My sister didn't go far – to my aunt's originally – but then Father fetched her home, not that she had wanted to come. Would you want to live with a mother who had forsaken you?'

We part once more, and I am full of new animosity towards Demelza Nightly.

'My mother is determined to force Evelyn out of magical society, out of our family, while Father and I are determined to keep her,' Nightly continues as if he never left my side. 'She has arranged for Evelyn to go to some island off the coast of Scotland, to be "rehabilitated" and to learn how to live a non-magical life. Evelyn is close to fleeing, running away from us all. Mother is usually relentless in her personal attacks on my sister, but this week she has done nothing but hound me about you. Evelyn has had a reprieve and I have become the sole focus of my mother's meddling and fury. So, here is my exploitation – if you want to call it that – we work together to find a cure, and, during that time, we will make it known, to my mother at least, that we are courting. Once we succeed, we can go our separate ways.'

He spins me again and dips me down, my hand holding on to his neck, his arm supporting me.

'But . . . what if that takes all Season? It might scare off a potential tether for you.'

He shrugs and returns me to an upright position.

'And what if we don't find a cure?' I continue.

'Then there will be three less witches in the world. If I can't save Evelyn, I don't plan on tethering.'

'Why not?' I ask before the dance forces us to part again. Here I am trying to think of ways to hold on to my magic, and here he is looking for a way to throw it away and implode his family.

'Because I can't leave Evelyn to that fate alone, because she is my sister and I'd rather be magicless with her than

97

to watch our mother push her from our family, from me. Because part of this is my mother's doing and I want her to suffer greatly, and with no one to carry on the Nightly's magical line, she will suffer. And most importantly because it is my magic, Ms Wycherley, and I can do with it whatever I please. I can have control over it just as you are seeking control over yours, so stop looking at me like that!'

As we spin apart I know exactly how I am looking at him – shocked, horrified, disappointed.

'So, unless we find a cure, you . . . you're going to give away your magic?' I whisper as he holds me close to him once more.

He must be able to see the hurt on my face. 'Yes.'

I push him away and stop still in the dance. 'I'll not do it, I'll not help you; I'll not give you access to the restricted library, and I'll not pretend to be courting you. I'll find the answers on my own.' I turn to walk away, but he reaches for me, grasping my hand.

'Please, Wycherley.' His voice is strained and full of desperation. 'If you don't do this, your magic will be lost too. But if we find what we are looking for then we will save all of our magic, not just yours and Evelyn's but every witch's. Besides, I promise it will be no large inconvenience to pretend to be enamoured with me.' He keeps his bright eyes on mine and lifts my hand up to his shoulder before grasping my waist and taking up the dance once more. 'It may even work out to your benefit – not just to your magic, but your heart too.'

I eye him again. 'Not for one moment do I intend on letting you anywhere near my heart.'

He gives a frustrated sigh. 'Not me. Crenshaw. Since we started dancing, he hasn't stopped looking at you. And I've seen the way that you moon over him.'

I push away from him a little too forcefully and snap into him hard when we re-join.

'I do not moon!'

He smiles. 'But you do – and now, so does he.'

Nightly spins me around so that I have a clear view of Sebastian. He is staring daggers into Nightly's back and when we lock eyes, I feel a jolt. I know I should scorn him as he has me, and I know that he has been unkind to me in my misfortune, but that look flows through me like a long-forgotten dance that I know all the steps to.

'Fine, I'll do it,' I tell Nightly, a snap decision I hope I won't come to regret. He spins me away one last time, and when we come together, the music stops. He is smiling broadly, a renewed flame dancing in his eyes. He lifts my gloved hand and brings it to his lips.

'Pretend to like me, or no one will believe us,' he says, his breath caressing my knuckles.

I stare icily at him. 'But you are a Nightly,' I say.

'Yes, and you are my foe, but for the Season at least, we will call a truce and be accomplices.'

I think this over in a moment before smiling sweetly at him and batting my eyelashes.

'Very good, Wycherley. You are so convincing in your deceptions.'

'Tomorrow, noon,' I say.

'It's a date.' He smiles and winks at me, and I feel like I might have just made a deal with some malevolent creature of the First Age. As he walks back towards his mother I shiver. I don't want to make a bigger enemy of Demelza Nightly than I already have, and I don't want to make an ally of Jules Nightly. But against my better judgement there is still a part of me that cannot quite give up Sebastian Crenshaw. Despite his actions, my heart is forever foolish and giddy, for presently he can't keep his eyes off me.

Nine

surprise myself with the vigour and excitement that I feel the next morning. Nightly is going to share all that he knows about the problem of tethering and together we are going to find a way for Evelyn and I to keep our magic. Being his shield against eligible witches, and a point of antagonism for his mother, is a small price to pay. I don't really believe that he will sacrifice his magic, not when it comes down to it how could he?

Constance and I walk to the Arcade together. The early October weather is crisp in the shadows but perfect in the light. I notice that the leaves on the trees are all the colours of Nightly's hair. As if knowing where my thoughts have strayed, Constance asks, 'What exactly is going on between you and Jules Nightly?'

'Going on?' I haven't quite figured out how I'm going to explain my counterfeit courting of Jules Nightly to

Constance, so for now, I don't. 'Oh, I think he was just a little surprised after we performed secondary magic the other day, and now he's quite interested . . . in my magic that is . . . for research purposes.'

'Really? It looked like he was interested in more than your magic, Aurelia, and I'm sure that if you see him again, he'll be *thorough* in his investigation of you,' Constance says, with a cunning smile. 'Who would have thought that a Nightly would be so interested in a Wycherley! You know, for research.'

'Wait up!' Vaughn calls from behind. As we stop to wait for him, I notice that Constance quickly smooths her dress before turning to face him.

'I see you two are off early, trying to nab the good instructors, or just avoiding me?' He glares in my direction before he nestles himself between the two of us.

'Definitely aiming for the good instructors,' Constance tells him.

'Try not to let Russo and Platz pair you up with any of the junior apprentices, and if they do, avoid the witches from Clune college – their reputation is not very good. Their teaching methods are somewhat lacking and their magical thinking is small-minded.' I get the feeling that he is trying to distract me, but I've known my brother too long to fall for his ploys.

'Why are you coming along to the Arcade anyway?' I narrow my eyes at him. 'You already covered all of this last year, you don't need instruction in primary magic.'

'True, but I wanted to offer you some moral support,' he

says. I don't believe him for a moment. 'Besides, Mother is concerned that there is something going on between you and Nightly.'

'Going on!' I exclaim. 'What exactly does she think I am doing with Jules Nightly?'

'I think it's more what she thinks *he* is doing with *you*.' I blush. 'He is a Nightly; never to be trusted. I said that I would keep an eye on you, even though I'm sure he was only dancing with you to fulfil a bet or something. If so, maybe I should duel him for your honour.'

I feel my cheeks get hotter. 'A bet!' I say, before Constance cuts me off.

'Oh, he's just interested in Aurelia's magic, for *research* purposes, you see.'

'I see.' Vaughn's voice has that edge that he reserves only for the Nightlys.

As we approach the entrance to the Arcade there is a steady stream of witches making their way through the arch. The domed space is full of light, and in the centre stands a group of tethered witches all wearing purple in various shades, from pale lilac to deep plum: the purples of the Coven of Knowing.

There are more light-grey witches in the group than I expected, and a few dark-grey ones too. I guess not making a match yet has them thinking that they might need to work on their magic. I look over at Vaughn and wonder again why he is here – it's not like he needs the practice – but then I see him looking at Constance. Not just looking . . . taking her in. I think my brother might be seeing something in my friend that he has never thought to notice before. I imagine them forming a tether in the future, and the possibility fills me with happiness for not only both of them, but me too.

Once in the Arcade the three of us find a space in the large hall, its arches high above us, and I smile to see that our rose bush is still there, trailing towards the nearest pillar that supports the domed roof.

'Witches,' Russo calls for attention and the crowd grows quiet. 'Over the next year, you will learn the basic elements of primary magic. When testing your connections with other witches, you will touch on some secondary forms of magic, but you cannot perform the more powerful, sophisticated secondary magic without first mastering the primary discipline.'

The group of purple-clad instructors fan out around the room and Platz steps forward, allocating each of us in turn to a pair of instructors.

Constance and Vaughn are sent off to the far end of the Arcade with a pair of witches in amethyst robes, whereas I am directed to a pair in pale lavender.

'Kit!' I exclaim as I take in the instructors. Kit Thorne hasn't changed much from the boy he once was. He is a little taller and his jaw has a more defined angle to it, but he still has the shock of blonde hair that he inherited from his mother and the dark, enquiring eyes of my father's tether, Jonathan Reid. Kit's easy good looks are all his own I realize

as he scrutinizes me, not able to place me for a moment . . .
because although he has not changed greatly, I have. Then
his face clears and his eyes widen.

'Little Aurelia Wycherley, is that you?'

'Yes, it is, although my looks might try to deceive you.'
I smile shyly. 'And not so little any more.' I gesture to my
height, although he is still a little taller than me.

'I was sorry to hear of your . . .' He gestures awkwardly
then puts his hand down.

I change the subject swiftly as I can feel my emotions
rising at the thought of my father. 'I thought you had gone to
live in America with your mother.'

'I did, we did, but we returned some years ago, just before
my debutante year. My father insisted we return so that I
could attend Faustings Coven College after tethering – he
didn't want me at one of the American schools of magic.'

'Have you been in contact with your father recently?' I ask.

'Not for a few years now,' he replies, looking strained at
the thought of it.

'I haven't seen him since just after my father died.'

Kit scoops up my hand. 'I was sorry to hear of his passing,
I always remember him with fondness.' I can hear the
American twang to his voice now as he turns and introduces
his tether.

'This is Cora Stewart,' he says. Cora is a sweet-looking,
round-faced witch with dimples. Her robes complement her
soft brown hair. She gives a small smile which falters almost

instantly. She looks over at Kit. He nods at her approvingly and she beams back at him in a way that makes me feel a little awkward.

'This is Ms Aurelia Wycherley, an old family friend,' he tells Cora.

'A pleasure to meet you, Ms Wycherley. I think we're about to start, so you had best take your place, if you don't mind?' Cora says, a little anxious as she looks over to where Platz and Russo are standing in the middle of the Arcade.

For the next few hours, Cora and Kit instruct us on how to ground ourselves in our magic, feeling for the subtle strains around us and connecting them to the deep reservoir that exists within us. Whenever Cora passes, she gives gentle encouragement and praise. Kit is more direct in his instruction and I remember that he was always serious and to the point as a boy – another trait he shared with his father. We were never particularly close; he was better friends with Vaughn than with me. He and his mother were estranged from Jonathan when I was about seven and left for the Americas during one of the long periods of silence and distance from one another that my father and Jonathan also sometimes had.

It feels odd to see him again. As he stands behind me instructing me in my spell casting, he places one hand on my shoulder, pushing it down while explaining why the extension of my arm is important to the magic and will improve the reach of my grounding.

'Thorne!' I flinch at the ferocity of the voice that booms

through the Arcade and turn to see Nightly charging towards me. If this is part of our counterfeit courting then I think it might be a little heavy-handed.

'Thorne, I called you out the Beltane before last and you left London with a duel debt unpaid,' Nightly shouts. The Arcade is now silent, every eye is on the two of them and I am standing between them. I look from Jules to Kit, trying to piece together why Nightly is talking of magical duels.

'What is going on?' Platz calls, as he makes his way towards us. 'Oh, I see.' He looks from Nightly to Thorne. 'I thought this would happen eventually, and I guess now is as good a time as any to get it over with.'

Nightly has not stopped staring at Kit Thorne, his teeth clenched so hard I think they might break. Thorne is standing his ground, but he is still close to me and I am sure that I can feel him trembling.

'Kit Thorne, Jules Nightly issued you with a duel for dishonouring his sister and her magic. Do you concede, or will you duel?' Platz says.

I turn my head to look at Kit Thorne. 'You,' I say under my breath, fixing my stormy eyes upon him. 'You jilted Evelyn!' He flinches.

I watch as a resolve passes over Thorne and an arrogance shifts into his features – an arrogance that I also remember belonged to his father. Kit takes a few steps past me, towards Nightly. 'I accept,' he declares. 'Under the usual rules, I call my tether, Cora Stewart, as my second.'

Cora moves swiftly past me to stand next to Kit. The other witches in the Arcade have now created a large fighting ring around Nightly and Thorne, with Platz and Russo standing in the middle. I skirt around the crowd near to where Nightly is standing. Magical duels are few and far between, reserved for resolving only the strongest of grievances. A duel is never issued lightly because no magical spell is withheld in a duel, and the consequences can be fatal. Though that type of malevolent magic is frowned upon, there is always the possibility that it might be performed by an immoral witch, and if Kit Thorne can give up on his tethering oath, then I wouldn't put anything past him.

I have never seen a magical duel before, but I have heard of them. Witches are creative with their magic, spells that don't kill are often far worse. Duels were a lot more popular in the Second Age of Magic, but then magic was more abundant – another reason why fatal spells are now discouraged.

'Nightly, who is your second?' Russo asks. Nightly shakes his head. 'I don't have one. No second,' he says.

A second is there to complete the duel if necessary, but also to channel their magic to the lead witch. Kit Thorne will have access to secondary magic and therefore a huge advantage over Nightly if he doesn't have a second to draw from.

Without thinking I step up, slip my ungloved hand into Nightly's, and push a little of my magic into him before he realizes.

'I'll second for Jules Nightly,' I declare.

There's a gasp from the crowd and I make the mistake of looking over at Vaughn, who is outraged. I can already imagine what Mother will say, and what the gossipers in the crowd are already whispering.

'What are you doing, Wycherley?' Nightly says in a low hiss.

'I'm not entirely sure.' I suddenly feel like this was a foolish idea. I had been so incensed by Kit and by a strange feeling of betrayal, not only for Evelyn Nightly but also for the memory of my father and the tether he had had with Jonathan.

'I don't need a second,' Nightly says, setting his jaw and giving me a dark look that is so much like his mother I feel a little put off.

I pull my shoulders back and tell him straight, 'Well, you've got one now. If I let go, you will succumb to the effects of my cursed magic, and then you'll lose your opportunity to hex Thorne.'

'Please, Aurelia, don't let go.' He squeezes my fingers as if I might. 'I need to do this, for my sister's honour, for the pain I have felt every day watching her magic fade.'

I feel my insides pull tight as I realize that, soon, Vaughn will have to watch my magic fade. I'm sure that if he had the opportunity to duel with Heston Nightly for bestowing the curse − on Mathilde, on me and on all the other Wycherley women in between − then he would. By the moon, I'd do it myself if I could.

I give Nightly's hand a squeeze back. 'I won't let go. Just tell me what I have to do.'

'This is enough,' Nightly says, lifting my hand. 'I can do the rest.'

Platz and Russo cast a dome around the four of us. We all have our wandlets in our hands, and I can hear Vaughn from outside protesting to Russo about me being Nightly's second.

'You know the rules: first to land a hex is declared the winner. On my mark,' Platz says and Nightly raises his wand arm. Thorne does the same.

I try not to feel scared as I stand side by side with Jules Nightly. I'm sure that Nightly would not use a deadly curse, but Thorne . . . he broke a sacred vow, he undid the first knot of tethering and cast Evelyn aside. Who knows what he is capable of.

'Now!' Platz calls, and Nightly and Thorne both strike at the same moment. I don't have time to feel terrified as my magic streams out of me, through Nightly and into the hex.

Thorne's hex is off target and explodes in the dome next to Nightly. But Nightly's hex hits home and Thorne stands ramrod straight for a moment, looking as if he hasn't a thought in his head.

'What did you do to him?' I ask.

'A nostalgia hex. He is currently reliving every moment that he spent with Evelyn, every promise he ever made her, every deep connection they had. The hex will last a lifetime, it will be the first thing he experiences on waking. For the rest of his life he will have to remember it all: the way she loved him and the way he broke her.'

I shudder as I think of it. Russo and Platz remove the dome of protection and the duel is over, with Nightly the victor. But a moment later Thorne regains himself and his face is a perfect mixture of misery and anger. His arm is up before I can react. 'Nightly!' I shout, but again Thorne's aim is wide. The hex is heading straight for me. I should act but I freeze.

Nightly, however, does not. He turns his body towards me, covering me, his back to the hex, as he faces me, wrapping his arms around me, pulling me to him as he did when we danced. But it doesn't hit. Russo and Platz have deflected it back towards Thorne, and when it hits him, he collapses into a violent fit.

'Bad form, Mr Thorne,' Platz calls out. 'You cannot cast once a duel is done.'

I look up at Nightly. 'Thank you,' I say.

'It's the least I can do. You are my second after all.' I know how much the duel meant to him; how much Evelyn means to him. 'Now, while Thorne is out of action, I think you should release me and let me suffer the consequences of a past Nightly's folly.' He gives a small smirk and I pull my hand from his. He doubles over, throwing up instantly.

Vaughn is at my side. 'What were you thinking?' he reprimands. Then he looks at Nightly in disgust and rage. 'If you put my sister in danger again, Nightly, then I will be the one issuing a duel to you, and my aim is as true as my word.'

'Glad to hear it, Wycherley, glad to hear it,' Nightly says before succumbing to the next wave of nausea.

Ten

'I hear that my roses were well received, apparently you were delighted,' Nightly says. He is sitting in a large chair in the foyer of the Royal Magical Library, a smile on his lips that stretches to his eyes. It's been almost a week since the duel and my mother has only just allowed me full possession of my liberties, although she is convinced I am taking too many of them where Nightly is concerned.

'Delighted? Who told you such lies?' I come to a stop next to his seat and look down at him.

'I have my spies, Wycherley.'

'I wouldn't doubt it for a moment.' I narrow my eyes, but then sit in the chair next to him.

'Don't worry. I made sure that my spies announced the fact loudly while Crenshaw was in hearing.' He looks amused.

'That was good of you. The flowers are beautiful. The

same colour as the roses we grew in the Arcade – nice touch.'

'The same roses. I had them . . . harvested, collected? What do you do with flowers?'

'I think you pick them.'

'Anyway, our rose bush is still giving Platz and Russo trouble, and I have it on good authority that flowers are customary when courting and essential after enduring a duel together.'

'Even fake courting.'

'Especially fake courting.'

'Your sister is the good authority.'

'She is. She wanted me to extend her thanks to you in helping me defend her honour, even if she wasn't exactly happy with me about it. She used the phrase "idiotic clot".'

I smile. 'Well, I might agree with her there.' Nightly pretends to look offended. 'The note that came with the flowers leaves a lot to be desired.' I wave it in the air and he snatches it from me.

'What's wrong with it?' He reads it back. '"Wycherley, meet me at the library Wednesday, ten a.m. sharp. Nightly". It served its purpose, you're here.'

'Yes, but if anyone else read it, they would know that this is not a . . . a love letter,' I reply.

He tilts his head to the side. 'I see your point. I'll work on it for next time just in case your mother finds it. Nell Wycherley is a formidable witch, so my mother tells me.'

'She is furious with you, by the way, for the duelling.' I try to keep my voice light.

He stands then and looks down at me. 'As is mine, with

113

you, not for the duelling. Although I hope you set your mother straight and told her that you forced me to take you as my second.'

'I did no such thing. She sat me down and gave me a very long lecture about bad boys and how, apparently, they are quite attractive—'

'That we are,' Nightly interrupts with a smirk.

'But how they never amount to much and will break more than hearts; probably the law.'

'I see. Did you then tell her about your forgery exploits? You know, Wycherley, I think your mother has it all wrong and that we bad boys need to be on the lookout for sweet, cursed girls who are going to corrupt us from the inside out with a string of persuasive misdemeanours.'

I fix him with my stormy eyes. 'Shall we go and see if I can get you into any more trouble, Mr Nightly?' I wave the permission to the restricted section in front of him and begin to walk off.

Nightly adjusts his confident strides to fall in line beside my shorter ones. I hope the restricted library proves to be the key for both me and Evelyn . . . and Nightly. I still can't work out if he was being sincere when he said he would give up his magic if he couldn't find a cure. There is something about the way he speaks about his family, his mother in particular, that makes me feel on edge for him. I could see how losing his magic and being disowned by his mother, along with his sister, could be a blessing for him.

'Your parents – they are not a tether, is that right?' I ask, suddenly aware that I know little about his family apart from his sister's misfortune and the ill will that his name carries among all Wycherleys.

'No, not tethered. They were in the same debutante year, but they didn't match their magic . . . although they did fall in love. They barely tolerate each other now. But back then, they knew that the best thing for each other was to find other witches to tether to. My mother has always been ambitious, my father more duty-bound; he wears the red of the Coven of Accord, he fought with Nelson. He's been absent for long periods of my and Evelyn's childhood, off securing the realm with his magic for the Crown.

'My mother is a brilliant but complex woman. She's chief investigator of the Coven of Mysteries alongside her tether, Geoffrey Knott.' The way he says the name of his mother's tether is not pleasant, and I realize that Nightly has a lot in his homelife that he is battling against.

We walk beside one another as we descend the staircase to the lower levels of the library. I can't help but think of the way my parents made similar decisions for their hearts and magic. This sends me ruminating through my memories of Father in his yellow cloak, always black ink staining his fingers, always a book in his hand and spell on his mind. I miss him more than ever. I'm sure he would have helped me find a spell to set this curse straight. Then I wouldn't need to be here with Nightly.

I think about my father's spellorium, the door magically

sealed shut the moment he died outside it, I wonder if he used the last of his magic to seal it. I think about what lies beyond that door, what secrets might be in there, what discoveries and magical treasures? My father might not be here with me, but Mother has always told me that I have a lot of him in me and I'm determined to channel that bit of him into this search for answers.

I wonder if Nightly has ever thought to go to his parents for help. Something in me knows that has never been an option, and I feel sorry for him. His mother unreachable, his father's inconsistent presence. My parents were always there, and I think Mother and Frances would be here for me now, if only because they felt they ought to, not because they really believed that I would succeed. Nightly has the same frantic hope that I do, and I need that to keep me going in the face of impossibility.

There's a desk near the entrance to the restricted room and a stern-looking witch manning it. 'Passes?' he asks, and I hand him the letter. He examines it, looking from the letter, to me, then to Nightly, before going through the process of allocating us each the necessary passes, glaring at us both the whole time.

'You are not to remove any books from the room. If you do, we will know about it,' he says with a raise of his eyebrow. 'You must put everything back as you find it, or your privileges will be rescinded. Like all of the books in the library, you cannot magically copy those in the restricted section; any attempt to do so will result in . . . consequences.'

He waves us towards the door, giving us the passes,

keeping the letter.

The door is small and unassuming, just like any other door in the library, but I can feel the magical wards of protection rolling from it as the spell on the pass in my hand glows. I look up at Nightly. He smiles with genuine warmth and excitement at what might be behind this door: a cure for his sister, for me, for all of us. We might find a way for witches to never have to tether again.

'Ready?' Nightly enquires, motioning towards the door with his head but looking straight into my eyes, his expression eager.

'Ready!' I push open the door.

We are met with a vast triple-heighted room with two balconies that circle around it, accessed by twisting staircases. Every wall is lined with bookcases laden with grimoires, spell scrolls and volumes containing all manner of information deemed too dangerous for the average witch. The ceiling of the restricted library is cast from amber-tinted glass, the light reinforced by orbs that float around the room, casting their warm honey glow over all the shelves.

Nightly walks ahead of me, running his eyes over every shelf, his gaze lifting higher into the vast void surrounded by books and scrolls, his mouth dropping open.

'If we can't find answers here, then they don't exist,' he says solemnly.

My face cranes up at the books above me. 'How many do you think there are?' I ask.

'More than we could read together in two lifetimes.'

He follows my gaze. 'Thank you,' he says and it catches me off guard.

'What for?'

'For this.' He gestures to the room, to the books. 'I would never have got in here without you.'

'I'm sure you would have found a way.'

He shakes his head and looks at me earnestly. 'I'm not a master forger like you, my skills lie in other places.'

'Like extortion?'

'Precisely!' He makes his way over to a shelf. 'And research, and making plans, and being patient.'

I can't help but smile at him as his long fingers pull a small volume from the shelf and he turns the spine to face me. 'This might come in handy – for our fake courting, that is.'

'"Powerful Love Potions and Incantations of Infatuation"!' I read the title and wonder what dangerous spells it holds that have deemed it worthy of the restricted section.

'It's a good job that, like you, I am not at all interested in making a match. Besides, us Wycherleys are impervious to all Nightly charms, just not their curses.' I smile. 'Although, I think my mother believes that you have some spell over me.'

'Mine is sure that I have set my wand at you just to spite her, which I have in a way.' He shoots me a look. 'She is currently conspiring to introduce me to every eligible witch of the ton that she feels is worthy. I narrowly missed afternoon tea with Bevis Nash today, but I made my apologies and said that I was coming to meet you. She was furious.'

I take in his grey cloak and feel a pang of guilt. He should be looking for a match, a real match. He catches my eye and as if he knows what I'm thinking says, 'If we succeed . . . no, *when* we succeed, none of that will matter. We'll both keep a firm hold on our magic and not need to rely on anyone to do so.'

'But you should have a backup plan. Besides, I hear that some witches do think of you as somewhat of a catch.' I roll my eyes at him.

He laughs at that, his merriment deep and untroubled. 'I know what people think about me, Wycherley. They think I am only little more a catch than they think you.' His words sting, and it must show. 'But what do they know? They should all be falling over themselves to tether with us both. If they really knew you, they would realize that you are the type of witch to stand up and second for a practical stranger at a moment's notice; that you are determined and resourceful and brave. If they bothered to look, they'd see this curse does not define you. You are just a witch looking to make her way in the world, no matter the cards a curse has handed her.'

I try not to blush at his kind words, but fail. 'And if they knew you, or more likely if you'd let them know you, then they would see that you have a heart as big as this room, and loyalty to those you love. You are very kind, Jules Nightly, and not only to your sister.' His cheeks flush and I feel a little bit of pride at that.

I feel something shift in that moment. Jules Nightly and I are no longer two strangers from warring families, we have become fellow explorers, united in our quest.

'So, where shall we start?' I ask him, looking up at the spines in front of us.

'Not here?' he asks with a frown, raising *Powerful Love Potions and Incantations of Infatuation*. I take it from his hand and push past him as I put it back on the shelf. I move further down the wall of books and place one hand out, hovering just in front of the bookshelf. I can feel the magic pushing on my hand, then, when I feel a little tug, I stop and pull out the book in front of me. *Mysteries of the First Age*.

'Here is as good a place as any,' I say, and Nightly begins pulling books from the shelf.

For the next few hours I use my magic to seek out books, and after a while Nightly stops pulling his own and instead he relies on my magic to guide us in our exploration. Some of the books have incantations placed upon them that require spells to open them, spells of secondary magic that neither Nightly nor I could perform alone. He offers his hand to me but I bat it away. 'The last thing we need is you throwing up over the books,' I tell him.

We place them to one side until the librarian comes to check on us. He reluctantly opens the books, tutting as he leaves.

'He doesn't like us very much.'

'This is my second Season in the library – he doesn't like anyone very much. But he is tolerating us, which is something,' Nightly says, not lifting his face from the book he is examining.

We continue in companionable quiet, only speaking when

we find something of interest. Nightly then writes it in his notebook, and I do the same on one of the many scraps of paper that I have been collecting my thoughts on. He eyes the scraps with horror, shaking his head when I rummage through them to find something that I have jotted down.

It feels as if we have only just got started when the library is set to close. We put the books back where we found them, and I collect all of my pages together in a rough pile which I secure with string.

'Tomorrow?' I ask as we leave the restricted room then make our way out of the library. The sky is a dusky grey outside, and I pull my cloak around me as a chill autumn wind blows through the ton.

'I can't. Evelyn and I are going away for a few days with our father.'

I nod and don't ask about his mother. 'I'll keep looking then, while you're gone.'

'I can send you a list of books to look up, things I have found reference to in my past endeavours but could not get to before,' he says. I nod in agreement, hoping that one of those books might hold what we need.

As he walks me home, we speak in hushed whispers of all the things we've learnt, of powerful wild magic, and magical history – of dark acts that happened long ago. I have the impression that we are searching for not one thing, but a collection of things, like my little bundle of notes, and that the solution will be the string that binds them all together.

Eleven

A few days later, I walk through the door and deposit my tied scraps of paper on the hall table before searching for more in the pocket of my cape. My fingers brush the letter that arrived from Nightly the evening of the day that he left, and I look about for my family before pulling it out and reading it again.

Wycherley,

While I am gone I will think of you often. I will picture you in the library studiously reading all of the books that I have taken the liberty of noting on a separate piece of paper and including here in.

If you are to find anything that you would like to share with me, then be sure to make a note of it.

I myself have taken a small volume with me titled Writing from the Heart. *As I have yet to begin studying it, please do not judge this attempt too harshly.*

Imagine that I have compared your storm-filled eyes to the swirling emotions that the sight of you stir inside me, a hurricane of want and desire and winds that will only be quelled by your gentle caresses.

Yours,

Nightly

I blush and stuff the letter back in my pocket. It arrived two days ago and, since then, I have sought out nearly all of the books on the list and read the letter often. Even if it is a fake love letter, it is the only such letter I have ever received – or am ever likely to – and there is a part of me, a very vain part of me, that forgets to breathe when I read that last paragraph.

I hear movement from the sitting room and turn towards it as I remove my cloak.

'No, leave it on!' Vaughn says.

'Something came for you today.' He has a broad smile on his face and a mischievous look in his eye as he beckons for me to follow him.

I enter the sitting room and see a vase full of flowers and a card tucked in them. The scent of the camellias, lilacs and forget-me-nots surrounds me and I feel a little thrill run through me.

'Are they for me?' My heart suddenly leaps as I think of Sebastian and the look he gave me at the Arcade, just before the duel, and at the Prior-Okore ball.

I reach for the card as Vaughn says, 'Um, no.' The flowers are for him, the card signed: 'Your constant admirer'. I smile at Vaughn, they may have been from his 'constant admirer', but whoever that is is not his *only* admirer. Since Mabon he has received a daily stream of gifts, flowers, chocolates, invitations to tea, dinner, dances. I have received nothing until now, except the flowers and notes from Nightly, but neither of those count as tokens of admiration; they are just evidence of the misdemeanours Nightly and I are committing.

'Mother said I should give it to you when you got back. She and Frances have been called away.' He hands me a black envelope. I take a sharp breath in and crack the official black wax seal, pulling out the black paper within.

Her Majesty the Princess Regent,
Georgianna,
and the Royal Magical Council
request the presence of

Ms Aurelia Wycherley

at the Samhain Rite

on Sunday the 31st October 1813,
at Nessbrugh coven college, Winchester.

Arrivals on broomstick at nightfall,
departures before dawn.

All witches are to wear black.

For the kingdom and the magic.

I give a little squeal of delight before looking at Vaughn. 'A broomstick!' I yelp. I was so envious of Vaughn last year when Mother had taken him to get his broomstick the day he received his Samhain invitation.

'Come on, let's go shopping,' he says with a smile.

'Really? But Mother!'

Vaughn is already shaking his head. 'She didn't want you to miss out. You know how the witches of the ton are about these things, and it's already late in the day. You'll be lucky if there are any decent brooms left in the whole of London,' Vaughn says. 'Where have you been all morning?' He suddenly looks at me suspiciously.

'The library,' I tell him.

'Has Nightly been bothering you?' he asks, his voice has that low menace that he has every time he mentions a Nightly.

'Vaughn, I have not seen Jules Nightly for days,' I tell him truthfully, and his shoulders relax a little.

'He spends a lot of his time at the library.'

'Does he?' I try to keep my voice nonchalant as we walk to the front door.

I throw his cloak at him. 'Come on, like you said, all the good brooms will be gone.'

And he was almost right. It was not so much that there were no brooms left, it was more that, like tethers, none of the brooms wanted me. It is almost dusk by the time we reach the last shop on Vaughn's list of acceptable makers. 'Croucher and

Fox, Traditional Broomsmiths of London, and Alberobella, Puglia', one of the less fashionable broom-makers in the ton.

'You're just in time,' the witch at the desk says in a sombre whisper. 'We are about to close, on account of the troubles.' I look over at Vaughn, wondering if he has any idea what she is on about. Most of the broomsmiths stay open late into the night on Samhain letter day, it is good for business.

'What troubles?' I ask, and the witch looks at me properly for the first time. My hood is still up but I see her eyes flicker from my stormy ones to the hair that is peeking out from under my cape. Her face takes on a look of wary warning and I feel a shift in her energy.

'You must be the Wycherley girl. I've heard all about you. Not every day a curse like yours strikes.'

'No, I don't suppose it is.' I pull the hood of my cloak defiantly down.

She looks away and Vaughn moves a little closer to me, just as he has in the six other broomsmiths we have already visited, once they realized who I was. Part of me thinks that the broomsmiths in those establishments were all a little relieved that none of their brooms took a liking to me, not wanting their craftmanship to appeal to cursed magic.

The witch at the desk avoids looking at me now.

'So, what troubles?' I ask again, and for a moment I think that she might not answer me.

'Another protest, this morning, targeting the broomsmiths. Even had a group of them outside here.' She sounds quite proud of that. 'The Coven of Justice dealt with it swiftly, but still, best to close up early than to call on trouble.' She eyes me then, no doubt assessing if *I* am trouble. 'Stay here. I'll get Mr Fox, he'll be able to assist the two of you with your needs.'

I glance over at Vaughn. 'I guess that's why Mother couldn't be here then.' I don't mean for my voice to sound quite so harsh.

'We knew it would be something important,' he says, glaring through the open door that the witch just left by. I do the same. She's talking to a small, squat man with a large moustache that could rival any broom bush.

'It's always important,' I say. Mother is always so busy with coven business, and I had hoped that when I came into my magic we would become a little closer.

When the curse first hit, I thought that things might change – that she might stay close to me, to protect me. I needed that, I needed her, but it hadn't happened. I guess, in a way at least, she didn't treat me any differently because of my curse, unlike some people. Unlike Sebastian.

Mr Fox greets us, concentrating his efforts on Vaughn, who, in turn, tries to pull me firmly into the conversation.

'I do hope that your brooms are up to the challenge, Mr Fox. My sister is in search of a one-of-a-kind broom for a one-of-a-kind witch. Not all broomsmiths are skilled enough for that challenge, many of the establishments I had previously thought to be very fine indeed have failed us today. I hope that you will rise where they have fallen.'

Mr Fox's demeanour alters, a glint appears in his eye. 'Those that boast to be the best rarely are; I know for a fact that Hollinger's mass-produces their brooms, working from design plans rather than feeling the magic in the wood. Here we have used the same broom-making techniques for over four hundred years. Our brooms saw action in the Great Witch War at the end of the Second Age and we are proud that we were the first officially licensed broomsmiths in London. Please, Mr Wycherley, Ms Wycherley, come this way.'

We follow him through the door. I trail behind, preparing myself for another disappointment.

The warehouse beyond is vast: a huge building that reminds me a little of the restricted section at the library, except, instead of books covering every surface, here hang brooms.

The broomhouse is not the biggest I have been in today, but I think it is definitely the most well stocked. I allow myself a tiny spark of hope . . . which instantly extinguishes as I see the two witches gathered in the circle painted on the floor.

'This is Cora Stewart and Kit Thorne, they'll be assisting you,' Mr Fox says.

I glare at Kit Thorne, and to his credit he doesn't look away, but his face does twitch, and I hope it is a side effect of his rebounded curse. Serves him right.

'Thorne,' Vaughn says in something similar to the tone that he usually uses for Nightly. After the duel, when Kit Thorne had fired a second spell that had almost hit me, Vaughn tore into his former friend. I can almost feel the tension seething from my brother, his magic fizzing in the air.

'I am well versed in the art of summoning, Mr Fox, and will not require any assistance,' I say. 'You may leave.' I glare at Thorne.

Mr Fox steps forward. 'As you know, Ms, it's the law that there has to be an instructor to talk you through the techniques, and on hand to deal with any . . . unwanted side effects of summoning.'

Cora Stewart moves towards her tether. She reminds me of a timid mouse, with her unsure smile, and soft brown hair. She stares adoringly at Thorne.

'Ms Wycherley, it is our job to assist you!' she says, her voice low and soft, like she is comforting a small child. 'I know that Jules Nightly has probably told you all types of things about us, about Kit, but they are not true.' She slips her hand into Kit's and he turns away from me, smiling at her.

I wonder if Cora Stewart is the reason that Thorne threw off his attachment with Evelyn, a true love match?

'Mr Nightly has told me only the basic details. You, Mr Thorne, swore an oath to his sister, Ms Evelyn Nightly, at Ostara, tying the first knot of tethering with her, an oath and a knot that you broke by Beltane, leaving her tetherless and soon to be magicless.'

Mr Fox takes in a loud gasp at the revelation, then tuts, glaring at me for saying such scandalous things out loud.

'Ms Wycherley, you really should not judge my actions. You of all people should be wary of the Nightlys – are they not the reason you are cursed and now a magical pariah?' Thorne says in a low voice. 'That same streak of malice that cursed your ancestor still runs through the Nightlys today – their conceitedness, their aloof attitude, their disdain – they think they are above us all. You might think that Jules Nightly is on your side, but he no doubt has some plan to disgrace or dishonour you. You are nothing but a source of entertainment or advancement to him, and he will give you up when he has had his fill. Don't be too foolish to realize that he is using you; I know from experience.'

I hold Thorne's eye as I listen to him suggest that there was something untoward about Evelyn's intentions with him. I can't help but think that it's untrue; however, I can't say the same about Jules. He *is* using me – to get into the restricted section, and as a pin in his mother's pride. But I am using him too. I know what I'm doing with Jules Nightly and I know why I am doing it.

Thorne moves away, Cora beside him. 'We will wait to the side. When Ms Wycherley realizes that she will be a broomless witch without our help, and her summoning has failed, we will be there to instruct her,' Thorne says loudly to Mr Fox.

I hate the arrogant way that he thinks I will need his help, and I am already determined to prove Kit Thorne completely wrong.

'Are you ready, Ms Wycherley?' Mr Fox asks.

I walk into the circle, collect my thoughts and tap into the instructions that I have been given at the other broomsmiths.

I empty my mind, then open myself up to the possibility of finding a broom that is right for me. I move swiftly through the sequence of magical movements, shifting my weight back and to one side, sweeping my arms out and then pulling them towards me as I step forward, attempting to summon the broom to me and moving to greet it.

And, just as all the other times that day, nothing happens.

I stand in the circle alone, with my empty hand outstretched. A broomless witch, just as Kit Thorne foretold. I guess it is quite fitting for a witch that in a few years will be magicless too.

Kit is staring at me with a smug look on his face, and Mr Fox looks disappointed – in me, not in his brooms.

Only Vaughn is looking about the room. 'Can . . . can you hear that?'

'Hear what?' I ask, and as if in answer I hear a *tap*, *tap*, *tap* that in moments becomes a *bang*, *bang*, *bang*.

Mr Fox turns and with a little run he makes his way deeper into the broomhouse, towards a heavily bolted door right at the back. With every step he takes, the banging gets louder. He hasn't quite reached the door when a splintering sound fills the air and the door splits open. Mr Fox jumps out of the way, his wand glittering in his hand as he pulls an arm back and fires off a quick spell.

The broom rolls to the left, avoiding the spell, before continuing to hurtle towards me, pulling up sharp and slipping into my outstretched palm.

I look at it for a long while, my eyes wide and breath

coming fast. Carved into the end of the handle is a rune that I don't know, glinting with the light of my own black flame magic. It reminds me of the mystery rune on my wandlet.

I can feel the quivering of magic seep out of the broom and into my palm, into me. Tentatively I begin to wrap my fingers around it. I worry that the broom might up and leave, that I might startle it in some way, or it might change its mind about me. But it stays hovering in place, as I curl my fingers securely around it.

Vaughn is beside me with his mouth open. 'What tree is that wood from?' Vaughn cocks his head to one side. 'I've never seen wood as black as that, it looks like polished obsidian.'

Vaughn is right, although within the blackness of the wood are tiny white lines that shoot across the handle and lace in knots that whorl out in concentric patterns. It's like a sky full of shooting stars. And the brush is made with twisting twigs that are the same, shining black and white flecked.

'It's perfect!' I say, already feeling a strong bond to the unique broom.

'Why was this broom locked away? What is behind there?' Vaughn asks.

'It came from the vault,' replies Mr Fox, looking from the broom to me and then back again. He gives a small nod of his head. 'It's where we keep all of the old brooms; the brooms that no one claimed in the lifetimes of their makers. Some of the brooms in the vault are hundreds of years old. Some have a history attached to them, a story of their making. Some of them even have a name. That broom is known as Ankoth.'

'This broom . . . does it have a story as well as a name?' I ask. I already know that it does, I can feel it in its wood, in its magic.

Mr Fox clears his throat. 'In the early days of the Third Age of Magic, when witches were trying to find a way to keep hold of their magic and tethering was newly discovered, an apprentice to John Croucher made that broom.

'It was crafted the day before the apprentice tethered her magic. She was a powerful witch with many accomplishments, one of which was being a skilled broom-maker. But Ankoth was to be the last broom she ever made. Once tethered, she changed her profession.

'She said she made this broom from a branch that she found on the battlefield during the last stand against malevolent magic in the Great Witch War. My ancestor, Samuel Fox, and his partner, John Croucher, definitely thought that could be true; the wood is not natural, you see, it has been magically altered in some way, as if it had been caught up in the spellstorm of that final battle. And the young witch had indeed been there, alongside the witch that she was later to tether with.

'Personally, I think that the wood was most probably enchanted in some way, a small trick of magic that the apprentice put into her last broom – after all, every broomsmith hopes to be remembered for the one broom above all others, the finest display of their skill and magic, and it was her last chance to make something spectacular.

'It's been waiting here ever since, for the right rider to claim it,' Mr Fox concludes.

'Waiting for me,' I whisper as I feel the broom vibrate happily in my hand.

'Well, it's quite an impressive story,' Vaughn says, eyeing the broom suspiciously.

'I haven't told you the best bit about this broom: the name of its maker.' Fox pauses for dramatic effect.

'Mathilde Wycherley.'

Twelve

I'm excited to tell Nightly about my broom, about its story and about the mysterious runes I've found. One I could dismiss of as a twist of magic . . . but two? That feels significant.

The very next day, I rush through the large doors to the Royal Magical Library, only to be called by a young witch carrying a stack of books.

'Ms Wycherley, I have a letter for you,' she says, reaching inside her light-purple cloak and pulling out a note. I thank her as I snap the Nightly seal and read as I walk; his handwriting elegant, with soft lines, and towards the end, words that are just as dulcet.

Wycherley,

I arrived when the library opened and have been

studious. I've left a pile of books in the restricted library for you (I assured the grumpy librarian that you would put them away; he said he would remove our passes and hex us both if you didn't. I can take the hex but not the rescinding of the passes). These are books that I have not yet read myself but ones that you and I have both found reference to. I have family matters to deal with today, but rest assured I shall be back to our cause in the morrow, sooner if at all possible.

As for the other matter – I shall think of you every moment that we are separated and no doubt that when my heart beats it shall do so to the beat of your name – Au-re li-a.

Nightly

As I walk towards the restricted section, I can't get Kit Thorne's words out of my head: *He's using you.*

What if he was right? Nightly was supposed to be helping me, but where is he? Can I really trust a Nightly?

On the table I find a considerable pile of books.

I sit down and start reading, scrawling down anything interesting on pieces of scrap paper.

Jules, unexpectedly, arrives a little after lunchtime. His long hair is so unruly, his curls are like knots of fire as he strides towards the table, his brow low and jaw set.

He looks more troubled than usual, which is saying something because Jules Nightly is as brooding as a sea swell before a storm. I smile up at him, just a small twitch of my mouth, mostly because I'm amused at the notion that has occurred to me, the thought that though my eyes look like a storm, he is one.

He picks up the large wingback chair from its familiar resting place at the side of the stacks and brings it to the desk. He doesn't sit; he stands, looking down at me as I gaze up, then his face clears and he lets out a large sigh and reflects my small smile back at me. 'It's good to see you, Wycherley.'

I feel the weight of his words and wonder how bad his troubles must be that the sight of his greatest family foe brings him solace.

His eyes dart to the books that are strewn across the table and the paper covered in my messy scrawl.

'I see you've been busy.' He hangs his cloak on the back of the chair and sits next to me. I can feel the heat rising from him like a merry bonfire, and realize that his cheeks are a little flushed.

'I wasn't expecting you till tomorrow; what have you been up to?' I ask him.

'Family business,' he says, picking up one of the scrap notes from the pile, then another.

'Family business that you ran away from by the look of it?' I say, motioning to his tousled hair, his dishevelled shirt collar. I look down to see his boots are filthy and there is a trail of mud marking his way through the library.

'I only ran once the business was dealt with, and I didn't run away, I ran towards something; I ran to you, Wycherley. We have work to do, after all,' he says and I feel as if I have been dismissed.

I close the book that I have open and look straight at him. 'Tell me.'

He shakes his head. 'It's nothing.'

I see the lump in his throat move as he swallows. 'Liar, it is something, a big something, I think . . . Evelyn?' I ask.

He nods.

I feel my chest swell as I ask. 'Her magic . . . has it gone?'

'Not yet. But time is running out, and she is not doing well. Mother has returned to bullying her into leaving.' His voice is thick. 'Father is away, his battalion moved out yesterday. Before that, Evelyn and I accompanied him to our family home in Cornwall – we thought the space would be good for Mother but . . .' His voice breaks and I reach out and place a hand on his arm. He doesn't look at me. A tear hits the desk and he wipes his face with his cuff. I fill with anger towards Demelza Nightly, sorrow for Evelyn and worry for Jules, for all he is going through.

I reach out and slide my palm down his arm to his hand. He looks at it, turning his palm and twisting my fingers in his, just like when we perform magic. 'As soon as our father left our mother was . . . well, she was her usual cruel self. Evelyn turned up outside the library this morning. I escorted her to our aunt's house – she's going to stay there for a few days while I try to . . .' He takes in a ragged breath, and my heart breaks for him and Evelyn.

'Jules, shouldn't you be with Evelyn?'

He shakes his head. 'No.' He wipes his face again. 'I should be here, doing all that I can to help her keep her magic. To help you keep yours too. What's happening to Evelyn . . . I can't bear to think of it happening to you as well.' He looks at me then, his eyes watery, his jaw clenched. And in that moment, I realize that I was a fool to have ever thought that Jules Nightly was like his mother, was like any of the other Nightlys I have been warned about. I want to help him, to ease his discomfort. I want to lift the burden of his responsibilities from him. Most of all, I want to hex his mother for him.

'Is there anything I can do to help? Maybe we could think of a way to distract your mother, bring the attention back on to you somehow?'

'Gladly. What exactly would you suggest?'

I point towards a pair of witches dressed in blue, poring over books on the opposite side of the library. I have noticed they are often there when Jules and I are. 'I have long suspected that they are two of your mother's spies.'

Nightly nods. 'As have I.'

They are both looking in our direction and as Jules turns to face me. I run my eyes over his lips and say to him, 'Kiss me.' The feelings that have been growing in me from the moment Nightly walked into the library, upset, rise. I surprise myself when I realize that I *want* Jules Nightly to kiss me, not just to spite his mother, but for many other reasons that I can't quite give a name to.

'What? No, Aurelia!'

'Jules, kiss me.' I say each word slowly as I lean towards him, glancing behind him to see that the two witches are still watching.

'Don't tempt me with more of your outrageous actions or we'll be adding "debauchery" to the list of your crimes.' He is watching my lips intently and I can see his pupils growing large, his breathing a little heavy.

'Kiss me, or I will kiss you.' And what started as a notion to annoy Demelza Nightly has shifted into something else. I want him to kiss me, I want him to *want* to kiss me.

He leans towards me and whispers into my ear, 'Aurelia Wycherley, I appreciate the gesture, but I would not steal a kiss from you and ruin your reputation in such a way.'

My heart is pounding as he moves back and straightens his waistcoat before pulling a book towards him. My stomach sinks at the thought of my wanton folly.

I gain my composure and sit back too, noticing the disapproving looks on the witches' faces. I hope it will be enough to turn Demelza's attention, and I try to quell the little spark in me that is running wild at the thought of Jules Nightly's lips. I pour water on it by thinking of what Mother and Vaughn would have said if a report of us kissing had reached them.

'Shall we get to it?' I say, trying to focus on the task at hand.

He looks at me, and I can tell that he wants to say something about what passed, about what did not happen, but I am slipping into mortification at my hasty actions.

'I found some runes that I want to talk to you about,' I say as I search for the scrap of paper that I drew Ankoth's rune and the rune from my wandlet on.

Jules turns and rummages in the pocket of his cloak. 'Just a moment, Wycherley. When I first started using the library last Season it took me a while to feel at home.'

'You? If someone said that you were born in a library I would have believed them.'

'I found my way around a library out of necessity and discovered that the most important way to organize my thoughts was to create a capture system.'

'A capture system? It sounds like you are stalking prey.'

'We are, in a way; we are hunting down knowledge!'

The spark in his eyes as he talks reminds me of the look my father would get when he was researching something that captivated him.

'I learnt the hard way that you can't expect to find anything of value unless you keep it safe. The ideas on these pieces of paper deserve better than a piece of string.'

He nudges what at first I think is his notebook towards me but then I realize that although it is the same size and shape, it is not. Made from black leather, it looks like a large envelope.

'What is it?' I ask.

'It's a document wallet.' He unclasps the lock on the front and pulls back the black leather flap to show the space within – enough to fit all my notes and more. The silver clasp matches Nightly's name embossed in the corner. He closes it and hands it to me.

'For me?'

'If you please,' he says. 'I want you to have this wallet. I know that you like to collect your notes loose and I prefer my notebook anyway. I've never used the document wallet and it will be good for it to be of use.'

'But it's yours . . . it has your name on it. I couldn't use it.' I nudge it back to him.

'You could, and I would like you to have it. And as for the name, we can fix that.' He takes my hand and holds it in his.

'Transformation is secondary magic. You know what will happen.'

He smiles. 'I do. But it will only be a small spell and it will be worth the headache . . . and probably the vomiting.'

I look around and see that the blue-clad witches have gone and we are alone in this part of the library.

There is a stirring inside me, a longing to feel his magic flowing through me, mine through him. I feel my heart rate pitch as I curl my fingers around his and he stands, pulling me to my feet. 'Do you know the sequence?' he asks.

'Of course.' I am desperate to move through the motion of the spell, to feel our magic combine, the intoxicating power of it. I know my magic is strong, but when we performed secondary magic in the Arcade it felt limitless.

'Hold in your mind how you would like your name to be written,' he says. I imagine it in an elegant looping script.

I feel his magic seeping into me slow and steady, mixing with mine as my wandlet glows and we both bring our hands down together, sweeping them over the leather of the document wallet. I see that it is no longer black. It is red, 'Wycherley' written in the corner where 'Nightly' once was. I recognize the handwriting – it's Nightly's and in the centre of the document wallet is the outline of a golden rose bud.

'Did you do that?' I ask.

'I can't give you kisses, but I can give you this,' he responds, gazing into my stormy eyes, and I feel the heat run through me again. Our hands still joined and our magic flowing freely between us, I hesitate, lingering in the feel of him, before I pull my magic back and feel his leave. As soon as we are no longer magically connected, he crumples. I grab him and lower him back into the chair, pushing his hair back from his face.

'Nightly,' I say in a hushed voice as I run my hand down to his cheek. 'Nightly, wake up.' I hold his face in my hands. His eyes are closed, his lips slightly parted, and again I think about how they would feel pressed upon mine. Would his kisses feel like Sebastian's?

I move my lips close to his ear. 'Nightly,' I whisper again and this time he begins to rouse.

'How long was I out for?' He grimaces and places a hand to his temple.

'Seconds,' I reply. 'Was it worth it?'

'It is always worth it.' He smirks.

I remove my hands from his shoulders. He looks a little green. 'Can I get you anything? A glass of water? A bucket?'

'No, thank you,' he says, his jaw tight, and I know that he is trying not to be sick.

'Thank you,' I say to him, as I run a hand over the wallet.

He shows me where the pencil is tucked with a little loop, inside is a collection of thick ivory paper for me to make notes on.

'Are you looking to wear purple when you graduate?' I tease. He looks offended.

'The Coven of Knowing? Just because I like stationery and being organized doesn't mean that I want to spend my day collecting information. Besides . . .'

'Oh yes, you intend to throw your magic away at the end of the Season. I forgot.'

He glares at me.

'I'm sorry, Jules, but just as you are trying to keep Evelyn's magic and help me keep mine, I feel that you need to make preparations to secure yours too.'

'About these runes!' he declares, staring at me. I know when I'm beaten.

'I'm guessing you know that back in the First Age of Magic, before the unification of spells and the treaties between the witch clans standardized magical practices, there were two distinct magical systems, each with its own symbols and rites, and that these two were merged to form the modern principles of magic that we use today.'

'Of course, any witch worth their weight in salt understands about the unification. The facts and the mythology too.' Nightly is looking at me intently, waiting for more.

'Well . . . did you know there was a third system?'

His eyes narrow in confusion as if I'm trying to trick him. 'Go on,' he says.

'This third system is mentioned twice. Once in a book about wild magic –' I point to the book that is sitting on the desk – 'and again in this scroll that outlines how the unification of the systems will work. They describe the runes that make up the third system as –' I read from one of my scraps of paper – '"emanating with a magic that glows in darkness". The scroll refers to the system as the Tavas Golowhe Arwodh. I have no idea what that means, or even how to say it correctly, but I think I have recently found some of the runes from this lost third system of magical discourse.'

'Really?' Jules is all interest.

'Yesterday, when I summoned my broom, it had a strange rune on the handle.'

I push a sketch of the symbol towards him. He lifts the paper, examining it closely.

'It's an old broom – made at the beginning of the Third Age of Magic, just after the Great Witch War – and it was made by my ancestor Mathilde Wycherley, just before her tethering with—'

'Heston Nightly.'

'Indeed.' I raise an eyebrow, satisfied that he finds this connection as intriguing as I do. 'Things keep happening to me that are connected to her – the curse, meeting you, and now her broom. And the broom has a name. Ankoth.'

'Ankoth.'

I tell him the story that Mr Fox told me.

'And there's another rune, here on my wandlet.' I hold my hand out to show him, and he takes ahold of my wrist. The rune on my wandlet glitters with that same darkness of my own witch-flame, as if it is sucking the light into it rather than reflecting it out.

'Fascinating. I've never seen anything like it,' Nightly says. I pull my hand away, then reach for a book.

'I don't think that many people have, not in hundreds of years. These runes are from the First Age of Magic, when magic was free and wild, before it was tamed and unified – when creatures of magic still walked through our world, spreading their wisdom and wickedness.' I give a little shiver as I remember some of the old tales of the creatures – of their malice and might.

'It got me thinking that, if Mathilde knew about the runes, then maybe she told Heston too. The First Age of Magic was well before their time, but they did live through the end of the Second Age, when tethering was not necessary, and into

147

the Third when it was. Maybe they knew something that will help us. They might have left some information about these Golowhe runes somewhere.'

Nightly nods. 'Yes, I think you're on to something . . . with these runes and our notorious ancestors.'

I smile. 'Me too. I've been doing a little research on the two of them.'

Nightly moves a little closer to me so that he can read from the book as I flip through, his interest piqued. 'Did you know that they founded a coven college together? It was called "Wynne Hordes".'

'Never heard of it.'

'Nor I.'

'My mother would not have stopped going on about it if it was true,' Nightly says.

'Mine neither. But I'm pretty sure it is true – look.' I turn to a page in *Coven Colleges of the Ages*, in a section listing all coven colleges ever documented, many of which no longer exist, and point to the magical crest for Wynne Hordes.

Nightly gazes at it intently before taking up his notebook and pencil to sketch its likeness.

As he begins, I pull a scroll towards me. 'And there's this,' I add, unrolling it and showing him a petition for the Royal Magical Council to build a college, and then an approval scroll with the Royal Magical seal on it.

'So where is this college? Did they ever build it?' Nightly asks.

'I don't know, but I think we should find out.'

'Nice work, Wycherley. I would have never found any of this if it weren't for you.'

'I'm sure you would have,' I say, but I do wonder. I only found this because of the Golowhe runes.

This line of enquiry feels like our first strong lead. Something is drawing me towards the coven college that Mathilde Wycherley built with Heston Nightly. If it exists then I'm certain that some of their knowledge of the Golowhe runes will be in the library.

One rune I could pass as a mystery, but two finding me is surely a sign. My father would have said there are no such things as coincidences where magic is concerned, and I agree with him, with regard to the runes and to Nightly too. I feel like he and I are meant to be following this path together. Nightly looks up and our eyes meet, a little spark of his left-over magic stirs in me.

SAMHAIN

The Most Magical Season – A Debutantes' Guide

by Cathleen Kelly and Kate Walker

The wheel of the year turns full circle. Samhain heralds in fresh starts and new beginnings for all. On this day, the boundary between this world and the magical realm of Avalon is thinner – magic moves more freely.

Samhain is a rich Sabbat, a time of deep contemplation, for the passing of all things – time, loved ones, seasons – and a time of celebration for the now, for the living, for the future. For the debutante witch, Samhain is also a time of great importance and intrigue. This is when the magic of a debutante witch will seek out the connections that it wants to make, making itself known in an attempt to encourage a magical tethering.

The Samhain Rite will reveal all the magical connections available to an untethered witch. The magic is deep and wise and should be heeded, but it knows nothing of the heart or mind, or any other reasons why a tether might be made between one witch and another.

A witch's magic might choose you, but remember it is up to you to claim the connection!

Thirteen

I stand in front of the mirror and twirl once, twice, then a third time. The skirts of my black dress fill out from under my bust as I spin. My sleeves are long and made of a delicately embroidered diaphanous material that covers me from my collarbone down to the hem of the dress underneath, black moons and stars embellish the sheer fabric. I glimpse my boots in the mirror as my skirts lift; my thick black cape fans behind me like a raven's wings.

I feel beautiful and bold and something else too, something that makes my heart a little giddy. I run my hands over the material, smooth and soft beneath my touch, and I think of the dancing that will happen this evening. I wonder if anyone will ask me to dance. I think of the jealous looks that Sebastian has been giving me and Nightly, and although I know that I should put him down as firmly as he has me, I can't help but hope. Nightly, of course, will dance with me. I feel my heart race a little at the thought of it, and blush as I remember wanting to kiss him in the library. The fact that he refused has done nothing to calm that notion and I keep feeling a little thrill of excitement every time I think of being close to Jules Nightly – a thrill that I quell by thinking of what my family's reaction would be to such an act, and by reminding myself that Nightly does not want to kiss me. For him this is all just a ruse.

I look over at my broom. I hardly have to perform the summoning move and Ankoth flies to my outstretched hand. I feel as if it wants to be there, like a dog that is sad when its owner is away. The broom is unlike any I've heard of – it doesn't like being with the other brooms and almost broke the cupboard door down on the first night. Since then it has lived in my room and often follows me about the house, and sometimes, as dusk is setting in, it becomes restless and taps on the window to be let out. I haven't joined it on its night-time wanders: it is illegal for a witch to be on their broom without authorization, but tonight . . . tonight is different.

Nightly is eager to see the broom and I'm looking forward to showing him. As if the broom knows what the date is, it vibrates eagerly in my hand, wanting to be airborne.

I pull up the hood of my cape, my white hair piled up on my head beneath. My stormy eyes look clear and calm, and I feel more like myself than I have in moons – cast in the colour of night and shadows. If I can find a way to keep my magic, I want to wear the black of the Coven of Justice, just like my mother and Frances. The work they do is important: keeping law and order within the magic of the kingdom.

I try not to let my smile fade at the challenges ahead of me. First I need to keep my magic. Of course, one way to do that is to find a tether, and although the Royal Magical Council have forbidden it, after tonight, I will know for sure if there is even a possible match out there for me and my cursed magic.

There were a few members of the council who objected to me taking part in the Samhain Rite, but part of the oath that all debutantes take at Mabon means that, as long as we are physically able to, we must take part in all of the Sabbats, not just for our magical traditions but as a sign of respect to the Crown.

Besides, the council are sure that no witch's magic will want to match with mine, and I can't help but agree with them. Mother has been gently warning me all week that magic as unusual as mine is unlikely to call to anyone else's. I know that she is trying to prepare me for the disappointment that I am going to face, although I think that she might also be a little worried that if someone's magic *does* seek me out, that will cause me greater disappointment. And, no doubt, if the magic of one person in particular might be attracted to mine, then that would cause a disappointment for *her*.

Samhain is one of the few occasions where all witches are allowed to wear the traditional black, to light their cauldrons in public view and fly their brooms at will. A night of the old ways, a night of connecting to who we were before the war, before tethering, and I fully intend to embrace it.

As well as marking the thinning of the boundary between the worlds, Samhain also marks two important moments in magical history – it is the day when the First Age of Magic ceased, when all the gateways between our world and the magical world of Avalon were closed off.

It was also the eve of the Great Magical Battle, when malevolent magic sought to reopen the gateways but was thwarted, bringing an end to the Great Witch War and seeing in the beginning of the Third Age of Magic. Tomorrow, there will be quiet contemplation, a family feast and the paying of respects to those witches we have lost. But tonight is a celebration of magic.

I am reassured by the same deeply peaceful feelings that I have always had at Samhain, but now there is another layer to it. Excitement, yes, but also a deep connection – that my magic is linked to all those witches who have been and all of those who will be.

I make my way out of my room and go in search of Vaughn; I find him outside the broom room next to our arcade. He too is dressed in black, from his boots to his shirt. His cape is on but his hood is down, his chestnut-brown hair glinting in the light from the small witch-flame he has conjured in his hand.

'You look very dashing!' I tell him, as he turns with a little jolt.

'Aurelia, you look . . . positively otherworldly! But in a good way,' he hastens to add, 'like a witch from the First Age of Magic: all wild and awe-inspiring.'

'Well, I never thought I'd live to see the day that I inspired *awe* in you,' I tell him with a smile.

'Oh no, not me.' He turns back to the broom room, turning the handle and opening the door. 'In other witches, ones who haven't grown up with you and don't know all of your annoying habits.'

I lift my broom and he eyes it suspiciously. He hasn't said anything, but I know he doesn't like Ankoth and finds its behaviour a little strange. But that's fine, my broom isn't for him, it's for me and I love it.

He takes a big sniff and sighs. 'Ah, nothing smells better than a broom cupboard.' On this, we agree. The seasoned wood and the magic clinging to the brooms is intoxicating.

Vaughn grabs his broom: a long sturdy oak handle with a brush full of hazel twigs. 'Are you ready?'

'I think so.' I clutch my broom a little more firmly.

'Shall we?' he says, motioning to the door that leads through the herboritum and on to the lawn at the back of the house.

The sun has just set and the sky is the washed-out grey of autumn twilight. Mother and Frances are standing on the lawn both dressed in black, both holding brooms.

'When did you land?' I call as I run over to them, my cape ballooning behind me as Vaughn follows, pulling his hood up as he crosses the lawn.

Mother hugs me close and I breathe in the smell of her:

sandalwood and lavender. 'We have missed so much of your debutante Season so far, with all that is happening. I wanted to see you off this evening.'

I smile broadly and hug her tight again, then move to Frances. Her hugs are lighter but just as warm. 'We'll be here when you return so you can tell us everything!' she says with a smile and a raise of her eyebrows. She does not feel the same way about Jules Nightly as Vaughn and Mother do, and I know that she has a quiet hope that something will come of our friendship, something that she would be willing to fight the Royal Magical Council for on my behalf. I don't have the heart to tell her that it is all a lie.

'You look amazing, Aurelia,' Mother says. 'Every inch a true witch, no matter what others might think. Just remember how those that love you feel about you, and try to heed their opinions, not those of strangers.' Mother is smiling, but I can't help hearing the warning against Nightly in her words.

'Remember to stay with the flock, and if you get lost, just head west and someone will pick you up. Don't land till you get there. There have been reports that the New Dawn are planning to demonstrate again this evening – it feels as if they are growing in number.'

Vaughn straddles his broom and I copy him as Mother starts fussing with my cape.

'Nell, they'll be fine,' Frances says as she wraps her arm around mother. 'Fly safe and true! Stick together.' She glances at Vaughn.

'We will,' I promise.

I look up into the sky; high above is a constant stream of little black shapes all moving in the same direction, like crows flying home to roost. Witches on their brooms; debutantes off to the Samhain celebrations.

I shout my goodbyes as I push off from the ground, eager to be in the sky. I ascend quickly, thinking for a moment that I may have left my stomach behind. Vaughn is shouting at me as he catches up. 'We have a way to go, you might want to pace yourself!'

I smile at him – there is no way I am going to be able to go slow.

Flying makes me feel so incredibly free. I don't think about what I'm doing but let Ankoth glide through the air smoothly and it feels as if the night is moving around me. As we fly out of London, I see a torchlight procession; the flame bearers are not wearing black or witches' cloaks. I think of the murdered witches and want to fly away from the troubles that are brewing and the worry of what might be to come.

'Aurelia!'

'Constance!'

'Isn't this just the most fun!' Constance waves and her broom dips into a dive as she relinquishes her grip. Both Vaughn and I dive towards her, but before we get close, she rights herself and starts laughing.

'Sorry, I couldn't resist.' There's a twinkle in her eye, and

I laugh along with her. But Vaughn isn't laughing. He looks like he's going to be sick.

'Are you all right, Vaughn?' I call out to him.

'Definitely! Just . . . don't do that again, I thought . . .' He's looking at Constance and she stops laughing.

Then Vaughn swoops in close to me and says, 'I'm going to find Martyn. Why don't you fly on with Constance?'

'But Mother and Frances said to . . .'

'Mother says lots of things; you'll be fine.' He looks pointedly at Constance, then pulls his broom to the right and heads towards Martyn.

'Where did Vaughn go? Is something wrong?' Constance asks, looking after him. She's gnawing on her bottom lip in that way that she does when she's worried about something.

'I don't think so. You know how he gets sometimes.'

'Yeah, but it's only because he thinks so deeply and feels so keenly.'

'Is that what it is?' I answer. 'I thought it was because he is a brother and all brothers are annoying.' I smile at her.

'Oh, sisters can be annoying too!' Constance replies, then glances again in Vaughn's direction.

There is something in the way she is looking – wistful and longingly – that makes me turn and look too.

I am pretty sure that Constance is falling for Vaughn, and he for her. In fact, I am almost convinced, by the way he just reacted to her stunt and is now avoiding looking in her direction, that he is not falling . . . he has already hit the ground.

I am itching to ask Constance about it, but I won't interfere. They are two of the most important people in my life, and if they are going to find each other in that way then it needs to be because they genuinely have feelings for one another and not because I am meddling.

'Vaughn once told me that he and Martyn have a pact: if they are both untethered by their dark-grey year, they will match. Maybe he's making sure that option is still safe?' Constance says, and I hear a hitch in her voice.

'Oh, I just think he wanted to get away from me, to be honest. I've been quite annoying today.'

'You have?'

'Oh yes,' I say with a mischievous smile. 'After all, you know what sisters are like.'

That puts her at ease. But I glance back over at my brother, wondering what he is about. Maybe he is nervous about this evening – that if his magic seeks out Constance, things might change, or that her magic won't find him.

Before long, the airborne procession of witches starts to descend. Below us is Nessbrugh House, home to the coven college that shares its name. The house is more of a castle estate, with large gardens surrounding the imposing turreted building. Like all coven colleges, the six disciplines of magic are studied here: Nurturing, Knowing, Justice, Accord, Mysteries and Curiosity. And also like most coven colleges, Nessbrugh has its specialism – most witches who enter the Coven of Nurturing train at Nessbrugh. I know this is where Vaughn is hoping to go.

The grounds are lit with witch-flames – large magical fires in metal grates showing us where to land.

Constance glides gracefully to the ground, landing with a little run as she pulls the broom from under her.

I come in close behind her, stumbling, almost falling, but righting myself at the last moment with a little guiding nudge from Ankoth.

I can't see Vaughn and assume that he must have started walking towards the college with Martyn.

Constance is a step ahead of me when there is a yell from behind. I turn quickly and have just enough time to push Constance to safety as Sebastian Crenshaw crash lands on top of me, the handle of his broom hitting me in the face and sending me sprawling to the floor with a skull-crunching blow.

I blink several times as the world swirls around me. I can hear Constance calling for help and everything goes black for a moment. When I next open my eyes, I see a blurry face before me, hands holding my cheeks gently, lips moving as I try to concentrate on the words they are saying.

'Sebastian,' I say, reaching my hand up to touch his face.

'Aurelia, are you all right?' His voice sounds different, and as my eyes swim in and out of focus, I realize that it's *not* Sebastian who is holding my face and speaking to me in an urgent tone. It is Nightly.

Sebastian is standing stock still on the lawn, witches

landing behind him as the light from the beacons dances on his face. He looks straight at me.

'Should I help?' Sebastian's voice is full of worry, and although this is more than he has said in my presence for months, my ears are ringing and my head swimming, so I can't be entirely sure that I haven't imagined it. I lift a hand to my head and feel sticky blood at my temple.

'I think you've done quite enough, Crenshaw,' Nightly says in a gruff voice laced with malice. 'Ms Prior, would you be so kind as to bring Ms Wycherley's broom and accompany me to the coven house,' Nightly says as he scoops me up, and gently carries me along the avenue of hedges, his steps long and swift.

My head swirls again. It feels so heavy I rest it on his chest, closing my eyes as the world blurs once more. I breathe in the smell of old books and ink.

'Nightly,' I say.

'It's all right, Wycherley, I have you,' he replies, his too-long hair brushes the top of my head and I can hear the hurried beating of his heart as he moves towards Nessbrugh House. I smell something beneath the books and ink, something deep and earthy and sweet – the smell of his magic. I feel my body relax as I enjoy the sensation of being so close to him, close to anyone. I had expected many moments of such closeness during my debutante year, but it would seem that the only way I am going to get a witch to sweep me off my feet is if a serious head injury is involved. I give a slightly hysterical laugh at the thought of it and Nightly looks down at me with a worried stare.

As soon as we are in Nessbrugh House, Nightly calls out for a healer. He places me down gently on a small couch and a pair of tethered witches move forward, muttering swift incantations. I smell the sharp twang of magic mixing with herbs. Then a cup is being placed to my lips. The mixture tastes sweet and warm. My head clears and the world slips into focus.

'Aurelia,' Nightly says, and I look in his direction. I can see a red patch of my blood on the side of his face and I move a hand up to my head again. Nightly clenches his jaw, and I move my fingers away, looking at the blood on them. I've never been particularly squeamish but this makes my head swim again.

'Hold still now.' One of the healers passes his wandlet hand over the cut and I see a little glow come from it. Then he wipes at my forehead with a wet rag, removing all the blood from my face, and I realize he is the same witch that healed me at Mabon. I can instantly think and see in a straight line again, to Jules Nightly, then beyond him to Constance . . . and next to her is Sebastian.

'I just wanted to see . . . to make sure . . .' Sebastian says then looks away; Constance and Nightly are both fixing him with looks that might hex. Sebastian turns on his heels and walks from the room and I surprise myself by feeling glad he has gone.

The healer turns my face to examine his handiwork. 'There will be a small seam of magic, but for the most part the scar will not be noticeable.'

The second witch produces a mirror, and I examine the scar. If I tip the mirror a little, I can see the ripples of magic holding the skin together.

Nightly kneels down beside me, his eyes run over my face and he smiles and says in a whisper for my ears only, 'You look radiant, Wycherley. I think the scar is very becoming of you, like you have breached the line from misdemeanour to full-on felony.' He strokes his fingers along it and my breath hitches in my throat.

'What is my crime?' I ask.

'Theft, I think. You have stolen a great many things this night, including Crenshaw's tongue, but this scar looks like a stolen thread of starlight and, if at all possible, it makes you look even more dangerously beautiful.'

'I see you've been reading *Writing from the Heart.*'

He smiles at me. 'I'll have you know that was all my own work.'

Nightly holds out his hand and I take it, swinging my legs off the couch. He stands and pulls me up with him.

'Aurelia!' Vaughn calls out as he runs into the room, followed by Martyn. I drop Nightly's hand. 'I should never have left you. Are you all right? Crenshaw told me what he did. I have half a mind to challenge him to a duel. Do you want to go home? I'm sure we can arrange some horses.'

167

I shake my head and it only hurts a little. 'Vaughn, I'm fine, really. The healers have taken such good care of me, and, of course, Nightly and Constance too.'

Now Vaughn reluctantly acknowledges Jules's presence with a hostile look. 'Thank you for your service to my sister, Nightly. I am sure that you will, no doubt, give me another lecture on how I should ensure her safety. Rest assured I will stay by her side for the rest of the evening and make sure that no more harm comes to her.'

A tense moment passes between them as Nightly takes a step closer to Vaughn, his hands outstretched. 'No lecture tonight, Wycherley.' Nightly is using that tone that I know holds more humour than malice. 'Ms Wycherley, I am glad you are well, and I will take my leave of you for now.' Nightly bows before bidding farewell to Constance, Martyn and the healers.

'Do you have to be so unreasonable towards him!' I snap at Vaughn.

'Yes!' he replies flatly. 'And so should you be. Don't forget what he has done to you, Aurelia.'

Except it was not Jules that cursed me. He has only done things *for* me, not *to* me. I can't forget that either.

Fourteen

t the very centre of the lawn, overlooked by the towers of Nessbrugh House, is an enormous monument of dried wood. A bonfire in waiting.

I hold on tight to Vaughn's arm as we walk towards it. We've been joined by Vaughn's friend Layla, trailing behind with Martyn, who is enthusiastically retelling the broom incident from pure hearsay.

Constance walks on Vaughn's other side. I notice them look shyly at each other a few times and I feel like I'm intruding. I'm sure that if I was not there, the two of them would be walking arm in arm, but I am glad of Vaughn's attention, because even though the swimming feeling in my head has gone, it seems that my legs have not yet received the message, and every now and again I feel them buckle a little.

'Are you sure you don't want to go back inside, or go home even?'

'Yes, Vaughn, I'm sure. It's Samhain! I'm not going to miss this because Sebastian Crenshaw doesn't know how to control his broom,' I say.

'Too right!' Constance adds, giving me a broad smile.

Usually, I would make some kind of excuse for Sebastian, but I don't feel the need to, and I notice the absence of the usual pang of longing I have when I think of him.

We form part of the black sea of witches making their way along the lantern-lit pathways towards the dark shape of the pyre. Wandlets glowing, hoods and hopes up – even mine. When we reach the bonfire, I let go of Vaughn, taking a few steps from him and Constance to stand with Martyn and Layla to the other side of me. I sway a little but hold fast and breathe deeply; I am feeling more sure of myself by the minute. I glance over at Vaughn who is looking at Constance with an expression of anxious expectation. I am intrigued to see if their magic chooses each other in the Rite – I'm sure it will.

Just like us, all the other witches have come to a halt, forming a scattered circle around the bonfire. I find myself looking for Nightly, but I can't see him.

Excitement wells in the silence. *The Most Magical Season – A Debutantes' Guide* details how the Samhain Rite works: witches send out their magic in fire form and in return they receive a spark of magic from any witch whose magic is a match for theirs. Even though the Royal Magical Council have deemed my magic too dangerous to be tethered, I'm intrigued to see if a spark might be a possibility.

The book also says that the form of the fire magic changes each year and I am excited to see it in action, to perform the Rite with my fellow witches, even if I have no idea what exactly is about to happen. It is one of the mysteries of the Magical Season; a certain amount of trust needs to be placed in one's magic – looking for the nudges, following the flow – and this is reflected in Sabbats.

There isn't long to wait before the beat of a drum starts up. Then a second drum sounds, soon to be joined by a third and a fourth. While the drumming fills the air, the witches in their grey years light small balls of witch-flame in their hands. Following their lead, I gather my thoughts and my magic and turn my hand over. In the palm of my right hand sits a ball of black flames.

The first time I called a witch-flame, commotion ensued in the Arcade. By then, Platz and Russo were used to my magic bringing a state of tumult with it, but even Platz raised an eyebrow and Russo a sad smile when they saw my black witch-flame. 'Ms Aurelia Wycherley, your magic truly is something; what a shame it will most likely come to nothing,' Platz had remarked.

The ball of black fire burns happily in the centre of my palm. The other witches are all holding balls of flame in every other colour: golden like Vaughn's, green like Martyn's, Layla's is a cobalt blue and Constance's is a reddish pink. Sebastian is standing not too far away from me, his amber flame burning bright, and our eyes meet for a moment. I feel a rush of hurt rise up in me for all the ways he has behaved towards me since the Thunder Moon. Maybe the bump to my head has worked something loose, because I now realize that although I am the one altered by my magic, he is the one who has changed. I had the curse forced upon me against my will, but his behaviour is a choice. All I can see in my mind is him watching as Nightly carried me away. He didn't even try to help me.

The drumming suddenly stops, and I stand in the silence with this realization. Then a chanting begins, low and quiet to start with, but as the witches in the crowd hear it and add their voices, it gains in volume. I listen through once, then join in the chant myself: 'In the deep and dead of night, in the burning, bold and bright, in the shadows growing thin, flows the magic of Samhain. I cast my magic into flight, to seek out honour, truth and might. For the kingdom my flame will catch, and thus reveal my magical match.'

Five times we make the chant, and on the fifth time, the drums all stop on the word 'match'. Again, I take my cue from those around me as they throw their glowing orbs on to the bonfire.

The wood catches immediately, the different coloured flames spreading up and over the scaffold. Straight up out of the twists of coloured flames flies a massive dragon. Each scale is made from a different coloured flame. It soars high into the sky, then swoops towards us. I wonder where my orb is, and then see that the dragon's eyes are made of the blackest black. The crowd of witches whoop with excitement as the dragon pulls out of its dive and circles overhead.

I squeal with excitement, and duck down as the dragon streaks above us before flying towards Nessbrugh House, where it stretches out its flame-filled wings and lands on the top of the tallest tower. There, it opens its mouth and breathes out a long stream of fire. It is as if the dragon is blowing itself inside out as the flames that formed its body disappear from the tail up, and all that is left are thousands of tiny floating specks, each one a different colour, each one floating above us witches like fireflies. We stand still, waiting for the magic to claim us. I hold my breath as a deep-red orb floats towards me, then it veers off towards Vaughn and Constance. I notice they are surrounded by many orbs which gently dance around them before deciding to settle or not. If they don't, then they drift off. If they do, they burst like a bubble popping as they touch them. I wonder what it feels like.

All around me, orbs are landing on other witches. I wonder if my magic is landing on anyone and I look over to Sebastian, who is looking in wonder at a large green orb. It lights up his face for a moment before it kisses his cheek, then pops. I see out of the corner of my eye an orb that is so white it almost has a violet tinge to it. I lean to one side, but it tracks me, as if it is deciding whether or not it wants to land on *me*. I hold stock still, watching it drift a little closer, excitement filling me. I hold out my hand to it, as if it is a small bird and

I am trying to entice it to me. The orb moves a little closer . . . and then a little closer still.

I blink at it, not daring to breathe in case I scare it away. I could reach out and grab it, curl my fingers around it and claim it. But I don't, I hold my hand out flat and wait.

My body is tense and I can feel the curiosity in my magic and the wonder in my heart as the violet-white orb slowly lowers itself on to my outstretched hand, then pops like a bubble. As it does, I feel a rush from the magic it contains flood over me. I close my eyes tight to savour the feeling. It feels like a heavy calmness and a deep desire to understand, one which matches my own curiosity perfectly. I smell autumn leaves and warm cinnamon buns. The magic feels as if it has a signature to it, a taste that is running through me. It's strong at first, and it makes me feel supported and powerful as if, for a moment, I am not alone, that my magic has something to lean towards, to grow with. The sensation slowly fades, and the second it is gone, I want it back. In that moment, I know whose magic has sought me out and marked me as a potential match. My pulse races and my breath catches. There is a lump of disbelief in my throat and tears are filling my eyes, I dash them as my mind races, my magic stirs, and my heart thumps.

When all the orbs are gone, the world looks a little darker, despite the multi-coloured flames of the bonfire still burning. The witches have started to murmur excitedly among themselves.

'The *magic* wants to match,' I whisper to myself. Since my curse arrived, I have known that witches wouldn't want to match with me, even if they were allowed, but I have never thought about the magic. That it might have a say.

One match. My magic matched with one other person, one witch, and he happens to be the only witch that I can never tether with, not just because I know how greatly my curse affects him, or because our relationship is based on a mutual understanding of wrongdoings, or because he recently rejected my suggested kisses, but also because he is a Nightly.

Fifteen

It is way past midnight by the time Vaughn and I arrive home. After the ceremony there was feasting and dancing, music and merriment. Vaughn stayed close to me all evening. I wanted to dance with Jules and to ask him if my orb had landed on him, but even if Vaughn had left me to my own devices, I was too terrified of the answer. Terrified that it hadn't . . . and also that it might have. I did not see him dance all night, he stayed in the shadows of the hall, and when I caught his eye, he gave nothing away: no indication that my magic had found him too. By the end of the evening I was sure that it had not, otherwise he would have declared it, no matter how protective Vaughn was being.

On the flight home Constance told me that she received eight orbs, and described each one in graphic detail. Vaughn was uncharacteristically quiet; I'd asked him if he had matched his record of eleven orbs of his debutante year.

'I bettered it with fourteen – but it doesn't matter how many orbs you get. You only need one match: one witch and their magic that will last you a lifetime.' Then he returned to silence. Part of me thinks he was speaking about me, even if he did not know it. I could still taste the flavour of Nightly's magic, but it was fading with every moment that passed.

It was not till we landed in Hemlock Square and I saw Sebastian walking up the steps to his house that I realized I was not at all disappointed that it wasn't his magic that found me.

Vaughn walked Constance home, and as I reached our door I looked back to see that he had slipped his hand in hers. I felt a warm rush of happiness for the two of them.

I greeted my bed with enthusiasm, diving deep beneath the covers and even deeper into a sleep filled with Nightly carrying me about in his strong arms.

'Where were you last night?' I call to my mother as I make the bottom of the stairs and meet her in the entrance hall. She looks tired, and I'm sure that she is wearing the same clothes as last night. 'Did you sleep at all?'

She shakes her head. 'Frances and I just got in, there was another murder last night.' Her voice is strained, and I hold out my arms to hug her. The unrest and murders, in addition to her usual council duties, are taking their toll on her, and on Frances too, who is yawning as she lays out breakfast, pouring tea into three cups.

A feeling of dread pools in me and I want to ask about the murder but I can tell that now is not the time, and besides it is bound to be in the paper soon.

'Where's Vaughn?' I ask instead as I sit at the table and take up my tea.

'You just missed him. He saw the flowers that you received and rushed out on an errand. I suspect he has a young witch that he needs to send a bloom or two to,' Mother says. I smile and hope that I know who the witch is. I lean back a little on my chair and look through the door to the drawing room and see a bouquet of my and Nightly's roses.

'Aurelia, what happened to your head?' Frances asks as she sits down next to me. Mother is by my side in a moment and I explain what happened with Crenshaw and how Nightly carried me to safety.

'I see. That would explain why the Nightly boy has sent you flowers . . . again.' There's an edge in Mother's voice that has nothing to do with her weariness. 'Demelza Nightly was very short with me the last time I saw her. I think it was because of you and this attraction that Jules Nightly has towards you.'

I splutter into my tea. Nightly is anything but attracted to me. I am his ticket to getting access to the places that he wants to be and payback on his mother for her treatment of Evelyn. His magic might have its own ideas, but it is not in alignment with Nightly's heart. I feel embarrassed about the way I asked him to kiss me and he did not, and cooled by the way he kept his distance last night.

I give my eyes a little roll as I walk into the drawing room, my back to Mother and Frances as I pick up the note in the roses and break the seal.

Dear Ms Wycherley,

I hope that the injury you received last night has not caused too much discomfort and that you are well recovered.

I have tried to write this note several times and employed all that I have learnt from Writing from the Heart, but I am a poor student when it comes to the language of love, and I hope our blooms speak to you instead. If they do, I hope they tell you that I am very glad that no serious harm was done last night.

They will also no doubt inform you that the next time I see Crenshaw, a duel may be in order. I hope you are ready to stand by me, if you please.

Nightly

P.S. Meet me at the library, two p.m. sharp.

I read it through quickly; I can almost feel my mother's gaze on me. My cheeks grow hot and then I remember that this is all part of our ruse and that any feelings that may be forming are surely not real, just a side effect of our fabricated feelings.

'Should I be worried?' Mother asks with a raised eyebrow when I return to the table. She sips her tea.

'No, Mother,' I reply, placing the letter in my pocket.

'I like the Nightly boy,' Frances remarks. 'Nell, you can't hold him responsible for the actions of all his family. He has a quick mind and reflexes from the sound of it, and I think he must also be a decent sort, wise beyond his years if he's set his wand at you, Aurelia.'

My mother gives Frances a serious look before softening as she turns to me. 'Aurelia, it is good that you are making . . . new friends,' she says. 'I know that since your magic arrived it has not been easy for you. I just don't want the Nightly boy to be another source of sadness. No tether can come of this, and that makes me worry about his intentions for you.'

'I assure you, Mother, he has no more nefarious intentions for our . . . friendship than I do,' I lie. 'Jules Nightly and I share a common interest, that is all. He is the only witch brave, or foolish, enough to perform secondary magic with me, and I am grateful for that.'

'That's what I'm worried about, that he is filling you with unrealistic expectations. Demelza Nightly seems convinced that there is something more between you.'

I shake my head. 'She is mistaken, and my expectations are perfectly realistic. At the end of this Season he will make a match and go on to a coven college, and I will look forward to my light-grey year, and enjoying the magic that I have for as long as I have it.'

Mother nods and I am glad that one of us is satisfied.

'Now, tell us all about the more fun things that happened last night,' Frances says.

Nightly is waiting in the foyer of the library when I arrive. He's sitting in one of the low chairs but, uncharacteristically, he doesn't have a book in his hand. I see him through the glass of the door, deep in thought.

I push the door open and as his eyes meet mine. I feel a funny flutter in my stomach: embarrassment from when he found me sprawled on the ground, gratitude that he scooped me up and got me to a healer, nervousness that his magic sought me out.

He's on his feet and walking towards me, his strides long, his dark-grey cloak billowing a little behind him. I'm reminded of the first time I saw him on my way to the Mabon celebration, before I knew who he was. I had thought he was handsome, and I realize that I was doomed from that moment, fighting a losing battle trying not to develop feelings for Jules Nightly. I try to convince myself that these emotions are not real, that it's a trick of his magic calling to mine and nothing more.

He stops in front of me, and I look up at him. 'How are you feeling today?'

'I'm fine, thank you,' I say a little curtly, trying to keep my emotions in check.

He eyes the side of my head where Sebastian's broom struck. 'May I?' he asks and I give a small nod as he places one hand on my cheek and uses the tips of his long fingers to push back my hair. He examines me like a specimen, running a finger over the silvery scar. It sends a delightful shiver down my neck, and further still. I close my eyes briefly and breathe through my nose to control the sudden leap in my pulse.

'You're lucky Crenshaw didn't kill you. I have half a mind to kill him. After all, he is my rival for your affections . . . and we *are* fake courting. I'm sure people will gossip if I don't at least try to end him,' he says with a raise of an eyebrow and a wicked smile.

Ah yes, fake courting . . . Except my feelings don't feel quite so fake any more. 'Then you'll have to get in line behind Constance and Vaughn,' I tell him.

He strokes my hair back down then holds my face, cupped in both of his hands, for a moment. I swallow because the way he is looking at me makes more than my magic stir.

'I have something for you,' he says and hands me an envelope.

'This isn't your handwriting,' I say to him.

'No, it isn't.'

182

I turn the envelope and see the seal of the Royal Magical Council.

'Have my forgery skills been rubbing off on you?'

'Well, a lot of your bad habits have been making an impression on me.' He reaches out a hand and takes the envelope back with a flourish. 'But on second thoughts, this might take a little explaining first.' He slides the envelope into his cloak pocket. 'Fancy an educational trip?' He offers me his arm.

As we walk through the ton I pester him on where we are going. 'You'll see soon enough,' he replies. Before long, we are outside the British Museum.

'Oh, we really are going on an educational trip,' I say as we walk up the short flight of stairs and into the vast building.

'Yes, but you do know that this is also where I would probably bring you if we were really courting,' he says.

'I see. Keeping up the pretence.'

He shrugs. 'Only if anyone is looking.' And I wonder if anyone is.

Littered among the exhibitions from all over the world are magical relics. I can feel their magic vibrating as I pass. I think of the way that magic calls, the way that it is imbued with many subtle elements from the witches that create it, full of the uniqueness of the land it is forged in, and I can't help but feel that many of these objects would be happier in their home lands where their vibrations would be matched, where they would be in harmony once more.

When we reach the section on magic of the British Isles, I can feel the large, concentrated gathering of ancient magic tingling over my skin, calling to the magic in my marrow.

'I've been following your lead.'

'Mathilde Wycherley and Heston Nightly?'

Nightly nods as we walk deeper into the rooms dedicated to magic, past the First and Second Age exhibitions and into the Third.

'You got me thinking when you said that Mathilde obviously knew about the third set of magical runes, the Golowhe runes, and that these runes existed in a time when magic didn't need to be tethered. Not only that, but you have found two of these runes since getting your magic – there is no such thing as coincidence when it comes to magic.'

'My father used to say the same thing about magic and coincidences.'

Nightly's face softens. 'My father always says that Ulric le Fay was the most brilliant witch of his generation. I'm sorry that you lost him.' His voice is full of feeling and I turn away.

'It was I that found him, when he was already gone. But I hate to think of him as not being here. It's easier to think of him being behind the sealed door of his spellorium or, and I know this sounds foolish, that a small part of him is in the wild magic – a part that maybe is nudging these magical coincidences towards us. I know it's impossible.'

'A great many impossible things are only so until someone proves them to be possible,' Nightly returns. 'I think the idea that your father had about magic guiding us is right, and I think it is no coincidence that you inherited your family curse, or that you and I are working together to puzzle this out. I can't shake the idea that we, a Wycherley and a Nightly, are walking the same path as Mathilde and Heston – finishing something that they began. Remember that missing college?'

'Of course, Wynne Hordes College. We searched all the records and couldn't find any mention of it, except in the original documentation which said it was supposed to be somewhere near Cambridge.'

'It is,' Nightly says, his eyes dancing with excitement.

'No, it isn't, I've checked.' I'm sure of myself, until I see the look on his face. He leads me into an antechamber where there is an exhibition of the history of the twelve witch colleges of Briton. He pulls me over to a display.

'Neoards?' Nightly says. 'Say it quickly with a W in front of it.'

'Similar, but not the same.' I shake my head.

'The same. Look.' He points to a scroll, the original architectural plans for the college, and in the corner it is signed.

"H. N. and M. W.",' I say, a little taken back.

'Heston Nightly and Mathilde Wycherley,' Jules says with a pleased smile.

I gasp . . . could it really be? Then shake my head again. 'These plans are different to Neoards: for one thing the plan is in the shape of a square and Neoards is a triangle.'

Nightly looks at me, and I feel the weight of his gaze as he says, 'Plans change.'

I know I'm blushing as I think of how my plans for him are most definitely adapting. 'But I still don't see what this has to do with the runes.' I try to change the subject.

'Well . . .' He begins to walk around the exhibition, and I follow. 'I started to read everything I could about Neoards, and in an art history book I found a reference to the Tomb of the Untethered Witch. And here is a painting of it.'

Before us is a watercolour painting of a large tomb with an effigy of a witch sculpted on top of it. The witch looks as if he is sleeping, his hands laced over his chest, his cape drifting down the sides of the tomb, and around the edge of the tomb is a kind of fresco of strange dark runes. 'The Golowhe runes!' I say.

'I think so,' Nightly says with a smile.

'And is that . . . Heston Nightly?' I ask, looking at the witch's face. Nightly pulls out his notebook. In it is a copied portrait of his ancestor linked by a red thread to one of Mathilde Wycherley.

'Did you paint these?' I ask and he nods. 'They're very good.'

I look from the painting of the tomb to the miniature. 'It is him,' I declare.

'I think so too,' Nightly agrees. 'And look at the description.' He points to the plaque by the painting and reads, '"The grave marks on the Tomb of the Untethered Witch may very well give us a clue to his identity, but they are written in no rune system known to magic. The question of his identity and why he was buried alone and not with his tether, which has been the custom since the introduction of tethering magic, is yet another mystery. It is obvious that he was an important witch in his time, as evidenced by his prominent burial at the centre of one of the most prestigious coven colleges in the land.'"

'Runes – more than just the two that I've found. A system. If we could see them, maybe we could find out what they are.' The excitement is evident in my voice and Nightly is nodding in agreement. 'We need to visit Neoards. We need to see these runes.' This feels like the next piece in the puzzle.

Nightly hands me the crisp envelope again. I break the seal of the letter and pull it open.

Her Majesty the Princess Regent,
Georgianna,
and the Royal Magical Council
request the presence of

Ms Aurelia Wycherley

at the Yule Ball

on Wednesday the 22nd December 1813,
at Neoards coven college, Cambridgeshire.

Arrivals from dusk, carriages at one a.m.

All witches are expected to uphold the Yule tradition
of the festive mask and to keep their identities hidden
till the striking of the bells.

Your Yule animal is: <u>a swan</u>.

Glamours are allowed, but must be removed
upon the stroke of midnight.

For the kingdom and the magic.

Sixteen

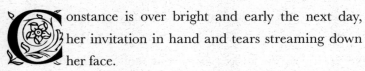onstance is over bright and early the next day, her invitation in hand and tears streaming down her face.

'What's wrong?' My mind races through a million possibilities.

'Peacock,' she says, shaking her invitation at me. 'They want me to be a *peacock*.'

'But that's great!? I got a swan. I've been wearing white all Season and I was looking forward to a change.'

'My sister Joy was a peacock, so when Mother sees this, she's just going to give me her old dress to wear. Everything I've worn so far this Season has belonged to one of my sisters and I . . . I just wanted to feel special and like I had something that was all mine.' She wipes her tears as she looks up. 'I know that's foolish, and I know that it sounds selfish . . .'

'No, it's neither of those things. But I have two questions

189

to ask you.' I look at her seriously. 'Have any of your sisters ever been a swan? And would you be willing to risk sickness, possible unconsciousness and a massive headache for the chance to be one?'

Moments later we are standing in my family arcade, my document wallet from Nightly in my hand as I rummage through and pull out two spells that I have copied down. I'd come across them in my research and thought they might come in handy, but had never thought this would be why. One for duplicating the written word and another for the transformation of it. Both of the spells are transformative in nature, and so require the use of secondary magic.

'We will swap your name on to my invitation and visa-versa, then you can give it to your mother and she will be none the wiser. And you'll get a new dress.' Constance's face lights up. 'But you know what happened last time we performed secondary magic,' I warn her.

'I'm not likely to forget that anytime soon,' she says with a grim look. 'But if it works it will be worth it.'

I start chalking out the symbols on the floor.

'Have you performed secondary magic with anyone else? I mean, outside of the Arcade?' I ask.

Constance shakes her head. 'Only with a few witches at the Arcade, just trying some potential matches. Some were a disaster, a few were better. What about you?' she asks, and I can tell that she regrets it immediately.

Since the beginning of the Season, Constance and I have

not engaged in conversation about magical matches. We've spoken of the primary magic that we have been performing at the Arcade, the type of magic that a witch can do alone, we have recounted the activities surrounding the Sabbats, and we have gossiped about other witches making matches, but we have not spoken about our own prospects, or lack of in my case. As long as we don't speak of her making a match and me being left behind, we can just pretend, like when we were children.

'I mean I haven't seen you at the Arcade, except the time with Nightly of course,' she adds, trying to keep her voice light, like it didn't matter, like it isn't the whole reason for the Season.

I feel a little sad. I don't want Constance to feel like she can't tell me things just because she thinks she might upset me, or I her in some way. Deep down we both know that Constance will make a match and will move on and I will not, no matter how much we don't want that to be true.

'Just before Samhain, Russo forced a few witches to perform magic with me, and they were all ill afterwards. Claire Millard was unconscious for a week. The only witches to perform secondary magic with me willingly have been you, and Nightly, and we all know what happened to the two of you too.'

'But Nightly . . . he's still very keen on you and your magic, if you ask me,' Constance says, giving me a look and a smile.

I wince a little as I shake my head. I've never told Constance about my and Nightly's deception, I know what she would think if she knew either of our true motivations.

She would think us both foolish for seeking the impossible and then she would take pity on me, and I have had almost as much pity from my fellow witches as I have disdain, and I can't bear receiving either from Constance.

'Not only does no one want to share their magic with me – not even Nightly – but no one *can*, not without repercussions. Imagine living with that every day?' My voice sounds harsher than I want it to. 'If Nightly and I were to tether, then every act of magic that we performed would hurt him, and although the magic is great, better than great – it's exciting and powerful – knowing that it would distress him afterwards . . . I won't do it. He deserves better – a proper match that can fulfil his magical needs.'

Constance looks at me, her eyes wide. 'Aurelia Wycherley! I think you are in love with Jules Nightly,' she declares.

I adamantly shake my head. 'Constance, no. Nightly and I, it's not what you think. And I certainly can't tether with him. I can't tether with you. I can't tether with anyone. Beside the fact that the council have forbidden it, it's too dangerous; who knows what the long-term effects of my magic will be. The short term is grim enough.'

'I would tether with you if you would let me, in spite of the throwing up and unconsciousness.' She sounds as if she is defending herself in some way and I instantly feel bad.

'I know, and I love you for that. But I'm never going to let you do it.' I continue with the chalk markings. 'This isn't going to be pleasant,' I remind her.

She chuckles. 'I know, but it's weeks till Yule. I'll be recovered by then and I'll have a new dress too.'

I stand up and head towards the altar. It's full of all the signs of late autumn and early winter: a large pumpkin with a crown of holly around it, golden sheaves of corn laced through with lavender and rosemary, and a bowl full of horse chestnuts, acorns and fir cones. In the next few weeks, the pumpkin will be replaced with red and white berries and more greenery. I light the candles and say the opening chant with Constance, inviting the magic in and preparing ourselves for the circle spell we are about to perform.

'Come on, let's get you a new dress for the ball,' I say when we're finished.

Constance stands in one half of the circle, and I stand in the other, the two invitations on the ground before us surrounded by the chalk lines of the invocation.

A standing circle spell is not like a sequenced spell: there is little physical movement, most of the magic is done by moving through the sigil, directing the magic and manipulating it from within. I kick off my shoes and place my feet on the ground. Constance copies me. I start to tune into the magic that is rising through me. My wandlet is glowing and the feeling of a soft vibration begins to swell in me. Just as we both raise our hands, ready to connect, Vaughn comes down the stairs.

'What the blazes are you doing?' he barks as he rushes towards us. I look from him to Constance; her eyes are wide and she turns a little pale.

'You know what happened the last time the two of you performed secondary magic. Why would you want to put Constance through that again?' Vaughn challenges me.

'We need to swap the animals on our invitations. It's important – we wouldn't be doing it if it wasn't,' I tell my brother.

I expect Vaughn to ask why, but he keeps his gaze on Constance and nods. 'It must be if you are willing to go through all that again.' He raises an eyebrow. I know that look, he is mulling something over, deciding if it's a good idea or not.

'I'll do it,' he says, crossing the circle. 'Constance and I have performed secondary magic before, we know that our magic is compatible and strong. This way you'll have what you want, and no one will need a healer.' I've already moved to one side and he's standing in my place by the time he has finished speaking. 'That is, Constance, if you don't mind performing magic with me?'

'Yes . . . I mean no, I don't mind,' Constance answers, a little breathily. 'Are you sure? I mean if . . . if you are willing.'

I step out of the circle and turn to watch them. Constance is running through the spell, telling Vaughn how he must direct his magic, giving him the same instructions I have given her.

There are two conversations taking place, one on the surface and one beneath. I can see them speaking, but it is in the silences between the words and the space between their bodies with which they are communicating their true feelings for one another.

I pass Vaughn the chalk and he rubs out the part of the spell that holds the sigil for my name and replaces it with his own.

He takes his boots off and reaches out his hand to Constance.

She looks at me, as if asking permission. I smile at her and give an enthusiastic nod. She reaches out her hand and I wonder if I should still be there. I can already feel the shift in the room, the magic concentrating on the two of them, flowing through them.

Vaughn takes his lead from Constance. She moves her right hand up, their palms touching then fingers lacing as they bring their hands down in a wide arc. The invitation nearer to Constance rises from the floor and hovers just above waist height.

Constance nods and smiles at Vaughn, who smiles back at her; a boyish smile that reminds me of long-ago summers. He raises his right hand, palm to palm with Constance's left before they link fingers, and the second invitation rises as their hands arc out.

They're looking at each other intensely, and again I feel like I'm prying. They repeat the movements over and over, as they slowly step widdershins around the circle, purposely scuffing the chalk as they go, muttering an incantation soft and low. It looks as if they are dancing, and between them, the invitations flutter and glow.

When Constance is standing in Vaughn's original place and he in hers, they stop, and the invitations flutter to the floor as if an invisible hand has let go of them. Constance and Vaughn don't let go of one another for a long time. Their breathing is fast, and each of them has a glow about them. I take a step back, up against the door to my father's spellorium, turning swiftly I try to seem enthralled by the glyphs on it. I focus on a rune right at the top. It is strange and dark, and I instantly know that it is one of the Golowhe runes – it glows black like those on my broom and wandlet. My breath hitches. I reach into my pocket and pull out my document wallet, retrieving a piece of paper I scribble down the shape of the rune, wondering why I have never noticed it before.

Then I hear Vaughn say, 'Constance, at Samhain I . . .' His voice is low, and I wish that the door to my father's spellorium wasn't locked so I could just sneak inside and leave the two of them to it.

'I . . . me too, Vaughn,' Constance replies, and I quietly make my way towards the stairs, and up into the parlour.

A few minutes pass before they join me, looking at each other awkwardly and smiling.

'It worked; you are to be a peacock, Aurelia,' Vaughn tells me as he hands me my invitation.

'All went well then?' I say with a raise of my eyebrow. I can't wait to tease them both about it but at the same time I realize that this might be it for them: a genuine connection. Magic *and* love. I hold a little hope deep inside me that they will bloom now that their magical connection has been confirmed by the Samhain Rite.

I take the invitation from Vaughn. A peacock it shall be.

Seventeen

'**D**o you want to come with us, Vaughn?' I ask.

'No, no, you two go ahead and have your fun without me. Martyn and I are going shopping tomorrow, and you wouldn't believe how long it takes me to pick out the right outfit. Martyn too – he has a thing about making sure his hats match his shoes. Besides, I want it to be a surprise,' he says with a glance at Constance. 'I'll wait till we're at Neoards to see your gowns. I'm sure you'll look quite lovely.' Constance beams as we leave the house, clutching our invitations.

I'm still not sure how Nightly managed to get them to hold the Yule Ball at Neoards, and I fully intend on getting that information out of him the next time we meet. It does feel as though magic is leading Nightly and me to the Golowhe runes, and for the two of us, the Yule Ball is more important than glamours, dancing and matches – although I am still looking forward to those. The three runes I have found swim in my mind, and I fight the urge to write to Nightly and tell him immediately of my latest discovery. But as Constance takes my arm and excitedly talks about the ball, I push thoughts of runes from my mind and instead fill it with new dresses, love and magical matches, specifically between my brother and my best friend.

As Constance and I make our way through the witch-laden streets, I want to ask her about Vaughn, but I don't quite know the best way to do so. I want to know how serious she is about him, about his magic, about the idea of them possibly tethering. I am sure that he is interested, although they both have so many options, but even so I don't want him to be disappointed. And because I love Constance almost as much as Vaughn, sometimes more, I don't want her to have to be the one to let him down if her feelings are not mutual.

'Did you get any flowers? In response to the events at Samhain?' I ask, thinking of how Mother said that Vaughn had rushed out to send some.

'A few.' She sounds a little disinterested.

'From anyone I know?'

'Probably – we are all debutantes together after all.' Then she adds, 'Bertram Downing and Saskia Von Hess signed theirs, but there were also three without names.'

'Any idea who they might have been from?'

She shakes her head. 'I saw you had some blooms too, from Nightly.'

'Yes, after Sebastian—'

'Attacked you!'

'It was an accident, Constance!'

'Ha, you know, the worm didn't even *apologize*. Not properly. He should have begged for your forgiveness with a field of flowers, for that and for every other small injury he has dealt you since the Thunder Moon.

'The way he just stood there – after he had struck you down, when you were bleeding on the floor – with his broom in his hand, doing nothing.'

'Maybe he was in shock?'

Constance snorted. 'Then it must be his natural state. Nightly on the other hand, that witch is all action. The way he just kind of swept in,' she says, her eyes sparkling. 'You should have seen him. I mean, you did, but you were all . . .' She rolls her eyes back and dramatically leans her head back too.

'Don't!' I say in a half laugh at her impression of me.

'Nightly was calm and collected and truly gallant. Oh, and absolutely livid at Sebastian – I thought he was going to hex him right there!' She lets out a little sigh. 'If the two of you weren't . . . whatever it is you're doing, and if I hadn't got my eye on someone else, I would set my wand at him.' She smiles. 'I don't know why you don't; he is obviously smitten with you, but it's like you keep holding back. I know that you can't ever be tethered to one another, that you can't share a lifetime of magic, but you could share a lifetime of love together.'

Except he isn't smitten with me at all. He is just a very good showman, I tell myself.

'Constance, he's not interested in me like that. It's complicated.' I can't tell her that it's all an act, that he doesn't think of me as anything other than a tool for antagonism, and that he rejected my kisses.

'Well, it doesn't look very complicated to me.'

I don't want to be having this conversation, I am trying to quell my feelings for Nightly, and knowing that he has none for me is becoming harder to deal with by the day. I try to distract Constance. 'You know, Sebastian has had a lot to deal with. Maybe he really did just freeze?'

Constance stops walking and turns to face me.

'No, Aurelia. I'm sorry, but you are my best friend, and it is time that you heard this. *You* are dealing with a disappointment; *he* is running away. Is that what you really want? Someone who runs away from you? Wouldn't you rather someone who runs *to* you, who scoops you up and does all they can to help you? I know it's hard, I know how you felt about Sebastian, and even if he did once feel the same way, deep, deep down, is it worth it? Magical matches always work best when magic and feelings are aligned, those feelings don't have to be love just as the magic doesn't have to be ridiculously powerful, but it does have to be *mutual*. And if you tell me you love him, I might have to duel you into your senses, because he doesn't love you, Aurelia, not really, not as he should.' She stops and takes a shaky breath.

I know she is right – I've almost accepted it already, but it still hurts.

'And what do you know of love and tethers?' I say, feeling the last bit of bitterness bite.

'Nothing of tethers, yet, but I know about love. I love *you*, Aurelia. And I don't want to see you giving up something good for the futile hope of something bad.' Constance sighs as she scoops up my hand. 'One of the reasons why we are such good friends is because I know that once you set your mind to something, there is no stopping you. But I'm asking you to please look at everything objectively. To change your mind. If someone was treating me the way Sebastian is treating you, what would you say to me? What would you do?'

'I would have already done it, and they would have the magical scars to prove it,' I say, and I mean it.

I turn my face up to the sky and let out a long breath. I have held on to the last little thread of Sebastian so tightly, the idea of letting him go entirely fills me with dread. But Sebastian hasn't been mine from the moment I received my magic. Tears run from my stormy eyes, and I let them fall. Constance hugs me tightly. I'm crying because, by cutting that tie, I feel free. I didn't realize how much I needed to release Sebastian, that I was the one holding myself to him the whole time.

'Come on, let's go and get the most amazing outfits for Yule – not for Sebastian or Nightly or any other witches, but for ourselves.'

'I'd like that,' I say, linking my arm in hers and wiping the tears from my cheeks.

The Yule Ball is one of the highlights of the debutante Season. Last year, the theme was constellations, and I remember that Vaughn wore the most beautiful golden suit, with a mask in the shape of a star. I'd asked him if it was a bit too much, and he had told me that 'for the Yule Ball, nothing is ever too much'. As we skip through the ton, I listen to Constance reel off the dresses and masks that each of her sisters had worn through the years. I was beginning to understand that Vaughn was right.

'I think I might go for something large, with more layers than a sponge cake,' she says with a grin. 'I just can't decide if I want to be a white swan or a black one.'

'You can always be both. Use your glamour to change the colour at midnight.'

Constance takes in a loud breath. 'That's perfect!'

Glamours are instable primary magic; a glamour gives a witch the ability to alter the appearance of any living thing for a short period of time. Being primary magic, glamours don't have the lasting power of transformation a secondary magic spell, and they are easily broken. Due to the deceptive nature of this type of magic, it is generally banned by the Royal Magical Council and punishment for using one without licence is . . . severe. However, there are times, like at the Yule Ball, where glamours are a traditional part of the Season. For debutantes, it is one of the highlights of the year: the chance to be incognito for the night, to magically become a different version of yourself . . . the idea is intoxicating.

'I'm looking forward to wearing a glamour,' I admit. 'I thought I might turn myself back into how I used to look.' I imagine my white hair returned to its former chestnut, my smoke-filled eyes a lighter soft brown. In my mind I'm smiling too, my warm skin glowing with a renewed lustre.

Constance frowns slightly. 'Doesn't that defeat the point of being incognito at a masked ball?' she asks before adding, 'Besides, I've grown so used to seeing you as you are now, it'll be strange to see you as you were.'

But I know exactly what I am going to do. I've been taken by the notion ever since Nightly passed me the invitation and I saw the word 'glamour' on it. If I am being honest with myself, I want Nightly to see me as I was, and if I'm being *very* honest it's because I wonder if he would have wanted to kiss me if I wasn't cursed.

A thrill of excitement runs through me as I think of Nightly and his lips. I take Constance's hand and lead us to Seven Dials where all of the most magical modistes' shops reside.

We pause outside Taylor and Hughes and look up at the window. Turning serenely behind the glass is a beautiful dress: the top is the fresh green of summer buds, adorned with small pink blooms, but as the dress cascades down to the floor, the green becomes darker and the flowers on the vines that lace the gown are as large as my palm and deep pink. Constance and I give a contented sigh before looking at each other and laughing.

The street is teeming with witches, all holding their

invitations and looking about excitedly. Inside, Taylor and Hughes is crammed. Constance stands close to me as a little circle opens up around us, our fellow witches all giving us a wide berth – well not us, just me.

The shop falls quiet, and every eye turns towards us. Standing on a raised podium with Ms Taylor, who is magically manipulating a length of rich satin into a beautiful gold gown, I catch eyes with Emeline Hunt. She looks very happy with herself in the dress. I hold her gaze as I think of her and Sebastian at the Season Gardens. I saw them together at the Arcade recently too, and watched them perform secondary magic when they thought no one was looking.

Emeline stoops down and whispers something to Ms Taylor before standing up straight and fixing me with a victorious stare. The modiste looks around at me, then as she rises from her crouch and moves towards us, a feeling of dread lodges in my stomach.

Constance takes a step forward, presenting her invitation. Ms Taylor is joined by her tether, Ms Hughes, who abandons Bevis Nash, leaving him to tie his own cravat.

Ms Hughes smiles at Constance: bright, radiant and completely false. 'Ms Prior, we would be honoured to make your gown for the Yule Ball, and as you know, our dresses are the very finest in the ton.' She gives me a withering glance. 'However, it is unacceptable for your friend to be here. The energies that we create with are subtle and easily upset by . . . well . . . I am sure you understand.'

My cheeks feel hot, although I am sure that my face is now pale.

I watch as Constance smiles sweetly at both Ms Taylor and Ms Hughes. 'I understand completely. Like the energies that you work with, I too am easily upset.' Constance raises her voice. 'And so, unfortunately, I am unable to give you my patronage. Not only because your opinions are backwards and outdated, but also because your designs are too. Why, I am sure that when my older sister Amity had her Yule gown made here some eight years ago, her dress looked identical to the one that you are currently fitting, quite poorly, to Ms Hunt. And while that tired, old design does suit her complexion, I am a modern witch in need of the freshest design for my gown. No, this won't do, and neither will you. Good day to you both. Good luck, witches.'

Constance casts her eye around the room at the witches who have all stopped to look. Then my friend turns and smiles at me, takes my arm and whispers suspiciously loudly, 'I hear that Moore and Kettle is dressing the Princess Regent for the ball. We really should have gone there directly, though I fear they may be overrun with witches. Let us make haste now in the hope that they can accommodate us.'

Constance steers me out of the door, and I notice that we aren't the only ones to leave. Most of the witches in the shop follow us and rush further up the street to Moore and Kettle. Constance keeps hold of my arm and leads me straight past them, past the bay-fronted shop, where a very startled Ms Moore is staring at the influx of witches pouring through her door.

'How did you know about the Princess Regent?' I ask, focusing on that rather than the way that I felt in the shop.

'Oh, I have absolutely no idea where Her Royal Highness is going to get her dress from.' Constance smiles at me. 'But I do know that it definitely won't be Taylor and Hughes!'

'Constance!' I am only a little shocked.

'Are you all right?'

I nod, my cheeks almost back to normal. 'I'm fine. It's something you get used to.'

'But you shouldn't have to. Ignorant witches.' Constance glances back towards the shop. 'You're still the same Aurelia you've always been.'

I smile at her, but I can't tell her that that isn't true. I don't feel the same. Everything I thought I was, everything I thought I was going to be, has been altered. At first, that terrified me, but now I feel like I am growing into this new Aurelia, and I am excited by who I am becoming.

Constance gently guides me towards the door of another dressmaker. I pull back slightly. 'You know, I think I'll just have Mother order me something.' I shake my head as I look at the door, the elegant sign above it declares 'Goth and Drake: Attire for the Sophisticated Witch'.

'Please, Aurelia, for me. You don't have to get a dress, but I need you to help me to choose one because . . . well, because there's a witch that I like very much, and I want to make a good impression.'

I hope with everything I have that the witch in question is Vaughn, and the way Constance is looking at me tentatively makes me feel quite confident that it is. 'Whoever they are, they would be a fool not to like you back. I will happily curse them if they break your heart – no matter who they are.' I hold her gaze, then take her hand and lead her into the shop.

The shop assistant smiles at me, then at Constance. 'Ah, witches, no doubt you are here for your Yule gowns and accessories. Please allow me to show you to one of the private rooms that we have set up for just this occasion, for there is nothing more important at a masked ball than the secrecy surrounding one's identity, is there not? And here at Goth and Drake we take the wishes of our clients very seriously indeed.'

He leads us down a short hallway, each side filled with doors leading to beautifully decorated fitting and dressing rooms. I think on his words. If I use my chance of glamour to make myself look like the old Aurelia, there will be people who will recognize me for who I used to be.

I'm full of contradicting opinions as the assistant opens a door to usher us into a dressing room. Just then, one on the opposite side of the hall opens and Nightly steps out, adjusting his collar and tugging it into place.

My heart gives a little skip and I can't help the smile that spreads across my lips, the tingle that makes its way into the pit of my stomach. 'Ah, fancy meeting you here. First a new suit and then . . . I expect you'll be at the barbers next.' I reach up to touch his too-long hair, and it feels natural to do so.

'Steady on there, Wycherley. There's nothing wrong with my locks.' He feigns hurt, placing a hand over his heart, and I let out a laugh.

'Jules, you forgot your hat,' a girl calls from inside the small room and I immediately stiffen. He was in there with another witch! I'm quite a stranger to jealousy, but the thought of him being with someone else burns right through me.

Then, Evelyn Nightly follows her brother out into the hallway, and I feel myself relax and my cheeks burn. I dart a look at Nightly and he raises a puzzled eyebrow at me.

'Hello.' Evelyn looks from Constance and me to her brother, who has become uncharacteristically shy. 'I don't believe that we've met, and my brother is so devoid of polite company that it seems he has forgotten the proper etiquette.'

Nightly stirs into action. 'Ms Wycherley, Ms Prior, please allow me to introduce my sister, Ms Evelyn Nightly.'

'A pleasure to meet you both. Ms Prior, I know your sister Felicity, we debuted the same year. How are she and her match? Elizabeth Doble, I believe?'

'Yes, they are well, thank you,' Constance replies with warmth.

'And of course, Ms Wycherley, you need no introduction. My brother has told me so much about you I feel like we are good friends already. I was too quick when I said earlier that he was devoid of good acquaintances, for he has you.'

I realize in an instant that of course he would have told his sister about me, about our work together – after all, it is of as much benefit to her as to me.

I wonder how much time she has left with her magic and my heart aches for her, for the way her mother is trying to push her from magical society and how she will no doubt be cast out if Jules and I are unsuccessful in our search for a solution to her plight.

'Ms Nightly, are you free on Thursday?' I enquire. 'I would like to invite you to tea. You and Nightly . . . I mean, Jules.'

Nightly's eyes are wide and a smile dances on his lips.

'I . . . I would love that, thank you, Ms Wycherley,' replies Evelyn. 'It has been some time since I was in the company of other witches, with the exception of my family, that is, and besides, I would like to get to know the witch who has stolen my brother's heart a little better.'

I look from Evelyn to Jules – he looks furious, his jaw set and brow low, so like the Nightly I first encountered on Mabon. 'Evelyn,' Nightly says, a hint of warning in his voice – because of course his heart is safe, although mine is now beating too fast in my chest. 'We should be getting along.'

Evelyn gives Jules the kind of intense stare that only a sibling can. He ignores her.

'Ms Prior, it was a pleasure to see you again. Wycherley, I will see you soon.' As he passes me, his shoulder brushes softly against mine in the narrow hallway.

'He is insufferable, but I'm sure you already know that,' Evelyn says to me with a smile and a quick hug. 'He is so . . . well, the Nightly is strong in him!' They both make their way along the corridor, and I rummage in my cloak pocket for my document wallet.

'Nightly,' I call as I hasten after him.

Evelyn goes ahead, opening the door to the shop with a ring of the bell, and Nightly turns to me. 'Aurelia, I need to—'

'I found another one.' We both speak at the same time.

'Please, go on,' he says, and I wish I had not interrupted him.

I extend the piece of paper with the drawing of the rune I found that morning. I lower my voice and glance behind me to check that Constance is in the dressing room. 'I found another of the Golowhe runes. It was in my house, at the top of the door to my father's spellorium, sitting there in plain sight among all of the other magical glyphs and symbols.'

'Do you think your father knew about the runes?' Nightly asks.

'Maybe,' I say. 'He knew a great many things and he was always researching the past as part of the work he did for the Coven of Curiosity.'

'May I keep this?' he asks, motioning to the piece of paper. 'Of course.'

'As you have yet to write me a love letter, I will have to make do with this.' He tucks it in to his breast pocket. 'I will see you on Thursday for tea.' He smiles before bowing to me and taking his leave.

I watch him walk down the stairs of Goth and Drake. When he reaches the street, he pauses and looks back at me. Then he takes Evelyn's arm and travels out into the world.

Eighteen

Mother is delighted when I tell her that I am to have guests to tea on Thursday, then outraged to find out that it will be the Nightlys.

'Aurelia, after all they have done to this family – to you,' she says, and for a moment I get a flash of the steel that has earnt her a formidable reputation on the Royal Magical Council.

But I hold my own. 'Evelyn and Jules Nightly have done nothing to me. Besides, she may lose her magic at any time, and once she does every magical house in the ton will close their door to her, just as they will to me at the end of my three Seasons.'

I can tell that my words have hurt my mother, but this is the truth of Evelyn's situation and mine too.

'I think that you have been very gracious, Aurelia, and that your kindness towards Evelyn Nightly should be commended,' Frances remarks. 'I for one am looking forward to meeting them both. I knew their father well in my younger years, it will be interesting to see if they aren't more Hallow than Nightly.'

Vaughn harrumphs at that. 'Jules is a Nightly through and through.'

As the week advances towards Thursday, the anxiety of my family meeting Jules and Evelyn builds in me. When the bell eventually rings, I rush to the door. I take a deep breath before I pull it open wide. Nightly is walking up the stairs, holding two large bouquets of flowers. He joins Evelyn on the top step just as I usher her into the hall. Mother is there now, saying her cold hellos and taking Evelyn's cloak.

'Are you all right?' Nightly asks.

I nod my head and he looks at me doubtfully, then lowers his voice and says, 'I'm a little terrified.'

'You? I don't think you've ever been scared of anything in your life, have you?'

I look at him then, and see that he is, indeed, tense.

'Your mother?' I ask. He looks a little pale at the mention of her.

'She was quite displeased with me and Evelyn for accepting your invitation.'

I reach out a hand and squeeze his arm. 'I'm sorry, I didn't really think through how she would react.'

'You have nothing to be sorry for,' he says as I close the door, then go to take one of the bouquets. They aren't our

212

roses, I notice, and Nightly moves them out of my reach. 'Not for you, Wycherley,' he says playfully.

He gives the flowers to Mother and Frances; they are both delighted with them – even Mother – and I try to remember the last time either of them received flowers. I make a mental note to send them some at Yule.

I see Mother soften a little as Frances takes Evelyn into the parlour and she follows them. I help Nightly with his cloak, reaching up to his broad shoulders and making a mess of removing it. As he turns back to face me, he has a single red rose in his hands.

'One of ours?'

'One of ours,' he says and places it in my hair, brushing a finger along the magical scar on my temple. I laugh at him.

'Beautiful.' He gazes at the rose and I think my cheeks now match the colour of the flower. I will him to look at me and not the flower but instead he offers his arm. 'It was very kind of you to invite Evelyn; she has missed out on the company of many witches since . . . her disappointment.' I hear that strain in his voice; it's always there whenever he speaks of his sister.

'I'm sorry others have reacted that way towards her, I guess I have the same awaiting me.'

'Not if I have anything to do with it. For either of you.' He gives my arm a small squeeze, which sends a shock wave through me.

Vaughn is on his feet, hand out as he goes to greet Nightly.

He's wearing the look of contempt that he reserves only for Jules.

'Aurelia tells me that you are interested in botany,' Nightly says, engaging Vaughn in conversation. As the two of them discuss the wonders of the natural world, they go over to the window, and I instantly feel on guard. I force myself to join Mother, Frances and Evelyn at the table. *It's good for Vaughn to get to know Nightly better*, I tell myself. Besides, I'm looking forward to chatting with Evelyn.

Mother being Mother, and not one to skirt around any issue, has launched straight into asking Evelyn what her plans for the future are. I almost choke on my tea when she says, 'Is there anything that the council can do to help facilitate your transition?' I see the look on Evelyn's face. Like me, she was not expecting my mother to be so amiable.

'To be fair, Madam Wycherley—'

'Oh, please, call me Nell.'

'There is nothing that can be done, I have accepted that now. I will lead a magicless life, but that doesn't mean that I won't be able to find the magic in living. Do I regret what has happened? Immensely. At the time, I was too distraught to consider another match, although if I could go back in time, I would snap up the first witch that came my way.' She says this with a light laugh. 'But I can't now, so it is no use me replaying my misfortune or musing over the magic I could have had. I am determined to be happy and to make sure that those I love are happy too.' She glances to the window where

Jules and Vaughn are sitting, then to me with a marked look before she reaches for her teacup. That look makes me feel terrible. Evelyn thinks that Jules and I are truly growing an attachment. When she knows the truth, that we are faking it and he may give up his magic in solidarity, I fear it will hit her harder than the loss of her own magic.

'I think that is very commendable,' Frances says, 'and full of wisdom that we can all apply to our lives.' She looks from Evelyn to Mother and then to me, and I wonder if she's thinking about my own loss. I think of the orb that landed on me, the orb I haven't dared to talk to anyone about, not even Nightly – especially him. I'm convinced my magic did not land on him at Samhain. If it had, he would have said something.

We continue to talk for a while. Mother is softer now, more like her private self, as she warms to Evelyn. After a while, Mother makes her excuses and goes over to join Vaughn and Nightly. I shoot a look and mouth 'sorry' towards Nightly; he smiles back.

'Aurelia said that she first met you while shopping for Yule,' Frances says.

'Yes, I was helping Jules with his outfit choice,' Evelyn replies.

I can't help the big smile that spreads across my face. 'When it comes to clothes, if he is anywhere near as picky as he is when it comes to his stationery and books, then I don't envy you that task.'

Evelyn leans towards me, her eyes wide as she touches my arm. 'Oh, he is exactly the same with all things.' We both laugh. 'Have you found a dress yet?'

I shake my head. 'Not yet. Maybe you could help me look? Mother and Frances are usually so busy, and although I do appreciate the opinions of my good friend Constance Prior, another view is always welcome.'

We make plans for the three of us to go shopping early next week, then I add, 'I'm excited to go to Neoards too. Have either of you been? Or do you have any connections there?' I still can't work out how Nightly arranged for the Yule celebrations to be there.

'We have a cousin who was there, Finneas Hallow — he and Jules are particularly close. He and his tether are now part of the debutante overview committee,' Evelyn says.

'And does the committee arrange the particulars for each of the Sabbats during the Season?' I ask.

She nods. 'They do.'

'My parents attended Neoards,' Frances says.

'Really?' I ask. Frances' parents are like an additional set of grandparents to me and Vaughn, but I have never thought to ask either of them about their college years.

Frances nods. 'It's a fine coven college: the instructors are thought to be some of the best in the world, not just Briton. It is not without its history or quirks. My parents attempted to persuade me and your mother to go there — they even tried to tempt me with the story of the lost quarter.'

'The lost quarter? Well, you're going to have to tell us all about that now,' Evelyn says, leaning in closer to Frances.

Frances drains her cup, then leans in too. She is a natural storyteller and used to read me bedtime stories all the time.

'Before the coven college was established by Naylor Selwyn and Alice Boone, the basis of the college had been formed by two other witches. They created the buildings of Neoards with magic and masonry and secrets, so the story goes. They were said to be quite a mysterious pair, interested in old magic, and they called on the deep enchantments that run through the earth to create the coven college. You see, Neoards is built on the joining of two ley lines and it is said that they used that energy, that wild magic, when conjuring the foundations. Of course, wild magic was far more abundant then than it is today.

'Anyhow, the coven was originally designed in fours, directly aligned with the cardinal points: north, east, south and west. It was a perfect square, and within the square were four equal quadrants, each housing classrooms, libraries, accommodation and arcades. But when the founding witches parted ways and left Neoards, a part of the coven was lost too. Still to this day, a quarter of it is lost – it went missing overnight. There one moment and gone the next. And the three remaining sides of the coven college magically shifted to compensate for the loss, becoming a triangle in appearance and function. What is strange is that if you were to measure the corners you would find that they are still set to ninety-degree angles. It is as if the laws of geometry have been magically manipulated. Most experts agree that the missing quarter is still there, just inaccessible, unseeable.

'You can walk all the way around the three sides of Neoards, inside and out, and not come across any sign that anything is missing. I could disregard the story of those founding witches as nothing more than college legend if it wasn't for the hard proof of the mismatching geometry; it is a very strange piece of old magic.'

'How very odd,' Evelyn says.

'It's even more disconcerting to see it in real life, it was the main reason why I persuaded Nell we shouldn't go there; the whole place felt off kilter and made me feel a little seasick.'

'Is there a book about this at all? The first two witches, do we know who they were?' I ask, because in all of our research, I've not heard anything about a missing quarter, and because I know those founding witches are Mathilda and Heston.

'Oh dear, I fear that my brother and his books are rubbing off on you, Ms Wycherley. Unless you have always been a bookish sort of a person too,' she adds.

'I have.' I smile.

'I don't recall there being a book about it, although I guess there must be,' Frances adds thoughtfully. 'But if I remember correctly, when your mother and I went on a tour, there was a tomb in the middle of the central courtyard: the Tomb of the Untethered Witch. There was a romantic notion among the students that he guarded the lost quarter because his tether was lost in it, and so he had made his tomb there so that he could watch over the entrance for eternity and be there when she returned.'

'Do *you* think there's any real truth in the idea of the lost quarter?' I ask Frances, feeling excitement running through me.

'I think that, like anything built on the fulcrum of magic, strange things often happen.'

'I wonder if Mother might know anything more, being part of the Coven of Mysteries,' Evelyn adds. 'Although, I suppose even if she did, she would never tell. You know, I think that's the bit that I'm most upset about when I think about losing my magic − not getting to know all of the mysteries, all of the archaic laws.'

'Does that interest you then? The hidden and unknown?' Frances asks. There's a look on her face − the one she often gets when she's just had a brilliant idea and she's thinking things through.

'It does. I've always been . . . curious. I like exploring the world, and not necessarily only in books and facts, which Jules has been doing a lot of lately.' She glances quickly at me. 'He's much more of an outdoors, action-type person usually, like me and Father.'

Frances smiles, like she has been proved right: Jules and Evelyn are definitely more Hallow than Nightly.

'You know that there are some elements of magic that need

the objectivity and separateness of a non-magical person to explore,' Frances continues. 'Why don't you come along to Carlton Palace next week to discuss it further. A bright young woman like yourself might just be what we need.'

Evelyn blinks. 'Are you sure?'

'Yes, I think you could be the person we've been looking for.'

I have never loved Frances more.

Evelyn smiles and looks as if she might cry. I cut the cake while Frances makes another pot of tea. As soon as it has brewed, Mother, Vaughn and Jules join us. We all sit around the table and pass the rest of the afternoon discussing everything from the best way to brew a rejuvenating draught to how exciting it would be if dragons were to exist once more. Nightly sits next to me, his sister on my other side. I worry that Vaughn and my mother have spent the last half an hour or so interrogating him, but he looks relaxed, and so do Mother and Vaughn, as if something in their manner towards Jules and Evelyn has shifted. Every now and again, Jules glances my way and I forget that we are pretending; it feels natural to have him and Evelyn as part of our family circle.

After the Nightlys leave, as we are clearing away, Mother pauses with a cup in hand and turns to me. 'I was a little unsure about this connection between you and Jules Nightly, but after seeing the two of you together and getting to know the Nightly boy a little better, I am inclined to agree with Frances. You make a merry match; it's a shame, really.'

'Oh.' I'm unsure of what else to say.

'He's also not so much of a pompous ass when you get him alone,' Vaughn concedes.

'I've heard the same said of you,' I tell my brother. He pulls a face in reply.

'Jules Nightly is a good witch, and a good person, I can see that; they both are,' Mother says with a raise of her eyebrow, as if she can't quite believe the words that are coming out of her own mouth.

Nineteen

On the eve of the Yule Ball the importance of the event looms large in my mind. If our plan works, we may find some of the answers we need. At the very least I am expecting us to add to the three runes that I have thus far been guided to. If we can find a way to decipher them, to unlock their meaning, maybe they can point us to a cure for tethering.

I sit close to Nightly in the restricted section of the library, the two of us leaning over our notes, plotting and scheming, finding the right moment to slip away from the Yule Ball and investigate the tomb. We have a modern schematic of the coven college open on the table and are currently trying to find the best routes out of the main hall and into the courtyard at the centre of the coven. Through his cousin Nightly has discovered the locations of the chaperones at the ball and which exits will be unlocked. To make things doubly complicated, Nightly is insisting that we depart individually from the ball.

I have found the perfect dress design. Evelyn and Constance helped, and I am excited to wear it and spend the *non*-criminal portion of the evening dancing and losing myself in the magic of pretending to be someone else. And even though Nightly and I have been pretending for months now, I know that when I am with him, I am truly myself. Save for the part that can't tell him how I am beginning to feel about him.

'How will you know it is me?' I ask him. 'It's a masked ball.'

'Aurelia, I would know you in a sea of witches.'

'Well, how will I know it is you?'

'Oh, you'll know,' he says in a low voice that stirs at my insides.

'But we'll be wearing glamours,' I add, feeling awkward about mine, which I haven't perfected yet despite my extra tuition at the Arcade. Kit Thorne and Cora Stewart have been thorough, but I can't help feeling like a traitor every time they help me. I had asked Russo and Platz if I could change instructors, but they had not seen the need for it. After all, the duel was not with me but Nightly, and they argued that if they let me change instructors then they were setting a precedent for other witches to do the same, and they couldn't have that!

'We will *all* be glamoured up. Till midnight anyway. Look, if you really can't find me, then I will meet you in the central courtyard under the clock tower at eleven on the

223

'dot,' Nightly says, pointing to the spot on the map.

'But what if . . .'

'Wycherley, I am not about to tell you what my costume is; it is part of the fun of Yule. The idea is that you go on what you can feel, not what you can see.'

I look around and lower my voice. 'I know, but it makes a break-in and possible robbery a little difficult if you can't recognize your accomplice!'

He smiles. 'I do so love our couple's activities: forgery, bribery, extortion, trespass.'

I nudge him with my elbow, then I lean close and say in a low voice, 'You forgot theft.'

'Ah, yes, but there may not be anything to steal. And it will only be information that we will be taking.'

'But information is priceless,' I tell him. 'Anyway, how are we even going to get into this lost quarter?'

'I'm trusting in magic. Your magic, to be more exact,' he replies earnestly. 'It has been pointing you in the right direction so far; it brought you to me, after all. If there is any truth to this lost quarter then I have a feeling that Heston Nightly will show the way. Besides, I'm also hoping that because it was a Nightly and a Wycherley who built that quarter, perhaps a Nightly and Wycherley can discover it again – and who knows what secrets it may hold.'

I don't want to get my hopes up, but this does feel exciting – as if we are about to do something daring and epic, like the witches of the First Age.

The clock in the library chimes and I start to collect my things. 'I'm meeting Constance. She's having last-minute nerves about her dress and mask so we're off to the boutique, again!'

'It's a bit late – it's Yule tomorrow.'

'Constance needs everything to be perfect.'

'For Vaughn?' Nightly raises an eyebrow.

'Oh, you picked up on that too, did you?' I say with a smile.

I pick up my cloak and pull a long, thin package from the inside pocket.

I hesitate for a moment with it in my hand as Nightly looks at the gift all wrapped up with a red bow and a note.

'Merry Yule, Nightly.' I lean down, my lips level with his ear and lower my voice. 'And just so we're clear, this is not a fake-courting thing. This is a me-wanting-to-give-you-a-gift thing.'

He looks at me. The lump of his throat moves as he swallows, and his eyes lock with mine, filling me with a burst of fire that I know is dangerous and might burn right through me.

'I . . . I didn't know that we were . . .'

'We're not. I just wanted to give you something to say thank you.'

He stands up. He's close to me, so very close.

'But I haven't . . .'

'It doesn't matter, but if you really want to give me something, you can dance with me at the Yule Ball.'

'I was going to anyway,' he replies. I remember how

we danced at the Prior-Okore ball. That dance was full of awkwardness and tension. This time, the tension will be of a different kind. But there will be no awkwardness.

'I have to go,' I say. Nightly takes my cloak out of my hands and swings it over my shoulders. Then, with one hand, he lifts up my chin and leans forward, his too-long hair flopping over the side of his face. My breath catches as he fastens the clasp at my throat, his eyes not leaving mine.

The door to the restricted library slams as someone enters and I turn, breaking the moment. I hasten towards the door, and as I reach it, I look back. He is holding the brightly coloured box in his hand, pulling it open and looking at the Phoenix-feather quill inside. The stationer assured me that it was real, that the quill would never break, would never need sharpening, and the lustre of the red-gold feather would never fade. Nightly looks up and for a moment I think about going back to him, to that moment we just shared. But for him this is still just a pretence, isn't it? The look he is giving me right now is a very fine ruse indeed, it has my heart pounding.

The streets of the ton are busy with witches making final preparations for Yule. The early-winter wind is cooling my hot cheeks, but they are still flushed by the time I get to Constance.

'Have you been waiting long?' I ask.

'No, did Nightly hold you up?' She is smirking.

'Something like that.'

We visit three boutiques before Constance returns to

the first one and buys a new gown and mask. It is not very different from the one sitting in her closet at home, except for the colour. This one is white and full of fluffy feathers.

'You looked beautiful in it. But then I think you looked stunning in the black gown too.' The black gown was sleek and cast with a shimmer of feathers that glittered whenever she moved, like ripples in water.

'Are you sure this new one is all right?' Her eyes are full of worry. 'I need to look perfect.'

I stop still and turn to her. 'Who do you need to look perfect for, Constance?'

She squirms.

'If you are going to say yourself then I am all for that,' I continue, 'and if you are going to say another witch then I am going to confront you on that, and if you say Vaughn then I'm here to tell you that you could wear any of your sisters' most appalling out-of-date gowns fashioned to look like a swan, even a dead one, and he would still be smitten with you.'

Constance blushes, deep crimson. 'I . . . I didn't think you knew.'

'Oh, please, the two of you have been mooning after each other since Mabon,' I say with a smile.

'You didn't say anything,' Constance says, her eyes wide.

'Neither did you.'

'I . . . I didn't want to risk anything, not with Vaughn, but with you. You are my oldest and dearest friend, I love you more than most of my sisters, and you know me better than

227

anyone in the world. I couldn't bear it if this came between us.'

I scoop up Constance's hand in mine. 'I swear to you that no witch, especially my brother, will come between us, ever. I'm delighted for you, and for Vaughn, although I feel that he is gaining more than you are. I love you, Constance, and if you and Vaughn do decide to tether, then that will only bring you and I all the closer.'

She throws her arms around me and we hug for the longest time.

She smiles at me shyly. 'Has he mentioned me? Said anything about his intentions?'

'No more than you have. The two of you have been silent in your words but loud in your actions. I love you both and I am glad that the two of you are forming a connection. But, Constance, that connection is because of who you are. That is what Vaughn is drawn to, just as you are drawn to who he is. So don't try and change for him.'

'Oh, Aurelia, you're so right. I've made a terrible mistake.' She turns and runs towards the shop, her bags jostling around beside her. 'I have to take it all back.'

I follow Constance as she rushes up the lane towards the modiste's. As I pass Mason's Magical Books, I see Kit Thorne coming out of the door, followed by two older witches. I stop dead on the pavement on the opposite side of the street and stare as the three of them say their goodbyes. One of the older witches I have never seen before, but the other is someone

I know so well that even the years since I last saw him have done nothing to dampen my memory of him: Jonathan Reid, my father's tether. I am shocked at seeing him after all these years. I had no idea he was back in London – in Briton even. Mother told me he had moved to Italy shortly after Father's death and none of us have seen or heard from him since. Even Kit had said he didn't know where his father was. And yet, here he is, and the two of them reconciled.

I watch as Kit leaves with the stranger and Jonathan walks the other way. I glance back over my shoulder and look through the window of the shop where Constance is talking animatedly to the dressmaker.

I turn back to see Jonathan moving away down the street, and I panic that he is going to leave again. I can't let him just go, not without saying hello. Not without telling him how much I have missed him.

My heart is racing as I hasten across the road and try to follow him among the late-Yule shoppers.

He looks behind him a few times, his eyes brushing over me but not settling. I wave but he doesn't see me. I realize that I have altered so much from the little girl that I was into the witch that I now am – I doubt that he would know me even if my hood was down and I was standing right before him.

He breaks off down an alley and I apologize to a pair of witches as I push past them to follow him. As I turn into the alley I watch, astounded, as Jonathan Reid stands in front of a side-door that leads into the back of the bookshop, and calls on the wandlet on his wrist to remove the ward on the door.

I see the archway around the door light up with magical symbols, then the door itself glows and opens. My own magic is curdling, I can feel the magic he is using and it has a tinge to it – a strangeness, a wrongness. He was a tethered witch who has a tether no more: he should not have magic, it should have died with my father. But here he is performing a spell, opening a magical doorway. As I watch, he walks through the door. It closes behind him, and the glow is gone.

My legs are shaking. I am without doubt that the witch I just saw is Jonathan, but how can it be? He performed magic, secondary magic. Magic that, after the death of my father, he should not have. My head swims and I feel unsteady as I make my way to the door.

I try the handle. It's locked.

I call on my own primary magic with a simple unlocking spell. Nothing. I look at the arch around the door, and there, cast into the brickwork, is a rune. It glows black. Nightly is right, the magic is guiding us and it has led me to Jonathan of all people.

Breathlessly, I stumble back to the street and think about the only two possibilities. The first I dismiss immediately – I know beyond a doubt that my father is not alive. Therefore, Jonathan must have found what Nightly and I are looking for: a way to have magic without a tether! Although his magic . . . it felt malevolent.

Twenty

ule has always been my favourite of the Sabbats. Not just for the presents – although when I was younger that was probably the main reason. All of us being together is the true focus, and since Father's passing it has also become a time for us to remember him. He so loved Yule.

Every Yule I miss my father, but this one is different. I feel him close to me, and I know it's because of seeing Jonathan. I can't shake the image of him performing magic, the oddness of it, the strangeness of his magic.

'Aurelia!' Vaughn calls from downstairs and I reluctantly leave my musing to join him, Mother and Frances.

We exchange gifts. I give Frances a novel by one of her favourite authors, and Mother a new potion kit – she doesn't have as much time to create potions as she used to, nor does Frances to read, but I hope they will both find the time to relax and do the things that they enjoy. I give Vaughn a copy of *Writing from the Heart*, and some letter-writing supplies, to which he gives me an embarrassed look.

With presents exchanged, we then sit down to a feast. The table is covered with small dishes of all of our favourites and my plate is soon spilling over with a combination of food that I would never normally eat together.

'Yesterday, when Constance and I were shopping, I . . . I thought I saw Jonathan,' I say as conversationally as possible while we eat. I know that my family will want to know, that it is important, but after seeing Jonathan perform magic, I feel a little unsure about sharing the information. I decide to leave that bit out and just focus on the fact that I saw him.

'Really?' Vaughn asks, putting down his knife and fork and looking at me intently. I notice Mother and Frances avoid looking at each other. Mother has put down her cutlery too, but in a more measured way, and Frances has frozen, her mouth full of dauphinoise potatoes.

'I thought he was in Italy or somewhere?' Vaughn continues.

I concentrate on cutting into the small pastry parcel on my plate. 'I am sure that it was him,' I say.

'Where was he going?' Mother asks, reaching for her wine glass, which is an odd question – not 'how was he' or 'did you speak to him'. Her voice is cold, and I instantly know that something is not right.

I shrug, pretending that it's not important. 'He walked off towards Mason's bookshop. I tried to follow him, but it was

Yule Eve and the streets were busy. I lost sight of him.'

Mother drains her glass, then fills it from the decanter. 'Was he with anyone?'

'No.' I should really tell my mother and Frances everything: who he was with, about the door and the magic. But they are holding something back. There is only one person that I intend on telling everything to and he is not at this table.

'You must have been mistaken, Aurelia,' Mother finally says. 'Busy streets, Yule. Although, it would be good to see Jonathan. We've been trying to track him down for a little while now.' She glances at Frances.

'So, no one knows where he is?' I ask. 'Not even Kit?'

'I very much doubt it. I'm sure that you and Vaughn knew more of Jonathan than his son ever did.' Then Mother firmly changes the subject. 'Are you both all set for the masked ball?'

We continue to eat and make small talk, but inside I am reeling and the world feels like it is spinning very fast. I have never had any reason not to trust Mother and Frances before, but I know that they are withholding something, something connected to Jonathan, and I can't help but think that also means it has something to do with Father too.

It's late afternoon by the time we finish our feast, and I scoop up my pile of gifts: a broomstick-maintenance kit from Frances, a book on common herbs and potions to make with them from Vaughn, and a new white winter cloak from Mother. I place them all on my bed, along with a gift from

Constance: a snow globe that has a small Constance and Aurelia inside, who dance when you shake it as snow falls around them.

Vaughn received a gift from Constance too, but was very secretive about it.

I had another gift, but I tucked it in my pocket when I saw it, and now I am alone, I pull out of the box. It is small and red with a little tag on it.

To Aurelia,

I hope the roses that we made together in the Arcade will last many years, but here is a memory of them that will last many lifetimes, as will my admiration for you.

Merry Yule,

Jules

My heart races as I read the words and I wish that they were true. I think of the way that he looked at me in the library just before the door closed, and I want to hope that he feels something for me too.

I run my fingers along the lid of the box, then, tentatively, lift it. Inside is a beautiful, long golden chain of roses linked together by delicate leaves. I put it on immediately, feeling its closeness to my heart.

My dress is hanging on my wardrobe door, and I slip into it before setting about performing my glamour.

Glamours are only allowed to be performed under special licence or on certain occasions like this. Punishment is severe for those witches who break the magical laws surrounding glamours. I close my eyes as I connect to the image that I want to project; the glamour that I want to show to the world. I feel my wandlet slither into my hand and a warmth pass over my body as I begin to perform the steps of the spell. When I open my eyes and look into the mirror, it's me – not as I am now, but as I was.

My hair is chestnut brown and my eyes a soft light ash brown. I examine my reflection, turning my head from side to side. This is the girl who disappeared when my magic arrived. I don't feel the way I thought I would – pleased, happy – instead I realize that I am not this Aurelia any more and I don't want to go back to being her either. I don't intend on wearing this glamour to the ball; I will wear one more in line with my peacock persona for the evening, but I keep it up for a little while longer. I never got to say goodbye to this version of myself properly and I take a moment to do that now, taking in who I was and acknowledging that she has gone.

I spin in a circle, and as I do, Ankoth startles, scuttling back and crashing into the desk by the window with a bang before hiding underneath it.

There's a knock on my bedroom door. 'Aurelia, are you all right?' Vaughn calls.

'I'm . . . I'm fine, it's the broom,' I say as I try to coax it out.

'You can come in,' I call to Vaughn as I leave Ankoth under the desk and stand to face the door.

'Wow,' Vaughn says as he stands frozen in the doorway for a moment before walking into the room. 'I had almost forgotten what you looked like before. Your glamour is very good. Are you going to keep it up all night?' he asks.

'I just wanted to remember how I used to look, who I used to be,' I tell him.

He shakes his head. 'I . . . it's peculiar seeing you like this. I've become so used to who you are now, it doesn't feel like I'm looking at you.' I let the glamour fade, and he smiles. 'That's much more you,' he says, and I can't help but agree with him. Ankoth obviously does too, appearing out from under the desk and drifting over to check that I'm me again.

Vaughn pulls out his watch. 'We have a little time till the coach comes, which is good, because I wanted to talk to you.'

'To me?'

'Yes,' he says, looking a little nervous. 'You see, I . . . I have been growing in fondness . . . that is to say, do you remember when we were young children, Grandma le Fay had that little cat?'

'Chester.'

'Yes, Chester. I was scared of him and he would chase me and scratch me, but then as we grew up and both Chester and I matured, we got along better, and he would seek me out and curl up on my lap to sleep, and when he died I cried and cried because, over time, I had grown very fond of

Chester . . . even grown to love him.' He says all of this in a rush.

'Yes . . .' I say, not knowing where this conversation is going.

'Well, the same kind of thing has been happening of late. A kind of slow evolution of feeling that I did not realize I had until recently.'

'But Vaughn, Grandma le Fay doesn't have a cat any more.'

'Not a cat, Aurelia, Constance. I have been growing in fondness for Constance Prior.'

'Ah, Constance.' I smile at him.

'This isn't coming out right at all. I'm terrible at things like this.' He stands up and paces back and forth. 'I like Constance,' he says.

'I know.'

'No, I mean, I think I love her – I *know* I love her. I've always liked her as a friend, apart from that one summer a couple of years ago when I first got my magic and the two of you were really annoying. But that's not the point. The point is that I like her as more than a friend; I like her the same way that plants like sunlight. I find myself turning to face her and growing towards her. When she is not there, I feel drained and empty and I can barely breathe. I want her to be the one that I grow with and help grow, I want to be her sunlight too. I love Constance Prior.'

I reach out and hug Vaughn close. 'I know,' I tell him again.

'You . . . you do?' He looks surprised, as if he thought he

had covered his intentions and feelings well.

I pull back and hold him at arm's length. 'Why do you think I gave you that book for Yule?'

'I did wonder about that, but I guess after the cat thing it makes sense.'

'Well, I guess it is more of a gift for Constance than it is for you — you should definitely use it to help tell her how you feel!' I say.

'So you're fine with the possibility of me and Constance Prior tethering?'

'Vaughn, I love you both and I think you should tell her. Tonight. Tell her exactly how you feel.'

'But what if she doesn't feel the same about me?'

'Do you think she doesn't?'

He smiles broadly and shakes his head. 'No, no . . . I think she might feel the same.'

'Then you should definitely tell her, exactly the same way that you just told me. Not the bit about Chester, but the other bit. Show her who you are and how you feel.'

'I will.' He hugs me tight and makes for the door. Then he stops and turns back to me. 'And you should do the same, Aurelia. It's nice to see that old version of you, but it's not who you are any more.'

I realize that I've been giving Vaughn and Constance advice about being themselves when the whole time I've been denying who I am. Ugh, it is so vexing when your older brother is right!

YULE

The Most Magical Season –
A Debutantes' Guide

*by Cathleen Kelly
and Kate Walker*

The jewel of the Season, the Yule Ball, gives debutante witches a chance to seek out matches that they feel might be favourable for them, under the anonymity of the mask.

Many a witch has been equally snared and scared by a Yule glamour, and while some witches feel that the use of a glamour is deceptive, it is worth noting that, often, courting starts off in the same way, as we show our best sides to our potential tethers.

Matches of magic are made after the performing of spells, matches of power are made after the sharing of family identity, and matches of love after a joining of hearts, but Yule matches are made after a dance and a glance.

At a masked ball, all that matters is you and the witch that you dance with. Many a match has been made and broken thanks to the freedom that Yule brings.

If we can give any advice on the matter it would be this: wear the glamour, disguise your appearance well, but let who you are in your heart shine out for all to see. If you do this, then the connection you make at Yule might well become a tether by Ostara.

Twenty-one

My dress is the perfect riot of colour: emerald greens, deep purples and royal blues. Each peacock feather on the skirt is outlined in glittering, golden thread that laces its way delicately over the bodice, skirts and sleeves.

After speaking with Vaughn, I feel a bit like a fraud. I'm surprised at how much I now identify with the cursed version of myself, with my white hair and stormy grey eyes. However, tonight, just for one night, I get to be me with no judgement. No one will look at me and see my curse; all they will see is Ms Peacock, and I fully intend on making the most of it.

As Vaughn and I get close to the college, I put on my glamour. I change the colour of my hair so that it is the same gold as the thread in my dress, and my eyes are a blue that they have never been in my life. They shine like sapphires from behind a golden mask that is lined with small peacock feathers, more of which are placed in my hair, and on the top of my head is a small, tall crown, like that on a peacock but in glistening gold, adorned with emeralds and sapphires.

Vaughn is a hare; his long ears protruding from his chestnut hair brush the roof of the carriage and, where my mask is all gold and feathers, his is fur and whiskers – the same soft beige and brown of his gold-embroidered suit. When I look closely, I see intricate embroidery: hares, sheafs of corn, oak leaves and acorns. It is beautiful magic.

'Remember, don't enter the ball with me and resist the urge to dance with me once the ball gets going,' I tell him. 'I'll be fine.' Partly because I will be, and also because once Nightly and I make our escape from the ball I don't want my brother to realize that I am gone.

'I'm not going to dance with you, Aurelia. I'm going to be far too busy enjoying myself to worry about you. Besides, I'm sure Nightly won't let anyone else get close.' And for the first time, there's no edge in his voice when he speaks of Jules.

I alight from the carriage, pulling the hood of my peacock-blue cloak over my head. There is a stream of costumed witches making their way along the torch-lit drive of Neoards. I join them, skirting away from Vaughn.

Nervous excitement is rising in me, not just for the evening's festivities, but for the forthcoming felonies too. I scan the outline of the college as I walk towards its south entrance. I feel as if I know it so well after all the blueprints, maps and drawings Nightly and I have studied. I know the layout of every wing, the name of each of the rooms and where every corridor leads to. The avenue that I am currently walking up leads directly to the entrance hall in the middle of the south wing. On the right I can see the astronomy dome that sits on the top of the east wing. In the west wing is the clock tower, and I know that to the left of that is the Great Hall, with its triple-height ceiling and stained-glass windows.

There is a buzz of magic and excitement as voices fill the air. Below them, the melodious playing of strings from a quartet stationed at the top of the avenue. I walk through the doors where I take off my cloak and hand it to an attendant. I feel magnificent and bold, my disguise giving me a freedom that I have never had. I could be anybody, but I choose to be me.

I glance at the large clock in the entrance hall and realize that I have hours before Nightly and I are to rendezvous. I intend to use that time catching up on all the dancing that has eluded me so far this Season.

I follow the line of witches to the ballroom. There's a strange mixture of animals among the dancing witches; I spy a magpie with a fox, a wildcat with a doe. The fizz of glamours hangs in the air and the night feels free and lively in a dangerous way that I have never experienced before. I roll my shoulders back and walk confidently into the ballroom. I pass a tawny owl and a frog, whose glamour has made the whole of their skin green and scaled. They both watch me intently and I finally understand the term 'peacocking' – that is definitely what I am doing.

The frog is the first to ask me to dance and I instantly know that he is not Nightly. We set off around the dance floor, the frog dances well but his conversation is boring.

My next dance is with a witch dressed as a firefly. I like her energy and we talk about all manner of topics as we glide across the floor. I ask her how she has managed to make the back of her dress glow.

'Oh, it only glows if I like the witch that I'm dancing with,' she says with the raise of an eyebrow, and I find myself watching her plump lips as my cheeks flush.

A witch in a beautiful pink dress approaches me, and I smile politely as we dance. Her black curls are piled high on her head, covered in budding roses, and as we spin, some of them open into blooms. Her face is half covered by a delicate rose-petal mask. The top of her dress is a bright green, the bottom made of the same delicate petals in every shade of pink I've ever seen. I soon realize that they aren't petals, but butterflies, and as the dress fans out, a few of them take to the air and settle again. She is beautiful and I'm enjoying the small tingle of magic that happens whenever I pull her close.

However, if she knew it was me beneath this mask, I doubt that she would even be holding my hands. I feel a thrill at the anonymity that the ball gives me, and suddenly I want to dance all night, with everyone. I force myself to not get carried away, to keep checking the clock. This part of the evening might be fun, but it's paramount that Nightly and I succeed in reaching Heston's tomb.

As the music stops, I curtsy and make my excuses, heading over to the window and glancing at the clock. There is plenty of time, but I don't want to be late meeting with Nightly.

I had hoped that, despite the costumes and the glamours, I would know him; he was certain that he would know me. And then I remember the violet-white orb that landed on me at Samhain and wonder if I could use magic to seek out Nightly. A thrill runs through me as I remember this is exactly what Yule is supposed to be about. A time to look inside a person, at their magic, to the very heart of them. I close my eyes and remember the essence of the magic that was in the orb, the magic that flowed through me when we made the flowers, when we transformed the document wallet, when we duelled. I use my magical senses and the vibrations around me to try and find Nightly.

As I open my eyes, I see a witch dressed all in black – a crow. He is looking at me as I am looking at him and I can feel a tension between us, as if there is a string extending from me to him.

As the music strikes up again, I take a confident step towards the crow as he makes his way towards me. The way that my heart lifts and my magic stirs tells me that this is Nightly.

Before he reaches me, a witch with a stag's head sweeps in and pulls me into the dance. I look back as the stag turns me, and I can see Nightly on the edge of the dance floor, his stare focused on us.

'Sir, I . . .' I look at the stag properly for the first time. Sebastian hasn't tried to shield his appearance, his mask is little more than a few sprouts of fur and his glamour extends no further than his grand antlers.

We mirror each other's steps as we once mirrored each other's thoughts and desires. I don't speak to him, instead I look over at Nightly and wish that I was in his arms.

'Are we to dance in silence?' Sebastian asks.

'I feel that one learns a great deal about their partner through observation,' I reply. He smiles and it feels like a knife twisting in me.

'I have always found that a more direct approach is more to my liking.'

'Yes, I suppose you have.'

Sebastian is not a witch who is extravagant with his imagination, he is not a deep thinker. He likes the facts of a matter. I know that the facts are thus: if he knew who he was dancing with, he would be repelled.

'But I can tell that you like a bit more mystery.' He spins me around and we part before finding one another again.

'This is true, I am curious – aren't all birds?' I suggest, moving my gaze firmly to the crow behind him.

'A peacock, of course, puts on a wonderful display when they feel most threatened. Maybe your silence is to scare me in the same way?'

'Hardly,' I blurt. 'It is just that I don't know what to say to you, how to tell you what I think.'

'You are doing a fine enough job of talking now.' He gives me that winning smile that once made my heart melt. Now it just makes me feel sad.

'I guess so.' We turn away from one another again. When we come back together, our eyes meet and I feel something in that look that, in the past, would have given me hope.

'I've missed you, Sebastian. But I have moved on – from you, from our friendship, from our love.'

He stops mid-dance and takes a step away, pushing me from him. 'Bad form, Aurelia,' he hisses. 'You tricked me. How could you?'

'And you thoroughly dismissed me, how could *you*?' I hiss back, the feathers of my dress rising high so that many eyes are glaring at him, added to by the witches in the hall who are all staring as the music plays and we stand still. 'We were friends, we were . . . more than that.' He winces at my words as if I have slapped him.

'That was before you had become . . . unnatural, malformed, cursed.'

I laugh at him. 'Is that what you think I am?'

'No, that is what you *are*, and I wish that this had never happened to you.' He takes a step closer to me, then says in a low voice so that only I can hear, 'I had such plans for the two of us, Aurelia, such hopes. We were going to be a powerful pair. But the truth is that the council need never have forbidden you from making a match . . . for I, and every witch here, would rather lose our magic than tether it to an abomination such as you. Now, for the friendship we once had I will not embarrass you by calling out the deception that you are wearing – hiding who you are from these good witches who do not deserve your deceit.'

'Sebastian, you do know how a masked ball works, do you not?' I wonder if I have ever truly known Sebastian, or if the version of him I had once let into my heart was more of an illusion than the costumes we are all wearing tonight.

I take a step closer. He doesn't move, but my knee does, making solid contact with his groin, sending him doubling over in high-pitched pain. There are gasps and giggles from the witches who are still watching the two of us.

A shadow looms behind him. I expect to see Vaughn in his hare costume, or the brilliant black of Constance's swan ready to hex Sebastian, but it is the black of the crow, with feathers expanding over his cheekbones up and into his hair, wild, dark and long, with tufting black feathers. His nose is beak-like, and his eyes are as golden as my glamoured locks.

'Nicely done,' Nightly tells me before he leans close to the stag and says in a whisper that carries to me: 'Crenshaw, if you have quite finished being the king of jackasses instead of the noble stag you are meant to be, I would like to dance with Ms Wycherley.'

Sebastian looks from me to the crow, then back again as Nightly cuts in front of him, slipping one winged arm around me. He holds me close then spins me around so that my back is to Sebastian, and he levels his gaze at him.

'And, Crenshaw, if you ever upset her like this again, I will challenge you to a duel, and you will lose. We all know how slow you are in all things, manners and magic being at the top of that list.'

Nightly deftly swings me away from Sebastian and we begin to dance. The rise and fall of the music matches our steps rather than the other way around. He doesn't speak as he guides me around the room, and when the music stops, he continues to hold me close. We pass another dance in that manner. Both of us twirling and turning without speaking, without needing to, as I feel more and more sure that I have fallen completely in love with Jules Nightly.

'Thank you, Nightly,' I murmur towards the end of the third dance as I look up into his golden eyes.

'Not at all. Crenshaw is a grasping climber, you are the richer for the loss. I know that you . . . have feelings for him, but you deserve so much more.'

'I know. But it is a terrible thing to give your heart to another and for them to not even realize you are there.'

'I agree, it is,' he replies. I wonder if there is a witch that he has given his heart to, or that refused him, and I feel irresponsibly jealous.

'Thank you, for coming to my rescue. How did you know it was me?' I ask.

'Aurelia, you hardly needed rescuing, and how could you

be anyone other than you? The way that you walk, the way you clench your fists when you're nervous, and push your lips together when you're excited.' Nightly raises a hand and runs his thumb over my lips, and my stomach twists delightfully.

'I do not,' I say with a chuckle.

'You do.'

My stomach flips again as I think of my lips and his and remember the way I had wanted him to kiss me in the library, the way he refused.

'Well, *you* clench your jaw when something vexes you,' I comment, 'and something is almost *always* vexing you. And when you are angry, your nostrils flare. And when you're engrossed in something, you focus on it completely to the detriment of everything else.' *But in that moment, you are still and serene and I catch a glimpse of something private, something that I'm sure you do not mean to share*, I add to myself.

He laughs and it resonates through my being.

'Well, I am glad that we both know each other,' he says as the music stops. He pulls away from me to bow and I resist the urge to pull him back to me as I curtsy. He leans in close to whisper, 'I'll meet you under the clock tower in half an hour. And because you were worried about not recognizing me, I'll be the one dressed as a crow.' Then he strides off into the crowd of witches, to return to the shadows.

Twenty-two

I stand in the shadow of the clock tower. Here, the feathers of my dress look as if they are almost as black as those of Nightly's crow.

After he left, I continued to dance, first with Vaughn, who sought me out to enquire about what happened with Crenshaw, then Constance, who did the same. But after I insisted that the two of them dance together, telling them I was looking for Nightly, they left me alone and I slipped from the hall. I knew exactly where to go and traversed the corridors and staircases quickly and quietly, then walked out across the gardens to the clock tower.

The night is cold, and I can feel my feathers rustling in the wind. Across the garden, the tall, thin stained-glass windows of the coven college hall are glowing from within. I track a shadow, and as it makes its way towards me, the bell strikes quarter past eleven.

'You are late.'

He looks up at the clock tower. 'Sorry, I had an unwelcome dance partner that I needed to shift.'

'Oh?' I'm unable to hide the curiosity in my voice. 'Anyone I know?'

'I didn't know them myself,' Nightly says, disinterested. He is carrying my cape over his arm and promptly swings it over my shoulders and fastens it for me. I have no idea how he got it.

'Nightly, I need to tell you something . . .' I begin to tell him all about Jonathan and the bookshop but just then, he pulls me quickly to him and pushes me further into the shadows, my back up against the wall of the clock tower, my heart pounding at the closeness. I look up at him but he is tracking a witch dressed as a cat.

'Your unwelcome dance partner?' I ask, a spike of jealousy flooding me.

'Indeed.' He is looking intently at me and it is all I can do not to rise on my tiptoes and push my lips upon his. A long moment passes then he shakes his head a little and looks over at the cat who is moving back towards the ball.

'Come on, before he comes back.' Nightly extends a wing. I take his hand and all I can think of is the missed opportunity to finally find out how his lips would feel on mine.

I cast a simple hovering charm on my shoes as I take my first steps on to the gravelled walkway. I extend the charm to Nightly as his first step crunches.

'Wycherley, have you got form with sneaking about?' he says, looking down at his boots.

I smile. 'It goes hand in hand with forgery, bribery and trespass.'

We walk towards the tomb, which, if the legend is correct, protects the entrance to the lost quarter of Neoards.

'Are we really going to do this?' I say with a gulp.

'It's what we are here for, isn't it? The answers lie in there, I know it. This tomb will lead us to a way for you to keep your magic. Evelyn too.' He looks at me earnestly and I feel a twang that runs through my body.

'And any other witch, too,' I add, thinking about the immensity of this. He looks towards the huge tomb. It is out in the open, right in the middle of the triangular courtyard. There are so many windows looking out, anyone could see us.

My wandlet snakes its way into my hand, the crystal tip glowing, as we reach the tomb and walk around it. The stone effigy of Heston is lying on the top, above my head – I have to stand on my tiptoes to glimpse him. Around the bottom of the tomb, the elements have not been kind, and the marks that I had hoped would be the full set of Golowhe runes are now little more than scattered scratches in the stone.

At the foot of the tomb, however, is a crest as tall as I am, and in the centre of it, faint but clear enough to identify, is one of the same black, glowing runes that we have been pursuing.

'Here.' I raise a witch-flame and spot a glimmer of something. 'Do you see that?' I point at it. 'There it is again.' I shift my flame and there is a definite ripple of magic on the surface of the large crest.

Nightly runs his hand over the stonework. 'It's warm,' he says. 'I can feel a ward of some kind.'

He takes my hand and slowly pulls my glove off, before holding my hand to the stone. The rippling deepens, and I can feel it vibrating through my fingers, my magic itching inside me.

'A Nightly and a Wycherley made this place, a Nightly and a Wycherley can find out its secrets,' Jules says. He pulls off his own black gloves and holds out his hand.

I hesitate. 'You want to perform secondary magic together? But you know what will happen.'

'I do, and I am willing to risk the consequences.'

Still I pause. I hate to think of him suffering because of me.

'Come on, Wycherley, this might be our only chance,' he say, looking back at the clock tower.

'Very well.' I let my witch-flame turn to an orb to hover above us. As I pull off my other glove and take his hand, I push my magic out through my fingers and into him, and as I do I hear him gasp, and a second later, I know why. Nightly's magic moves through me and there is no doubt that his magic was in the orb that landed on me at Samhain. I smell the autumn leaves and the taste of cinnamon buns as our magic combines. The power of it builds inside of both of us and I can't tear my gaze away from his.

I take a small step closer to him, and he reaches out his other hand to me, but as he does, his wandlet curls into his fingers and glows. I can feel that mine has done the same and I intuitively lift it till it's level with Nightly's. A spark of magic shoots from both of our wands and straight at the crest. The magic covers it, running over the stone of the tomb and revealing the outline of a door.

'Ha!' I call, my eyes almost as wide as my smile. 'A Wycherley and a Nightly.' Excitement races through me as I pull Jules forward. Keeping hold of his hand, I move towards the door and give it a shove. 'It's locked.'

'An opening spell?' Nightly suggests.

We run through the sequence, moving smoothly, then we stand in front of the tomb watching and waiting . . . but nothing happens.

'Let's try it again?' I can hear a worried edge in Nightly's voice.

'Yes, but let's draw the rune on the crest with our wands as we move through the sequence,' I suggest, as I gaze at the black flame rune in the crest that has burst into life thanks to our magic.

Nightly nods and we set to work, hands locked, magic flowing between us. I pull it into me greedily and send my magic into him. It feels deeper than before, and I wonder if that has anything to do with the Samhain Rite or the introduction of the Golowhe rune to the spell. Together we move as one, tracing the rune and passing through the movements associated with unlocking.

I stop moving as I hear a deep rumbling sound followed by the sound of grinding stone. Jules takes a step closer to me, our hands still joined and both of our magic thrumming. I feel Nightly give a jump of surprise beside me as the stone effigy of Heston Nightly sits up and extends his arms in a stretch. A light dusting of stone falls from him as he moves his stone limbs.

I squeeze Nightly's hand, feeling the comfort of him as I stare up at the animated stone Heston Nightly.

'Who doth wake my slumber?' His voice sounds like the grating of stone on granite. A small thread of magic and emotions is flowing between Nightly and I: awe, surprise and a little fear too.

'We did, we woke you.' My voice is little more than a whisper.

'And, pray tell, who are you?'

'I am Aurelia Wycherley, and this is Jules Nightly.'

The stone Heston lets out a low grumble. I worry that someone might hear him, but I can't pull my eyes away to check if we are still alone.

'A Wycherley and a Nightly.' He leans forward, looking from me to Nightly then back again. 'You are strange-looking witches. I fear I have been gone so long that I have missed much. Do witches still use brooms to fly? Or have you all grown your own feathers?'

'Oh, no, these are just costumes,' I say, and he smiles and chuckles low.

'As you can see, Ms Wycherley, I was not conjured yesterday. I know what you are wearing, and I can see the magic in your glamours. While I have slumbered here, I have listened and have tasted the magic of this world, just as I can taste the magic within the two of you. I think you will both do well at what lies before you . . . but I am sorry for it.

'I know why you have come. You are looking for a cure to the blight that fills all witches of this age. But I have to warn you both that witches greater than you have sought this cure and failed.'

I feel Jules squeeze my hand in reassurance as he says, 'We won't fail.'

Heston smiles. 'Spoken like a true Nightly. What you find within this tomb may not be what you are expecting. Are you ready to face what is behind the door? In opening it, it will become your fate. Do you accept that?' I look at Nightly. 'Whatever we must face to find a way forward, we will. Will we not, Wycherley?' he says and gives my hand a small squeeze.

'We will. Together.'

Heston gives a sad smile. 'Only a Wycherley and Nightly could have made me stir. You are the heirs to the lost quarter and all you find in it. But also, it is your responsibility to guard it, and each other. I was one half of such a pair, and I am much ashamed of how that ended. Mathilde and I, we gave our magic to one another, and I gave her my heart, but she loved another, and I could never forgive her. I now wish I had.'

'We know,' I say, and I let the glamour fall from me. My golden hair becomes white and my eyes smoky.

Heston looms over me. 'Your eyes . . . the curse. You carry it? The curse I gave to the witch I loved. I have had long to think, and now I know that if I had truly loved her, I would have wanted only her happiness. But I do not understand how you now have the curse?'

'One Wycherley woman always carries it,' I say to him. 'And because of it, we cannot tether. Our magic is . . . incompatible. That is the curse you gave Mathilde and me and all of her descendants in between.'

Heston looks confused as he continues to stare into my eyes. 'No.' His voice shakes. 'That is not the curse that I intended to bestow. The pain of her not loving me as I did her was too much to bear, but I never meant for the curse to extend beyond her lifetime. In my hubris and folly I made a deal with a magical force that I should have left well alone. I did not know the strength of the old runes, or the old magic that I called upon, and now it would seem that I am responsible for the sorrows of many more Wycherleys than my sweet Mathilde. Forgive me.'

I believe that he is indeed sorry, this remnant of Heston Nightly who wanted so desperately to be loved by the one he adored.

'You said there are secrets within the lost quarter. Is one of those the cure to tethering?' Nightly asks his ancestor.

Heston turns to him, his stone head grinding sharply. 'Some believe the secret to tethering is to find a witch that you can spend the rest of your days with, to live in harmony. Others want something different: to have their magic without the need to match. I know the latter is what you seek, but I don't have a direct answer for you without delving into the realms of malevolent magic – which I must caution you against, from my own catastrophic experiences.' His eyes narrow in warning. 'I can give you two things, both await you within the tomb, both you will need to claim for yourself, and they will help you, I am sure. But in taking these gifts you will become responsible for them and for the lost quarter. Once again, I ask, do you accept that responsibility?'

How could we not? I turn my head to Nightly and see that he too has removed his glamour, his black feathers removed, his long hair back in place. We both stand there, side by side, hands joined and magic flowing, as ourselves but together. He gives me a nod.

'We accept,' I tell Heston.

'You must do it together, a Wycherley and a Nightly, that is the only way that this will work,' Heston warns.

'We accept,' Nightly seconds.

'Very well. Prick your fingers then place your hands and blood upon the door and send your magic into the stone together.'

'May I?' Jules slowly reaches up to my hair and pulls from it a golden pin. I hold out the index finger of my free hand and he pushes the pin down. A small bead of blood collects on the tip of my finger.

As I look at it, I am reminded of Mabon and the debutante ceremony, when Nightly was still my enemy. And now we stand united on the precipice of something bigger than both of us expected, not just a possible cure for tethering but a call to protect this place. The responsibility sits heavily on my shoulders, but how can we turn away from it? I need this, Evelyn needs this and so will countless other witches, but that doesn't stop me from feeling apprehensive – a little scared even.

I take the pin from him and he holds out his finger.

'It takes but a drop,' Heston says. I look at Nightly as we extend our hands and place them on the stone, sending our magic forth. The crest lights up, the sound of locks and the grating of stone fill the air as the crest swings inwards like a door.

'This is your covenstead now.' Heston's voice echoes. 'The magic will awaken, slowly, within it. Henceforth, the tomb will open at your command, for it too belongs to you, the entrance to the lost quarter and all the ancient secrets it holds.'

I glance at Nightly, he swallows deeply, and when he looks at me, I can tell that he is having the same feeling of swimming out of his depth as I do.

'Together, you will need to raise your number, form a full coven and make the magic stick fast – or it will be gone forever, and with it, all hope.

'As I have lain here for well over a hundred years, I have felt the shifting in the tides of magic. Tethering has tried to keep magic in place, but one day it will be no more . . . witches will be no more. I fear that not only is that day fast approaching, but it is being aided in its departure. Magic as we know it is being tainted with malevolence, and it will fall to the two of you to stop this fall of magic. It is a heavy fate indeed. You came here seeking an answer to keep magic for yourselves and now you will have to find a way to keep it from disappearing from this world altogether. Blessed be, young witches. Blood of my blood, blood of my love.'

Then Heston Nightly lies back down on his stone tomb, and it is as if he has never risen at all.

Twenty-three

ou saw that, right? I didn't hallucinate the last ten minutes?' Nightly is staring at the tomb, at his ancestor.

'I saw it,' I reassure him, then gesture towards the open door.

'What . . . what just happened, Wycherley? What exactly did we just agree to?' Nightly's voice has an edge to it that I have never heard before.

'I think we just promised to fix the world.' I let out a wild giggle at the absurdity of it.

Nightly looks at me and breaks into a smile too, then a deep rumbling laugh. 'Oh, is that all!?'

We are both a little hysterical for a moment.

I start to sober as I say to Nightly, 'Come on, it's just a little thing, restoring the balance of magic in the world. How hard could that be? We should be done by teatime tomorrow.'

'Maybe even sooner,' he says, his laughter trailing to a halt. 'Wow, that's a lot, Wycherley.'

'It sure is.' We both stand in silence for a long moment, looking at the open door and feeling the trepidation of what might lie within.

'Together?' I say.

'Always together,' Nightly says, looking at me seriously. My heart lifts and I remind myself that I cannot fall in love with Jules Nightly, but it is too late for that.

'If you please.' I gesture towards the open doorway, and he smiles, his eyes glinting at me, and I almost come undone and ask him again to kiss me.

'I do please, very much, but keep hold of my hand. When we are connected, when our magic flows through one another, I feel fine, but if you let go . . .'

'I know, I'm sorry.'

'Don't be, it's his fault,' Nightly says, gesturing to Heston.

A low rumble fills the air and my wand glows as I take the first steps into the tomb. My orb of black witch-flame is ahead of me and I see a broad staircase leading down. I expect the steps to be dusty, marked with age, but they are crisp and pristine. My witch-flame is joined by Nightly's bright white one, and our footfall echoes together too. I'm not surprised when the door shuts behind us. I bid my witch-light seek out any torches; Nightly does the same and the staircase is flooded in a pattern of dark and light flames.

The stairs twist as we descend into what appears to be

a large, circular arcade. The round room has doors in its walls, and the centre of the floor is marked with an ornately decorated circle. Inside is a smaller circle of upright stones, each one taller and broader than me. Nightly's breath catches.

'It's a henge.'

'A what?'

'A henge. From the First Age of Magic. I've only ever read about them. They are focus points for energy; I remember that there is one at the centre of the Season Gardens. It's a place where wild magic is plentiful, or was, back in the day. Standing stones mark them – nearly all were destroyed in the Great Witch War by non-magical folk.'

I count the roughly hewn stones. There are twelve around the perimeter of the circle, and in the centre is the smaller base of one that looks as if it has been broken off.

We walk around the room, holding hands. Nightly casts another orb, brighter and bigger than the first. As he creates it, I feel some of my magic racing out of me and into him, boosting the spell. He throws it towards the ceiling high above us and his light catches on a low-hanging chandelier, spreading through it like lightning down the branches of a tree.

I can see the floor clearly now, an intricately painted pentacle of colour, and I can see four doors carved into the wall on one side of the circle, I am sure that one of them must lead off into the lost quarter.

'Look.' Nightly points to the smaller broken standing

stone in the centre of the circle. And I watch as two objects glisten into being.

'Heston's gifts?' I ask and as Nightly nods a rumble from above fills the air in confirmation.

Together we move towards the stone and Nightly reaches for a small book and I for a key. I lift it up to the light to see on the bow two interwoven initials: a W and an N. The same are on the cover of the grimoire. Nightly runs a finger over it before opening to the first page.

'Herein are recordeth ye magical practices of Wycherley and Nightly,' he reads. 'Read at ye peril. Use at ye risk. Ignore at ye cost. For ye kingdom and ye magic. For ye Nation and all witch-kind.'

A bell chimes in the clock tower, swiftly followed by another one.

'Midnight. Vaughn will be looking for me soon.'

'As he should be.'

I place the key inside the pocket of my cloak.

'I wish we had more time to explore this place.' Nightly looks about longingly.

'He said it was ours. We can open it any time we want to.' I look around the henge again as Nightly places the small grimoire in his breast pocket.

We begin to make our way up the stairs, but it feels as if I am leaving something important behind.

'We can always put our excellent breaking-and-entering skills to use again.' I smile, but something about the serious way he is looking at me makes my smile falter.

'I guess I know which coven college I'll be attending next year,' says Nightly, and I feel a little pang of sadness. He leads me up the stairs as the last of the midnight bells chimes.

'So, you've decided to make a match?' I ask.

'I think I have to. You heard what Heston said: something is coming, something that needs to be stopped, and whatever is hidden in here can help with that.'

'I see.' My heart and my magic are both being unreasonable. I remember what Heston said: *'if I had truly loved her, I would have wanted only her happiness'*.

Jules stops and turns to face me. I crane my head back, the extra step making him look impossibly far away. 'I don't think I can give my magic up, despite what I said after you stormed into the library and demanded that I share all of my secrets with you. However, there is one secret I have not shared.' He reaches down and pushes back a lock of my hair. 'Aurelia, I . . . I know that your heart has been otherwise engaged, but I cannot pretend any longer. I have been in love with you since the first moment I saw you at Mabon. I tried to ignore it, but then your stormy eyes flashed at me, that day in the library as you bribed and coerced your way into my soul, and I knew it was only ever going to be you.'

My heart skips and magic pours out of me and into Nightly.

'When you charged towards those protestors and I told you to leave and you wouldn't, I thought you were reckless, and impulsive, and dangerous, but I didn't know that the person you were most dangerous to was me and my plans,' he continues. 'I don't think I can ever give my magic up, but I know for certain that I can't ever give you up either. I felt your magic on Samhain. Our magic calls to each other, and you call to me.' He places his free hand on my cheek. 'If you don't feel the same, I'll understand. I know that you have an attachment, that Crenshaw—'

'No, not any more, not for some time now,' I say, taking a step up and then another so my face is level with his. 'You, Jules Nightly, have grown in my heart as true as those roses that we made at Mabon.'

I push Nightly's mask up. He gently pulls mine off too, letting it fall to the ground.

'There you are,' he says with a smile that makes my insides twist. The space between us evaporates as I press my lips against his, and our magic explodes inside us. My hand is in his hair, his is wrapped around my back, pushing me to him.

As soon as my lips leave his, they want to be on him again. Our kisses grow deeper and more urgent, and he pulls his hand from mine. I move to grab him but in that moment his kisses stop, his breath catches, and I feel him fall back, away from me. Time seems to slow as Nightly's eyes close and he plunges down the twisting stairs.

'Nightly!' I scream.

I don't think, I just act. My wandlet is in my hand and a lasso of magic flies from it, wrapping itself over Nightly as I send out the levitation spell.

I can feel the strain of it, the secondary magic that was flowing through our connection is fading fast and I'm not sure my primary magic will be able to stop him from falling to his death in the hidden henge.

We are only a few steps from the entrance, so I fling out my arm and the door opens. I can see the night and the gardens beyond. I pull on the lasso of magic with all that I have, lying flat on the steps as Nightly flies over my head and out of the door. I'm on my feet and running after him as he hits the ground with an almighty crunch.

I rush over, the door closing behind me.

Running my hand from his brow down his cheek, I cup his jaw in my palm, smoothing my thumb over his chin, his lips. My magic has done this to him; my blasted cursed magic has almost killed him.

His eyes twitch and I lean in close. 'Jules! Jules, it's me, Aurelia. Please wake up,' I whisper, tears threatening to fall. His eyes flutter again, once, twice, then open.

'Aurelia.' His voice is distant. He lifts a hand to my face warm and soft. 'Wow, your kisses pack a punch,' he says and I laugh, although I shouldn't. 'I don't suppose if I told you another one would make this pounding in my head stop that you would believe me?'

'No, I don't suppose I would,' I say, even though I desperately want to.

I pull him to his feet. He's unsteady and slips back down to the ground and out of my arms. I almost lost him, just at the moment that he declared he had feelings for me.

'I need you to stand. Can you do that?'

'For you, anything.' He stands with his arm wrapped around my shoulder for stability. We start walking slowly along the path, gravel crunching beneath our feet. The last chime of midnight has long since sounded, and glamourless witches are moving about the grounds freely, waiting for their coaches to arrive.

'I am so sorry,' I say.

'Don't ever be. I intend to kiss you again, just as soon as there stops being two of you and I know which set of lips to kiss.' He smiles, wavering with every step.

'Not for the kisses. I am sorry for my magic, for the curse.'

'Please don't apologize for your magic, Wycherley. It makes you who you are, and no one should ever apologize for being who they are.'

He halts for a moment and takes some deep breaths. I know that he's trying not to be sick.

'There you are!' I groan as I hear Vaughn. I quickly turn to check that the entrance to the henge below the tomb has sealed itself.

'Nightly, um . . . fell and hit his head. I think he needs a healer,' I say.

I don't expect Vaughn to believe me for a moment.

'I'm quite all right now, Ms Wycherley,' Nightly says, his jaw clenched. 'I was observing the heavens; there is a minor conjunction of planets this evening, Mr Wycherley. I must have lost my footing.' He makes a show of gazing into the cloud-filled sky, and I realize that for all of his wonderful gifts Jules Nightly is a terrible liar, and that makes me realize that every word he has ever said to me has been true. My cheeks flush.

'Yes, and I came out for some fresh air and found him over there on the floor.' I point back in the direction Vaughn has just come from.

'I see! All of this must have happened quite fast, because I only passed by a few minutes ago looking for you, Aurelia.'

I glare at Vaughn; he knows that we are lying. 'Yes, very fast. Where is Constance, by the way?' I ask casually. He turns a little red as I reach up and wipe lipstick from his cheek.

Flustered he says, 'Shall we?' He points in the direction of the coven college hall, eyes us again suspiciously, then walks ahead.

Nightly makes it into the hall before passing out again. A pair of healers are called. I realize they are the same ones that attended to me at Mabon and again at Samhain. 'You two again?' the healer says, looking from Nightly to me. 'Do you need a pair of healers with you through all of your courting?' he adds with a smile.

'So he fell, did he?' the other healer adds.

Vaughn whispers in my ear as the healers whisk Nightly away to the infirmary, 'If he fell, then the only thing he fell for was you.'

I can feel the heat rising in my cheeks.

But as I watch the healers lead him away, I realize that despite how we both feel about each other, even if we were allowed, I can never be Jules's tether. My magic will make him sick every day. However, I know that, against my better judgement, one kiss from him will be all it takes to have me sharing my magic with him again.

As I stand there, I make myself two promises: I will never perform magic with Jules Nightly again. It's too dangerous for him. And I will never kiss him again. It's too dangerous for me.

Twenty-four

Almost a week later, Nightly is still suffering from the effects of my magic. I've been dividing my time between the Arcade, the library and trying to track down Jonathan. I've returned to the alley almost every day, checking Mason's bookshop too.

I need to tell Nightly about Jonathan, about the new rune on the bookshop door. I wish I had been able to tell him at Yule. If only I had picked up Mathilde and Heston's grimoire, I could have read the whole thing twice by now, and who knows what I might have learnt. But most of all I wish my magic had not made Nightly so ill.

I've been doubling down on my promise not to kiss Nightly again, telling myself frequently that his lips are off limits to me, but that doesn't mean that I'm not thinking about him. Kissing will lead to magic, and magic will make Jules ill.

This morning, I went to the Arcade after my daily visit

to the alley at the back of Mason's bookshop to cut roses for him. For every one I cut, two more grew, and Russo and Platz chastised me for the bush again. Not a single visit to the Arcade goes by without them mentioning what a beautiful monstrosity the rose bush is.

I took the flowers to Nightly's house and left them with Evelyn, who told me that Jules was exhausted and sleeping. I could tell she was worried. She invited me in, but I saw Demelza Nightly pass behind her and fix me with such a stare, I was surprised it wasn't a hex. I spoke to Evelyn briefly about the work she had been doing for Mother and Frances at the Coven of Justice and could see that she was holding herself with renewed confidence and glowing with purpose. I wrote Nightly a quick note to go with the roses, wishing him a speedy recovery, then left for home.

As I walk through the door, the smell of cake and tea hits me. Mother and Frances are in the parlour so I go to join them. They ask after Jules, and even Mother seems genuinely concerned for his well-being.

I then turn the conversation to Vaughn.

'He's taking tea with the Priors,' Mother says with a wide smile. 'I do so like Constance.'

'Me too.' I smile and sip my tea, almost spilling it at a sudden hammering on the door. Mother sweeps from the room and then trails back past the parlour with Emery and Jackson, both in black. Frances is already on her feet following. I have learnt over the past few years that if Emery and Jackson are near, then so is trouble.

I wait a few moments before curiosity gets the better of me and I creep towards the library. There is a large crack in the jamb of the door and I look through it into the room.

'Another witch dead? Who is it this time?' Mother asks.

'A young witch in her second college year. Cora Stewart. She had been sequestered to the Arcade for the Season as an instructor with her tether, Kit Thorne.' Emery's voice is low and grave.

My head spins and I place a hand to my mouth to stop from gasping.

'Oh my goodness, Nell, that's Jonathan's boy,' Frances says. I can't help but think of how unlucky Kit has been to suffer the same fate as his father, but then I remember that Jonathan somehow still commands magic and something in me stirs in an unpleasant way, something that I can't quite get a grip on understanding.

'He had reported the breaking of the tether the day after Yule, but it has taken us all this time to . . . locate her and verify her death.' I don't like the way that Jackson says this and it makes me feel squeamish.

'Was it like the others? Did she have a mark?' asks Mother.

'The way she was murdered was different, but the strange mark was there just like on the others,' Nita Jackson, Emery's tether, says.

'Eleven witches murdered. Ten since . . . Ulric.' I hear my

mother's voice catch. 'I never thought that he would be the first of many.'

My heart pounds.

Murdered.

I had always thought that Father's death was an accident. I take a step closer to the door. I want to know everything.

Murdered by whom?

'It's odd: witches with no connection to one another, killed on Sabbats but, again, no pattern to the timings of the Sabbats or the victims,' Jackson says.

'Except there is a link now,' Mother says. 'Jonathan Reid and Kit Thorn, father and son, have both lost their tethers to this same murderer – this Magimancer, as the papers call them.'

'We should go over all the victims again, looking for any connections – not just between them, but between their tethers too. Maybe the Magimancer killed these witches to take away the magic of their tethers. Maybe they were the intended victims of this crime and not the dead witches,' Frances says.

There is a long pause as everyone takes this in.

'That is a new way of looking at it,' Mother says thoughtfully.

'We still think we are looking at an escalating situation,' Emery says.

'There were two murders in that first year – Ulric at Imbolc, then another murder at Ostara. Then three witches killed the following year at Litha, Mabon and Yule,' Jackson says.

'And last year. Three – at Beltane, Lughnasadh, Samhain. One of them even made it into the papers despite our best efforts. And that was when we first became aware of the marks. They had been there all along, tucked away at the crime scenes. Although it feels as if they haven't even bothered to hide them with the three this year,' Emery adds.

Ten other witches have died since my father, and it sounds as though all the deaths are connected by strange marks. It's too much of a coincidence, and I bet that the marks are the Golowhe runes. Magic is never coincidental.

I watch as Hobbs Emery hands my mother a drawing, and for a moment I catch a glimpse of it, and my heart skips a beat. It is the exact same rune that's on my wandlet.

'Again, it isn't like any magical symbol I've ever seen before. It's as if someone is playing at magic. I'm sure that the members of the New Dawn are behind all of these murders and that there is, indeed, no connection,' Emery says.

'That makes them even more terrifying, if true,' Nita adds. 'Any witch could be next and until the Magimancer is stopped, I fear that they will continue to kill at random.'

'With the other two murders this year having made it into the papers, I need you to do all you can to keep this one quiet. The last thing we need is mass panic,' Mother says. 'Who found her?'

'A non-magical. We're liaising with their authorities who

have detained the woman; there might be a link between her and the New Dawn.'

Frances shifts, and through the gap I can see her shaking her head. 'I've told you, it's not them. I know you think these weird marks are an attempt by the New Dawn to blame witches, but there is something off about the murders, like someone is trying to frame the New Dawn. I think we have to seriously consider that the murderer might be someone from the magical community. A fellow witch,' she says. Mother has a look on her face that I know well. It's the look that says 'I don't want to hear any more of your nonsense'.

'Given how precious magic is and how we all know its importance, especially in the light of its decline, I just can't see how any witch could ever do such a thing,' Emery says.

I love them for their optimistic view, but agree with Jackson when she says, 'Come on, Hobbs, you know, as we all do, that malevolence is growing. A witch could definitely do this; they have done worse in the past – in the Great Witch War.'

Everyone is quiet again.

'What has young Kit Thorne been told?' Frances continues.

'Nothing yet. We will tell him the usual lie: that she suffered an accident,' Emery says flatly, like lying to someone about the death of their tether was acceptable. An accident . . . just like they told me and Vaughn about our father. A trip and fall down the stairs, they had said, and the way his body was lying when I found him had definitely looked that way.

But they had known the truth. I wonder, what did they tell Jonathan? Did he know the truth? Surely he deserved to. We all did.

'I don't want to visit the scene and draw any attention to it. Emery, Jackson, conduct a thorough investigation and get your findings to me as soon as you can.'

It sounds as if their conversation is coming to a close, so I hasten towards the front door, where I quickly grab my cloak. I don't want to be anywhere near my lying mother and Frances for a moment longer.

As I walk into the dreary late December afternoon, drizzle starts to fall. I wander aimlessly, my mind reeling.

Father was murdered, which means that when I found him on the floor of the arcade, someone else had been there first. Who? Why? And why are they still killing witches? Eleven in total now.

Father always said there was no such thing as coincidences – that when we stumble across something that feels like it might be significant, it usually is . . . like a signpost, a nudge of wild magic pointing you in the right direction. Nightly and I have had so many of those along the way, and now here was another. These murders are connected to the Golowhe runes, as is my and Nightly's investigation. I decide to find out all I can about the dead witches, their murders and their tethers, in the hope that exploring one thing will lead me to information about the other.

It's no surprise that I find that I've walked to Kestrel

Lodge. Nightly's house. I want to tell him everything so that he can help me make sense of it all but also so that he can sweep me up in his arms and tell me it will all be all right.

But Nightly is still incapacitated. Because of my magic. I look up at the house and try to figure out which of the rooms is his. I could float my way up to him, knock on his window, tell him everything I know, hold him close. But who would that be for? Me. It would make me feel better, and Nightly would let me. He would listen, then he would hold me, cup my face in his hands, lower his lips to mine . . . but he would be the poorer for it, because, soon enough, I would want to feel his magic running through me, and after my magic had run through him, he would be sick.

Heston Nightly's words echo in my head again: *'If I had truly loved her, I would have wanted only her happiness.'*

And for the second time today, I walk away from Nightly's house.

Twenty-five

It is another week before I hear from Nightly. In that time, I have amassed all the information I can about the murders, even visiting a non-magical newspaper archive to collect any nuggets of information that they might have gathered on the New Dawn and the Magimancer over the years. I was not surprised to find anti-magic rhetoric in the newspapers, but I was shocked at how the witches' deaths were reported – not exactly with relish, but there was a definite hint that the witch in question deserved their death. It sickened me and for the past few days I have been careful not to travel in any parts of the ton without magical affiliation.

Nightly's letter offered the perfect diversion from my troubled musings.

Dearest Aurelia,

You and I have much unfinished business.

Of all the discoveries the two of us made at Yule, finding out how your lips feel upon mine was most definitely my favourite.

Meet me at the library at two p.m., bring the key . . . and your lips.

Your Jules

I give the butterflies that swarm up in me a stern talking to. *No more magic, no more kissing.*

The weather has taken a cold turn; for days now the clouds have been the grey-purple of snow, but they have yet to release. Vaughn and I haven't been to the Winter Gardens yet, but he and Constance have. The two of them have been inseparable since Yule, and the sight of them together makes me feel so happy. They are everything a perfect match should be.

I throw my white, wintery cloak over my shoulders and scoop up the key from Neoards. My need to be out the door quickly betrays my resolve not to pursue Nightly for any other purpose than the hunt for knowledge.

I get to the library before him and make my way to the restricted section. Instead of pulling his wingback chair from the fireside, I pull the desk towards it, dragging it along the floor with a noise that makes the witches around me *tut* loudly. I don't want to be responsible for Nightly catching a chill after the first day of recovering from something that I'm to blame for.

So much has happened in the last fortnight that I am struggling to piece it together. So far, Cora's death has been kept from the magical society, and I'm angry with my mother for that. She and Frances have been busy – no doubt covering up more misdoings – but when we are all together, I am frosty with them. They lied to me, they are still lying to me and Vaughn, and now I am lying to him too. It all feels like such a mess.

My head spins, my heart aches and my magic reels at the thought of it all. Not just this latest batch of revelations – my father's murder, the other witches – but also finding the henge, discovering the runes, Nightly, Nightly's lips, Nightly kissing me and almost dying because of it. It's all so unfair.

I wipe a tear and try to hold on to being angry, an emotion I know will stir me into action.

I start to pull all of my notes from my wallet, and as I arrange them on the desk, I try to focus on what I have learnt, what I need to share with Jules.

Every time the door to the restricted section opens, I snap my head up, only to be disappointed. It's gone three in the afternoon before I look up to see Nightly. He looks well, not at all like a witch who has spent the last fortnight convalescing. His hair is flopping forward in that way that makes me want to push my fingers into it, then I want to run my hand over his jaw, push my lips upon his and . . .

No, no kissing.

He locks eyes with me, and I feel more than my magic swirling. I am definitely in over my head. In fact, I am completely lost in Jules Nightly. He has cast a spell on me that I am never going to break free from . . . that I never *want* to break free from. I stand but my knees feel weak and my breathing is fast. He walks with purpose as if I am the only place in the world that he wants to be.

'Wycherley,' he says, standing in front of me. He smiles, and it is infectious. Then he pulls a rose from nowhere, one of our roses, and hands it to me, leaning towards me, his lips to my ear. 'I've missed you,' he whispers, making my skin tingle as his lips gently graze just below my ear.

No more kissing.

I decide that his lips on my neck do not count and I fight hard to resist the urge to bury myself in him.

He takes off his cape and drapes it over the wingback chair before sitting down. I stand still for longer than I should. When I sit, he nudges his chair closer to me, his knee resting up against mine, and when he runs his hands down his legs and his fingers graze my thigh, I feel that shoot of electricity running through me. I want to turn and look at him, to get lost in his eyes, in his kisses, in his touch.

No kissing.

'Much has happened while you have been sitting at home doing nothing,' I tell him.

'Hardly nothing, Wycherley, you should know me better than that. I have been examining the grimoire, and I have been thinking.'

'Thinking. Yes, I can see how that might have kept you incapacitated for a fortnight,' I tease, chancing a quick glance at him.

'Well, it was a very great deal of thinking,' he says with a smile that makes me want to throw my arms around him. 'About the runes – which are fascinating, and we will get to – but also about everything that happened at Neoards. Heston, the lost quarter, the threat of malevolent magic, the henge, the way that our magic ran through each other, you, your lips, how much I want to kiss you again right now, Wycherley, I don't care who sees.'

His voice is low and the tingles that are running through me are threatening to undo me.

'I care,' I say to him, and it takes all of my strength to turn to him and not to reach my fingers up into his hair and pull him to me. 'I care about you, Nightly, and, because I care, there is to be no more kissing, no more magic.'

His hint of a smile dies on his lips.

'Oh . . . you mean it, don't you?' His eyes flash with worry.

I take a deep breath. 'Yes, I mean it. Because I too have been thinking. You know what happens every time we perform magic, so what happens if, next time, I can't catch you? What happens if you get seriously hurt – or die?' I'm

286

crying, and Nightly reaches into his pocket and hands me a handkerchief before placing an arm around my shoulders and whispering to me.

'Wycherley, I'm not going to die.' I just want to sink back into his embrace, but I stay upright. I turn to him and hope that he feels the full effect of my stormy gaze.

'You were falling down the stairs and I only just caught you. Even then, it's taken you a fortnight to recover from me.'

'I am never going to recover from you,' he says, his chin low as he looks up at me through his eyelashes, and the sparks of feeling rush through me again.

I shake my head. 'Don't do that, it's not fair. I refuse to share my magic with you any more. I can't be responsible for what will happen to you.'

'I understand why there is no magic, but why is there no kissing?' He holds my gaze, and I look away to save me from leaping on him.

'Because kissing will lead to places that neither of us can go. You need to tether, you need to go to Neoards, and I don't want to scare off any potential matches for you.'

'Well, I don't want them if they are scared of you.' He looks at me seriously.

I take a deep calming breath. 'There will be no kissing because I need to be responsible for what happens to me too, and one kiss from you and all my resolve will disappear.'

'Wycherley, I don't think you are giving yourself enough credit, I have seen your determination. I am sure that you can do one – kissing – without the other – magic.'

'And I don't think that you understand just how deep my feelings for you run. I can't have kissing without magic. I want all of you, and one sip, one kiss, will have me draining my cup.'

'Are you sure I can't kiss you right now?'

'Jules,' I say, and fix him with a hard stare that is barely skin deep.

He sits up straight, pushing his hair back from his face, and lets out a deep breath.

'Very well, I understand, I respect your wishes. No magic. No kissing. But I want you to know that I want you. I want all of you, Aurelia Wycherley, and that includes your cursed magic.' He leans towards me and I turn to face him. He is so close that I can see the tiny flecks of gold in his dark blue eyes, just as clearly as he can see every cursed storm swirling in mine.

'But the thing is, Aurelia, I want you for more than a single spell, a single kiss. I want my magic to flow through you forever. I want my kisses to be the last thing on your lips each night and the first thing every morning, and I want my touches to slip over every part of you. Until you feel comfortable with that, then no kissing, no magic. But as soon as you tell me you want me, I am never going to stop kissing you, and if I have to duel every member of the Royal Magical Council to force them to permit us to tether, so be it.' He lifts my hand and links his fingers with mine. 'And our magic, it's going to be unstoppable.'

'It's going to get you killed.'

'It might just be worth it.'

'Even if the person who kills you is your mother? She would never stand for . . . us.'

'Yes, even then,' he says, but I don't know if that is entirely true.

I take my hand from his. I will never tell him that I want him, even though every single speck of me does. I shake my head and pull out the key.

'I can't give you my kisses, but I can give you this,' I say, using the same words that he did after he stopped me from kissing him, sliding the key to him.

He picks it up and examines it before pulling the grimoire from his cloak and placing it on the table next to the key.

'This book is amazing. I don't understand half of it, but what I do understand is challenging everything I thought I knew. Mathilde and Heston, for all of their personal problems, were an amazing tethered pair. But let's start with the runes.

'There are thirteen of them. In the First Age of Magic, when covens consisted of thirteen witches and not twelve, each of the members of the coven used one of the runes as their own personal sigil, calling upon the power that it gave them to enhance and colour their magic. There is no set hierarchy to the runes, so it made for a more balanced and equal coven despite the odd number. Here . . .'

He turns to a page in the grimoire and shows me the thirteen runes. They are laid out in two lines of six with a rune named Dalleth – which means 'beginning' – sitting underneath them all in the middle.

I see the rune from my broom, and like the broom, it too is called Ankoth, which translates as 'unknown'. Next, I recognize the rune from above my father's spellorium. It's called Keniver Tra – 'everything'.

'This rune here is the one that I saw above the door behind the bookshop.' I pull the book towards me and read, 'Omlesa: expanding.'

'What bookshop?' Nightly asks, his expression quizzical. I love the way that he looks when he is perplexed and I smile at him.

'I tried to tell you this at the Yule Ball but—'

'But we were busy with our couple's activities.' He smiles and I know that he is remembering all of the kissing, and I am remembering him falling and me barely catching him.

I tell him about the door, about Jonathan, about the magic I saw him perform. Then I tell him about my father, about Cora, about the other nine witches, and Kit and the other witch I didn't know who was with Jonathan. I show him all the information I have collected.

'Too many coincidences,' Nightly says. 'Come on.' He stands up.

'Where are we going?'

'To see this mysterious door of yours – the one you saw Jonathan go through.'

Twenty-six

I pull my cloak around me as the wintery wind stings my cheeks. My footsteps are in perfect time with Nightly's and I know that he is shortening his stride to keep step with me.

More than once, he flexes his fingers by my side as if reaching for me but then, remembering his vow, pulls away.

The streets are not as busy as they usually are, and the wind is cutting. I pull my cloak around me, keeping my hands inside its warmth and away from Nightly. When we make it to Seven Dials, we find the shops almost deserted in comparison to the pre-Yule rush.

I lead Nightly towards Mason's Magical Books. 'There. That's where I first saw Jonathan. He was leaving the shop with Kit and the other witch.'

'Kit Thorne,' Nightly says, that note in his voice that he reserves for people he has a particularly strong dislike towards: Kit, Sebastian, even Vaughn, at first. 'I don't like the fact that both he and his father have lost their tethers now. Maybe their family is cursed too.' Another coincidence that has not escaped me.

'After Kit and the other witch went that way –' I point in the direction that we have just travelled – 'Jonathan carried on down the street, then turned into the alley.'

'To the door?'

I follow the path I took on Yule Eve, till we stand in front of the door with the rune Omlesa above it. Nightly fishes out the grimoire and holds up the page with the Golowhe runes on it. 'There. Just like you said: Omlesa, the rune of expansion.' He frowns. 'And this is where he performed magic?'

I nod and Nightly puts his hands on his hips, looking up at the rune. 'We know these runes are connected with old, deep magic. The fact that they're here, where Jonathan performed magic without a tether . . . do you think that this rune gave him magic somehow? He doesn't *have* magic but has *borrowed* it from the rune?' he ponders.

'Magic is stored in any object that is created with it, and all runes have their own magic about them. He could have done that, but wouldn't he have needed a spark of his own magic to call upon it in the first place?'

Nightly shrugs. 'Maybe old magic doesn't work like that. Maybe Jonathan is helping his son to regain his magic after Cora's murder?'

'Maybe . . . except I saw them on Yule Eve and Cora didn't die till Yule.'

Nightly is pacing as he stares at the door. He begins examining the alley and the wall around the door.

'What are you looking for?' I ask as he stands staring at the wall, shifting about from side to side.

'I think I can see a glimmer of magic here. It's hard to be sure. What do you think, Wycherley?' He invites me to take a closer look. I stand just in front of him, my back to him, and he lowers his head so that it hovers above my shoulder. Then, with his hands on my shoulders, he moves me slightly. 'There. Do you see it?'

I nod. There *is* a faint seam of magic running up the door. I follow it down and realize that it runs along the ground and off into the building on the other side of the alley.

'Oi, what are you two doing?' We jump as a witch calls out from the opening into the alley. She has an apron over her dress, and beyond her is a café, its door wide open. I guess that from the window she has a clear view into the alley.

'Excuse us Ms, we were just looking at the strange rune above this door. Do you know what it is, or where this door leads to?' I ask, pointing.

'It's a basement storeroom to the bookshop, but it often floods so Mason doesn't use it.' The witch walks tentatively towards Nightly and I. 'A strange rune, you say? Wouldn't surprise me – there's plenty that's strange about this alley.'

'Oh, like what?' Nightly asks.

'Witch-flames floating about,' the witch divulges. 'Sometimes I see people go in here, but they don't come back out. Mason thinks it's because of the ley line that runs right through here.' I think about the seam of magic that I just saw and realize that it must be the ley line. 'But I think it has something to do with that dead witch,' the woman continues.

'Dead witch?' I ask.

'Last Beltane, a witch, killed. Oh, what was his name?'

'Last Beltane . . . Miles Bracken,' I say, remembering my research.

'That was it. He was murdered right here, members of the New Dawn did it, mark my words. Business was terrible for months. I can't say I've noticed that mark up there before though.' She gestures to the door. 'But like I say, strange things happen down here.'

We follow the witch back across the road to her café and order tea and cake. Nightly and I sit in the corner, in front of the window, with a clear view of the street and speak in whispers.

'We need more information about the dead witches, all of them,' I say. 'Information not in the papers, information that the Coven of Justice prevented from being public. I don't like to do it, but Emery and Jackson visit Mother and Frances at home and often bring reports, and never leave with them. Would you be able to fish around too? Your mother's a member of the Coven of Mysteries – she might know something.'

'I'll try.' Nightly grimaces as he returns his cup to his saucer.

'How are things at home, with your mother, with Evelyn?'

'Mother is being more accommodating since Evelyn started working at the Coven of Justice, but she is livid that it was Frances and your mother that found her a position and that now both her children are . . . how did she put it? "Fraternising with the Wycherleys".' His impression of his mother is so good that I let out a laugh, but a movement from out of the alley draws my attention.

'Nightly.' I grab his arm and he follows my gaze.

'Is that Kit Thorne?' he asks. I nod. 'I've been keeping one eye on the alley the whole time we've been here, and I didn't see him enter.' Nightly makes to stand.

I hold his arm. 'Let me talk to Kit – you'll just scare him off. Out of the two of us I'm sure he likes me better.'

'I bet he does. Fine, but I'll be watching,' Nightly grumbles, sipping his tea again.

I hurry from the café and make my way down the street in pursuit of Kit. I look back over my shoulder and see that Nightly has swapped his seat so that he can keep me in his sights.

'Kit! Kit Thorne!' I call lightly. I remind myself I'm not supposed to know that Cora is dead. There wasn't any mention in the papers – not even in the obituaries. I have been scouring them all fortnight.

He turns and smiles at me. Not the response I was

expecting. 'Aurelia! How are you? How was Yule? Did your glamour work?'

I am instantly on my guard – something is definitely not right. I know grief works differently for every witch, but still.

'Perfectly, thank you. I . . . I haven't seen you at the Arcade lately and I wanted to say thank you for the extra tuition you gave me and to let you know that I've been rethinking my attitude towards Jules Nightly. As you said, he is arrogant and full of Nightly pride. I suspect his sister was too.'

'Oh, she was, terribly full of it,' he adds.

I look about me then ask, 'No Cora?'

'No, she's spending the Yule season with her family.'

I suddenly think about the lies that my mother has told me, the lies that the black-clad witches must have spun. Maybe he doesn't know she's dead, maybe Emery and Jackson still haven't told him. But I recall he reported the snapping of their tether, he would have known the moment that she died, the very second his magic disappeared. Or, at least, it should have.

'Does she have a big family?' I ask.

He gives a sad little smile. 'Not really. No siblings, and her parents died in magical service to the Crown a few years ago. She has an uncle; he's quite old, lives in a little village in the highlands. She doesn't get to see him much, it's quite a journey.'

'I'm sure it is,' I say, my mind reeling. I'm sure that there's no mistake, that Cora is dead, but Kit is acting like nothing has happened. Then he lifts his hand to pull his cloak around him and as he does, his wandlet slips, and on the side of his wrist I see the same rune that is on my wandlet – Gwrians: creation – branded on his skin, the same rune as was found at Cora's murder.

My wandlet snakes into my hand and I have a foolish idea, but one that might prove what I need to know, irrefutably. And if my suspicions about Kit are wrong . . . well, I just hope that I know Nightly well enough to trust that he would never stay sitting in the café.

Timing is essential. I glance about me and see a stagecoach making its way down the street.

'When you write to Cora, do send my thanks,' I say to Kit cheerfully. Then, still looking at him, I step off the kerb and into the path of the oncoming coach.

In that split moment my wandlet glows, knowing that I am in danger, but I bid it to stay and send no magic through it to aid me in my plight, even though fear slams into me as I turn my head away from Kit and see the horses careering towards me. I close my eyes and then I'm in the air, flying back to the kerb, back to Kit Thorne, as he uses his magic to pull me from harm's way. The coach thunders past, the driver shouting obscenities at me, as Thorne holds me to him, shaking.

'I . . . I shouldn't have done that!' He pushes himself off me and runs away. I stand there, breathing heavily, as adrenalin, fear and shock course through my body.

'Wycherley!' Nightly spins me around, runs his hands

over my face, his eyes over my body.

'He still has magic,' I manage to choke out, my breath shuddering. 'Kit Thorne has magic. How is that possible?'

Nightly is breathing hard, his eyes wild and frantic. He pulls me to him, wraps his arms around me and buries his lips in my hair. 'I thought that you were . . . I couldn't get to you quick enough . . . If Kit hadn't . . . What were you thinking, Aurelia!?'

He holds me at arm's length and I swallow, suddenly realizing not only how rash my actions were but also how deep Nightly's feelings for me are.

I place my hand on his cheek and he closes his eyes, leaning into it. 'I'm so sorry, I didn't . . . I wasn't thinking. But I was sure that he had magic, and if not, I thought you would be there.'

Nightly shakes his head and pulls back. 'But I wasn't, not quickly enough. Promise me, Wycherley, that you will never do anything so reckless again. Never put me in a position to be without you.'

'I promise,' I tell him. And if it wasn't for all of the witches watching us, the no-kissing rule would be history.

HER MAJESTY THE PRINCESS REGENT,
GEORGIANNA,
AND THE ROYAL MAGICAL COUNCIL
REQUEST THE PRESENCE OF

Ms Aurelia Wycherley

AT THE FIRE TRIAL AND FEAST OF IMBOLC

ON TUESDAY THE 1ST FEBRUARY 1814.

PLEASE REPORT TO THE LONDON ARCADE
VIA YOUR NEAREST ENTRANCE.

ARRIVALS FROM TWO P.M.,
COACHES AT MIDNIGHT FROM CARLTON PALACE.

ALL DEBUTANTES ARE TO WEAR THEIR ASSIGNED COLOURS.
ONLY THOSE IN WHITE NEED ATTEND BOTH THE TRIAL AND
FEAST. THOSE IN GREY WILL BE FEASTING ONLY AND CAN
ARRIVE AT THE PALACE ANY TIME BEFORE SIX P.M.

FOR THE KINGDOM AND THE MAGIC.

Twenty-seven

The autumn leaves, which had filled the magical metal railings that encircle the Season Gardens, have been replaced with falling metal snowflakes, each one different, each one sparkling like a real snowflake. They float to the ground and gather in a pile that never grows any higher. The streets of the ton are wet, dirty and dreary. Heavy rain clouds hang low in the sky and the pavement has not been dry for days. I look at the skates in my hands and feel a little foolish carrying them, but that morning I sent a letter to Nightly.

Dear Nightly,
    As much as I love spending time with you in the library, it has been brought to my attention by the arrival of the Imbolc

invitation that I have almost missed the beginning of winter. The season, like life, can often be too short and, after my recent recklessness, I feel the need to be out in the world, living a little. Vaughn is taking me to the Winter Gardens today, Constance will be joining us and if you are not busy it would be nice to see you. We will arrive at noon.

I'm looking forward to spending time with you without a book or ten between us, but I may have a file or two about my person.

If you please,
Aurelia

P.S. I'll meet you on the pond at one p.m. – bring your skates!

I was pretty sure that if the invitation to the Winter Gardens was not enticing then the promise of files would be. It has been well over two weeks since the incident with the coach. In that time I have often caught Nightly looking at me like he wants to scoop me up in his arms and hold me close. And every part of me wants him to, but I think he is beginning to realize how I feel every time we perform magic, every time he becomes ill, and how utterly afraid I was at Yule when I only just saved him from falling to his death.

Inside the gardens everything is white and crisp and wintery. A full-on blast of Arctic chill hits me in the face as we enter the gates, making my cheeks rosy and my ears cold. As we walk towards the amphitheatre I pull up the hood of my cloak. The fur lining instantly warms me, and when I push my hands into the fold of my cloak I check the files are still safe.

A Winter's Tale is aptly the play of the moment.

'Oh, would you mind if we watch it?' Constance asks. Vaughn is eager to say yes, and we find seats in the audience next to Martyn. After the first act, I go and get us hot chocolates, and when I return, I make my excuses and leave them to meet Nightly on the pond.

I turn back to see Vaughn trying awkwardly to put his arm around Constance. As he pulls it back, she grabs it and drapes it around her shoulders. The sight makes me smile.

I know that Nightly would never hesitate or stumble; he would smoothly wrap me in his arms and pull me to him if I let him. I walk slowly listening to the sound of the crisp snow crunching underfoot. The skeletal deciduous trees are all wearing icicles that glint like diamonds and the evergreens hold a cape as white as mine. The red burst of berries on a holly tree catches my eyes and as I look up, I see a mistletoe curling itself towards every pair of witches that walk close to it. Then I look down the path to see Sebastian.

'Crenshaw,' I say with a nod.

'Wycherley,' he replies with a scowl. I look behind me as he passes. Beyond him on the path I see Nightly. The wintery air catches in my lungs and as I breathe out, a little cloud of dragon's breath appears.

'You brought your skates then.'

'As requested – but I must warn you, I am a terrible ice skater.'

I shake my head. 'I don't believe you for one moment. You are good at everything.'

'Far from it, Wycherley.'

The mistletoe's white berries hang above his head and its leaves are tapping him encouragingly as it grows towards me too.

'I can't,' Nightly tells it. 'Wycherley has forbidden me to kiss her. Although I have made no such sanctions on her.' He raises an eyebrow.

The mistletoe has reached me now, its leaves haranguing me.

'It's not happening,' I tell it, and it drops several of its white berries on my head. 'Fine,' I say with a sigh, and I put a hand on Nightly's arm, lift up on my tiptoes, and kiss him on the cheek. The lurch in my stomach makes me want to throw my arms around his neck and lose myself in his lips.

I pull away, but stay on my tiptoes, and as he turns his

head to me, his nose touches mine and he lets out a deep sigh that is almost a growl. My whole body tingles. I quickly put my heels on the floor and begin to walk towards the lake.

'We can skip the skating and get straight to the documents if you want,' I say when Nightly catches me up in a few long strides.

'It has been brought to my attention that you have missed much of the beginning of winter and the fun it brings already by our . . . sleuthing and criminal activity. So fun first, murder investigation second.' He says the last part in a low whisper.

'Ah, another thing to add to our courting activities.'

He was not trying to be gracious when he told me that he was no good at skating. I hold his hand and try to guide him, but still he spends most of the first half an hour lying on the ice. After another half an hour, we make it around the pond once, and just as I'm starting to feel like a block of human ice, he lets go of my hand and manages to skate half the lake on his own . . . till he falls again.

I look down at him, his cloak strewn around him, his hair a tousled mess.

'Shall we go and get something to eat?'

'Only if we can find a healer for all of my bruises too,' he moans as I help him up.

'Where does it hurt the most?' I ask as we skate to the edge.

'My pride.' He smiles.

We remove our skates and find a seat in the small

promenade café where all of those months ago I hid from Sebastian, where I saw Nightly and Evelyn collecting pond weed and first heard him speak of finding a way to keep magic without tethering.

So much has happened since then.

We sit off to the side where it is quieter. Nightly pulls out a chair for me and I thank him as I sit down. We order a pot of tea for two and a bowl of stew each.

I look about, then pull out the files and hand it to Nightly. 'This is just the highlights. I copied what I thought was important.'

'More forgeries! You really do give me the best gifts.'

'The real files are much bigger than this one − they go back to when my father . . .' At this, my voice catches, and Nightly reaches out for my hand.

'I'm sorry, Aurelia,' he says.

I place my hand on his. 'It's all right. It's good that I know, and I feel like I'm doing something to help. But I also feel like I'm being deceitful to Vaughn. I remember how angry I was towards Frances and Mother for not telling me, and if he finds out I know and I kept it from him . . . I'm worried he will feel that way about me too.'

'We could tell him . . .' Nightly says.

'We will, just not yet. When I tell him I want to have a *why* to tell him too. That's the thing that is eating away at me. Why did my father die? And I'll only know that if we can discover who killed him . . . who killed all of them.'

Nightly flicks through the files and I watch as he takes in

the information, his expressions running through familiar patterns: a single eyebrow raise for something that surprises him, the joining of both eyebrows for something perplexing, a blank expression for the things that distress or appal him, and there is much in the file to do that. The descriptions of the murders, the bodies and the scenes are thorough. I tried to take in all the points that were important but also skimmed over the things that made me feel most uncomfortable.

He closes the files when our food arrives and as we eat, he tells me his observations.

'Do you mind?' he asks as he pulls out his notebook. 'It's terribly bad manners.'

'Not at all, you go ahead.' I watch him eat his stew and put his thoughts down on paper as we talk things through between spoonfuls.

'There is a connection and a pattern with the runes, each . . . incident has a different rune associated with it. The reports say that not only was a rune at the scene – carved or burnt or painted somewhere – but an identical rune has been magically placed on the victims too. All are in the same place: on the outside edge of the wrists on their wand hands. Just as you saw on Kit. I wonder if that has something to do with the tether, if the murderer placing the rune on the victim also makes it magically appear on their tether?'

I think about that for a moment. 'You know, there was no mention of that in any of the reports. If that was so, I wonder why Kit didn't mention it?'

'Maybe he did but the investigators didn't think it was important?' Nightly suggests.

'I very much doubt that Emery and Jackson would have missed out that detail.' I muse on that a little more as we eat. 'He also failed to let them know that he still has his magic.'

'Maybe something about the way Cora was killed means that the magic takes longer to fade away. That would explain why Jonathan can perform spells too. Maybe his magic is fading slowly – like Evelyn's,' Jules says.

'You know, I also noticed that none of the runes have been used twice,' I add. 'Which has led me to think about the part in the Neoards grimoire, the bit about the structure of the old covens – the thirteen runes and the thirteen witches, each one having their own rune.'

'Oh . . .' Nightly says, putting down his spoon, his eyes wide as he hurriedly says, 'Now, I know this might sound a bit outlandish but I wonder . . . I mean I hope not . . . but you don't suppose that someone is using that old magic to create a coven of dead witches, do you? Some kind of malevolent necromancy. Heston did say malevolence was on the rise.' The thought makes me sick, but during the Great Witch War, when malevolent magic rose, acts of the most abominable magic were reported, including necromancy.

'I hope not,' I say, dabbing my lips with a napkin. Nightly suddenly looks unsettled.

'Oh, Aurelia, I'm sorry. I didn't think before I spoke. I am sure that is not your father's fate.' He reaches out a hand to me and looks horror-stricken at what he just suggested.

'It's all right, Nightly, it is important that we think through all of the possibilities, no matter how uncomfortable they may be.' I pat his hand. 'I know that was not my father's fate. When I found him, he was very much dead and not at all reanimated.'

'It is obvious that the murders are linked to the runes, and that so far there have been eleven victims, each one with a rune connected to them. So it stands to reason that there will be two more murders to finish the full set of runes, but why?' Nightly turns to the page in the Neoards grimoire and we list off the eleven that have already been used, leaving Dalleth (beginning) and Daskor (return).

After our bowls have been cleared, Nightly orders us apple crumble and custard – my favourite – then he turns to me and asks, 'Have you been able to get a lead on Kit Thorne?'

I shake my head. 'No one at the Arcade has seen him. Russo and Platz definitely know about Cora, from the way that they spoke to me. Platz was gentle when he spoke of her and Russo was more cagey and less direct than he usually is. I've also written to Jonathan at his last known address, and I went to visit his old house in Pimlico but it was still all locked up.'

'You should have said – I would have come with you,' Nightly says. 'You promised me you'd keep safe.'

'And I was safe.'

He raises one eyebrow. 'Well, next time you rush off to do something dangerous, send me word. If you please.'

I smile and promise to do so.

IMBOLC

The Most Magical Season – A Debutantes' Guide

by Cathleen Kelly and Kate Walker

The fire festival of Imbolc: the most feared Sabbat of the first-year debutante. A trial by fire. Once faced and passed, it is never to be repeated, and the reward is gaining the means to tether your magic should you find a worthy witch.

The trial is different for each witch and corresponds to the frequency of their magic as embodied in their witch-flame. Because of this, there is very little that a witch can do to prepare themselves. The only comfort that you can take is that everyone passes. Eventually.

Most trials are over in minutes; however, the record for the longest trial sits at seventeen weeks, five days, two hours and thirty-five minutes. Unfortunately, the tethering thread that Mr Thaddeus Evans gained in that trial ended up not being used that year, as Ostara had been and gone by the time he emerged – as had the feast and ball that is held in Carlton Palace as the reward for all witches on Imbolc.

We wish you a speedier completion of your trial than Mr Evans.

Twenty-eight

'm reminded of that first trip to the Arcade after making my pledge and receiving my wandlet. Just as she was then, Constance is by my side, only today she's stamping her feet on the cobbles and hugging herself.

'I knew I should have worn a thicker cloak, but this one is so adorable,' she says. I throw my cloak out and over her shoulders too. She snuggles into me as the line proceeds more slowly than the snowflakes falling on us.

'Fire festival. Ha!' she says, the snow catching in the dark curls of her fringe.

'Have you and Vaughn come to an arrangement?' I ask to distract her from the cold.

Constance beams. 'We have, but we are thinking of having another Season before we tether. He has his final grey year and I quite like the idea of making my parents wait it out. What about you and Nightly?'

We take another step forward. I can't very well tell Constance that our arrangements involve no magic, no kissing, and a let-me-know-if-you-are-about-to-do-something-dangerous clause.

'It's complicated,' I say instead.

Constance gives me a serious look. 'I hear that his parents are still looking for a match for him.'

'Yes, they are. Nightly says that they are quite keen on someone.' I try to keep my voice light.

'Does he know who? I heard it was Liam Long.'

'Oh, that would make sense. I like him – he has such a graceful way of moving through his magic,' I say, fighting down my feelings.

'Aurelia, you are not supposed to like, or even compliment, the witch that is going to steal away the person that you love!' We move a little further towards the entrance and again I hear the words of Heston in my head: *'If I had truly loved her, I would have wanted only her happiness.'*

'Constance, Nightly is not mine for someone to steal from me. My magic is cursed and I can't – I won't – share that curse with anyone, especially Nightly.'

'Exactly. Because you care deeply for him.'

'I do.' I sigh. 'And because of that, I am letting him go.'

'Oh, Aurelia. I really thought that love could change everything, that it really was the strongest of all magic, but if two witches who love each other as much as you and Nightly do can't make it work, then what chance do the rest of us have?'

'Constance, you're being dramatic. I wouldn't say that we are so very much in love.' *I just think of him endlessly and can't bear to be apart from him, and I imagine his lips kissing every part of me.*

'Well, I would.' She shrugs. 'And I'm your best friend and I know a thing or two about love.'

'Because of Vaughn?'

'Because of Vaughn.' She smiles dreamily, and we are at the front of the line.

'You go first,' I tell her and she walks forward. Russo greets her and leads her inside.

As I stand outside the Arcade, I can think of nothing but Nightly. Constance is sure that I love him – but love doesn't seem like a deep enough word to explain how I feel about him.

'Ms Wycherley,' Platz calls, and I break off my musing to follow him into the Arcade. We walk past the rose bush. I smile as I see it, then Platz side eyes me, and tuts.

The Arcade is strangely quiet. I was expecting to see all of the witches that had been ahead of me in the line, but instead all I see is a collection of doors, each with a dancing flame covering it: purple, blue, green, white, red, orange, yellow, the seven colours of magic.

'Summon a witch-flame please, Ms Wycherley,' Platz instructs, then groans as he sees my black flame. 'Nothing is ever simple when it comes to your magic. I am going to need you to do some additional magic before your trial can begin.'

'Why?' I ask, looking at the flame in my hand.

'The doors for the trials are cast from flame spells by a witch who has a corresponding-coloured flame to the door they are creating, one for each of the seven colours of magic, or I guess now that is eight.

'To create a door such as this, tertiary magic is required, the type that can only be performed by witches linked to a coven; a high-level one at that. We wouldn't normally entertain the idea of a debutante performing such high-level magic, but you are no normal debutante, and for the Fire Trial to work for you, we need to create a door with the corresponding-coloured flame to your magic. As no one else in the world, to my knowledge, can conjure a black flame, a hitherto unknown eighth colour of magic, you will have to assist us in forming the magical foundation for your trial,' Platz finishes, then walks me through the sequence needed.

Once I am sure of the spell, the movements and invocation required, Platz stands to one side of me, I can see Russo on the other side of the Arcade ushering Bevis Nash towards the door with the blue flames.

'I will channel the magic of my coven. It will be stronger than any magic you have accessed so far. I will send it through you, you must send your magic into me—'

'But it will make you ill,' I blurt, and he gives me a withering look.

'Ms Wycherley, I am no debutante; my magic is robust, as am I. I am sure no harm will come to me. You will send your magic into me and it will travel through my coven via my tether with them, and we will all perform the spell together. When you are ready, Ms Wycherley.' Platz holds out his hand.

The second we connect, I can feel the magic of not only Platz and Russo but the ten other witches in their coven. It is flowing through me like a melody, all of the different notes coming together in chords and harmonies. As I perform the moves, I find that I can move along the threads of magic, picking out the witches within the coven, drawing on the idiosyncrasies within their individual magical abilities that I need to pull the spell into being. The power moving through me is exhilarating and intuitive. I watch in wonder as a door forms in the middle of the Arcade. It soon outstrips the doors around it, reaching high into the arches of the room. I know instantly that it is made of the same black wood as my broom – Ankoth. Engraved on the front of it is a giant tree that burns in a black flame, and around the frame are the thirteen Golowhe runes, catching in the flicker of the witch-lights in the Arcade and the black flame burning on the door.

I let go of Platz and he instantly falls to the ground, as does Russo across the Arcade. Not only that, but the echoes of the coven magic running through me tell me that all twelve of its witches have been affected by my cursed magic and have fallen unconscious. Unconscious debutantes is one thing, but a whole coven is another. A wave of panic floods through me, as I wonder where the other ten witches are, what they are doing, if I have put them in danger.

'Help!' I call. 'I need a healer.' Two green-robed instructors rush in, looking shocked as they notice the massive door behind me and then Russo and Platz lying on the floor.

I quickly tell them what happened. Platz starts to come round, holding his head, his skin ashen as he tries not to be sick, and fails.

'I'm sorry,' I say.

'You have nothing to be sorry for, Ms Wycherley.' He takes calming breaths and then allows himself to be lifted and placed on a chair that has been conjured. Russo is now conscious but still on the floor. 'Your magic is like nothing I have ever experienced. Look what you have created.' He extends a hand to the door.

I have to admit it is impressive, if a little terrifying.

'The after-effects of your magic leave much to be desired.' Platz looks like he might be sick again, but he holds it back.

'The other witches of your coven – can you feel them? Are they well?' I ask.

Russo looks at me blankly. 'Can I feel them?' he asks slowly.

'Through your coven tether, your magical connection, are they all right?'

'Ms Wycherley, I'm not sure that I follow. Are you telling me that when you connected to my coven, you could feel the magic of each witch the spell drew from?'

'Yes, doesn't every witch feel those that they are connected with magically?' I say slowly.

'Tell me, what does it feel like to you?' he asks and I can see that his interest is piqued despite his slightly unfocused eyes.

'When we performed the spell, I was holding hands with you, but I was connected to the whole of your coven, I could feel along the threads of your magic, along your connection to Russo, which was strongest, but also the other ten. I could feel who they were, all of them a little surprised by the magic. A few of them were excited by it, one was quite taken aback, a little scared even, his magic felt shy, as if it had never been comfortable blooming into its full potential.'

'Ah, that would be Jordan Jones,' Russo says from behind me and I turned to see him walking slowly towards us. 'What else, Ms Wycherley?' he asks, and I tell them things about all of the witches in their coven, remarking on the resonance of their magic, the feelings that I gained from them while the magic was happening.

When I finish, Platz, Russo and the two healers are looking at me with a mix of unease and awe.

'Ms Wycherley, I have only heard of a very few witches who have been able to feel along the magical connection of their tethers and never one who could feel further than that, never along their covens,' Platz says and he exchanges a look with Russo.

'We need to explore these interesting connections a little more, Ms Wycherley, but not now – now your trial by fire awaits you.' Platz stands with a little wobble and extends a hand towards the door we just made. I look back at it and my head swims not just with the enormity of the door before me, or what waits behind it, but also the revelation that what I thought was normal for all witches is particular to only a few.

'When you enter the door it will take you to your trial, at the end of which you will see the door once more. Your aim is to reach the door and step through it we will be waiting here to greet you when you do.' He looks at me intently. 'Keep your witch-flame blazing and listen to your magic.'

I nod and turn to face the door, I call my witch-flame forth and split it between each of my hands, I let it run over them, sparking between each of my fingers and trailing up my arms.

As I approach the door, it swings open.

Twenty-nine

I step over the fiery threshold of the gigantic black-flame door, the Golowhe runes shine around me and I find them a comfort as I lift my hand up over my eyes to shield them from the intensity of the light. The black flames lick my body but don't burn me as I pass through them, just like my witch-flame.

I'm in a forest full of tall, black trees, so wide that I would need three of me to wrap my arms around them. They reach up into a grey sky full of stormy, swirling clouds that remind me of my eyes. A deep, unsettling feeling is mounting in me. This place feels wrong . . . off kilter somehow.

The door I entered through is nowhere to be seen, but through the trees, in the far distance, I can see an identical door, large and looming, surrounded by a henge of white stones.

As I walk towards it, my fear grows. I hear whispers

rustling through the bone-white leaves of the trees.

'Who is she?'

'How did she get here?'

'Why is she here?' the whispers ask.

'Shall we kill her?'

'We want to kill her – rip her magic from her, split her body into pieces.'

Their voices sound sweet and childlike but their words . . .

I walk faster, my boots crunching on the leaves, my wandlet responding to my fear, snaking into my hand and glowing fiercely.

'She's a witch.'

'She has the old magic.'

'She shouldn't be here.'

'She shouldn't *be* at all.'

'We should kill her.'

'We should tell him.'

'Yes, he will want to know!'

The whispers follow me, and I'm running now, as fast as I can towards the henge, my magic screaming to me to leave this place.

From behind the trunks of the dark trees, smoky tendrils reach out, slow and stealthy. They remind me of the tendrils of smoke that reached for me on the Thunder Moon, that held my curse and burrowed into me.

They make their way towards me as I run faster and faster, my breath coming in snatches, my heart pounding.

I look behind me and see that the smoke has morphed into a tall figure with long limbs that twist and ripple, and claws that are deadly sharp. From his head split massive antlers, and his eyes glow black with a fire like my witch-flame. I realize that until that moment I have never felt real terror.

He doesn't whisper. His voice rings out high and clear across the forest. 'Witch, whence didst thou steal that magic from?' he screeches after me as I make it into the ring of the henge and run straight up to the door. I place my hands on it and my witch-flame sets the tree engraving alight. I send my magic out into the door, begging it to open, using everything in me to open it. I take a step back, throw my magic at it and hear a boom run through the wood. I do it again and again, boom, after boom, after boom, as the creature of smoke and claws moves closer. I know with complete certainty that if he reaches me, I am dead. I think of my mother, of Frances, of Vaughn and Constance and Nightly – oh, how I wish that he was here with me.

'Be not afeared, little witch of stolen magic, I will cut the burden from ye, take back what is not yours.' He is almost upon me as I strike out again, using the Golowhe rune Anter in my spell as Nightly and I did to open Heston's tomb. The door begins to open: a crack then a little more. I get one arm in and begin to squeeze myself through. My heart leaps as I feel someone grab my hand on the other side and pull. Inch by inch I slip through the gap, but not fast enough as I feel his claws, as cold as ice and sharp as steel, slice through my flesh.

I don't know if the creature screams or if I do as I fall through the door straight into Nightly. He pulls me behind him, his wand up, and through the door a clawed arm reaches.

I take hold of Nightly's hand and push my magic into him, pulling his into me as we send out a closing spell to shut the door. It closes with an ear-splitting scream as the creature's arm falls to the floor this side of the door. Another spell and the door is sealed shut with our combined magic.

I instantly let go of Nightly's hand and his magic. He closes his eyes and shakes his head, as a small knot of tethered witches in black and green and red, holding their wands up at the door, flood in front of us. I look behind me and realize that I am standing on the balcony overlooking the hall at Carlton Palace, that the door behind me is the one I entered through at my presentation on Mabon, and below, in the hall, is a crowd of frightened debutantes, huddled close together.

A witch pair in yellow robes rush forward, moving Nightly and me to one side, and demanding to know what happened.

'A-a creature of smoke, with antlers and claws,' I stutter and point at the arm on the floor, as the room around me buzzes with worry. The witches move towards the arm, midnight-blue blood pooling on the floor. It is starting to fade, the flesh turning into smoke and twisting up into the air and away.

'What in the name of magic was that?' one of the witches surrounding the door says, and the witches in yellow exchange a look but say nothing.

'Aurelia! Aurelia, you're bleeding,' Constance cries as she

and Vaughn rush up the stairs towards me. I place a hand up to my upper arm and when I pull it away it is covered in blood.

One of the yellow witches starts to give instructions while the other examines the door, and even though my and Nightly's magic has sealed it shut, I watch as the red-clad witches of the Coven of Accord set up additional seals and wards of protections.

My head spins and I feel my magic quivering inside me as the danger of what just happened hits me. That was no trial, that was not an illusion of magic. That wood, those whispers, that creature, they were real, and now they know that I am too. I start to cry, big uncontrollable sobs, and the crowd of witches begins to whisper. I cover my ears with my hands at the memory of the whispers in the trees, then I close my eyes tight. I feel overwhelmed.

Safe hands cover mine and I hear Nightly's muffled voice. 'It's all right, Aurelia, you're safe. I'm here, I'm not going to let anything happen to you.'

I open my eyes. He's stooped so that his eyes are level with mine and I throw my arms around his neck.

He holds me close as my blood seeps into the dark grey of his coat, turning it black.

The witches in yellow try to usher me away, but I hold on to Nightly with one hand, and clutch Constance with the other.

'We're not leaving her,' Constance says. 'If you want to take her somewhere then we're all coming.'

The witches relent and lead the four of us away.

Thirty

'You were gone for six hours, Aurelia,' Vaughn tells me after the healers have stopped my bleeding, after the witches from the Coven of Curiosity have stopped interrogating me. I told them everything that happened to me from the moment that I stepped into the Arcade. I don't name the runes around the black-flame door, but I say that they were strange, with a pointed look at Nightly. Now just the four of us sit in a side room of the palace, its opulence in stark contrast to the wood beyond the black-flame door.

'Six hours . . . But it felt like six minutes,' I say, looking from Vaughn to Constance in disbelief.

Nightly is pacing up and down in front of me, and I know it's because he is worried, because he is trying to understand everything.

All the other debutante witches had entered their doors

and faced a trial by fire that resonated with their magic and their essence. Constance's trial involved her having to get through her house while each member of her family tried to detain her or lead her astray, making her feel guilty and ashamed for wanting to leave. She is uncomfortable as she tells me, and I know that letting her family down is one of the worst things in the world for Constance to face.

During the trial, a tiny red piece of string had formed, looping around her wrist and wandlet. This string is the reward that each witch receives for passing the trial, and when I look down, I see one twisting around my own wandlet.

Each of the witches, Constance included, had exited their trial through the same door that they had entered by. The door *I* had burst through had been a normal door until I had breached it with my magic. Everyone in the hall of Carlton Palace had heard the pounding on it, the booming that my magic had made as I had tried to open the door in the henge.

'I knew it was you. The moment I heard the knocking. I could feel it,' Nightly says, holding his hands over his chest. I remember what Russo and Platz said about my connection with them and wonder if Nightly is able to do the same.

The door opens and Mother and Frances rush over to me, scoop me into their embrace, then check me over. I forget I am angry with them both and hold them tightly. My wounds are healed, my clothes repaired, my hair almost smooth again. But inside, I still can't stop my magic from quivering.

'Mother . . .' My voice breaks.

'Aurelia, there is no time for you to tell us all that has happened, though we have heard most of it from the witches here.' I look at Mother quizzically. 'Nightly's mother and her tether are here too.' I see out of the corner of my eye that Nightly suddenly grows very still.

Frances gives my arm a little squeeze. 'They are here in an official capacity, as investigators for the Coven of Mysteries. They need to speak with you alone.' Her expression is solemn. 'When they speak to you, it is important that you tell them *only* the truth. They will know otherwise.'

There is something in her voice that makes me shudder. I'm sure that Mother and Frances' rivalry with Demelza runs deeper than Heston Nightly's curse.

'We will be right outside. If you feel uncomfortable at any point, just call out for us.'

'I'll stay with her,' Nightly says. 'At least until my mother insists that I leave.'

Mother looks over at Nightly and gives him a look far softer than any I would expect. She nods in agreement. 'Vaughn, I need you to make sure that Ms Prior gets home safely. The carriages have been called and the other debutantes have all left.'

Constance hugs me tight. 'I'll be over first thing,' she whispers. Vaughn holds me close, and I squeeze him back. The four of them leave the room and, as they do, Nightly comes and stands next to me, lacing his fingers with mine.

'Wycherley, you promised to let me know if you were going

to do anything dangerous,' he says, and I feel the worry in his voice ripple through me as I look up at him. I can't speak. I can't tell him how when I was breaking through that door, I thought of him, of being with him, of getting to him.

'We've already broken the no-magic rule . . . so I think it's fine for us to break the no-kissing rule too,' he says. My heart skips a few beats, and I reach my hands up into his hair and pull his lips to mine. I kiss him like he is air.

'You need to stop finding ways to leave me,' he whispers as he pulls away from me enough to try and smooth my hair down. I feel my heartstrings pull tight because I am not leaving him, but he can never fully have me nor I him.

I let go of Nightly and turn sharply towards the door as I hear it open.

Just like at the Prior-Okore ball all those months ago, it is Demelza who commands the gravity in the room. I'm fixated on her as she strides towards us, her blue cloak so dark it's almost black, sweeping out to reveal a beautiful black dress covered in shimmering blue crystals. She is assessing every inch of me. It is not till she stops in front of us that I turn my gaze to her tether, Geoffrey Knott, and I do a double take. Because I have seen him before . . . leaving the bookshop with Kit Thorne and Jonathan. My mind starts racing. Is the Coven of Mysteries involved in giving Jonathan and Kit back their magic? Does Demelza know? Has she kept this from her own daughter? Questions fill my brain, and I feel muddled and sick when I think of Evelyn.

'Ms Wycherley,' Demelza says curtly. 'Leave us, Jules. There is a carriage waiting to take you home.'

'I'm not leaving Aurelia,' he replies firmly.

'Yes, you are.' Her face is stony. 'We need to speak to her, but we promise that is all. If you must, you can wait outside until we are done and we can go home together.'

Geoffrey gestures towards the door, reinforcing the cue for Nightly to leave.

I look up at him. 'I'll be fine. Your mother will take good care of me, and besides, they need to know what happened. It's important for the magic and the kingdom.' I know that those are the two things that Demelza holds above all others, even her children and their happiness.

Nightly nods hesitantly, then whispers, 'Don't forget that you are to tell me if you are about to do anything dangerous. I'll be right outside.'

A small, sorry smile dances over my lips as I watch him leave. He turns and our eyes lock just before he slips through the door, then closes it with a click.

The mood in the room immediately shifts. It's tense and quiet. Demelza tells me to sit, the two of them remain standing in front of me.

'We hear that you have had an eventful night, Ms Wycherley. You incapacitated a whole coven of witches when you conjured that black-flame door – a door that, by the way, cannot be conjured away, it would seem. In fact, that rose bush that you and Jules are so fond of has become quite protective of the door. When I visited it earlier with a full battalion of elite witches, the roses grew over it and started spitting thorns at us.'

I try to keep my face neutral as I imagine the scene in my head.

'Tell us what happened when you stepped through the door,' Geoffrey says as he sits on a chair in front of me. Demelza takes a chair to the side of us and reaches for my wrist. I don't resist as she pushes her magic into me, but I don't send my magic into her. His voice is smooth like satin and I instantly feel safe; I want to tell them everything, but my wandlet stirs, warning me to be on my guard.

'I'm sure that you have heard it all from the other witches.'

'We have, but we want to hear it from you, and we may ask questions to help you unlock any details that you might have unwittingly omitted . . . things that, at the time, might not have appeared important.'

So I tell the story again, and as I do, Geoffrey asks me questions. 'What did it smell like?', 'How many different voices whispered to you?', 'What type of stone was the henge formed of?'

I speak as truthfully as I can, and the whole time Demelza is quiet, but she is not subtle in what she is doing. I can feel her magic probing into my mind, into my magic. I have never experienced anything like this before but I have read about it. It is a very rare and particular ability but she is not skilled at it; I can feel every push she makes into my mind, like a shout or a disruptive thought, trying to pull my attention in a certain direction. But it is easy to distract her and I only let her see the things that I want her to see. I fill my mind with Jules and I can feel her agitation as she pushes harder.

As soon as I have answered all of the questions I probe back. I send my magic along the invisible connection that Demelza has made to my head and I can see everything that is at the forefront of *her* mind. It is easy to slip into her thoughts, in a split second I absorb it all. I see Cora on the floor, dead, the rune on her wand wrist; the scene is in vivid colour and detail. Poor Cora, she was so young. Demelza has all of the dead witches connected together in her mind, so I see another dead witch, another, then another, desensitizing me to the horrors of each death. I take in the details, analysing each one, detached . . . until there is my father.

All of the emotions of finding him that morning hit me in a flash and flow through me, threatening to pull me back into myself and Demelza with me, but I don't want her to see me like that. I turn away from those thoughts, and find her thoughts of Nightly and Evelyn. Nightly is arguing with his mother as she is insisting that Evelyn must leave. 'Her magic is all but gone, she is not a true witch, not a real Nightly any more,' Demelza is saying. And then she is challenging Jules, 'To maintain this family's good name, you *must* tether as we have arranged . . .'

Just then, Demelza pushes me forcefully from her mind. She has finally been able to rid herself of my intrusion. I gasp as I come back to myself, reeling from what I've seen, and she slumps in the chair.

Geoffrey stands and I think that he is going to her, but instead he doubles over and throws up.

'Help! We need a healer!' I call.

'What did you do?' Geoffrey hisses from the floor, as the door opens and Mother, Frances and Jules enter the room.

'She connected to my magic,' I tell Geoffrey. 'This is what happens. And just like the coven that was affected when Russo and Platz linked to me through their tertiary magic, when Demelza used secondary magic, you were connected to me too.'

'She's right,' Nightly says, giving me a knowing look from the door. 'It will pass. Your head will feel like it's cracking open, and your stomach like you're on the roughest of seas, but it will pass.' Nightly tenderly helps his mother to sit up straight. As she regains her senses, she shakes him from her and sits up tall, closing her eyes and holding a hand to the bridge of her nose.

Geoffrey is still on the floor, looking at me in awe. 'When you pushed your magic forth, I've never felt anything so powerful.' He breathes deeply.

Demelza is in full possession of herself when she hisses, 'I warned you all that something like this would happen.'

Mother and Frances are instantly on guard and I feel as if I should be too.

'There is a reason why no cursed Wycherley has ever been

allowed to partake in the Season, to enter into the Sabbats and find a match,' Demelza goes on. 'She took out a full coven of advanced witches, she just corrupted Geoffrey and me with her curse and she has opened a door to magic knows where. She's *dangerous*.'

'I'm not,' I say, at the same time as Nightly says, 'Honestly, Mother.' And Frances adds, 'She is not the dangerous one in this room.'

Mother moves forward. 'Demelza, I stand by what I said to the Royal Magical Council before Mabon. Aurelia's magic is cursed; we know that she will never get to become the witch that she could have been. In another three years or so, her magic will leave her. As a mother you can understand how I wanted my child to experience all that she can, before it is taken from her.'

'And that time is now. If she were anybody else's daughter, she would never have been given this chance; she would never have been presented, never have entered her debutante year, never have been allowed to grow such dangerous magic.'

Nightly shakes his head and gives my hand a squeeze. 'Mother, Aurelia is not dangerous. She is magnificent.'

'Don't be a fool, Jules. She has no doubt bewitched you, convinced you to share your magic with her by devious implementation of her curse.'

'Careful, Demelza. It sounds like you are accusing my daughter of malevolence.' Mother's voice is icy cold and Demelza stands with only a slight wobble.

'Aurelia Wycherley, I will petition the council and the Crown to remove your debutante status, to withdraw all privileges that this brings and to remove you from magical society at the earliest convenience. After all that has happened today, I am sure that they will realize that this action is necessary.'

'Mother,' Jules starts, but Demelza Nightly raises a hand, casting a spell on her son. She freezes Nightly in place, and the look on his face is a mixture of embarrassment, rage and fear. I make to move towards him. 'You are never to go near my son again,' she tells me. 'Your magic, Ms Wycherley, should be allowed to drift away untested, untrained, just like all the other cursed witches in your family.' Demelza releases her hand and Jules is freed. He stumbles forward, taking deep breaths. I want to hex Demelza Nightly as she makes for the door, Geoffrey just behind her, gesturing for Jules to follow, but my mother reaches out an arm to halt me.

'I won't let her do this to you. I'll make her change her mind,' Nightly tells me. Then he follows her from the room.

I already know that he will fail, even before Mother tells me that she and Frances will mount a defence for the council, but that I should prepare for the worst.

Thirty-one

aughn pulls me into a tight embrace. 'The way Demelza Nightly was looking at you, I thought she was going to tie you to a stake.'

'Not funny, Vaughn,' Mother says.

Constance did not go home, she is in the parlour too and holds me close.

'I wasn't joking, and I wouldn't put it past her,' Vaughn replies, his expression grave.

'Then you don't know the first thing about Demelza Nightly. She is a stickler for the rules and traditions of magic,' Mother says.

I tell Constance, Vaughn, Mother and Frances everything that happened when I was inside the room alone with Demelza and Geoffrey. I only leave out the part about Demelza forcing Jules to tether . . . I can't bear to think of it just now.

'She did *what?*' Mother says when I explain how Demelza

tried to rifle through my memories.

'She is within her rights; it was part of an official investigation by the Coven of Mysteries,' Frances counters.

'What will happen at this council meeting?' Constance asks. 'Will we be able to tell them that Demelza Nightly is wrong about Aurelia and her magic?'

Mother shakes her head. 'The hearing will take place in a closed court. The Princess Regent will be called – she was at the original hearing that decided Aurelia was allowed to partake in the Season.'

'You should have told me about that. About how opposed everyone was to me entering the Season,' I say, feeling angry, upset and so very tired.

'I wanted you to enjoy your magic while you could. I didn't tell you for your own good.'

'Just like you didn't tell us that Father was murdered by the New Dawn.' It slips from my lips before I can stop it, and once it is out, I instantly feel regret. Vaughn doesn't deserve to hear it like this.

'What?' Vaughn says.

'How do you know about that?' Mother asks, pain and shock etched across her face.

'I overheard you talking to Emery and Jackson about Cora Stewart.' I hold my mother's eye. I think she might deny it, tell me that I've got it wrong. I'm not expecting her to break down. Frances wraps her in her arms and holds her while she sobs, and again, I feel terrible.

'Mother . . .'

'No, you're right, I did lie to you. To you both. I didn't want you to know the truth, and as the New Dawn murdered more witches, I didn't want you to know that it had begun with your father.'

'More murders?' Vaughn's voice is distant. Constance is next to him, her hand in his. 'Father was killed by the New Dawn here in our house?'

'We can't be sure of that,' Frances says.

'All the evidence points towards them. It's the one thing that Demelza Nightly and I agree on.' Mother wipes her tears, giving us a wry smile.

'You should have told us!' Vaughn says. 'Maybe not when it happened, but before now.'

'Yes, we probably should have,' Frances admits, 'but as time went on and more witches died, we weren't sure how to tell you.'

'You said there have been more murders. How many have there been?' Vaughn asks.

'Eleven,' Mother says. 'But you are not to let anyone know. That is top-clearance information.' She gives Constance a stern look as well as Vaughn and myself, but I know that we won't say a word to anyone. Well . . . except to Nightly, that is.

'You mean to tell me that there is no Magimancer out there killing witches? Or, rather, The New Dawn is the Magimancer and they have killed a whole coven's worth of witches, and another left behind, magicless?' Vaughn is shaking his head.

Except it's not a coven, I think. And it isn't – at least not in the way they thought of it in the old days of magic, when they used the runes that are being left on the bodies, and when they didn't need to tether to keep their magic. A coven in the old days of magic was thirteen, and at least two of the witches left behind still have magic.

It is all connected, but I can't see how. The answer to tethering, the old magic, the Golowhe runes, the dead witches – all of it. In that moment I think about telling my mother and Frances all that Nightly and I have found out but I still can't make it all fit, and Mother looks worn out – not just with the dead witches, but with me, my magic, my thoughtless exposure of my father's murder – and I can't burden her any more.

'It's been a long day, let us talk about all of this properly in the morning,' Mother says. 'The council will meet early. You won't be allowed to attend, but I will let you know what they decide.'

'Mother, we all know what they will decide – my magic is cursed.'

When I get to my room, I scribble a letter to Nightly.

Jules,
When I was trapped in that place and trying to get out. I thought of you – of never seeing you again, of never feeling

your magic running through mine, of never feeling your lips on my own.

I am certain that in the morning, the Royal Magical Council will decide that I am not fit to be a witch. No more magic. It will break me and leave me hollow.

I know this is a lot to ask, but is there any chance that although there will be no more magic, can there still be something between us?

Go off and find yourself a tether, and magic for the both of us, but keep the kissing only for me, and I will fill my hollow self up with your caresses.

Thank you for pulling me from the door, thank you for accepting my bribery and thank you for extorting my heart from me.

I love you, Jules Nightly.

Aurelia

I fold and seal the letter, and think about how to get it to him.

Ankoth floats towards me and nudges me gently. It has taken to sleeping on the end of my bed when I am not in the room, coming to greet me when I enter, and every now and again it will bang on the window wanting to be let out.

'Will you take this to Jules for me?' I ask.

If the broom had a tail it would be wagging as I tie the letter to it, then open the window and it slips out into the night.

I wake to the sound of Ankoth tapping on the window. The early morning air is cold as the broom drifts back into the room and I pull the window shut after it. A note is tied to the handle.

Aurelia,

I will only ever be yours, for as long as my heart beats, my love, my kisses, and if I have any say in it, my magic too — it is all for you.

Forever yours, if you please,

Jules

It is the best start to the day that I could have imagined. But it is not the only letter that I receive that morning. Mother holds one out to me as I rush to meet her at the door on her return from the council meeting.

'What's this?' I ask, tentatively taking it from her.

'It's your last invitation.' Mother says. She seems pleased, but sad at the same time.

HER MAJESTY THE PRINCESS REGENT,
GEORGIANNA,
AND THE ROYAL MAGICAL COUNCIL
REQUEST THE PRESENCE OF

Ms Aurelia Wycherley

AT THE OSTARA FASTENING CEREMONY

ON MONDAY THE 21ST MARCH 1814,
AT CARLTON PALACE.

THE PLEDGE BEGINS AT NOON, SHARP.

THOSE WITCHES INTENDING TO TETHER THEMSELVES
AT BELTANE WILL PLEDGE THEMSELVES BY TYING
THE FIRST KNOT AND BINDING THEIR INTENT.

FOR THE KINGDOM AND THE MAGIC.

'I don't understand. I was sure that they would banish me from the Season,' I say.

'It was an eventful meeting,' Frances replies with the raise of her eyebrow.

'Demelza Nightly presented her evidence, then each of the council pairs asked questions about your magic. It would seem that Russo and Platz have not only been keeping reports on you, but that they have been reporting to their council representatives for the Coven of Knowing. They are very highly regarded members of the Royal Magical Council and they feel that your magic warrants further exploration.

'Demelza objected, of course. But it was decided that if you and your curse could be understood, it may be of great benefit to the Crown, the nation and the future of magic.'

'She couldn't argue with that,' Frances adds with a small smile.

'The Coven of Justice also reminded the council that all witches who are presented at Mabon, and who are still alive at Ostara, are bound by the traditions of the Season to pay their thanks and respects to the Crown and the magic at the Ostara Pledge Day.

'It was agreed that you will see this Season out. But before you get too excited –' Mother pauses, looking at Frances – 'this will be your *only* Season, and for the rest of it, you are not to mix with any other witches unless it is at the Arcade and under the supervision of Platz and Russo.'

I panic.

'No library?' I ask, thinking of Nightly and our investigation.

'No library, no Season Gardens, no anything but the Arcade and only when you are requested to be there.'

My mouth runs dry and my mind reels.

How will Jules and I be able to finish what we started now?

'What about Vaughn? They can't stop me from mixing with him.'

'Vaughn is an exception, as are any tethered witches.'

'What about Constance? Nightly?'

Mother shakes her head. 'And they are not allowed to see you. If they do, there will be consequences. They will be notified today of the court's ruling and told to keep away.'

I don't like the way that Mother says 'consequences', but I know that no notification is going to stop Constance or Nightly, I'm sure of it. As if she can read my thoughts Mother adds, 'Emery and Jackson will be stationed outside. You are not to leave the house alone for the next six weeks or so, not until Ostara.'

My heart is heavy. But it is pointless trying to argue with her, with the Royal Magical Council, with any of them.

'Is your brother here?' Mother asks. I shake my head as I put the letter away, already trying to find holes in the sanctions that have been placed on me.

'I want to speak to the two of you about your father.' My attention is suddenly entirely on my mother. 'Yesterday there was so much going on – I didn't get a chance to properly explain. Let's talk now. I'll do the same with Vaughn when he's back.'

Frances leaves the room and Mother bids me sit with her. She takes my hand. 'Your father was bright, vibrant and brilliant. His mind was amazing: there wasn't a problem that he couldn't work out given enough time and access to a good library. You remind me so much of him.

'Before he died, he was working on a project that he and Jonathan were excited about. From the moment I'd met him, he'd been interested in "the great problem" as he called it: why was magic disappearing from the world? Why did we need to tether it to keep it, when that had never been required before?'

I try to keep my face neutral, but my heart is beating fast and my thoughts are racing, my father was researching the same thing that Nightly and I are looking for. I listen intently to see if I can glean any new information that might help me in the investigation.

'He told me that he had found something important to do with wild magic. He and Jonathan travelled all over the country tracking down pockets of it, trying to find the old tracks of magic – ley lines. So many of the old henges that once marked them were destroyed during the burning times just before the Great Witch War. I know that, given time, he would have discovered both the reasons for and solutions to the problem.

'When he was murdered, I thought for the longest time that it was because of his knowledge. But as more witches perished, I realized that the murders were just acts of violence against witches.

'I didn't want you and Vaughn to be scared of the world, in or outside our magical wards. I didn't want you to know that your father had died at the hands of another. I didn't tell you because I wanted to protect you, and then as time went on and more and more witches died, it got too hard to tell you the truth, not least because it is the responsibility of the Coven of Justice to find who is doing this and stop them, and I can't. I know deep in my magic that this is the work of the New Dawn, it has to be, but I have yet to find any concrete evidence.'

'Maybe it's not them, maybe it is murder by magical means?' I say slowly, thinking of the Golowhe runes, deciding if I should tell my mother everything, wondering how she will react if she knows all of the things I have done. I suddenly feel scared as I remember Demelza using her magic to hold Jules in place and punish him. My mother would never do anything like that, even if instructed to do so by the rest of the coven council, by the crown; it would break her.

'I just can't see another witch ever murdering their magical kin in this way,' she says and I know she believes that deeply.

I lean forward and hug her. 'I'm sorry I was so rash last night. We all have secrets, and we often keep them because we don't want to hurt those around us. Thank you for telling me now, I know that was not easy for you.' I hug her closer. Now that I am the one keeping secrets, I know how awful she feels.

Sudden shouting outside has Mother reaching for her wandlet. I put a hand on her arm. 'It's Constance. I think you might have a little more explaining to do.' She leaves me in the parlour as she goes to speak with my best friend.

When I get to bed that evening, I try to push aside the disappointment that Constance was the only one who had fought to see me. I kept expecting Nightly to do the same but he hadn't tried to visit me. Then again, I haven't tried to visit him either – yet.

Thirty-two

Another untethered witch falls to the floor of the London Arcade, unconscious. A healer rushes to assist, checking them over before levitating them off to a side room to recover. In the past six weeks, the healers have become skilled at remedying my cursed magic, limiting the side effects – no one falls into a coma now, which is a good thing. To be honest, I have become numb to seeing each of the witches fall.

'Extraordinary,' Russo says as he walks around the floating orb of metal that is in the middle of the room. While we were creating secondary magic, Jade Drew and I had concentrated on pulling non-magnetic metals together. Russo and Platz had hidden them around the Arcade, and we used our magic to seek them out. Drew's magic was thick and sticky like toffee, I had worked hard to manipulate it, to combine it with mine and make it as effective as possible. Once the metallic mass had been created, we set about charging it, making it magnetic. As a test, Platz pulls out an iron pin from his cloak and the moment his fingers release it, it flies to the ball.

I look over at Drew as she is being hovered away by the green-clad witches. She had been delighted as her magic mixed with mine, the initial fear abating as the thrill of weaving the complex spell took over. Her magic had felt naïve, but I coaxed the best out of it. I have become quite adept at tuning in to all sorts of magic, since Russo and Platz began their relentless investigation of mine.

My days have become nothing but tests. My magic has expanded exponentially but my heart has shrunk. I miss the company of witches, even their scorn. I miss being able to do the things that I want. I miss Constance and our smiles together. And Nightly . . . I miss everything about Nightly.

When not in the Arcade I feel physically drained. I'm still trying to carry on my and Nightly's investigation into tethering, following some of the leads that Mother mentioned that my father had been studying. I have been learning about ley lines, and henges and the old magic from our family library. Every evening, I write to Nightly, and Ankoth eagerly waits by the window to deliver my messages, but nothing returns with him in the morning. I don't know if they are being seized by Demelza or the Royal Magical Council as part of the conditions of me being able to see out the Season, but the lack of communication from him is like an ache that is ever present – even when I am fully occupied in the Arcade, there is a part of me that is pining for Jules Nightly.

Every untethered witch was sent a royal decree letting them know that Mr Platz and Mr Russo would call on them at some point, and that they were bound by their oath to the Crown to use their magic to assist them. Before joining me in the Arcade, each witch then pledges not to tell another soul what they are about to do.

Without the pledge, the witches of the ton would talk, and none of them would come if they knew that they were going to perform secondary magic with me. I keep hoping that the next witch will be Nightly – at this point, I would gladly make him throw up if it meant that we got to spend a few moments together.

'I'm going to need another one to undo it,' I say, pointing at the metal ball. But two apprentice witches roll out a large crate and begin to encourage the ball into it.

'The Coven of Curiosity need to study this,' Platz says.

'Will I get to turn it into gold next week?' I ask, only half joking. I am pretty sure that alchemy is not far from the Coven of Curiosity's mind. I can tell from the experiments they are making me do that each of the covens is keen to see how my magic can be of advantage to them. I have been testing the limits of my magic, and we have yet to find them, but I am sure they are determined to do so in the few days before Ostara comes along.

I arrived at the Arcade in the darkness of winter dawn and

have spent the day within its walls, it is now early evening and, so far, six of my fellow debutantes have been rendered unconscious or left in various degrees of sickness. When I see one of them succumb to the effects of my magic, I think maybe it is for the best that I will not be permitted to use it after the next Sabbat. But when I perform magic I feel so connected to everything that I never want it to end.

'Last one for the night,' Platz says, and I look up to see Sebastian Crenshaw. I fold my arms over my chest and shake my head.

'No. I will perform magic with anyone but him,' I say.

'You don't have a choice, Ms Wycherley. You took an oath at Mabon, and you are bound to use your magic in whatever way the Crown decides.'

'What is going to happen to me if I refuse? I'm already cursed,' I say.

'There are worse things than curses . . . the penalty for treason, for example.' He is right – the penalty for treason, for a witch, is burning at the stake.

'Well, I don't want to perform magic with her either. I'll die if I do, I know it.' Sebastian is looking at me as if I'm a piece of dirt on his overly polished shoes.

'Mr Crenshaw, only one witch has ever died in this Arcade, and that was not at the hands of magic,' Platz says. 'Now, Ms Wycherley, Mr Crenshaw, let's just get this over with, shall we.'

I glare at Sebastian.

'You and Nightly, are you still . . . close?' Sebastian asks, a smirk on his face, and my mouth feels dry, as I think of the unanswered letters.

I turn away from Sebastian, not answering his question. The apprentice witches wheel out a long, thin wooden chest. I tune my magic in to it, finding out its secrets. It is made from the heartwood of an oak, and I can feel that the tree was alive during the First Age of Magic, that it was harvested and worked into shape by a witch for a king. The box has a large metal lock on the front, and inside the magic of many, many witches buzzing.

My skills have dramatically increased over the short time that Platz and Russo have been drilling me, and I can feel every single spell that is on the chest.

'Do you know the sequence for unlocking?' I ask Sebastian. He nods. 'How about unbinding?'

'Isn't it the same thing?' he asks.

'No, it's not.' I run through the sequence with him and get him to repeat it a few times until he's memorized it. 'Undoing?' I ask. And again we go through the sequence. Russo watches me instructing Sebastian. Platz takes notes.

'Any other charms or enchantments on there, Ms Wycherley?' he asks.

I concentrate on the chest. 'I can feel sixteen individual spells on the chest. They are nestled one inside the other, like a Russian doll. The two spells at the centre are the strongest; I can feel a binding made by a full coven of witches as well as a locking. All the other spells were made by secondary magic, tethered pairs; different pairs for different spells, some of them were part of the two covens that cast the centre spells – three of the pairs to be exact. And there is something in the box . . . something familiar that I can't quite grasp yet, but I'm sure I will as we remove the other magic.'

Platz makes more notes, and I hold out my hand to Sebastian who is gawking at me like he can't believe what he's hearing.

'Follow my lead, don't break the connection till I tell you,' I say to him. I've been through this enough times now to know the effects of the curse and a small part of me, that I don't want to give voice to, is looking forward to Crenshaw being sick.

'When you are ready, Mr Crenshaw,' Russo says.

Tentatively, Sebastian places his hand in mine and I send my magic into him before he can pull his hand away. He gasps. I don't face him; I don't want to see his eyes widen when he realizes how much magic he has missed out on by rejecting me.

'Unlocking,' I say, and we run through the movements. I modify my actions to keep in time with him. I've found that the magic works best when I am in sync with the witches I am working with, when I move with them at their pace. Only Nightly has ever matched my moves perfectly. I almost lose my grip on the spell as I think of him.

'Unbinding,' I call, and we move again. Each time one of the spells is undone, I call out the next one and we continue. I can feel Sebastian's magic tiring as we reach the last few spells.

'Step it up, Crenshaw, those last two are going to be tough

353

and I can't do it all on my own,' I say as he stumbles through the sequence.

Finally, we get to the two coven spells. I don't think we can break them, not like this. Instinctively I kick off my shoes and pull off my stockings, while keeping hold of Sebastian's hand. I tell him to do the same but he refuses. 'Fine, it's your headache,' I tell him and I push the soles of my feet on to the hard stone of the Arcade. I remember reading in one of the books I have been studying that the Arcade was built on a ley line, and I begin to call it to me as Sebastian and I perform the unbinding. Now it is my turn to gasp as I feel a rush of wild magic move through me. Again and again, we perform the sequence.

'Aurelia, I need to stop,' Sebastian says.

'You should have taken your shoes off,' I tell him. 'One more round – I almost have it.' I push a little of the wild magic from the ley line into him and Sebastian rallies as the magical bindings fall away. Just the final coven lock is left.

'I really can't do this any more, Aurelia.' He goes to pull his hand away, but I hold his fingers tighter. 'One try and then you can quit,' I tell him, as I walk towards the chest, tugging him along behind me, to examine the metal lock. *If only I had a magical key*, I think.

There is something in the chest that is calling to me, to my magic, something that I want and won't stop until I have it. My eyes run over the wood and the lock and I see a crest – it is the crest of the Royal Magical Council.

'Crenshaw, do you have a key on your person?' I ask,

getting a sudden burst of inspiration.

'Yes, but not to that,' he says, gesturing to the chest.

'Give it to me.' I hold out my hand. I've learnt to listen to my intuition – to the small nudges that my magic gives me – and right now, with the wild magic running through me, all I can see in my mind is the key that Nightly and I retrieved from the lost quarter at Neoards.

Crenshaw pulls a key from his inside pocket and holds it out to me. I take ahold of it, examining it.

'Hold on to it too,' I tell him, and I keep hold of the stem as he holds the bow. I can feel the key biting into my palm, shifting as I direct my magic and alter its shape.

'Did you know, Crenshaw, that the part of the key that you insert into the lock is called a "bit", and that the bit is made of wards, just like protective magic is?' I say this with a smile, then I remove my hand and take the key from Crenshaw. I notice that the bow has altered, it now has one of the Golowhe runes on it. Delivra: release. I place the key smoothly in the lock and turn it widdershins. The magic completely falls away as the lock releases.

'We're done,' I say, and the two witches wearing the light green of healing rush forward. I let go of Crenshaw's hand and the witches catch him with their magic, lowering him to the floor.

'Very impressive, Ms Wycherley. What prompted you to use the key?' Russo asks. 'I have never seen that . . . technique used before.'

'I think I remember it from a book my father used to read to me. A story about a witch from the First Age of Magic who used a magical key to unlock a door to a magical realm. No doubt a childish witch tale, but as you have been saying, I need to follow my intuition.'

'It was an inspired approach, and one that evidently required little input from Mr Crenshaw.' Russo raises an eyebrow.

'The key was a risk, a last chance,' I confess. 'I don't think he would have made it through another unlocking, especially not a coven spell. To give him his due, he did well to get this far − but he will pay for it in the morning.'

I roll my neck, massaging out my shoulders with my hands, the wild magic has left me now and I feel weary to my bones.

'I'm tired. May I go home now?' I ask.

'Of course,' Russo says, like I am free to leave any time. 'But . . . don't you want to see what's in the chest?' he asks.

'No,' I say as I turn and walk towards the exit, past my and Nightly's rose bush. I reach out a finger and brush the petals as I pass. I know exactly what is in the chest. Excalibur: the sword that the Princess Regent uses at Mabon to secure the Oath of Obedience. The buzz of magic that I felt was from the blood of all the witches contained in the diamond in the hilt. That strange possessive call from the metal of the sword has me on edge and I add it to the many things that I will need to tell Nightly about. If I ever get to see him again.

Thirty-three

My world feels as if it has narrowed. The feeling of expansion that I gained on Mabon has been replaced, restricted to the daily monotony of being and not living. I sleep in late when I can – there is no point in rising early – and my family are being so gentle with me as I deal with my disappointments. When I am not exhausted, I attend to my and Nightly's quest, learning all I can. My room is littered with books from our family library.

I stand at the window waiting for Ankoth to return empty-handed. In my hand is the key from Neoards, I rub my thumb over the entwined N and W and think of nothing but Nightly.

Mother and Frances leave the house early, Emery and Jackson talking to them as they do. Mother looks up at my window and waves but I do not move.

Vaughn is next to leave; he makes his way across Hemlock Square to the Prior-Okore house. I miss Constance so much, and I miss Vaughn. The way he is acting towards me is reminiscent of the early days when I first received my cursed magic, being so careful, like the slightest thing will break me. The way I am keeping him distant is just the same too.

I watch as Constance opens the door to Vaughn and throws her arms around him. She steals a look around the square then kisses him, and I smile for them. I am sure that if I was not currently being held hostage by the Royal Magical Council that Vaughn and Constance would have announced their intentions towards one another. Two days till Ostara, and every day for the past fortnight the papers have been full of tethering intention announcements.

With the days running out on my magic as well as my happiness, Platz and Russo have been conducting their research with greater determination, leaving me feeling depleted each evening. I gladly meet the oblivion of sleep each night and wake each morning to the promise of the exhilarating feeling of secondary magic, which courses through me for a few blissful hours.

This morning I am feeling hopeful, and with the key from Neoards in hand, I go downstairs, pausing to pluck one of my and Nightly's roses from the vase. They are all still alive despite being picked many months ago.

As I descend the steps to my family arcade, I recall the last spell I performed with Sebastian last night. The idea of it lit a fire in me as I was travelling home and I decided to try it on the locked door of my father's spellorium.

The weeks of intense testing of my magic have made it strong. Platz and Russo have taught me magic far beyond the knowledge of any other debutante, and I know I will be glad of it if I can put it into action now.

I reach out and feel the magic on the door. A single, powerful spell, full of old magic, similar to that Nightly and I felt in the henge at Neoards. But there is something else here . . . a tinge around the edges. Darker, malevolent magic has been woven into this spell; it reminds me of the woods beyond the black-flame door and the creature within it. I realize that this is what I felt last night, on Excalibur. The sword was embedded with a magic that wanted to dominate and control, magic that's out of balance with the benevolent, wild magic that I had pulled from the ley line, and in opposition to the magic that I always seek to put out into the world. I wonder who placed this spell – was it my father? Or was it the witch that killed him?

I have the shape of the magic, a feel for it. It's deeper and more binding than coven magic, but I'm counting on the greatest magic of all to cast this spell.

I grab some chalk and quickly draw a circle to ground me. Around the edge I write the thirteen Golowhe runes. I've come to know them well since Yule, and have used each of them in my spell casting both here and in the Arcade – not that Platz and Russo have noticed, I slip the runes into my spell work and they fit perfectly, acting as a conduit for my magic and helping it to move more smoothly out into the

359

world. Nightly said that the runes were calling to me, but I think maybe there is something in my magic that calls to them. When I was beyond the black-flame door, the creatures said I had the old magic in me. This stands to reason – after all, Heston called on old magic to curse Mathilde.

Once done, I cover the chalk circle with salt; that malevolent streak on the door worries me.

I pick up the rose and hold it in one hand, the key from Neoards in the other. Concentrating on them both I begin to move through the opening sequence: my magic is latched on to the deep magic permeating through the door, my heart is latched on to Nightly and how I feel about him. The way he looks at me when he thinks I'm not looking. The way he makes my pulse race every time I see him. The way his lips feel on mine. His magic – how when it floods into me, it is always in perfect rhythm with mine.

My wand hand with the key in it grows hot as my other hand grows cold. The rose is withering, all the colour draining out of it and into me, all the magic that was both mine and Nightly's filling me in the same way that I feel when his hand is in mine and he pushes his magic into me. It dances through me in exquisite joy, and I miss him so much. I try not to be angry and disappointed with him and push those thoughts from my magic. Instead I think of all the ways I will kiss him when we are finally reunited.

When the spell is done, I let go of the rose. All the love and magic have been drained out of it, its petals grey. I thought the roses would last forever, and a pang of sadness fills me.

The key is warm, and the Anter rune for opening is now on the bow. I have altered the wards to match the magic on the door.

I place it in the lock, and turn it widdershins. The magic retreats and I push the door open.

My black witch-flame is in my hand instantly and I send out orbs from it to light the space. I was expecting the Spellorium to be covered in cobwebs and dust, but it looks exactly the way I always remember it: an organized mess of books and papers.

It's a small space, but it feels more daunting than the Royal Library of Magic. I'm not sure how I'm going to find what I'm looking for, or even if I know what that is.

On my father's desk is his open grimoire. His writing is a scrawling mess, and, with a lump in my throat, I read the last things he wrote in his book.

The ley holds the key, the henges of old need to be rebuilt.

Jonathan has made a breakthrough with the strange runes we found at the hidden henge ruin in Kernow. He wants to show me an exciting discovery he has made, he seems to think that it links to the work on ley *lines we have previously done together. I am glad we are speaking once again, and I hope that this return to our old work means that he has the nonsense of the past year out of his system. I have not felt that streak of malevolence that ran through our magic like a wedge since our altercation, so I hope he is on the right side of magic now. I still can't quite grasp how the tale of the untethered witch inspired such deep and troubling ideas in him.*

Ley lines, henges, the Golowhe runes – everything Nightly and I have found had already found my father. I marvel to myself: there truly are no coincidences where magic is concerned. I was meant to discover it all.

Next to the grimoire is the book of witch tales that I recognize as my own from childhood. It has in it the story of the witch and the key, and as I lift it I see the book is open on the story of the untethered witch. I quickly read through it. It is a grim tale of a tethered pair who fall out. One of them, seeking a way to break their connection but keep his magic, goes to a place of old magic. There he reaches into a past realm and speaks to a Creature of Magic from the First Age who gives him a spell in a strange language. He then tempts his tether to his house, offering a reconciliation, but once there he binds her to a chair and performs the spell he has been given.

He is indeed free of the witch, for she dies as part of the spell, and in killing her he has absorbed her magic, transforming his own into something malformed and malevolent. Unable to live with what he has done to his tether, he returns to the place of old magic and turns his magic against himself.

The story makes me think of Heston and Mathilde, though he did not kill her, he cursed her. None the less, I feel a little nudge of magic stir within me, just as I hear footsteps on the floor above.

I scoop up my father's grimoire and the book of tales. I close the door to the spellorium and lock it, expecting the magical wards to snap back into place, but they don't. As I place the key on the necklace that Nightly gave me, which I haven't taken off since Yule, I watch as the rune is replaced with the N and W, and the wards of the key return to their original form.

'Aurelia,' Vaughn calls from upstairs. I grab two other spell books from a small bookshelf we keep in the arcade, hiding our father's grimoire and the story book in plain sight and hastening up the stairs. I walk into the parlour and place the books on the sideboard next to another vase of my and Nightly's roses. They are all dead too.

'You've heard then?' Vaughn says as he walks into the

room to see me gently brushing one of the roses, its faded leaves falling to the floor at my touch.

'Heard what?' I ask vaguely as I realize that I must have pulled more magic from the roses than I intended.

'About Nightly.' Vaughn takes a step towards me, the day's newspaper in hand. I know from the look on his face that something is wrong.

'Is he all right? Is he hurt?' I can barely get the words out as I reach for the paper.

'He will be when I see him,' Vaughn mutters darkly as he tries to move the paper away from me, but my reflexes are fast and I snatch it from him.

I scan the page, searching for his name. And there it is:

Ms H Crenshaw and Mr C Pollock of Hemlock Square and Ms D Nightly and Mr O Hallow of Kestrel Lodge are delighted to announce the intended tethering of Sebastian Bartimus Crenshaw and Jules Horatio Victor Nightly.

If the roses were not already dead, they would have been in that moment.

Thirty-four

don't cry, although I feel like it, desperately so. Vaughn is watching me, waiting for me to break down.

'It's a relief really,' I say, my voice only wavering a little. 'I told him to find a match – one that doesn't leave him needing a healer after every spell.' I fold the paper and hold it out for Vaughn.

I remember what I wrote to Nightly on Imbolc and, despite those words, know that I can never be with him, not if he is tethered to Sebastian. I will have to watch them perform magic together after my own magic is gone. I will always be thinking of how it was, how it felt when Nightly and I were together. Now there will be no more magic, no more kissing – ever.

'I'm going to hex them both,' Vaughn spits.

Ever since I saw into Demelza Nightly's mind I knew

that she was set on Jules making a match. I didn't want to entertain the idea or give any thought as to who it might be, pushing the notion away whenever it surfaced . . . but *Crenshaw*? I never would have thought it would be him.

'You're not going to hex anyone,' I tell Vaughn straight. 'This is good for them. Do I wish it had been anyone but Sebastian? Of course. Is it up to me? No. And you better tell Constance not to go duelling as well.' I give a small smile.

'I always suspected Crenshaw was a weasel, but Nightly . . .' Vaughn shakes his head. 'He almost had me thinking he was one of the good witches. I thought he cared about you. But he is a Nightly after all. I should have never trusted him.'

'Jules *is* one of the good ones. He told me from the beginning that he had no intention of making a match with me and that his parents were in charge of finding him a tether. Let's be honest, even if the council hadn't already forbidden it, Demelza Nightly was never going to allow him to bind his magic to a Wycherley, cursed or not. I never had any design or expectations on his magic,' I lie, although nearly all of my designs and expectations involved the way Nightly's lips felt on mine and the ache that I felt any time he was close to me.

I scoop up the books and make for the door. 'Now if you'll excuse me, I'm going to my room to be alone.'

'You shouldn't shed any tears over Nightly, Aurelia, he is just as unworthy of you as Crenshaw is,' Vaughn says flatly.

'Vaughn, although I am perfectly fine with Nightly's tethering I am heart-shatteringly sad. So I will cry, as I did when I suffered the disappointment of my cursed magic, but in time I will rally, just as I did then.' I turn, leaving Vaughn in the parlour, and make my way to my room. With every step my heart sinks a little further. I will not rally as I once did, I realize, because my heart now has a crack running through it and no amount of time is ever going to heal it.

I place the books next to the vase of dead roses in my room. I start removing them from the vase one by one, placing them on the top of my dresser. In the centre of all the dead blooms there is one single live bud, not yet open. I think about pulling the head from the stem and placing it on top of the others but instead I leave it alone in the vase, an echo of what once was.

I feel completely hollow as I sit in the chair by my window and look out on to Hemlock Square. Ankoth has returned and nudges me a little before settling across my lap.

Everything looks exactly the same as it did this morning. A riot of daffodils fills the gardens at the centre of the square. The first leaves of the alder are a vivid green and life is springing forth in the world as it feels like it is dying in me.

I wipe my tears and reach for my paper and pen. I'm not sure if Nightly has received any of my letters since we were banned from seeing one another, but I feel that I owe him one last message. Not to tell him how hurt and disappointed I am, but to tell him that I am proud to have been part of his magic, and that I hope he will go on to greatness. Letting him go was the best thing to do for the both of us, but the hardest.

'If I had truly loved her, I would have wanted only her happiness.'

I stare at the blank page until my eyes well up, then, instead of filling the paper with words, I fill it with tears.

I hear Constance's voice shouting and go to the window to see Vaughn holding her back at the bottom of the stairs to Sebastian's house while Sebastian stands in the doorway.

I don't need to hear Constance clearly to know what she is shouting at him, and Crenshaw looks so smug I think about hexing him myself.

Vaughn is joined by Jackson and together they pull Constance away. She looks up at my window and I place a hand on it as we lock eyes. I hope she knows how much I miss her. The loneliness since Imbolc has been all consuming, but with Ostara just two days away, all of that will pass. Once the Sabbat is over and the Season with it, I will be free to do as I wish, so long as it never involves magic.

I intend to sit at my window till dusk comes, hopelessness consuming me, but in less than an hour a carriage arrives to escort me to the Arcade.

The first thing I see when we arrive is the rose bush: it too is dead. Where it was once green and red it is now grey and brown.

Russo and Platz are staring at it. 'Has something happened to your magic?' Russo asks in alarm.

'I happened to my magic,' I tell him and he blinks at me. 'What did you do?'

'I took it all back,' I tell him, which is kind of true.

'How did you do that? Why?'

I look over to the black-flame door. It is still there, the runes burning in my black fire, the roses that have kept everyone from it withered and dead. I feel a little afraid when I realize that the roses are no longer there to protect me from what is beyond it.

'Because I suffered a disappointment.' I feel the lump in my throat rising.

'Could you elaborate on that?' Platz asks.

'No, I don't think I can.' I don't want to discuss the matters of my heart with him. He makes his way over to Emery and Jackson, and of course they tell him everything.

When Platz comes back his expression is softer than it ever has been. 'I am sorry, Ms Wycherley. I know that you and Mr Nightly had formed a . . . friendship beyond the magic that you performed together, which is the most impressive and enduring that I have ever witnessed from a pair of witches your age.'

'Until now,' I say. I look back over at the roses and feel the loss of Jules Nightly threaten to take hold of me. I won't let it, not here.

'Ms Wycherley, may I ask a personal question?' Russo asks.

'You may ask. I may choose not to answer though.'

'At the Samhain Rite, did any orbs of other witches' magic land on you?'

I nod. 'One.'

'Mr Nightly's?'

'Mr Nightly's,' I confirm.

'Interesting,' Platz continues. 'When we were recruiting for these experiments with your magic, we asked all of the debutante witches in the ton if they had received a black orb at Samhain. An overwhelming number of them admitted they had, and then after performing magic with you, all of them said they recognized your magic. It would seem, Ms Wycherley, that your magic is a match for almost everyone, but only one witch's magic is a perfect match for yours.'

'That can't be true: Nightly is affected by my magic, the same as everyone else.'

'Ah, the side effects. We have a few theories about those that we will be working on tomorrow. I must admit, we were not expecting to call you in so early but the state of your roses gave us concern.'

And so, they set me to work. The unfortunate witches in the Arcade are rounded up and each one brought to me in turn. I try not to feel emotional towards them, I learnt in the first week to distance myself. But it's still hard to watch the look of fear that most of them approach me with, and then the pain and sickness that my magic leaves them with.

As dusk falls, a coven of twelve red-clad witches arrive, and I know that it is going to be a long night.

370

Thirty-five

That night, I sleep uneasily. There's a ferocious wind outside, howling past the house and banging at the windows. I dream that I am standing in front of the black-flame door, the roses gone, the door open. I can hear the whispering voices calling to me. *Come in, little witch, we promise not to rip your magic from you. We promise not to kill you.* They lie, but all the same I walk through the door into the forest and start to run towards the henge. When I get there, Nightly is standing in the doorway.

'I'm sorry, Aurelia,' he whispers in the same voice as the things in the trees, and closes the door on me. I pound my fists on it, then slam spell after spell into it, because behind me is the creature of smoke with the claws and the antlers coming to claim my magic, coming to claim me.

I wake up with a scream, and although I know that it was

just a bad dream, I can't get back to sleep. The dream has lingered, and the wind is even stronger.

I sit by my window and throw open the curtains. The sky is full of stars, and mysteries are being blown about in the world.

I reach for my father's grimoire, then a fresh stack of paper.

Running a hand over my document wallet, the memory of me and Nightly combining our magic to create the rose on the front pricks my heart like a thorn. I quickly open my father's grimoire and begin my research.

Father and Jonathan had been investigating the old henge sites and ley line energies for the Coven of Curiosity when they stumbled across the Golowhe runes, just as Nightly and I had. The thought that my father and I both found the same lost magic feels special, and I can hear him saying 'There is no such thing as coincidence; it's magic giving you a nudge to continue.' I do.

I look over at the single rose that remains in the vase and blink, trying to work out how long I've been sitting here. The small, perfect rose bud glows in the late morning rays that the sun casts through the window. It's Ostara Eve; tomorrow is my last day as a witch, as a member of the magical community, before I am cast out and forbidden to perform even the simplest of spells.

I hear a knock on the front door and look out of the window to see the last person I was expecting. Demelza

Nightly is holding on to her cloak, battling the storm as the wind whips it around her. I quickly throw on my dressing gown then creep out. I don't need to go down the stairs to be able to hear the conversation in the hall below.

'. . . you know that there is nothing I can do about that. The Coven of Knowing has jurisdiction here, her Majesty has put them in charge of this matter.' Mother's voice is firm and final.

I hear Demelza groan. 'Very well. As for the other matter, I have sanctioned two battalions of my witches to join in your plans to patrol key magical sites. It makes sense that, if there is to be another murder, it will happen today or tomorrow, marking the Sabbat. You have no doubt had the same information that we have about the protest the New Dawn are planning. As with Mabon, we think their protest will provide them with the cover they need to single out one witch and dispatch them.'

'Any idea where? Or who might be the target?' Mother asks. 'I would like to concentrate our combined forces if we can.'

'As with all the others, I suspect that this will be opportunistic. There are so many variables, but they do like to deposit the dead witches in places where we have magical interests, so I would advise that your witches be vigilant at places like Carlton Palace, the Arcade, maybe old henge sites.'

'Old henge sites?' Frances asks.

'Yes, one of our apprentice witches found that five of the

eleven murders happened on the site of a henge that was removed during the burning times. Here.' I hear the rustle of paper. 'A list of all the known sites and the two active henges in London. I don't need to tell you the clearance level on that particular piece of intelligence, but as both sites are in constant use by the magical community . . . well, I will leave it up to you on how best to direct resources.'

'What of my theory?' Frances asks.

'We see no validity in it. What advantage would any witch have to kill one of their own? No, these murders are happening at the hands of the New Dawn. I'd stake my magic on it.'

'I appreciate you letting us know, Demelza. And congratulations on your recent announcement,' Mother says. I freeze with the pain of her blessings on Nightly and Crenshaw's forthcoming union.

'Yes, a most suitable match. Sebastian Crenshaw is from a fine family and his magic is strong and pure. I'm sure that Jules will do well with him.' I can hear the gloating in Demelza's voice as she slates me, my magic and my suitability without even mentioning my name.

I return to my room. Two active henges in London. I flick through my notes. After we found the henge at Neoards, Nightly and I did a research dive on them.

My eyes skim my familiar scrawl: 'At the height of henge magic there were over a thousand henges in the kingdom, each one on a ley line of wild magic. After the burning times, before the outbreak of the Great Witch War, this number had diminished to less than a handful. Many are lost, and today only a few actively draw on the wild magic they are built on.'

There was no mention in my notes of any active henges in London, and I was sure that I would have remembered if it had been in the original material.

But then I remember the maps in the back of my father's grimoire. I glanced over some of them yesterday, but now I examine them thoroughly, one by one. The ley lines are marked on each: some are of small geographical locations, others are towns, counties, some whole regions of the land. Then I open one of London and smooth it out.

I trace my finger along the line that is drawn in gold on the map. A little thrill runs through me as I realize that marked on it are several old, lost and forgotten former henge sites; Father was already a step ahead. The line starts at the Season Gardens and I almost kick myself for not thinking of it. The island at the centre of the lake is off limits and it is commonly believed that there is a henge on it which gives the Season Gardens their magic. I follow the line with my finger, discovering several crosses along it, and close to them, in my father's writing, it says 'former henge site'. One of them is the alley behind Mason's Magical Books. Following on I see that our house lies on the ley line too. The house is old, but dates from after the destruction of the henges, so it may be on top of a former henge.

The line ends at a nondescript point in the southeast of

the ton that has a question mark on it and fathers scrawly handwriting says '*The Arcade?*' I remember Mother telling me that the interior location of the Arcade was a secret that only the Royal Magical Council knew – and Demelza Nightly, judging by the earlier conversation.

I copy the map on to a fresh piece of paper, and I add to it. I mark the points where the eleven witches were murdered, I write their names next to them and draw the lost runes that were found. Every single one of them was murdered in a place that falls on the ley line, only the Arcade and the Season Gardens don't have the name of a dead witch attributed to them.

I start to write down all of my disorganized thoughts: murdered witches, ley lines, old magic, lost runes and witches with untethered magic.

It's all here . . . I just can't see the connections. I need Nightly more than ever, I need to talk things through with him, for us to bounce our ideas off of one another. Just as our magic works best together I feel that our minds do too.

A knock on my door startles me.

'One moment,' I call as I fold up my father's map and put it back in its original place. I step across the room and open the door.

'Sorry, Ms, but the carriage has arrived,' Jackson says.

'I'll just get my cloak and be down,' I say, closing the door. I place the map I've made in my document wallet and then stuff it into the inside pocket of my cloak. Then I hear a *tap*,

tap, tap on my window and look, expecting it to be the wind. It's Ankoth, impatient to be let out. I walk over. 'Are you sure? It's very blustery out.'

The broom taps on the pane again and I pull open the window. Ankoth flies out into the gale that is blowing, but I know it will be back.

Jackson is still waiting outside my door when I open it. I follow her down the stairs and out of the house, bracing myself against the wind as we walk to the carriage. On the ride I think about ley lines, runes, dead witches – eleven so far, two more to form an old coven with the Golowhe runes – and witches who have no right to magic able to perform spells. How did Jonathan and Kit learn to regain their magic? And why are they keeping it a secret? Where does Geoffrey Knott fit into this? I'm so lost in my thoughts that it takes me a moment to realize we are travelling in the wrong direction.

'I thought we were going to the Arcade?' I ask.

'We are. We're expecting some disturbances this evening, leading into Ostara on the morrow, so we're using the south entrance to the Arcade.'

It takes us a little longer to arrive at the Arcade entrance than it would have otherwise, the constant rain and wind battling us back.

I've never used the south entrance, and I'm not entirely surprised to find that it looks identical to the west entrance I usually take. I run my eyes over the high, stained-glass windows, and as I climb the stairs I read the familiar declaration on the arch of the door, 'for the kingdom and the magic', then I stop dead. There on the arch is a rune, one of the Golowhe runes: Dalleth, meaning 'beginning'. A cold sweat moves over me.

'Ms Wycherley, are you all right?' Emery asks.

I am far from all right, but I nod.

My mind whirls as I walk through the arch and into the Arcade.

I pause as soon as I'm through. 'Emery, Platz once told me that a witch died in the Arcade; an accident, no magic involved, he said. It would have been about three years ago. Do you know anything about that? Do you know who it was?' I ask.

'I do. It was four years ago, during our training year. It was a high-priority case. You probably don't remember it – you were too young and had more interesting things to think about than politics. His name was Louis Heap, he was a member of the Royal Magical Council, former head of the Coven of Justice. When he died, your mother and Frances took the place of him and his tether on the council. What was her name?' Emery looks lost in thought.

'A few Sabbats before Father died?' I say.

They nod. 'I think in the end it was found to be a heart attack that killed him.'

'Was he quite old?'

'Not really, come to think of it. Why do you ask?' Emery narrows their eyes at me.

I shrug. 'Just curious and in need of a distraction. Who knows what Platz and Russo have planned for me.'

My heart is beating fast and I feel a wave of dread come over me, as if the magic in the Arcade is trying to warn me of something. Louis Heap . . . I am sure that he was the first witch to be murdered and not my father, and if I'm right then this means that there are twelve murdered witches, not eleven. *But thirteen witches does an old coven make,* I think, quoting the line of an old nursery rhyme, and I try to remember the rest of the rhyme as I walk boldly into the main structure of the Arcade. But I am distracted by the black-flame door; the roses have now fallen in a dead heap around the base and I can feel a steady vibration of magic just behind it, calling to me in a way it wasn't yesterday.

There, standing to the side of the door, by the remnants of the rose bush, is Nightly.

I lock eyes with him. I want to run to him, and when I get to him, I want to kiss him and hex him in equal measure.

His hair is still too long and tousled, and his jaw is locked so tight I fear for his teeth.

He makes a small movement towards me but then stops and looks away. That crack in my heart opens wide.

I follow his gaze and see that some distance from him at the far end of the Arcade is a raised platform and sitting on it are my mother, Frances and the rest of the Royal Magical Council.

Emery and Jackson hang back as Russo and Platz gesture

for me to join Nightly. I stand next to him, facing the council. If I were to reach out my fingers, I could touch him. I look straight ahead, trying to keep my breathing level and my wandlet in place.

He is better off with Crenshaw, I tell myself, but I don't believe it.

Platz and Russo stand between me and Nightly and the council, addressing them, detailing all of the experiments that they have performed with me over the past six weeks, all of the magic of merit that I have cast.

As I half listen, I run through all the things in my head that I desperately need to talk to Nightly about. *There are twelve dead witches not eleven and one more witch might die tonight, both our mothers think so . . .*

My mind catches on something.

'Wycherley, I need you to know that Crenshaw and I . . .'

I shush him and I can tell that he is taken aback. At the moment, the least important thing in my head is probably the only thing he wants to talk to me about, although it is the thing that matters the most to me.

Russo and Platz are commanding the council's attention, showing them the metallic ball I made the other day. I lower my voice and whisper to Nightly, 'Listen to me, we need to get out of here. They are going to make us perform magic, we need to do as they ask but when I give you the signal, I need you to follow my lead. Do you remember rune Kosoleth from the grimoire? It means "stillness".'

Nightly nods.

'Good. We're going to use it in the sequence for a locking spell. We're going to freeze time around us so that we can get out of here. Draw the rune in your mind, in your magic, with your wand and your body and your soul, but not till my say so,' I tell him in quick, hushed tones.

'We know that you all think that Ms Wycherley's magic should be left to wither,' Platz is saying, 'but we believe . . . No, we *know*, that she is the strongest witch of this Age, maybe of all the Ages.' I can't help but stare at Platz in disbelief as he says this, unable to marry up my magic with the accolade being bestowed on it. 'With her cursed magic she can amplify any witch that she is in direct contact with, be it a single witch or a coven of them . . . even a battalion. Last night, Ms Wycherley performed a spell with a coven of witches from the thirty-first Battalion of the Royal Magical Guard from the Coven of Accord. Her magic flowed through seventy-two witches. Twelve were here in the Arcade with her and the other sixty were stationed across the nation. When connected to her magic, they all felt it. We had instructed each of them to perform a simple spell: to raise a witch-wind.'

Mother leans forward. 'Are you telling us that the hurricane that is battling these shores is because of Aurelia?'

'Yes,' Platz says simply. 'From a basic witch-wind came this. Now do you see why it is imperative that you allow Ms Wycherley to keep her magic?'

'But the only way she can keep her magic for the duration

of her life is to tether, and if she did that, she would make the unfortunate witch sick. Just as it did my witches of the thirty-first Battalion,' Carmen Torres says. Her long white hair is gathered up in a bun looped with neat plaits, and her hand rests on the top of a walking stick. In her deep red robes of the Coven of Accord she looks as if she belongs in the First Age of Magic.

'They were affected, yes. But all of the witches have now made a full recovery . . . and we have a theory on how to negate these undesired side effects. You are here to see it in action.' Russo gestures towards me and Nightly.

'Ms Wycherley and Mr Nightly have a connection. Since Mabon they have been performing magic together, and at Samhain Mr Nightly's magic sought her out. Over that time, Mr Nightly has, like the others, suffered, but the magic they have performed together was by far the most enduring that Ms Wycherley has created.'

Platz takes a step forward. 'We have seen that Ms Wycherley's magic is strong while connected to the witch that she is performing with, but as soon as the connection is severed, the curse takes over, almost as if it punishes whoever she connected with.'

I think of Heston and the curse he gave Mathilde for loving another, and now I think I understand the curse he meant to invoke.

Platz continues, 'However, we believe that if Ms Wycherley and Mr Nightly form a tether – a temporary one, I might add, a single knot of magic – then the curse will not strike. Mr Nightly will suffer no side effects because the connection will not have been broken.'

'And what if it does strike?' Carmen Torres asks.

'Then we will remove the petition for Ms Wycherley to be allowed to keep her magic indefinitely.'

Mother looks along the line of assembled council members, they all nod in agreement. 'Very well,' she says. 'We will see if the magic sticks.'

Russo and Platz approach me and Nightly.

'You understand what is about to happen?' We both nod. 'Ms Wycherley, this is the last chance you have to keep your magic. Mr Nightly, this is the only chance you are going to get to keep Ms Wycherley. So I advise you both to put your all into this small piece of magic,' Russo says.

'Ms Wycherley, Mr Nightly, raise your wand hands please,' Platz says.

I do as I'm bid and watch as the tethering string that is wrapped around my wandlet unravels, growing long and thin until I can only just see the shimmer of it. Nightly's has done the same. Platz picks up both ends of the string and ties them in a single knot. As soon as the knot is pulled, both Nightly and I gasp. I can feel his magic flowing into me and we are not even touching. I close my eyes with the bliss of it, the feel of his magic moving through my marrow. I have missed it so much. It fills my whole body. If I look at Nightly, I know I won't be able to resist reaching out for him.

'Ms Wycherley, please go and stand by the south entrance, Mr Nightly by the north. And when you get there, combine your magic and grow those roses again. I miss not seeing them brightening the Arcade, and besides, I felt a lot safer when they were protecting that door,' Platz says.

I walk towards the south entrance of the Arcade, then look back at Nightly. He pushes back his hair, his wand in hand as he takes up position, and in perfect unison we move through the sequence of the first spell that we ever cast together. I can't help the smile that spreads over my lips as I feel our magic combine further, and watch as the roses bloom back, bigger, brighter, stronger than before. When the door is covered in blooms, I pull my magic away, and Nightly stays upright. No fainting, no retching, no clutching of his head or stomach. Instead, he smiles at me, and I desperately wish we were alone.

'You see!' Russo says, his voice triumphant. 'Once tethered, Ms Wycherley's magic would not have any negative effect, be it on a single witch, a coven or a battalion that she was linked to. She will enhance the magic of every witch she tethers to and with no ill effects. We petition that Ms Wycherley be allowed to find a suitable match.'

'Suitable match? What about me?' Nightly says.

'You are to be tethered to Mr Crenshaw, are you not? Besides, I'm not sure that your mother would approve of any other match,' Russo says.

I think of Demelza Nightly, and then I remember that

Geoffrey Knott was with Kit Thorne and Jonathan and feel that strike of fear run through me again, as if the magic is warning me.

'If there is to be another murder, it will happen today or tomorrow, marking the Sabbat.' Demelza Nightly's voice echoes in my head, and for some reason I suddenly think of the story of the untethered witch – not of Heston, but the version from the witch tale book in my father's spellorium. I feel a sinking dread as the last pieces of the puzzle fall into place in a sudden rush.

I push my magic back along the invisible tether and into Nightly. He responds, knowing now is the time to use the Golowhe rune. Wands in hand we move as one against the shouts of the council. When we don't cease our spell casting, Russo sends out a binding spell but it's too late. Our spell has been cast, Kosoleth has taken its place in the sequence, and the world has frozen around me and Nightly.

I run to him, and he to me, and in front of the rose bush our bodies collide and I hold him so tight that I'm sure we are only one person. His lips are on mine and my hands in his hair as I push all that I am into him: all my magic, all my love, all of me.

'Don't ever leave my side again,' I say to him.

'If you please,' he murmurs, his lips not leaving mine.

Thirty-six

'Jules, as much as I would love to do this forever, we need to go,' I tell him, taking his hand and running for the north exit. Outside the Arcade, time is still running and the wind is ferocious. I wonder how long we have before Mother and the others are after us. I have never attempted such a spell and have no idea how long it will last.

Nightly and I run against the wind, trying to put as much distance between us and the Arcade as possible before I pull us into a side alley to catch our breath.

'Looks like we can add "fugitives on the run" to our list of fun couple's activities.' He grins as he pulls me to him. 'Aurelia . . .'

'Nightly, where is your mother?' I stop him as his lips are making their way to mine. He pulls back.

'Of all the things I expected you might say to me in this

moment, that is most definitely not one of them.'

'Jules, it's important, please.'

'She's at home, probably in the same foul mood that I left her in,' he replies with a wary look. I pull my document wallet from my pocket and retrieve the drawing of London with the ley line running through it.

'Your house isn't on this line, is it?' I ask, remembering that his house is close to the Gardens. He takes the map.

'Aurelia, what's going on?'

'One moment.' I step away from him and perform the summoning spell, calling Ankoth to me.

'Aurelia, is my mother in trouble?' Whatever has passed between his mother and him, the concern is obvious.

'I hope not. I hope I'm wrong. Yesterday, I managed to unlock my father's spellorium and in there I found information about the work he and Jonathan were doing. They had discovered the Golowhe runes and I think that Jonathan worked out how to use them to do what we're looking for: he discovered how to keep magic without a tether. And now he's using the wild magic of the ley line, combined with the lost runes, to bind magic to a single tethered witch from a pair. But to do that I . . . I think they are killing the other part of the tether in the process.' Nightly is pacing up and down.

'They? Are you saying that the murdered witches were all killed by their tethers? But why?'

'I have no idea,' I say honestly.

'Jonathan killed your father, and Kit Thorne . . .'

'He killed Cora Stewart,' I say.

The colour drains from Nightly. 'If Evelyn had tethered with him . . .'

'She would have lost more than her magic.' I wonder if maybe Kit really did love Evelyn and couldn't bring himself to tether with her, knowing that he would kill her and take her magic. The idea that he would look for a witch with hardly any family, to murder and take their magic, makes me feel sick. Poor Cora.

'And my mother?'

'Do you remember that when I saw Kit and Jonathan together, they were with another witch? I didn't know who that was until Imbolc, when I met your mother and her tether, Geoffrey Knott.'

I can sense Ankoth getting closer and I put out a hand. A small thrill runs through me as it lands in my outstretched palm.

'Initially I thought he was there because the Coven of Mysteries knew how to regain magic and were helping Jonathan and Kit, but now . . .'

'You think he was there so that they could help him . . . and that he is going to kill my mother? He's going to take her magic and murder her. For what? For power? For greed or envy?' Nightly starts pacing, like he needs to be doing something.

I remember the feeling of unease I had when Jonathan performed magic, a similar feeling to the magic beyond the black-flame door.

'Malevolence – power, greed, control, envy, hatred. I felt it all in Jonathan's magic, but I don't know for certain why they are doing this. What I do know is that someone is going to die. Every time one of the witches has been murdered, it's been on a Sabbat, and there has been some kind of demonstration from the New Dawn. I hope your mother isn't the target, but I think I know where it will happen. And I know that this will be the last one: the thirteenth member of the coven, not the twelfth.'

I get on my broom and reach out a hand to Nightly. He climbs on behind me just as Emery and Jackson round the corner of the alley and run towards us. As Nightly casts a barrier around us to deflect any spells the Justice witches might send our way, I concentrate on flying.

Nightly holds on to me as I raise us into the blustery wind. The storm – apparently of my own making – is dying out, but the winds are still strong and we are flying against them.

Nightly's body is warm against my back and it feels so good to be close to him again. I've missed him, and when this is over, I intend to show him just how much.

It's close to midnight by the time that we get to the Season Gardens. We land outside the railings and as soon as we are on the ground, Nightly rushes towards the entrance. It's locked. As Ostara brings in the start of spring, at midnight the season will turn, and the gardens are always off limits on those nights.

'Are you sure that this is the right place?' Nightly asks. I let go of my broom and it hovers close to me.

I nod. 'We should tell someone.' I pull a page from my document wallet and scribble a hasty message on it, then attach it to my broom. 'Ankoth, find my mother or Vaughn. Don't stop till you get this note to one of them.'

The broom shoots off and I turn to see Nightly looking at me. 'That is definitely not usual broom behaviour,' he says and smiles.

'Since when has anything or anyone that chooses me been normal?'

'I guess I deserve that.'

'It's all *extra*-ordinary,' I add and he smiles.

'Later I will tell you just how extraordinary you are, Wycherley, but for now, we need to get inside.'

My wand is in hand. 'Can you feel the spells on the gates?' I ask as I move our combined magic over each one, plucking them like invisible strings.

'How are you doing that?' Nightly's eyes are wide, his voice filled with awe.

'I'll show you later, but right now I need you to concentrate on trying to match your magic to the same frequency as the spells. That's the fastest way for me to unlock them.'

Raising his wand, he moves through the sequence with me in perfect unison. The wards fall one by one and, after a few minutes, the doors swing open. Nightly rushes through them. I follow.

Inside the Season Gardens, the air is still as cold as midwinter. Our footsteps are left behind in the snow as we run, but they are not the only ones. I can see many footprints all leading towards the lake, where there are lights glowing on the island.

Nightly runs out on to the ice and immediately falls over.

'Wait,' I call as I follow him. I crouch down and call upon the winter around me, running my hands along the soles of his boots, making skates from icicles.

'You are a genius.' He gives me a quick kiss, then is on his feet, skating for the island, what he lacks in skill and finesse he makes up for in speed as he rushes to save his mother. I cast the spell for myself; the icicles that cling to the bottom of my shoes move smoothly over the frozen lake as I follow along behind Nightly, watching him stumble, but stay upright.

I can feel the magic around me. There are two sources: one I know is the wild magic of the ley line; it feels as if it is gathering like steam in a pot that will soon spill out into the gardens. The other magic is coming from the island – twelve witches, part of a connected coven but all with no tether, and two tethered witches. As I explore the magic, I know that Nightly can feel it too through our connection.

A thought hits me, and I skate as fast as I can to reach Nightly, but he is too fast, spurred on by the thought of his mother in trouble.

He reaches the island and I feel him strike a witch-flame and melt the ice from his boots, then he is off.

I wish he would wait – give me a moment to make a plan,

but would I hesitate if it was my mother?

The snow on the island is melting and I can sense that the gardens are on the precipice of changing from winter to spring. Whatever Jonathan, Kit and the others are planning it is going to happen soon.

I feel Nightly pulling on my magic and I move faster, entering a torchlit clearing to find him already locked in a duel with Geoffrey Knott. Around them stand twelve untethered witches. I recognize each of them from the drawings in the files of their dead tethers, tethers that they murdered, tethers whose magic they stole. Jules is on the far side of the fighting circle created by the untethered coven, closest to his mother, who is bound to a stake, but alive, her hands tied behind her back, gagged, blindfolded and on her knees. I have never wanted to be so wrong about anything in my life. Demelza Nightly is in the gravest of dangers and Jules has flung himself into the middle of this coven to save her. I freeze for a moment, unable to believe that this is happening and has happened twelve times before. That these witches have taken the life and magic of the witch closest to them. That Jonathan took my father from me.

I see the twelve start to move as one, combining their magic as a coven. I can feel their magic stirring, and I act before I have a chance to think. I don't cast a spell . . . instead I do what I know will incapacitate the twelve witches of the coven the fastest. I run towards Jonathan, who is closest to me. He turns just as I slam into him, knocking him to the ground. I place one hand on his face, and my other grabs the wrist of his wand hand. I push my magic into him, into the twelve murderous witches, and perform a shielding spell, using the magic of the untethered coven to bolster mine and Nightly's and place a protective guard over both Jules and his mother. I can see the dome surrounding them, and when I feel it is sound, I shift my attention.

I send my magic through Jonathan and along the magical connection between him and the other malevolent witches, binding each one to the spot that they stand on, before I let go and watch as all twelve witches succumb to the curse of my magic, falling to the ground in various states of fainting, weakness and sickness.

I see Geoffrey step back and into the small woodlands surrounding the henge. He's not yet part of the coven, and with Demelza safe behind the dome of protection he is no doubt fleeing. I pause for a moment, then throw up myself. My head is throbbing, and a lethargy overcomes me. It seems that my magic is misaligned with malevolent magic, and I have never been so glad to be ill.

I push myself up and, on wobbly legs, stumble towards Nightly. The protective dome is holding fast and stops me from reaching him. I watch as he unbinds his mother from the stake – she falls forward into his arms and holds him tight. I feel my way along the magic of the dome, trying to take it down, but just as I start to lift the ward, Demelza Nightly shouts out my name and reaches out her wand hand, sending something flying from it towards me. Her spell hits the dome as I am grabbed from behind.

Geoffrey Knott has cast a lasso of magic around me, fixing my arms to my chest and binding my hands. He pushes me into the exterior of the protective dome. It's hard and unyielding as my face collides with it. He stands behind me, wrapping his gloved fingers around my neck. The shock is powerful, the pain is excruciating. I try to get a hand out of the knot of light to touch him but I can't.

'Foolish little witch,' he spits into my ear as I cry out. 'I know everything about you, about your powers. Russo and Platz have been sharing it all with the Coven of Mysteries so that we might help as they seek to understand you, but I feel that I already do.' Nightly pounds on the inside of the dome, I can feel him pulling on my magic as he slams spell after spell into it.

'Jonathan had hoped that, in time, he might be able to persuade you to join us,' Geoffrey croons. 'Maybe set up your own coven of thirteen. Your magic is spectacular and with it we could finish what was started in the Great Witch War by the brave witches before us. They knew the way the world should be, with witches in their rightful place having domination of magic over all.'

He pushes harder on my throat. My lungs burn and I can feel my magic struggling to get a hold.

'Ms Wycherley, you have no idea how extraordinary your power is. They will use you. The Royal Magical Council, the

Crown, will use your magic against us and all who fight for the dominion of magic. For the kingdom but *not* the magic, that is how we have lived for too long. I'm sorry but it's time for the magic to win.'

My eyes haven't left Jules. He's still trying to bring down the dome.

I feel the air in my lungs run out. 'I love you,' I try to say and I send that thought out along the connection that is growing dim between us. The single knot is straining and about to slip undone, cutting our connection and restoring his magic to him before I die. Inside the dome he screams and lashes out with our magic. I feel the dome fall as the world fades away, and all I can see is Nightly moving towards me, and his mother behind him sending a spell that soars over Nightly's shoulder. I feel the spell thunder around me, as I fall to the ground. The earth is warm and soft, new, green grass, small, white snowdrops and purple irises bloom all around me as I suck in a sharp rasping breath.

Nightly pulls me to him, holding me tight and smoothing my hair from my face. 'Breathe, Aurelia, just breathe,' he says.

I look up from Nightly to see Demelza standing above him, looking down in horror. I turn my head to see Geoffrey, lying on the ground next to me, dead.

'What have I done?' Demelza cries. She falls upon him, shaking his shoulders, trying to rouse him.

'What you had to do,' a familiar voice calls. And I see

Mother and Frances swoop into the clearing, accompanied by a coven of black-clad witches.

'He's dead,' Demelza says. 'Nell, I didn't . . . I had no idea that he . . . I trusted him . . . He was going to kill her and I . . . I couldn't let him.'

'Go. Go to your mother,' I say to Nightly, my voice rasping.

My mother alights from her broom and scoops me to her, checking me over and hugging me close.

I watch as Nightly does the same with Demelza. She cries and holds him and thanks him, giving me a look that is so unlike any she has ever given me before that I am taken aback.

Frances pulls me and Mother to her, holding us both as we watch the untethered coven being taken away. She whispers in my ear, 'That was an impressive time-stop spell back in the Arcade! I have only heard of them being performed in the legends before.' I can hear the smile in her voice.

'You have a lot of explaining to do,' Mother says as she pulls away, 'but that can wait. I'll have someone take you and Nightly to the palace while we get things straight here.' She gives me one last hug, kissing the top of my head, before the two of them go to help the rest of the Coven of Justice witches collect up the malevolent witches and lead them away.

I watch on the edge of it all, trying to process what just happened. My throat is raw, my legs still feeling a little wobbly. I sit beneath a tree covered in spring cherry blossom, breathing in its sweet scent, as I rest my back against its trunk. A pair of witches lead Kit Thorne past me.

'Aurelia, I didn't want to. My father . . . he forced me to do it. Tell them. Tell them I am innocent. I don't want to burn at the stake.' He lunges towards me, places a hand on my arm and desperately sends his magic into me; it feels deep and oppressive, and instinctively my wandlet is in my hands. I hit him with a freezing spell. He stops moving but his eyes still stare at me. I turn aside as the witches pull him back and carry him away. I feel sick, and it has as much to do with the magical connection as it does with the thought of Kit, Jonathan, the whole untethered coven burning at the stake for magical treason.

I know that Nightly and I saved his mother this evening, but it also feels like we lost. The way to keep magic without tethering is abominable and I would never do it. Not only that, but Heston's warning feels real now, I have seen malevolent magic in action this night, and it has left me shaken to my marrow.

Thirty-seven

Nightly and I are bundled into the back of a carriage. 'Take them to Carlton Palace,' Frances instructs, before saying to me, 'We'll be with you presently, along with the rest of the council.'

Nightly and I sit together in silence for a few minutes. His hand is in mine, our magic still flowing between us.

'How is your mother?' I ask, my voice still hoarse.

Nightly conjures a witch-flame and, using its light to see, he runs his fingers gently over my neck, examining the bruises that I can feel there.

'If Mother hadn't killed Geoffrey, I would have,' he says. 'She's in shock, understandably. She has all of her power still, and his magic too – she says she can feel it in her.'

My eyes widen and I start to speak, but all I can do is cough. Nightly rubs my back and then my neck and throat, his fingers soft and warm, and I can feel him sending his magic into me, healing me.

'She doesn't know what this will mean. Your mother and Frances will no doubt need to call a special council meeting about her position as head investigator of the Coven of Mysteries.'

'What do we tell them?' I croak, trying to keep my thinking straight. The feeling of his hands on me is making more than my magic stir.

'Everything,' he says.

'Neoards?' I ask.

He shakes his head. 'Not everything. We'll tell them we learnt of the runes from your father's grimoire. They're in there, right?' I nod. 'But everything else, we tell them the truth.' He lowers his mouth to my neck and kisses the bruises. A slight moan escapes me and he kisses me again, slowly, and his hands run down from my neck, brushing the top of my breasts. Now it is his turn to moan, and I reach my hands into his hair and push his lips downwards from my neck.

Then I guide him back up to my lips and kiss him deeply, before shifting myself on to his lap, my thighs gripping his hips.

'Aurelia,' he groans between kisses. 'I want you. Just you.'

I pull back, my hands cupping his face. 'But what about Crenshaw?' I croak, keeping my face deadpan.

'I was never going to tether with Crenshaw. Yesterday, when that announcement was made, when you found out, when the roses . . .' He pauses and shakes his head. 'When

I saw the roses die, I feared that your feelings for me had changed. These weeks apart from you have felt like years. I didn't realize how deeply I had fallen in love with you until I couldn't be with you any more. Do you know how many times I tried to break into your house to see you?'

'You never did!'

He nods. 'Eight times, before the Coven of Justice put a ward around Hemlock Square just to repel me. But I knew it wouldn't work forever because it was only ever going to be you and me from the moment I saw you on Mabon, when you were fierce and defiant, and you rose into the air with so much grace and power. I grabbed you by the ankle and pulled you down because I didn't want you to fly off without me, before I had a chance to know you.'

'And now you do,' I tell him, as I kiss his cheek. 'Now you know who I am.' I kiss his jaw. 'Now you know my magic.' I kiss his neck. 'You know my heart.' Then I whisper into his ear, 'And soon you will know all of me.' I press my hips firmly on to his and kiss his lips, sending my magic into him.

'How long till we get to the palace?' I ask breathlessly between kisses.

'Not long enough for all the magic I have planned for the two of us,' he says.

OSTARA

The Most Magical Season – A Debutantes' Guide

*by Cathleen Kelly
and Kate Walker*

The ending of the Magical Season also marks new beginnings. Those young witches who have been lucky enough to find themselves a match will tie the first knot of tethering at the Ostara Fastening Ceremony. The first step along the way to binding your magic together forever.

For those lucky witches, a long summer lies ahead before they join their coven college.

Those witches that haven't yet found suitable matches need not fear, unless they are in their last year. Just as the wheel of the year turns, so Mabon will be upon us once more, and with it new balls and rites and pledges, and new witches all too eager to find a match.

Thirty-eight

ightly and I are separated as soon as we get to the palace. I'm told that someone will come and talk to me, but I'm so weary I soon fall asleep in the office they have placed me in. I wake, feeling not at all rested, to a knock at the door.

I can still feel Nightly's magic joined with mine. It nudges me gently as if he is saying 'good morning, Wycherley' with a push of his hair and a shine in his eyes.

I blush as Emery walks into the room and hands me a pile of fresh clothes, pointing me in the direction of a small washroom.

My hair is the wildest I have ever seen it, and I try to work out how much of the tangle was caused in the drama of last night and how much by Nightly. I wash and dress, and when I'm presentable, Emery escorts me to the Royal Magical Council's chambers.

Before the interrogation begins, Platz and Russo confirm that they will need to untether us but not until after the ceremony, otherwise Nightly will succumb to the effects of my magic. I wonder how long he will be out of action this time – a month?

Nightly and I are questioned by the Royal Magical Council and I tell them all that Nightly and I agreed upon. I tell them my father's spellorium is open, and a flurry of excitement goes around the room. Then I tell them where to find my father's grimoire, though I'm loath to when I haven't finished reading it.

Mother calls to Jackson, whispers to her, and she and Emery leave the room. They return just as I finish giving my account of what happened in the Season Gardens.

'Is there anything else that you would like to add?' Carter Jenkins, head of the Coven of Nurturing, asks.

I shake my head. 'No, but I would like to ask how Demelza Nightly is and, if I may, what will happen to the untethered witches.'

The council whisper among themselves before Frances replies, 'Of the untethered we have not yet decided. Their treason against the Crown is abominable, and it goes against all that is natural within magic. As for Ms Nightly, we are monitoring the situation, but no doubt she will be present at the palace later for her son's tethering.'

I guess that is all I can expect to get from them – no real answers. But I can't shake Frances' words on Nightly's tethering.

'Now, Ms Wycherley, we have much to discuss,' Jenkins says, 'not least the future of your magic, which we *had* been called to rule on before you stopped time and ran out on us.' I glance at Mother and see her look of pride.

I'm dismissed and sent to sit out in the corridor. Nightly is there, dressed in white, ready for the ceremony and the tethering that he told me last night would never happen. But I know that he has to accept it, he has to keep his magic – too much is at stake. As I sit down next to him, pushing away the churning in my stomach that I feel when I think of Jules and Sebastian, I brush my fingers along Nightly's arm and he stretches out a leg so that it is touching mine. Emery stands guard, watching us disapprovingly.

A voice from down the hall rings out. 'You will let me through this instance! My mother, her tether and my sister have been missing all evening and I have had no word and—' Vaughn's voice echoes down the corridor and is interrupted by Evelyn Nightly.

'And *my* brother and mother have been missing too! You will let us in and tell us what we need to know.'

I look over at Nightly and he smiles and rolls his eyes, but I can tell that he is delighted to hear Evelyn's voice.

There is more talking but I can't quite make out what is being said until Constance's voice fills the corridor, low and full of cold annoyance. 'I know all about you, Nita Jackson. My sister Honour was in your debutante year, and is the most gossipy of all my sisters. You'll not be surprised to learn that she joined the Coven of Mysteries. I wonder what little things she might know about you?'

Moments later, Evelyn, Vaughn and Constance run towards us before Emery ushers us into a side room at Constance's insistence that we need some privacy.

'What does Honour know about Nita Jackson?' Evelyn asks as we enter the room and I listen, full of curiosity.

Constance shrugs. 'Probably nothing, but she knows enough things about enough witches that they all think she has the measure of them and their secrets.'

Evelyn nods, looking suitably impressed.

Nightly and I proceed to tell them all that has happened. From the very beginning: our arrangement, our pursuit of a cure to tethering, and when we get to Neoards, Nightly looks at me and then tells Vaughn, Constance and Evelyn everything after securing an oath of secrecy from the three of them. I'm not overly convinced that they believe us, but when I pull out the key that I've been keeping close to me since opening my father's study, and they feel the old magic in it, they change their minds.

'Something big *is* coming,' Evelyn says. 'I'm sure of it from the work I have been doing for the Coven of Justice. I think that the warning from Heston Nightly was right, you need to open that henge and raise a coven of your own.' She looks from Nightly to me, then across to Constance and Vaughn.

'Neoards? What do you say, Constance? How do you fancy Cambridge?' my brother asks.

She looks at him thoughtfully. 'It's as good a coven college as any. Besides, they throw a good ball.' She smiles and I see Vaughn blush.

After we finish telling them what happened in the Season Gardens, Evelyn is on her feet and insisting that she find their mother. Jules goes to the door and asks Jackson if she will take them to Demelza.

I run after Jules out into the corridor and grab his arm and swing him round as I hastily say, 'Please don't lose your magic over me. Tether with Crenshaw. No magic for us, but yes to kisses.' I'm smiling, but he doesn't answer. His brows knit together in a familiar expression, I know he is, trying to work out a problem. The problem, I guess, is me.

I return to Constance and Vaughn and they ask me question after question about the runes and the untethered witches, Jonathan, Kit and the lost quarter. Just when I am hoarse from speaking, the clock strikes a quarter to noon and the door opens. Emery and Jackson enter and escort us, not into the council chambers, but into the great hall of Carlton Palace.

It is full of debutante witches all dressed in white, standing in the middle of the hall.

Around the edge stand their parents. I can see Ms Prior and Mr Okore near the front, looking expectantly between Constance and Vaughn. Mr Pollock and Ms Crenshaw are there in the crowd, looking very smug. I see Ms Crenshaw lift a hand and smile at Demelza Nightly and Oliver Hallow.

Evelyn is standing between them both, her arm linked with her father's. Demelza is not looking at Crenshaw or her son – she is looking at me. It is as if she has never seen me before and she's trying to work out who, or what, I am.

A witch in yellow directs us where to stand. I remain near the back of the hall, the others are ahead of me. Beyond the rows of debutantes is a large gap before the dais where the Royal Magical Council sit around the Princess Regent. She stands and so do they.

'Young witches of Briton, we hope that this has been a Magical Season in more ways than one. As you have moved through the seasons, so you have found your magic and hopefully your match too. At Mabon I pressed upon you all that it was not only your duty but your responsibility to this nation, to the Crown, to magic, to find a witch to tether to. We are delighted that some of you will now perform the first oath on the way to tethering. For those of you who have not had a chance to find your match, fear not, there is always another Season – unless you are in your dark-grey year.' The princess looks around the hall gravely.

I feel the tug on my magic as she looks at Nightly, and he reaches out as if to say *Magic be damned.*

'As is the custom, those of you wishing to tether are to dance now and let the first knot of your tether string be tied.'

The princess smiles and sits back on the throne as the music starts to play. I feel my heart rate rise. I look at the Royal Magical Council all sitting there watching my fellow debutante's ready to make their matches and I guess that they have not had time to decide my fate and by the time that they do, Nightly will be tethered with Crenshaw and our knot will be undone. And who knows what tomorrow will hold for my magic? Whatever it is, I know it will not be Jules Nightly.

All the witches are still for a moment. As the music gathers I am surprised to see that Martyn is the first witch to move. He approaches Bevis Nash, they bow at each other before taking to the dance floor. This starts a small flurry of activity as witches seek each other out. I see Constance look back over her shoulder towards Vaughn and smile. He smiles back, but neither of them move. I guess they have decided to wait till next year after all.

I watch as Russo, Platz and the other purple-robed witches from the Arcade stand in front of the dancing pairs, instructing them on what to do and knotting their magic together, just as they did with me and Nightly the evening before.

Nightly stands firm at the front of the crowd of debutantes, then I watch as Crenshaw approaches him, gives a long bow, and offers Nightly his hand.

My heart twists and I close my eyes and take a breath. Despite everything that Nightly said last night, despite knowing that he is the only one for me, I know too that the council have not allowed us to tether.

Go. Don't lose your magic for me, I think along our connection, and I see him bristle then turn his head a little in my direction. I wonder if he can actually hear me or sense me as I have him.

Then, as if it didn't happen, he turns back to Crenshaw and I know he is speaking to him. I see Crenshaw's face fall, his disappointment turning to anger as he storms back to his place in the crowd.

I want to run over to Nightly and tell him he's being unreasonable. But I can't. That is not how it is done, and I must stand here till the music stops, or dance.

I feel myself getting upset and look at Constance who is turning to look at Vaughn. She looks as sad as I feel.

'Vaughn!' I give a loud whisper to my brother who is only a few witches in front.

He turns and I gesture to Constance and mouth, 'What are you waiting for?' He looks at me and shrugs. 'Do it!' I tell him.

He turns to see that Constance is looking his way. Her face breaks into the most radiant smile as Vaughn walks towards her. He bows and she curtsies, then he holds out a hand and she practically pulls him to the dance floor, swirling him off his feet. Vaughn smiles so broadly that I think my heart might break with happiness for them.

I'm so distracted I don't notice that Russo is beside me.

'Ms Wycherley, the council didn't have time to deliver their resolution to you before the Ostara Oaths were called, but they have asked me to give you their decision.' He hands me a note.

From the Royal Magical Council of
her Majesty the Princess Regent Georgianna

Ms Wycherley,

On the matter of your magic, it is the decision of the Royal Magical Council, by the authority invested in them by the Crown, that you be allowed to return next year under the guidance of Mr Gerard Russo and Mr Linden Platz, to find a suitable match. Your magic and the potential that it holds has been deemed too important to the kingdom to be lost, therefore this council not only urges you to find a suitable match but insists upon it.

Next year will give you an opportunity to connect with a new collection of debutante witches. However, Mr Russo and Mr Platz have informed us that they believe Mr Jules Horatio Victor Nightly would prove to be a most suitable tether for your magic, and, if you would rather not return next year, the council will approve this match. After a brief discussion, so does Mr Nightly's family, and your own.

For the kingdom and the magic.
The Royal Magical Council

'Is . . . is this real?' I stare at the note in disbelief.

'It is, Ms Wycherley,' Russo says, then he glances towards Nightly who is still standing tall, facing forward, the only one of the dark-grey witches of the year who is not dancing.

'Platz and I will be very sorry if we see you next year.' He is smiling widely. Then adds, 'The dance is soon to end.'

I don't need telling twice. With the letter in my hand I start to walk and then hitch my dress and run to the front of the crowd.

'What are you doing, Wycherley?' Nightly says, staring at me.

'I could ask the same thing!'

'I told you: it's you or nothing.'

'And I'm here to tell you that if you want me, you can have me, magic and all!'

He stares at me with a raw intensity. 'Don't toy with me, Wycherley!'

'I'm not, I promise. I want you, Jules Nightly. I want you the way that you want me. I want your magic and your kisses and everything else that you have to give.' I pass him the note and I curtsy low. 'If you please.'

My heart thumps in my chest. I watch his face as he reads, his brow knitting, then breaking into disbelief and, finally, that smile that undoes me. He folds the letter and places it in his breast pocket. Then he bows, taking my hand before scooping me up in his arms, spinning me around and kissing me right there in the hall of Carlton Palace where everyone is watching. I feel my feet leave the ground and we begin to dance on the air, soaring together, above the other debutantes, above everything, and I know that every time I soar, Jules Nightly will be right there with me.

The End of an Age:
A Treaty and Examination of the Events that Closed the Third Age of Magic

by Chloe Barnes, first published 2025

My fellow magical historians have differing views on when the beginning of the end of the Third Age of Magic started. Some think it was with the first witch murder, others believe that the end of the Magical Age was sealed when Aurelia Wycherley gained her cursed magic, some say it was when she first opened the black-flame door. A few believe that it was when Jules Nightly tethered himself to the cursed witch. But I have more than ample evidence to believe that the tipping point occurred on the new moon of March 1814, and will lay out that evidence in detail within these pages.

It is, of course, worth noting that the new Worm Moon of 1814 happened to fall on Ostara, the very day that Jules Nightly and Aurelia Wycherley pledged themselves to one another. But it was not until the darkness of that night that the twelve malevolent witches – known as the untethered coven – mysteriously escaped from the magical prison they had been placed in and began to plan their assault against the kingdom and the magic of these blessed isles.

Every witch in the land knows of the atrocities of those last few years in the Third Age of Magic, as well as the heroics and the sacrifices of those who fought against the malevolent forces. Sacrifices that still scar our world today, sacrifices without which the world would no longer exist.

We witches of the Fourth Age owe our magic to the deeds of the Coven of Wynne Hordes, and the secrets they uncovered in the lost quarter.

THE COVEN OF ACCORD

Witches of the Coven of Accord are the first and last line of magical defence for the magical world. Well trained in magical combat, with excellent broom skills, and unrivalled ward casting charms, these red-clad witches protect and serve crown and country.

THE COVEN OF CURIOSITY

Witches of the Coven of Curiosity are explorers and adventurers of the magical world. Whether they are travelling the globe or performing magic in their coven arcade, these yellow-clad witches are always pushing the boundaries of what magic can do and looking for new ways to cast spells, brew potions, and perform magic.

THE COVEN OF JUSTICE

Witches of the Coven of Justice are the peacekeepers and protectors of magic. Ensuring the rights of witches and their safety is the priority for these black-clad witches, highly skilled in advanced magic and the laws that govern the world.

THE COVEN OF MYSTERY

Witches of the Coven of Mystery are the alchemists and magical physicists of the magical world. Their one drive is to understand and tame the fundamental nature of magic, to unlock its mysteries and bring them to light. These secretive blue-clad witches investigate and test, theorize and expand the understanding of magic in ways unknown to those outside of their coven.

THE COVEN OF KNOWING

Witches of the Coven of Knowing are the teachers and scholars, librarians and record keepers of the magical world. These purple-clad witches specialise in educating witches in the fundamentals of primary and secondary magic, as well as keeping records of the history of magic for all.

THE COVEN OF NURTURING

Witches of the Coven of Nurturing are the healers and the growers, the herbologists and the biologists of the magical world. Potions are the expertise of these green-clad witches, they tend to nature, encouraging it and learning about its innate magic while helping it and every witch around them to grow.

About the Author

Annaliese Avery is a former library manager and children's book editor who lives in Suffolk, England. She has an MA in creative writing and a life long interest in physics and astronomy and in 2013 she founded an astronomical society.

Acknowledgements

Writing is magic to me – it's where I feel most like myself. It brings me joy, excitement, and wonder. When I set off on a story, I carry a handful of ideas, a pinch of hope, and a cauldron full of possibilities. But the true magic in my creating a book comes from the people around me – the ones who add their spark to the process, whether by listening to my ideas, joining me in writing sprints, or working behind the scenes through editing and marketing.

If Helen Boyle lived in the world of *The Wycherleys*, she would undoubtedly be one of the Witch Queens of the thirteen clans from the Second Age of Magic. Helen brings her own enchantments to every book we work on together, and I'm honoured to have her as my agent.

I am so grateful to be part of an extraordinary coven of talented witches at Simon & Schuster. My brilliant editor, Ali Dougal – who wields a red pen infused with pure magic – has been invested in this story from the very beginning. I'm incredibly lucky to have her as part of my magical council, alongside the wonderful Arub Ahmed. Together, they have supported and nurtured me every step of the way.

But they weren't alone in casting their spells – Kathy Webb, Petra Bryce, Sorrel Packham, and Loren Catana each sprinkled their unique magic over this book, helping it shine.

To Jess Dean, Olivia Horrox, and Nina Douglas thank you for chanting the name of *The Wycherleys* loudly and connecting with readers in so may magical spaces, inviting them to the magical season and generating such a wonderful buzz around the book – broomsticks and ballgowns at the ready!

Everyone at Simon & Schuster has embraced *The Wycherleys*, pouring so much energy into sharing its magic far and wide. A heartfelt thank you to all of the incredible stars in the sales and rights teams for bringing Aurelia and Jules' story to readers in the UK and beyond. A most magical thank you to Rachel Denwood who has been a huge champion of *The Wycherleys* since receiving her first invitation to read it.

A special thank you to Kelley McMorris for creating the most stunning cover – it is truly breathtaking spell work. Watching Kelley's creative process unfold was a joy, and seeing the final cover come together was pure magic. We had many conversations about Jules Nightly and his autumn locks, which I think we both thoroughly appreciated.

To all my wonderful writer friends – thank you for sprinting with me, cheering me on, and sharing in the excitement of this book. Dominique Valente, Chrissy Sains, Vanessa Harbour, Teara Newell, Abs Tanner and Nicola Baker, your encouragement has meant the world. And to my spell sisters, Cathie Kelly and Kate Walker, thank you for lending your names to my witches and your support to me.

This book was written during a chaotic time in my life. Though the writing was a joy, I often felt uncertain. My gorgeous family kept me grounded, as they always do, never letting me drift too far. Jason, Liberty, Krystal, Oak and Gregson – thank you for tethering my magic and, when necessary, offering to hex me into action.

One of the most magical parts of writing is what comes after – sharing the story. Dearest reader, thank you for stepping into this world with me, I hope that you have enjoyed the magical season. To all the booksellers, librarians, teachers, and reviewers who help spread the magic of stories, I hope your witch-flame always burns bright.

For the kingdom, for the magic… and for the books!